THE BONE VAULT

"Chilling. . . . A richly detailed . . . and an authentically documented murder investigation. . . . The banter and give-and-take between Cooper and Chapman is enchanting. . . . Fairstein [is] a champion teller of detective tales."

—*USA Today*

"Satisfying. . . . The quick-witted Cooper is as likeable as ever."

—*Publishers Weekly*

"Fast pacing, colorful suspects . . . this is fun reading."

—*Library Journal*

"[The] romantic tension, the fast-paced plotting, and the New York setting will keep fans of Fairstein's series engrossed."

—*Booklist*

THE DEADHOUSE

Winner of the prestigious Nero Wolfe Award for Best Crime Novel of 2001 and chosen as a "Best Book of 2001" by *The Washington Post* and the *Los Angeles Times*

"A four-star tribute to good writing, strong characters, and the ability to translate expertise into a terrific story."

—*USA Today*

"Darkly woven . . . *The Deadhouse* conjures up a horrid past to solve a baffling modern murder."

—Patricia Cornwell

"Four stars out of four stars. . . . Absorbing and well-plotted."

—*Detroit Free Press*

"Linda Fairstein writes tough, beautiful prose about a world she knows firsthand."

—Lisa Scottoline

"A beguiling mix of murder, romance, and suspense. . . . Fascinating. . . . An extraordinarily well-knit mystery that the author wraps tightly in suspense before unfolding it with a flourish."

—Dick Lochte, *Los Angeles Times*

"Her novels are authentic and timely, with the feel of a true-crime drama and the writing style of a natural-born story-teller."

—Nelson DeMille

COLD HIT

A *People* magazine "Page-Turner of the Week"

"[A] fast-paced thriller [with] a view of today's art world unlike anything taught in Art History 101. . . . A stylish study in criminal expressionism."

—*People*

"Dazzling. . . . Fascinating, fast paced. . . . [Alex is] smart, sexy, and indefatigable."

—*Library Journal*

"Absorbing, intricately woven. . . ."

—Patricia Cornwell

"A shining protagonist, comfortable in the upper echelons of New York society but eager to roll up her sleeves at work, her heart aching for her staff and the victims they defend."

—*Publishers Weekly* (starred review)

"Thoroughly tension-filled and pulse-pounding."

—*Midwest Book Reviews*

LIKELY TO DIE

"An authoritative and scary view from one who has battled evil and locked it away."

—Patricia Cornwell

"With its taut plot and classy setting, *Likely to Die* is an uptown act."

—*People*

"This gritty, harsh book has a strong sense of authenticity."

—*Chicago Tribune*

FINAL JEOPARDY

"Raw, real, and mean. Linda Fairstein is wonderful."

—Patricia Cornwell

"Put down *Final Jeopardy* and you almost expect to find crime-scene grit under your nails. Dead-on details are no surprise in this taut mystery."

—*Us* magazine

"If it is authenticity you demand, *Final Jeopardy* has got it in spades. . . . There is an anger and a passion in Alex Cooper that is clearly not fictional."

—*The Times* (London)

THE KILLS

Linda Fairstein

POCKET STAR BOOKS

NEW YORK LONDON TORONTO SYDNEY

A Pocket Star Book published by
POCKET BOOKS, a division of Simon & Schuster, Inc.
1230 Avenue of the Americas, New York, NY 10020

This book is a work of fiction. Names, characters, places and incidents are products of the author's imagination or are used fictitiously. Any resemblance to actual events or locales or persons, living or dead, is entirely coincidental.

Copyright © 2004 by Linda Fairstein

Originally published in hardcover in 2004 by Scribner

ISBN: 0-7434-8749-4

Pocket Books Export Edition Printing February 2004

10 9 8 7 6 5 4 3 2 1

POCKET STAR BOOKS and colophon are registered trademarks of Simon & Schuster, Inc.

Manufactured in the United States of America

For information regarding special discounts for bulk purchases, please contact Simon & Schuster Special Sales at 1-800-456-6798 or business@simonandschuster.com

For
PATRICIA CORNWELL

Timidi numquam statuere trophaeum
The timid never erect monuments

With gratitude for
courage, friendship, and boundless generosity

THE KILLS

1

"Murder. You should have charged the defendant with murder."

"He didn't kill anyone, Your Honor." Not yet. Not that I could prove.

"Juries like murder, Ms. Cooper. You should know that better than I do." Harlan Moffett read the indictment a second time as court officers herded sixty prospective jurors into the small courtroom. "Give these amateurs a dead body, a medical examiner who can tell them the knife wound in the back wasn't self-inflicted, a perp who was somewhere near the island of Manhattan when the crime occurred, and I guarantee you a conviction. This stuff you keep bringing me?"

Moffett underscored each of the charges with his red fountain pen. Next to the block letters of the defendant's name in the document's heading, *People of the State of New York Against Andrew Tripping,* he sketched the stick figure of a man hanging from the crosspiece of a gallows.

My adversary had been pleased when the case was

sent out to Moffett for trial earlier in the afternoon. As tough as the old-timer was on homicide cases, he had been appointed to the bench thirty years ago, when the laws made it virtually impossible to take rape cases before a jury. No witness to the attack, no corroborating evidence, then there could be no prosecution. He clearly liked it better that way.

We both stood on the raised platform directly in front of Moffett, answering his questions about the matter for which we were about to select a panel. I was trying to divine my prospects as I watched the notations he was making on the face of the indictment I had handed up to him.

"You're right, Judge." Peter Robelon smiled as Moffett scribbled out the image of the doomed man on the gallows. "Alex has the classic 'he said–she said' situation here. She's got no physical evidence, no forensics."

"Would you mind keeping your voice down, Peter?" I couldn't direct the judge to lower his volume, but maybe he'd get my point. Robelon knew the acoustics in the room as well as I did, and was keenly aware that the twelve people being seated in the box could overhear him as the three of us talked about the facts and issues in the case.

"Speak up, Alexandra." Moffett cupped his hand to his ear.

"Would you mind if we had this conversation in your robing room?" My subtlety had escaped the judge.

"Alex is afraid the jurors are going to hear what she's about to tell them anyway as soon as she makes her opening statement. Smoke and mirrors, Your Honor. That's all she's got."

Moffett stood up and walked down the three steps, motioning both of us to follow him out the door, held open by the chief clerk, into the small office adjacent to the courtroom.

The room was bare, except for an old wooden desk and four chairs. The only decoration, next to the telephone mounted on the wall, were the names and numbers of every pizza, sandwich, and fast-food joint in a five-block radius, scrawled on the peeling gray paint over the years by court officers who had ordered meals for deliberating jurors.

Moffett closed the window that looked down from the fifteenth floor above Centre Street in Lower Manhattan. Police sirens, from patrol cars streaking north out of headquarters, competed with our conversation.

"You know why juries like homicides so much? It's easy for them." The wide sleeves of his black robes flapped about as the judge waved his arms in the air. "A corpse, a weapon, an unnatural death. They know that a terrible crime occurred. You've just got to put the perp in the ballpark and they send him up the river for you."

I opened my mouth to address him. He pointed a finger in my direction and kept going. "*You* spend most of every damn rape trial just trying to prove there was even a crime committed."

Moffett wasn't wrong. The hardest thing about these cases was convincing a jury that a felony had actually taken place. People usually kill one another for reasons. Not good reasons, but things that twelve of their peers can grab on to and accept as the precipitating cause. Greed. Rage. Jealousy. Infidelity. All the deadly sins and then some. Prosecutors don't have to supply a motive, but most of the time one makes itself visible and we offer it up for their consideration.

Sex crimes are different. Nobody can fathom why someone forces an act of intercourse on an unwilling partner. Psychologists ruminate about power and control and anger, but they haven't stood in front of a jury box dozens of times, as I have, trying to make ordinary citizens understand crimes that seem to have no motives at all.

Explain why the clean-cut nineteen-year-old sitting opposite them in the well of the courtroom broke into a stranger's apartment to steal property but became aroused at the sight of a fifty-eight-year-old housewife watching television, so he held a knife to her throat and committed a sexual act. Explain why the supervising janitor of a Midtown office building would corner a cleaning woman in a broom closet on the night shift, when the hallway was dark and deserted, pushing her to her knees and demanding oral sex.

"May I tell you what I've got, Judge?"

"In a minute." Moffett waved me off with the back of his hand, rays of the late-afternoon sunlight glancing off the garnet-colored stone in his pinky ring. "Peter, let me hear about your client."

"Andrew Tripping. Forty-two years old. No record—"

"Well, that's not exactly true, Peter."

"Nothing you can use at trial, is there, Alex? Now how about letting me finish without interrupting?"

I placed my legal pad on the desk and started to list all the facts I knew that would flush out the picture Tripping's lawyer was about to paint.

"Graduated from Yale. Went into the Marine Corps. Did some work for the CIA for about ten years. Now he's a consultant."

"Your guy and everyone else who's not employed. Everybody who hasn't got a job's a consultant. What field?"

"Security. Governmental affairs. Terrorism. Spent a lot of time in the Middle East, Asia before that. Can't give you too many details."

"Can't or won't? You'll tell me, but then you'll have to kill me?" Moffett was the only one to laugh at his own jokes. He slid the yellow-backed felony complaint out of the court file and flipped it over. "Made two hundred fifty thousand bail? Must know something—or somebody."

Peter smiled at me as he answered. "Our friend, Ms. Cooper, was a bit excessive in her request at the arraignment. I got it cut in half in criminal court. He spent a week on Rikers before I got him out."

"Sure doesn't look like a rapist."

"What is it, Judge? The blazer, rep tie, and wire-rimmed glasses? Or just that he's the first white guy you've had in the dock all year?" There was no point in losing my temper yet. The jury would be looking at Tripping the same way the judge was. People heard the word "rape" and expected to see a Neanderthal, club in hand, peering out from behind a tree in Central Park.

I had Moffett's attention now. "Who's the girl?"

"Thirty-six-year-old woman. Paige Vallis. She works at an investment banking firm."

"She knows the guy? This one of those date things?"

"Ms. Vallis had met Tripping twice before. Yes, he had invited her out to dinner the evening this happened."

"Alcohol involved?"

"Yes, sir."

Moffett looked at the complaint again, comparing the place of occurrence with the defendant's home address. Now his primitive doodles were a wine bottle and a couple of glasses. "Then she went back to his place, I guess."

It wouldn't have surprised me if he had said what he was undoubtedly thinking at that moment: What did she expect to happen if she went home with him at midnight, after a candlelit dinner and a bottle of wine? I had countered that logic in court more times than I could remember. Moffett didn't speak the words. He just scowled and shook his head back and forth slowly.

"She got injuries?"

"No, sir." The overwhelming percentage of sexual assault victims presented themselves to emergency rooms with no external signs of physical injury. Any rookie prosecutor could get a conviction when the victim was battered and bruised.

"DNA?"

Peter Robelon spoke over me as I nodded my head. "So what, Judge? My client admits that he and Ms. Vallis made love. Alex doesn't even need to waste the

court's time with her serology expert. I'll stipulate to
the findings."

Nothing new about Tripping's defense. Consent.
The two spent a rapturous night together, he would
argue, and for some reason that Peter would raise at
trial, Paige Vallis ran to the nearest cop on the beat
the next morning to charge her lover with rape.
Surely it couldn't be for the pleasure of the experience
she was about to undergo in a public forum, when I
called her to the witness stand.

"Did Judge Hayes talk plea with you two?"

The case had been pending since the indictment
was filed back in March. "I haven't made any offer to
the defense."

"You got rocks in your head, Alexandra? Nothing
better to do with your time?" Moffett cocked one eye
and stared over his reading glasses at me.

"I'd like to explain the circumstances, Your Honor.
There's a child involved."

"She's got a kid? What does that have to do with
anything?"

"He's the one with a kid. A son. That's what the
endangering count refers to."

"The father did something sexual to his own kid?
Now that's—"

"No, no, Judge. There's been some physical abuse
and strange behavior—"

"Stop characterizing this to prejudice the court,
Alex. She's on thin ice, Your Honor."

"The boy was a witness to much of what happened
leading up to the crime itself. In a sense, he was the
weapon the defendant used to compel Ms. Vallis to

submit to him. If Peter will stop interrupting me, I can lay it out for you."

Moffett scanned the indictment again, reading the language about endangering the welfare of a child. He looked up at Robelon. "How about it, Peter? Your guy willing to take the misdemeanor and save us all a lot of aggravation?"

"No way. The prosecution doesn't have the kid. She's never even talked to him. He's not going to testify against his father."

"Is that true, Alexandra?" Moffett was up and pacing now, anxious to get back in the courtroom before the prospective jurors got too restless.

"Can we just slow this down a bit, Peter?" I asked. "That's one of the things I'd like to discuss with you before we charge ahead, Judge."

"What's to discuss?"

"I'd like you to sign an order directing production of the child, so that I can interview him before I open to the jury."

"Why? Where is he?"

"I don't know, Your Honor. ACW took him away from Mr. Tripping at the time of the arrest. They've never allowed me to meet with him." The Agency for Child Welfare had relocated Tripping's ten-year-old son to a foster home outside the city when I filed the indictment.

"Judge," Peter said, picking up on Moffett's obvious annoyance with my case, "see what I mean? She hasn't even laid eyes on the boy."

"Why isn't the kid with his mother?"

Peter and I spoke at the same time. "She's dead."

Peter jumped in defensively. "Killed herself a few months after he was born. Typical postpartum depression, taken to the worst extreme."

"Tripping was in the military at the time, Judge. She was killed with one of his guns. I've spoken to investigators who think he's the one who pulled the trigger."

Moffet aimed his pinky ring in my direction, jabbing it in the air while he grinned and looked over at Peter Robelon. "She should have charged him with murder, just like I said. Pretty good self-restraint for Alexandra Cooper. So why'd Judge Hayes leave me with all these loose ends to tie up when he sent this over to me? What else are you asking for?"

Peter answered before I could open my mouth. "Alex, you know I'm going to oppose any request you make for an adjournment. You answered ready for trial, Hayes sent us out, and my client is ready to get this over with."

"It sounds like we got some housekeeping matters to clear up here before we start picking," Moffett said. "I'll tell you what I'm going to do. Let's go back inside, so I can greet the jurors and give them a timetable. I'll introduce each of you and the defendant, tell them we need the morning to complete some business that doesn't involve them, and have them back here at two P.M. Either of you have a list of witnesses you want to give me?"

I handed both men a very short list of names. This case rested squarely on Paige Vallis's shoulders. "I may have one more to add to this tomorrow."

Peter Robelon smiled again. "I don't want to lose

sleep worrying about who that might be, Alex. Want to give me a hint?"

"I assume you'd be able to do your usual devastating cross-examination, even if I conjured up Mother Teresa as an eyewitness. Let me keep you guessing."

Mercer Wallace, the case detective from the Special Victims Unit, had been contacted by one of the guys in Homicide at the end of last week. He had a confidential informant—a reliable CI, he claimed—who had been Tripping's cellmate at Rikers and had some incriminating information that he'd overheard in the pens in the hours after the two were first incarcerated together. They were producing this informant—Kevin Bessemer—in my office tonight, for me to evaluate the statements he was trying to trade for some years shaved off the time he was looking at in his own pending case.

Moffett waved his hand toward the door and the court officer opened it for us. He took my arm and steered me toward the hallway. "Nice of you to bring me a case that doesn't have the first three rows of my courtroom filled with reporters for a change."

"Believe me, Judge, it's the way I prefer to work, too."

"Do yourself a favor, Alex." Moffett turned back to look at Robelon, no doubt winking to assure him the whispering was to benefit his client. "Think about whether we can make this case go away by this time tomorrow. I'm amazed it survived the motion to inspect and dismiss the grand jury minutes. I'm not sure you're going to see a lot of rulings going your way under my watch, from this point on."

"It's actually a very compelling story—and a frightening one. I think you'll see that more clearly when I make my application in the morning."

He let go and stepped out ahead of me, into the courtroom, taking his place back up on the bench as Robelon and I walked to our respective tables.

Mercer Wallace was standing at the rail, as though he had been waiting for me to emerge from the robing room. Moffett recognized him from a previous trial. "Miss Cooper, you want a minute to speak with Detective Wallace before I get started with our introductions here?"

"I'd appreciate that, Your Honor."

Mercer reached for my shoulder and turned me away from the jurors in the box, toward him. "Keep your game face on, Alex. Just got news that you should know before you spill anything to the judge about how strong your case is. Hope I'm not too late to be useful."

"Ready."

He leaned over and spoke as softly as he could. "Heads are gonna roll as soon as the commissioner gets word about this one. Two guys were bringing Kevin Bessemer over from Rikers for your interview. The car got jammed up behind an accident on the FDR Drive, and the prisoner bolted from the backseat, right down the footpath on One Hundred Nineteenth Street and into the projects. They lost him."

"*What?*"

"Poker face, girl. You promised."

"But wasn't he cuffed?"

"Rear-cuffed and locked in tight, the guys say. Stay

cool, Alex, the judge is checking to see what the fidgeting is and why your blood pressure's going up. Your cheeks are on fire."

"I can't start picking this jury tomorrow. How the hell am I going to buy myself some time?"

"Tell the man what happened, kid. Tell him your snitch is gone."

2

"Good afternoon, ladies and gentlemen," Moffett said, clearly relishing this role as he swaggered on his small stage, higher than everyone in the courtroom and completely in charge. He stood behind his massive leather chair, gesturing broadly with both arms as he spoke.

"I trust you each had a good, restful summer, a pleasant Labor Day weekend, so now you're ready to settle down and get to serious business here."

Jurors liked Harlan Moffett. He was seventy-one years old, with a full head of thick white hair and a robust build. His three decades on the bench made him comfortable with almost every situation that might arise in the Supreme Court of the State of New York, Criminal Term. He was patient with nervous witnesses, never tolerated outbursts from sobbing relatives or defendants' girlfriends who showed up in court with wailing rent-a-babies to elicit the jury's sympathy, and he was the only person in the room who had not ducked the time a notorious killer had thrown the water pitcher from counsel table across the courtroom at his head, rocketing shards of glass all over the well.

When he finished telling the panel a bit about himself, Moffett extended his right hand, palm up, and asked me to stand. "This young lady is Alexandra Cooper. Paul Battaglia—he's the man you people keep reelecting to be your district attorney—well, he put Miss Cooper here in charge of all the sex crimes cases that occur in Manhattan."

I nodded at the group and sat down.

"She's got a real friendly smile, folks, but you're not going to see it again during this trial. So when you pass her in the hall or on your way into the courthouse, don't say hello to her or wish her a good evening. She can't talk to you. Neither can Mr. Robelon over there."

Moffett introduced Peter along with his second seat, an associate from his law firm called Emily Frith. I glanced over at their table and noticed the routine defense shtick that had become so commonplace at rape trials. The young and attractive Emily was necessary for one purpose only. She had her seat pulled up as close to Andrew Tripping as possible, her arm resting on the back of his chair. It didn't matter if she had a brain in her head or had passed the bar exam. She was simply there for the visual. Jurors were supposed to see this interaction and think to themselves that if she was comfortable being so intimately involved with the defendant, then maybe he wasn't really a violent sex offender.

Tripping, when called on, rose to his feet, mustering his most forlorn expression of presumed innocence, smoothing his tie into place before lowering himself back down into his seat. Here but for the grace of God goes any one of you, was the subliminal message he was sending to all the male jurors. He looked paler than the last time I had seen him, with muddy brown eyes and hair the color of a well-rusted metal wrench.

"Since it's already four forty-five, I'm going to let you folks be excused. You can all sleep late tomorrow while I make these lawyers work on some other aspects of the case in the morning. You're to be back here at two o'clock sharp, ready to go. At that time we'll be picking a jury."

Moffett came out from behind his chair, leaning over the edge of the bench and wagging a finger at the panel in the box and then expanding his admonition to the rest of the prospective jurors in the gallery. "And let me remind you people that those tired, old efforts to get out of your civic duty won't work in my courtroom. Leave your excuses at home. I don't care if you have two plane tickets to Rio on Friday, or that nobody will baby-sit for your cat if I sequester you in a hotel room, or that your cousin's niece's brother is being bar mitzvahed in Cleveland this weekend. Send him a check, and as far as I'm concerned, you can bring the kitty with you."

The jurors gathered their belongings and made their way to the double doors at the rear of the room. I swept my notepad and case folder off the table and waited for the judge to excuse me so that I could get downstairs to my office to deal with the slippery witness and my disintegrating case.

"What time for us, Your Honor?" Peter asked.

"Nine-thirty. And Alexandra, you'll have the agency people here?"

"I'll call over there right now, as soon as you dismiss us."

The corridors and elevators were packed with nine-to-five civil servants who set their schedules by the time clock, so as not to give the city an extra minute of their energy. Assistant district attorneys were swimming against that tide, making their way back to their offices from the dozens of courtrooms on both sides of Centre Street, to spend long hours readying themselves for the next day's legal battles.

Laura Wilkie, who had been my secretary for seven years, anticipated my return from the trial part. She was standing in my doorway, steno pad in hand, brewing a fresh pot of coffee to jump-start me for the evening ahead.

Clipped to my In box was a wad of telephone messages. "Those you can ignore. Friends, lovers, bill collectors, snake oil salesmen. This one you can't."

She gave me the yellow paper with the message she had taken from the district attorney. *See me as soon as you finish in court.*

It meant Battaglia had heard about the escape and wanted an explanation.

I walked into my office and dropped the files on top of my desk. Mercer was standing against the window, the dark outline of his six-foot-four-inch frame silhouetted against the granite gargoyles on the building ledge behind him. He was on the phone.

"Find out what you can. Alex is gonna tank on this one."

"I think it's already happened," I said to Mercer as he turned and saw me, then hung up. "I'm about to hit bottom. Battaglia wants the story. Any news on how this happened?"

"Bessemer's a predicate. Facing the rest of his natural days behind bars for a five-kilo sale of cocaine. Brooklyn Narcotics made the arrest. Their lieutenant insisted that they be the ones to transport him here instead of our squad. Everybody there's playing dumb."

"Sounds like they have the credentials for it. Any sightings of him yet?"

"I've called anyone who owes me. I'll get you an answer before the night is out."

"If it comes back in little pieces, even if the information is too late to save my tail, you know I'd be grateful."

I scanned my security pass to get into the executive wing. Battaglia's executive assistant, Rose Malone, looked relieved to see me. "Go right in, Alex."

Rose was my early warning system. Completely loyal to the district attorney, she had a superb ability to read his moods and transmit the data to me just as the most accurate barometer at Cape Canaveral could do for Mission Control.

"Do I get a hint about who ratted me out to the Boss?"

"It's not who you think."

I thought McKinney. The chief of the trial division, Pat McKinney was my direct supervisor. His eagle eye scoured my actions for every misstep and mistake, and he seemed never to weary of reporting them to Battaglia.

"Who then?"

"The commissioner. Don't worry, the Boss isn't angry. He just wants to know some background before he takes the call." She had intercepted the message and was giving me the opportunity to explain the situation to the DA, so he could be in the driver's seat during his conversation with the police commissioner.

The boss wasn't upset yet, because the screw-up was the doing of the NYPD. He just wanted to know the extent of our complicity before he pointed his finger at the cops.

Battaglia exhaled as I entered the room, the smoke from his Cohiba obscuring the expression on his face. "Why don't you sit down and bring me up to speed, Alex?"

Unless I was in his office to deliver good news—a DNA databank cold hit, the sentencing of a serial rapist, a bit of personal gossip he could deposit in his limitless storehouse of information—I preferred to stand and answer the questions he had ready for me, leaving as rapidly as I had arrived.

He glanced at the paper on his desk. "This—this Bessemer character. Why'd you need him brought down here?"

"I'm about to start a trial, Paul. The defendant is a guy—"

"Yeah, Andrew Tripping. That military nut who was disciplining his kid."

There were more than six hundred assistant district attorneys in Battaglia's office, the best training ground for litigators in the entire country. No detail was too small to engage Battaglia's attention, and there was no fact that I had ever briefed him on that he couldn't call up from memory unless it had to do with money I asked for to fund a special sex crimes project.

"It's a tough case, Boss. And last week Mercer Wallace got a call that one of Tripping's cellmates from the time he was in Rikers had some useful admissions to give me. Something that might put my rape victim over the top."

"Like what?"

"That's what I was supposed to find out, right about now."

The left side of Battaglia's mouth pulled back as he talked around the large cigar stub that hung between his lips. "You're losing your charm, Alex. Who thought a prisoner would prefer his freedom to tea and crumpets with you? How unusual was this arrangement?"

"Not very. The routine dance. He refused to tell the cops exactly what he had to offer until he eyeballed me to see what I was willing and able to do for him. I wouldn't talk possibilities till I knew what he was putting on the table."

"Promises?"

"Of course not. I was fairly skeptical." Snitches like Bessemer usually did more harm than good in a case like this. He had waited too long to make his offer seem sincere, and he was just as likely to be jerking me around as to have any tidbits of value. I couldn't refuse to see him without knowing what he might be sitting on, but I wasn't prepared to waste a great deal of time playing with him. CIs were the bottom feeders of the prison population.

"Worth the embarrassment of putting him back on the street while he's on his way to keep a date with you?" Battaglia asked.

"Not for a second. But, Boss, in more than a decade here, I've never heard of anything like this happening. I've had prisoners produced here scores of time—we all have. This was completely unpredictable."

"You had a loser of a case before Bessemer's phone call to the cops. So you still got a loser."

Now both sides of his mouth pulled back around the cigar into a broad smile. He went on to explain how he knew. "I just heard from Judge Moffett. Wants me to lean on you to be more reasonable."

I smiled back. That was one thing Paul Battaglia would never do. If my judgment call was a belief that the defendant was guilty as charged, and I thought I could prove it, then the district attorney's only rule was for me to do the right thing. It was one reason I loved working for the man.

"Is that why he called you?"

"In part. He wants to know what's in this case for Peter Robelon. How can Tripping afford his rates?"

Robelon was a partner in a small firm, a well-regarded boutique that specialized in white-collar litigation. His fees were among the highest in the New York bar—$450 an hour.

"I think there's some family money. Tripping's mother died about a year ago, several months before these events occurred. She had been raising her grandson until that point. She left everything she had to the defendant." I hadn't been able to discover anything unusual from the bank records.

"Interesting, but only if she had enough to cover the retainer and trial costs." Battaglia paused. "Robelon's dirty, Alex. I've got good reason to know. Watch your back."

"You want to tell me what you mean?" I asked. Peter Robelon had often been mentioned as a possible candidate to oppose Battaglia in the next election.

"Not for the time being." Battaglia protected his hoard of information like an eagle on its nest. The fact that I had spent the last year in a serious relationship with a television news reporter made him far less likely to trust me with something sensitive that could play into his political future. "Did Peter know about this Bessemer guy? Is his escape anything Peter could have had a hand in engineering?"

I was caught completely off-guard by his question. "That never crossed my mind."

"Well, keep it open, Alex. And if you're going to go belly-up on this case, do it fast. We've got a busy fall lineup and I'd like your help drafting some of the legislative proposals for the next session."

I returned to my office to find Mercer sitting at my desk, still working the phone. I motioned to him to stay put and sat facing him, waiting for him to finish his conversation. From over my shoulder I heard a knock on my office door, which was ajar. Detective Mike Chapman braced himself against the jamb, smiled at me broadly as he ran the fingers of his right hand through his thick black hair.

"Hey, Coop. What am I bid for one 'Get out of jail free' card? Only slightly used by the very nimble Kevin Bessemer."

I looked at Mercer. "Why do I think I'm about to be told what a sucker I was to fall for Mr. Bessemer's proffer of prosecutorial assistance? Do I owe Mike's appearance to the fact that you've run out of chits to call in?"

Before Mercer Wallace transferred to the Special Victims Unit several years ago, he and Mike had worked together at the elite Manhattan North Detective Squad. Like me, Mercer thrived on making the system work better for women who were victims of violence. Like the jurors of whom Moffett spoke, Mike preferred murder. There was none of the emotional baggage of traumatized rape victims to deal with, nor any hand-holding, dissembling, or cross-examination of living, breathing witnesses.

"He's my go-to man, you know that, Alex."

"And if I've got what you need, you buying dinner?" Mike asked.

"What I need is for Kevin Bessemer to walk up to a beat cop and ask for directions to my office."

"So where'd the guys from Brooklyn tell you this went down, Mercer?"

"Came off the ramp from the Triborough Bridge, heading here. Four-car pileup right in front of them—"

"And while they're watching some poor slob from Highway One clear up the mess, Kevin gives new meaning to E-ZPass, hops out of the unmarked narc-mobile, starts singing 'Feet don't fail me now,' and hightails it off into the sunset right in his own 'hood? That's what you hear?"

"Look, Mike, if you know something different, tell

me," I said. "Let me score a few points with Battaglia, so he can tell the PC."

"The real deal? These morons from Narcotics tried to sweeten the pot for Kevin. Gave him a slight detour on his way downtown."

"How'd you find out?"

"Walter DeGraw. His kid brother's in the unit." Maybe Mike wasn't joking. DeGraw was solid as a rock.

"Where to?"

"Seems whenever they want something from Bessemer, he's much more cooperative after he's had some fried chicken and a piece of uptown ass. They made a pit stop at his girlfriend's apartment. One Hundred Twelfth and Second Avenue."

"You can't be serious?" I was furious.

"It's not the first time. The cops were sitting at the kitchen table, nibbling on wings and watching *One Life to Live* while Bessemer was supposed to be relieving his sexual tension in the bedroom."

"And when they took a commercial break?"

"The window was wide-open. The bed had never been touched. The fire escape ran straight down five stories to an alleyway behind the projects. Bessemer and the girl were both in the wind."

3

"Tonight's 'Final Jeopardy' category is Astronomy,"
Alex Trebek told us after Mike had coaxed me away
from my desk shortly before seven-thirty to turn on
the television in the public relations office down the
hall from my own.

"Don't waste my time. I've got work to do so I can
go home and get a good night's sleep."

"Whoa, whoa, whoa, blondie. Throwing in the
towel 'cause you didn't take any science courses at
Wellesley? Well, I never studied it either. But I did
spend some time in the planetarium recently, don't
you remember?" Mike winked at me as I nodded my
head. "What do you say, Mercer, ten bucks apiece?"

The three of us had a long-standing habit of bet-
ting on the "Final Jeopardy" question whenever we
happened to be together at this hour, whether in a station house, a bar, or at a crime scene.

"A dime it is," Mercer answered, and I nodded
my head while the three contestants entered their
multi-thousand-dollar bids on their private score-
cards. "What did you tell Paige Vallis, Alex? You

want me to bring her to meet with you in the afternoon?"

"We won't get to her tomorrow. I spent so much time prepping her last weekend that I think she's really ready to go. If we get anywhere near finished picking the jury by midday Friday, we can get her in then. Meanwhile, let her stay away from my office and go about her normal routine. She's more likely to keep calm."

"The answer is," Trebek said, stepping aside to reveal the printed statement in the blue box on the large screen, "'Warrior who called Halley's comet his "personal star," sparking European invasion that massacred millions.'"

Mercer folded his bill in the shape of a paper plane and sailed it at Mike. "Who was Attila the Hun?"

"This was rigged." I laughed. "You must have known it was really a history question." Mike had majored in the field at Fordham, and knew more about military history than anyone I had ever encountered. "Before I hand over ten, how about William the Conqueror?"

"Not a bad guess for either of you." He clucked his tongue the same way Trebek did at our wrong answers. "Who was Genghis Khan?" That would be the winning ticket.

"Yes, Mr. Wallace, a comet did portend the sack of Gaul, and you were very close, Ms. Cooper. William embarked on the Norman invasion when Halley's comet streaked by, calling it a sign from heaven.

"But it was Khan who thought it was his personal star. Twelve twenty-two. Swooped down from Mongolia and killed everyone he could find in southeastern Europe."

"You don't mind if I go back to work, do you?" I headed out the door as Mike started to play with the remote.

"She almost had the right answer. Only off by two hundred years and one continent. I can't believe that guy I told you about called her a dumb blonde," I heard him say to Mercer before I was ten feet away.

"What guy?" I made a U-turn and stuck my head back in the door. "Who called me dumb?"

"Just a cheap ploy to get you back here with me. There's your man." He clicked up the volume as NY1, the local news channel, flashed a mug shot of Kevin Bessemer.

". . . convicted felon escaped from police custody earlier today. Bessemer, who has a long history of drug trafficking involvement, is thirty-two years old. He is believed to be extremely dangerous," the earnest young newscaster said, "and may possibly be armed."

"Yeah, with a drumstick and four stale biscuits," Mike said, shutting off the television. "C'mon, let's grab a meal. Gotta fortify myself for a midnight tour. I'm doing night watch tonight."

Mike would be working from twelve till 8 A.M., available to respond to every major crime that occurred in Manhattan.

"I really don't—"

"C'mon, Alex. You've done everything you can to get your ducks in order," Mercer said. He had been working with me on the Tripping case during the two weeks since my summer vacation ended after Labor Day weekend. "You're just spinning wheels at this point. We'll feed you and drop you off at home. Call Primola. We'll be waiting for you at the elevator."

I went back to phone my favorite Italian restaurant for a reservation, straighten up my desk, and pick up the file folder to take home to organize my questions for the morning's hearing. The message dial was illuminated on my voice mail, telling me that two calls had come in while I had stepped away.

I pressed the playback button. "It's Jake, darling. I was hoping to scramble to make the last shuttle home tonight. Whatever's rocking the stock market has the staffers jumpy down here, so I think I'd better stay overnight. I'll try you later. Pleasant dreams."

Jake Tyler and I had been trying to sort out our relationship these past few months. We had spent the end of August alone together at my home on Martha's Vineyard, and the weeks of playful solitude had pushed from my mind the reality of what a wedge our two intense professional schedules put between our attempts at a serious romance.

The second one was a short message, overridden by the static of a bad cell phone connection. I couldn't tell whether the caller was male or female, and the only word I could make out clearly was "tomorrow." I pressed the caller ID function and got only the indication that the message had come from out of the area.

I walked to the elevator and met the guys, who were deep in conversation about how far ahead of Boston the Yankees would end the season. The cop

who had the lobby security post bid us good night.
"Full moon, Ms. Cooper. I'd get rid of Chapman first
shot you get."

I gave him a thumbs-up and got into the passenger
seat of Mercer's car, parked up the street on Hogan
Place, telling Mike we'd meet him at the restaurant on
Sixty-fourth Street.

"Mercer, before you get in, remember to dig out
the pictures, okay?"

He nodded and opened the trunk, handing me four
packages of snapshots of the baby who had been born
in the spring to him and his wife Vickee. As we pulled
away from the curb, I turned on the interior light and
flipped through the photographs.

"It's amazing how much they change in just one
month. He's enormous."

Mercer Wallace was forty-two, six years older than
Mike and me. He was one of a handful of African
Americans who had been promoted to the coveted
first-grade rank in the detective division of the NYPD.
After his mother died in childbirth, he had been raised
by his father, Spencer, in a middle-class neighborhood
of Queens, where the elder Wallace had worked as a
mechanic at Delta Airlines.

His second marriage, to an equally talented detective named Vickee Eaton whom he admired and
adored, had ended a few years ago when she walked
out on him. But after Mercer was wounded in a
shoot-out during a murder investigation, Vickee had
come back to help him heal, and the quietly charis-
matic man had rejoiced at his great good fortune. The
remarriage and recent birth of Logan Wallace marked

the first go at establishing a family among what Mike, Mercer, and I liked to think of as our modern urban trio of musketeers.

I listened to Mercer's description of his new lifestyle, my head against the car window, mindlessly watching the overhead lights as we streaked past them up the East River Drive. Sleepless nights were nothing new for any of us. But bottles, feedings, formula, disposable diapers, and a wonderful little life for which both Mercer and Vickee were completely responsible was a whole new dynamic.

"I know I'm boring you to pieces, Alex."

"Not at all. I love hearing about him. I intend to try very hard to spoil him beyond imagining and be his favorite auntie," I said. "On the other hand, the minute you start proselytizing like Mike, I'll treat you the same way I treat telemarketers who call in the middle of my dinner hour."

I listened to him tell me about the joys of fatherhood while my mind wandered for the rest of the ride. Something had brought me close enough to formalizing my relationship with Jake that I had tried living with him in the middle of the previous winter. When I took a step backward from that move, it was without any regret that I was putting off a decision about marriage and raising a child.

I had often tried to figure out what it was that made me so content with my present single situation, since I had experienced all the benefits of a warm and loving family throughout my youth and adolescence. My mother, Maude, had met my father while she was at college getting her nursing degree. She had every superb nurturing quality of a great RN, but had diverted her skills and her own career to the paramount feature of her life: her marriage. My two older brothers and I were brought up in a household in which family came first—parents, grandparents, and siblings. Now it seemed the independence that everyone had worked so hard to instill in me had firmly taken root and made me entirely comfortable in my own skin.

"What do you hear from your folks? They okay?"

"They're fine. They're out West, visiting my brother and his kids," I said to Mercer.

My father, Benjamin, had retired from his cardiology practice years ago. The simple plastic tubing that he and his partner had developed three decades earlier had been used in all open-heart surgery in virtually every operating room in the country. It was the Cooper-Hoffman valve that had cushioned my lifestyle, providing a superb education—my degree in English literature from Wellesley and the subsequent Juris Doctor from the University of Virginia—as well as the means to maintain my apartment on Manhattan's Upper East Side and my beloved farmhouse on Martha's Vineyard.

But it was my father's devotion to public service in his medical career that led me to try something comparable in the law by applying to the Office of the District Attorney following my graduation more than twelve years earlier. I had anticipated spending five or six years there before moving on to private practice. As I rotated through the routine assignments of the young prosecutorial staff, I'd been fascinated and engaged by the work of the Sex Crimes Prosecution Unit. The endless challenges—legal, investigative, scientific, and emotional—kept me riveted, and committed to making a professional home for myself in this new specialty within the law, created just a generation earlier.

We pulled off the drive and circled the block before Mercer spotted a parking place on Second Avenue.

Mike was standing on the sidewalk with Giuliano, the owner of the restaurant. Both seemed to be enjoying the warm September evening.

"*Ciao, Signorina Cooper. Com'e stai?* How was your holiday?" He held the door open and ushered us to the corner table at the window, where Adolfo seated us and started to describe the specials.

"Fine, thanks. And Italy?"

"*Bellissima,* like always. Fenton," he called to the bartender. "Dewar's on the rocks for Ms. Cooper. *Doppio.* And your best vodka for the gentlemen. On me."

"You oughta stay away more often, Coop. Giuliano's so happy to see you he's giving away his booze. That's a first."

I ordered the veal special, a paillard pounded thin and lightly breaded, with arugula and chopped tomatoes on top. Mercer asked for sausage and pepper with a side dish of fettuccine, and Mike settled on the lobster *fra diavolo.*

"How's Valerie?" I asked.

"Pretty good. She never seems to pick her head up from the drafting table long enough to tell me." Mike had been dating a woman for the past year, an archi-

tect who was involved in planning the redesign of the
Museum of Modern Art. They'd met when Valerie
was in the early stages of recovering from a mastectomy, in treatment at Sloan-Kettering Hospital, where
Mike had gone to donate blood.

"How did the trip to California go?" Valerie had
taken him home to Palo Alto to meet her family over
the Labor Day weekend.

"I'm not sure Professor Jacobsen's first choice for
his daughter's beau is a New York City detective, but
the old lady handled it pretty well."

Michael Patrick Chapman was the son of a legendary street cop, a second-generation immigrant
who had met his wife on a visit to the family home in
County Cork. Brian was on the job for twenty-six
years, dying of a massive coronary barely two days
after turning in his gun and shield. That had been
during Mike's junior year at Fordham, and although
he'd completed school the following year, he'd ap-
plied for admission to the police academy before he
handed back his cap and gown. He had idolized his
father, longed to follow in his footsteps, and distin-
guished himself in his rookie year with a major arrest
following the drug-related massacre of a Colombian
family in Washington Heights.

I raised my glass and clinked it against the others'.
For the better part of the last decade, these two men
had become my closest friends. They'd taught me the
creative investigative skills they themselves had mastered, they covered my back whenever I was exposed
to danger or double-dealing, and they could make me
laugh at the darkest moments of my life.

Dinner was casual and easy. We caught up on each other's personal lives and reminded Mike of the details of the Tripping case. I wanted an early night, so Mercer dropped me in front of my building before ten, and Mike went on to his office to do paperwork, ready for the long tour ahead.

The doorman let me in and handed me the mail and dry cleaning that had been left in the valet's room. I rode up the twenty stories in the elevator, key in hand, opening my apartment door and flipping on the lights.

I spent an hour at my desk organizing my questions for the morning. Jake called at eleven-fifteen, when he got off the air after delivering his piece.

"Hope you don't mind that I stayed in D.C."

"Good timing, actually. I get to concentrate on the trial. The sooner I have it behind me, the happier I'll be."

"Remind me what we've got on for the weekend."

"Saturday night we've got theater tickets with Joan and Jim. Friday night I thought we'd have a quiet evening at home."

"That means I cook."

"Or Shun Lee delivers. Or we starve, and just nibble on each other." I was useless in the kitchen. Whipping up a tuna salad and removing ice cubes from their tray was a slim repertoire.

"*That* flight I won't consider missing."

I hung up, undressed, and drew a steaming-hot bath, filling the tub with something bubbly that smelled like vanilla. My friend Joan Stafford had written another thriller, and I took the manuscript with me into the tub, trying to discern the players who were so deliciously portrayed in the roman à clef.

Sleep came easily and I awakened at six, with time to make coffee and read the newspaper before making my way to the garage in the basement of my building.

"Good morning, J.P.," I said to the attendant, who pointed to my Jeep, which he had positioned at the top of the ramp.

"You got company, Ms. Cooper."

I opened the car door and found Mike Chapman dozing in the front passenger seat.

He didn't move a hair as I settled into the driver's side. I pressed the button to play the first CD in the deck, turning the volume up so that the letters *R-E-S-P-E-C-T* blasted out of the speakers.

Mike opened his left eye and shifted his weight. "If I had wanted to wake up with Aretha Franklin, I would have gone to bed with the woman."

"I guess you didn't exactly want to wake up with me, either. You could have rung the doorbell. There's always the sofa bed in the den."

"And all that temptation in the bedroom? Sorry, just came to pick your brain. Only got here fifteen minutes ago and I was afraid I'd miss you if I didn't head you off in the garage. Wild night in the naked city."

"What happened?"

"Caught two kills, so I gotta go right back uptown to sort things out."

That's what homicides were to Mike Chapman.

Kills. Hunters used that word to describe the slaughter of their prey, and fighter pilots spoke the same language when referring to the downing of enemy planes—the unnatural termination of lives.

"What kind of cases?" I asked.

"One's a shooting, probably justifiable. Bodega owner on One Hundred Tenth dropped a guy who pulled a knife on him and tried to steal a six-pack of Bud. Other one's really ugly. Thought you could help."

"Sure. How?"

"Break-in at a brownstone in Harlem, West Side. Place was ransacked, lots of old junk strewn all over the place," Mike said, shutting off the music. "Eighty-two-year-old woman. Looks like she was raped and then smothered to death with her own pillow. Thought you could tell me why."

"Why what?" I asked.

"Why somebody does that? Who am I looking for? What's inside his head? What the hell's the motivation for a sexual assault on an octogenarian who's already had a stroke and was partially paralyzed?"

"I can give you hours on this, but I probably still won't be able to answer your question. No one can. Last time I had one like that, I called my favorite court shrink. 'The guy either hates his mother, or he loves his mother too much. Your perp either has an Electra complex, or his mother beat him when he was a child. The guy either needed to control his victim, or has a thing about—'"

"How much does it take to control a semi-invalid eighty-two-year-old? I realize profilers are useless."

"Have you checked burglary patterns? Try Special Victims. We've had a few cases with a guy who pretends to be a plumber, sent by the superintendent. Gets in, beats the women up pretty badly, and usually tears the place apart looking for cash and jewelry. Then he rapes them, almost like an afterthought."

"Women as old as this?" Mike asked.

"No. But he's just opportunistic. He takes whoever is there."

He opened the car door to get out. "Will you look at the crime scene photos with me, and go over the autopsy report, in case I'm missing anything?"

"I'm in court all day today."

"What's this?" he asked, checking the date on his watch. "Thursday morning? I won't have much to show you in the way of pathology results until Saturday."

"Fine. Meanwhile, I'll get Sarah to assign someone to work on it with you."

Mike closed the door and I started the engine. He walked around to my side and leaned on the roof of the Jeep. "Did your mother let you wear white shoes in September when you were a kid?"

I was anxious to get down to the office. "What are you talking about?"

"The Chapman babes," he said, referring to his three older sisters, "after Labor Day my mother never let them be seen in white."

"Yeah, I know what you mean." I laughed, remembering my own mother's stories of the fashion rules of the fifties.

"So around two o'clock this morning, there's a

squad car parked in front of the projects where your buddy Kevin Bessemer disappeared. The guys see this fashion vision walking down the street. White high-heeled patent leather shoes and a white shoulder bag. The whole outfit just didn't seem to fit."

"With what?"

"Thermometer almost hit ninety last night. I'd give her a pass on the color of her footwear in that temperature, but she was sporting some kind of muskrat at the very same time."

"Coat?"

"Yeah, a full-length fur-bearing rodent. May even be a mink for all I know. Kevin sure was grateful to his main squeeze and her rear window."

"You got his girlfriend? Where is she now?" This brought us one step closer to getting a break on Besse-mer's whereabouts. "Talk about burying the lead. No wonder you came to deliver this news in person."

He tapped his hand against the car door. "She's up in the squad. I'll keep you posted. We're about to go interview her. Tiffany Gatts. And you can add a charge to Kevin's arrest warrant."

"What now?"

"Statutory rape," Mike said, backing away from me up the ramp to the street. "Little Tiffany's only just turned sweet sixteen."

4

"People of the State of New York against Andrew Tripping. The defendant, his attorneys, and the assistant district attorney are present," the clerk announced in a flat monotone.

There were only three other people seated in the pews behind Peter Robelon, on what Mike Chapman referred to as the groom's side of the courtroom.

Harlan Moffett put aside the racing sheet he was studying and asked each of us if we were ready to get started. The judge had a fondness for the ponies, and would often interrupt proceedings to check the off-track-betting phone line for the outcome of a wager.

"Who you got here today, Alexandra?"

"Your Honor, I don't think any of the parties in court consider themselves prosecution witnesses. I assume," I said, turning to look at the two women seated in the second row of benches, "that Ms. Taggart is present. I spoke with her last evening but she hasn't identified herself to me."

The middle-aged woman in a flowered dress that hung to the top of her ankles rose and stepped forward. "I'm Nancy Taggart, sir. I represent the Manhattan Foundling Hospital."

She motioned to the woman sitting beside her, who was younger but just as severe-looking. "This is Dr. Huang. She's the psychologist responsible for the supervision of the Tripping boy."

"And you?" Moffett pointed his gavel at the man sitting alone in the first row. "You a legal eagle, too?"

"Jesse Irizzary. Counsel for the Agency for Child Welfare. We placed the child."

"I got more damn lawyers in this case than I got witnesses. What's the deal here? Can we reach any agreement on how we're going to proceed?"

"Your Honor, last week I asked you to issue a subpoena directing the production of Dulles Tripping—"

"What'd I tell you? I didn't do it?" Moffett asked me. "No, sir."

His pinky ring circled in Tripping's direction. "What kinda name is Dulles? You name your boy for an airport?"

Both Peter Robelon and Emily Frith leaned in close and began whispering to their client, probably cautioning him not to open his mouth. Everything about Robelon's physical appearance was in sharper focus than his client's as their heads came together at the counsel table. His dark hair was well-groomed, his skin was tanned, and there was a reptilian veneer that made me distrustful of the earnest glances he flashed back at me from time to time.

"The child was named for Allen Dulles. Former head of the Central Intelligence Agency. I'm just reading from the statement the boy himself made during the hospital admission process, the day his father was arrested and Dulles was examined at Bellevue," I told the court. "It's relevant to the matter on trial. You'll hear more about it during the case."

Tripping was a control freak. Every detail Paige Vallis had told me confirmed that. He had started disciplining the child in military fashion from the time Dulles was a toddler, intent on being the spymaster for his own little soldier.

"You were saying?"

"That the subpoena was issued to direct Ms. Taggart and Mr. Irizarry to bring Dulles Tripping to your chambers, where I might interview him and make a determination, with the help of a forensic psychiatrist, about whether or not he is able to testify in these proceedings."

Nancy Taggart spoke up. "I'm moving to quash that subpoena."

Jesse Irizarry was connected to her at the hip. "I join in that application."

"Why do you want the boy so badly, Al—sorry, Ms. Cooper?" Moffett asked. "He a witness to this rape you got?"

"Not exactly. Obviously, since I haven't talked with him, I don't know exactly what he saw and heard. But no, he was not in the room when the sexual assault occurred."

"So what do you need him for?"

"He actually is part of the forcible compulsion, Judge. The treatment of the boy by his father that very evening is one of the reasons Ms. Vallis submitted to Mr. Tripping's sexual demands."

Peter Robelon read the puzzled expression on Moffett's face and took advantage of the judge's skepticism to knock my position. "That one is really a stretch for the prosecution."

Moffett decided this was the moment to give me some paternal advice. "I know you like to be creative, dear, but this is a novel application of the law, isn't it?"

"Ms. Vallis had never met Dulles Tripping before the point in the evening when she entered the defendant's apartment. The boy was invited into the living room. His father directed him to sit on a chair in the corner and be drilled on a series of questions. There was a discussion about a pistol, a reference to the pistol actually being in the apartment. And there was talk of what the punishment would be if Dulles answered incorrectly. One of his eyes was swollen shut and badly discolored. There were bruises on the child's forearm and—"

Robelon was on his feet. "We're getting ahead of ourselves here, aren't we?"

"Ms. Vallis was not going to leave," I continued, "unless or until she could take the boy with her and find out what had happened to him."

"So why didn't she just stay up and watch TV all night? Who said she had to go to bed with my client? If that's all Ms. Cooper has to—"

"I've got more than that, as you're well aware." Not a lot more, but Paige Vallis was a good witness, with a harrowing story to tell.

Moffett scratched his head. "What's this kid gonna say?"

"Quite honestly, I don't know what he's going to

say at this point, Judge. That's why I want the opportunity to speak with him. We've been at a terrible disadvantage in this matter."

"Ms. Taggart," the judge asked, "are you familiar with what caused the remand of the child to your facility back in March?"

"After Mr. Tripping's arrest and incarceration, sir, there were no living relatives to care for Dulles. There was a complete physical and psychological workup ordered, and the findings made it clear to the family court judge that even when the father was released, no one would authorize an immediate return to his custody."

"There was an Article Ten proceeding," I explained, "on neglect and abuse. Every eighteen months there's to be a hearing held about the continued care of the child."

"Have you got all the institutional records, Ms. Cooper?" Moffett shifted his attention to me.

"No, sir. Only the meds from Bellevue, the morning Ms. Vallis reported the crime."

"You two," he said, waving at Taggart and Irizarry. "Why can't you give the district attorney all your reports? She's got a job to do."

Taggart pursed her lips. "We've got serious concerns about the confidentiality of the material here. The foster parents don't want to be identified, nor do we want to reveal the location of the child, for his own security."

"So we redact the papers. Take out specific names and locations." Taggart and Irizarry huddled with each other to think of a response to the court's suggestion.

Tripping was agitated now. He was writing furiously on a legal pad, sticking his notes under Robelon's nose.

"Are you at least prepared to discuss the psychological findings, so I can make a decision here?"

Taggart nodded to Moffett as she answered. "I'll let Dr. Huang do that."

I rose to my feet. "Your Honor, I'd like the witness to take the stand so that we might do this under oath. I'd like to question Dr. Huang myself."

"Sit down, Ms. Cooper. I can handle this."

"Most respectfully, Judge Moffett, I'm more familiar with some of the history here and might be better able to direct the cross—"

He glared at me and I took my seat. "Don't test me, Ms. Cooper. I still got some tricks up the big black sleeves of this robe. I didn't get here just on my good looks."

The heavy old door creaked open behind me and I turned to see who had entered. Two men, suited like bookends, walked in shoulder to shoulder and sat in the last row of benches on the bride's side, behind me. If *Saturday Night Live* was doing a spoof of spooks, they would have cast this pair. Dark glasses in a dim courtroom on an overcast day, government-issue suits with drab patterned ties, and haircuts from the local PX.

I focused back on the witness. Huang stated her credentials and gave the background of Dulles's history, from his mother's death shortly after he was born, to his grandmother's care, to his placement with his father after her loss.

"It was my recommendation that there be no visits, no contact, between Mr. Tripping and his son. There is a strong bond between them, but it is a pathological one. Dulles is worried about losing his relationship with his father"—she stopped speaking and glanced over at the defendant—"but he is even more fearful of retribution."

Tripping was talking in Peter Robelon's ear, while Frith tried to ease him away so Robelon could follow the proceedings. Tripping had no use for Emily Frith, aware that she was just seated at the defense table for decoration.

Robelon interrupted Huang's narrative, fumbling through his notes. "And your colleague, I think it's a Ms. Plass, her view was entirely opposed to yours. Her opinion was that it would be good to arrange visitation between the two because this child adores his father and will eventually be given trial visitation opportunities with him at the conclusion of these proceedings."

"You'll get your chance, Mr. Robelon," Moffett said. "I want to hear what Dr. Huang has to say. Has there been any regular contact at all?"

"By telephone, sir. That was the compromise we reached."

"Monitored?"

"No, sir. But there were rules. Mr. Tripping was forbidden to discuss the allegations before this court, or anything to do with the criminal proceedings. And brief meetings. There were two meetings which I conducted at the hospital."

Now I was as agitated as the defendant. "*What?*

When did this occur? There has been an order of protection in place since Mr. Tripping's arraignment. There was to be *no* contact with the child. I'm not even blaming the defendant for the violation—I have to find out here in court that it's two professional agencies that are responsible? Your Honor, it would appear that everyone except for me has had the opportunity to talk with this child. What more do you need to hear?"

Huang was nervous, biting her lower lip as she ran her fingers across the top page of her records, looking for dates.

"Were you aware of the order of protection?"

"Yes, sir. The family court judge said she was overriding it. In the best interests of the boy." Huang gestured toward Ms. Taggart. "The lawyers told me to arrange the meetings."

Put that in the category of "nice to know."

"When were they held?" Moffett asked.

"I'm trying to find you an exact time. The first one was early on, when the defendant was still incarcerated. I remember that clearly. The second one was midsummer, before I left for my vacation in August."

There must be one enormous stretch of beach on the Atlantic coast where every psychiatrist and psychologist in New York disappear for the month of August, hoping the city's supply of antidepressants and mood elevators will hold all the patients at bay.

"How'd they go, these meetings?" Moffett asked.

"Perhaps you can understand my reluctance to respond to you, Judge. My conversations with the child are privileged in nature. If I betray that confidence to the court, especially in the presence of the father, I'm not certain I'll be able to get Dulles to speak with me again."

"Well, was there any discussion of these criminal charges in your presence?"

"No, sir. Not these charges." She spoke with hesitation. "But others. That's why I terminated the conversation."

"What did Mr. Tripping talk about?"

"Not him, sir. Dulles." Huang spoke softly and stared at a spot on the floor in front of her. "The boy asked his father whether it was true that Mr. Tripping had been involved in a plot to assassinate the president of the United States seven or eight years ago. The child had brought a news clipping with him. Something he had taken off the Internet."

Robelon was on his feet, pounding his fist on the table. "I'm going to object to this line of questioning, Judge. That case was never brought by the government. There's no need to add any mention of it to this record. I move to strike."

Moffett seemed to miss the point about the gravity and magnitude of the accusation, as well as the boy's concern about his father's possibly violent history. The judge seemed more interested in the level of the child's intelligence.

"Motion denied. The boy was able to find that news article by himself?"

Huang was on firm territory here. "On-line, on his computer. Dulles is a very smart young man. Tests way beyond his age range. Although he's only ten, he's capable of reading at a college level."

"So I don't have to worry about swearability?"

A child of ten could not be presumed to understand the meaning of an oath. Moffett seemed relieved to know he would not have to grapple with that problem, too.

"He has the intellectual capacity to have an oath administered. What I can't guarantee is whether or not he will choose to give false testimony in your courtroom."

"That puts Ms. Cooper in a very difficult position, Ms. Taggart. Suppose I let her call the boy to the stand, and you haven't allowed her to speak with him first. Suppose he testifies in an exculpatory fashion, denies that his father injured him. Let's say—and I never know what Ms. Cooper has in her arsenal—but say she knows the boy's statement is inconsistent with things he has said before."

"That's possible."

"Well, then Ms. Cooper's stuck. She can't cross-examine him. She can't impeach her own witness."

Taggart glared at me. "She can have Dulles declared a hostile witness."

I was back on my feet. "I don't know whether Ms. Taggart's ever tried a case to a jury. I would guess not. If you think I'm about to put a ten-year-old child through *that* experience, emotionally or legally, you need a refresher course in trial advocacy."

"Judge Moffett," she went on, "Dulles Tripping is at massive risk for the development of a mental disorder—"

"Which I certainly have no intention of compounding," I added.

"I've already told you to sit down, Ms. Cooper. How so, Ms. Taggart?"

"The risk factors start with the multiple loss of caretakers throughout his young life—mother, grandmother, and now father. Even a stepmother. You may not be aware, Your Honor, that Mr. Tripping remarried for a brief period, a few years back. Second, parental suicide increases the risk of his own suicidal ideation. Third, being abused—or witnessing abuse—by his father increases Dulles's risk of disturbing conduct. And—" Taggart's volume dropped as she made reference to Andrew Tripping.

"What?" Moffett asked, cupping his hand to his ear.

"I was talking about the paternal psychosis that's been diagnosed. Mr. Tripping is a schizophrenic. It increases some tenfold the probability that Dulles will inherit that same condition."

The swinging doors creaked behind me again. Moffett had turned his chair toward the wall, tapping his fingertips together as he tried to settle on a Solomonic solution.

I swiveled to see who had entered the room this time. The man who stood with his back to the door, getting his bearings, seemed out of place in the drab surrounds of the criminal courthouse. There was an air of elegance about him, with his charcoal gray bespoke suit, horn-rimmed glasses, barrel-cuffed shirt, and tasseled loafers. I guessed him to be in his early forties, and at five-eight, a bit shorter than I am.

I watched as he sauntered down the aisle, Robelon and Tripping engaged in an animated discussion as they eyed him, too. There was in him none of the strident urgency that blanketed so many of the earnest young defense attorneys who walked these hallways every day.

The judge pushed his chair around so that he faced us again. "This mention of schizophrenia by the doctors, Mr. Robelon, you're not gonna spring any kind of psych defense on us in the middle of the trial, are you?"

"No, sir."

Tripping looked over his shoulder at the man in the gray suit, now seated three rows behind him, who mouthed something—several words—to the defendant. I could not make out what he said.

"Just a minute," Moffett said, slamming his gavel on his desktop. "Mr. Tripping, you wanna pay attention to these proceedings or you wanna play charades with the people in the peanut gallery? You, you got business here?"

The man answered, "Yes, I do." Moffett's courtroom was more casual than most. The fact that the man did not rise to respond to the judge was not taken as a sign of disrespect by the court, but there seemed a touch of arrogance about it to me.

"You a lawyer, too?"

"Yes, sir."

"Jesus. I'm choking to death on lawyers here. Get me an Indian chief. Doesn't anybody go to medical school anymore? Who are you?"

"Graham Hoyt." He reached in his pocket and pulled out a small leather case, black alligator, and removed a business card from it, standing to pass it to the clerk to give over to the judge. Then he looked at me and nodded, passing another card.

"I'm the guardian *ad litem* for Dulles Tripping. The family court appointed me to protect his interests during the pendency of this case."

"You're late. *Ad litem. Come latum.*" Moffett chuckled to himself.

"No one informed me about this hearing. I just happened to call Mr. Robelon's office this morning and his paralegal told me what was going on today."

Great. He's obviously tight with the defendant. For every step forward I try to take, I get pushed back two or three.

"You here to oppose the prosecution's motion to interview Dulles?"

"Actually, no, Your Honor. Maybe I can broker some kind of arrangement that would be satisfactory to everyone."

I glanced over my shoulder to reassess Hoyt. This was the first time in six months anyone had even suggested listening to me to see whether what I wanted was reasonable. He smiled at me and I reflexively returned the smile.

"How about saving the court some time. You know what the kid's gonna tell her?"

"The truth, Your Honor. Dulles Tripping will simply tell Ms. Cooper the truth. He's going to say he was playing lacrosse the afternoon before he met Ms. Vallis and got hit in the face by a stick. Happens on playgrounds across America every single day."

5

"Be careful what you wish for," I said to Mercer as I dropped an armload of case files onto my desk.

"What now?" He vacated my chair and opened a paper bag with our sandwiches and two bottles of water.

"I pushed and pushed to get the kid. Looks like it's going to happen now, but he's clearly been sanitized. You think I'm better off without trying to use him at trial?"

Mercer's judgment and insights were sound. "What's to lose talking to him? Keep fighting for the interview. We always knew this case was a crapshoot. You're good with kids. Maybe he'll surprise you and respond to some warmth in his life."

"The judge wants us to go on with jury selection this afternoon and do our opening statements tomorrow. How the hell do I open when I'm not sure what my witness list looks like?"

He bit into the baguette full of roast beef and all the trimmings. "Nothing you haven't done before, Ms. Cooper. Understate what you're gonna give 'em the first time you talk to them. Robelon gets up next and reinforces that you got zilch. Then out of the bag, you pull a surprise witness. He's smart, sympathetic, sincere—puts you over the top. Bingo. Tripping's dead meat."

"And best of all is that we can try to get Dulles into a better situation as soon as it's over. Place him in a stable, loving foster home and keep him out of reach of his crazy father until he's college age. That would be the real blessing of a conviction in this case."

"Slow down and eat something."

I sat at my desk and picked at the wilted greens from the deli on Broadway. "You should see the courtroom. Five lawyers in the mix, not counting me. Everybody's got a piece of the pie and I'm sure we haven't seen the end of it. Then there's these two suits—came in and sat in the back today. Never saw them before and can't quite figure out why they're here, but they sure look like stereotypes of government agents."

"You want me to—?"

"No, no. You can't be the one to talk to them. You're going to testify next week. I'll get someone from the DA's squad to sniff them out if they show up again."

"You think the CIA still has an interest in him?" Mercer asked.

I had subpoenaed Tripping's records from the Agency, but as I expected, those had been purged. It was clear he had worked there for several years, and had some Middle Eastern assignment that followed the 1993 car bombing of the World Trade Center.

Then came the allegation that he had participated in conversations about some harebrained plot to kill the president that was exposed before any overt steps were taken, and the CIA seemed to have misplaced their files on the entire matter.

"I suppose it's possible. They didn't let on that they were the least bit interested in the evidence you found in his apartment after he was in custody, did they?"

"That's so typical. We put it under their nose, and they act nonchalant so they don't have to give you anything in return."

The day Tripping was arrested, and based on the information Paige Vallis had given me when I interviewed her at the hospital with Mercer, I had drafted a search warrant.

Mercer had executed it that evening.

Tripping's apartment was more like a military outpost than a family home. His bedroom had only a mattress on the floor, while Dulles slept on a cot in an alcove off the kitchen. The walls were hung with a variety of scimitars and scythes, primitive weapons that looked capable of beheading an enemy with a single swipe. There was a bayonet and casing on the floor beside the mattress, and several bowie knives on tables throughout the warren of small rooms.

Vallis claimed Tripping had threatened her by holding a cold metallic object against her head, telling her it was a gun. She never saw it. Dulles led Mercer to a closet in the bedroom, from which he recovered an air pistol, with its pellets and case. None of these things was illegal to own, and only chargeable if the defendant had actually used them against another person.

There had been books and papers everywhere. Beside a lamp in the living room, under a black-sheathed stiletto, was a leather-bound copy of *The Seven Pillars of Wisdom,* the private edition published in 1926 and signed by T. E. Lawrence. Mercer had vouchered all the scraps, receipts, and correspondence, and we had spent days trying to find anything of significance among the writings that were in our safekeeping.

"A guy just can't get any luckier than this," Mike Chapman said, walking into my office. "Here we are, less than one hundred shopping days until Christmas, and Ms. Cooper's gift just falls into my lap. Now, Mercer, I suspect you want to give a tired guy like me who's been up all night keeping the city safe half of that fat sandwich you're filling up on."

He laid out a full-length fur coat across my papers and files.

"Not that Tiffany Gatts has agreed I can have this yet, but it would look mighty snappy on you, come the first frost."

"What'd she say?" I asked.

"Her exact words were a bit too crude to use in this refined company, but it was something like, 'I don't have to be talking to you, do I? Get me a lawyer.'"

"You mean you didn't get a thing out of her? Nothing about Kevin Bessemer? Nothing about where the coat came from?"

"All she kept saying about the fur was, 'It's *mines.*' Over and over. I asked where she got it, whether she had a sales slip for it, whether Kevin gave it to her. No use. Then when I started asking her about Kevin, she clammed up completely."

"The coat's stolen, right?"

"Trying to find that out. Lieutenant Peterson's got guys working the phones, checking to see if anything like this has been reported missing lately. Precincts around the city, Major Case Squad, Robbery Squad. Brought it for you to look at. See what you think. I only know about one kind of fur and it isn't this."

"Keep that thought to yourself," I said, picking up the heavy garment and examining the pelts.

The deep mahogany skins had rich color and fine long hair. They seemed dry to the touch, but they were clearly of good quality and fine styling. I spread the coat out on my desktop to look inside at the lining and label.

"Ever hear of that furrier?"

I shook my head from side to side. "Matignon et Fils. Rue Faubourg, Paris. That's a pretty pricey neighborhood."

I picked up my phone and dialed a number in Washington.

"You calling Interpol?"

I laughed. "No. Joan Stafford." My girlfriend knew more about shopping on the Faubourg-St. Honoré than all the *flics* in France.

She answered on the first ring.

"You kept me up way too late last night reading the novel, which I adored. Your favorite detectives want to know if you'll help us solve a little caper this afternoon, since I'm so worn-out."

Joan was living in D.C., engaged to a foreign affairs columnist for a major newspaper. She was one of my closest friends.

"Will Chapman give me his gold shield if I do?"

"At least that. Think fur. Think France." I told her the name of the maker.

"You're out of luck to get a bargain, if that's what you're in the market for," she said. "Gregoire Matignon closed his doors in the 1960s."

"Was he a big deal?"

"Just the biggest, Alex. One of those old families that started out in Russia, dressing the czars and czarinas. Then moved to Paris to service the royal families of Europe. The Duchess of Windsor, Grace Kelly—you know that classic photo of her when she started dating Rainier, wearing a golden sable, stepping out of an old Bentley in front of the Grimaldi Palace? That kind of clientele. As the monarchies became threatened with extinction, the minks thrived and Matignon went out of business."

I ran my fingers over the faded red stitching on the old label. "That's a help. I'll call you later."

"What'd she say?"

"That it sure wasn't made for Tiffany Gatts. You find a monogram?"

"Where?" Mike asked.

I folded back the lapels of the broad collar and scanned the lining. "It's pretty traditional to sew the client's initials into the lining."

"Jeez. And to think my mother used to mark my labels with a felt-tip pen, so the other kids at school didn't make off with my leather jackets. This winter I'll get her to try embroidery."

"See?" Near the bottom of the left front of the coat, in a deep chocolate shade of thick silk thread,

was an elegant script monogram. I read the letters
aloud. "*R du R.*"

"That should narrow my search."

"I'd say you concentrate on the Seventeenth and
Nineteenth Precincts," Mercer said, smiling. "High-
rent districts on the Upper East Side. Lots of European diplomats. Some Eurotrash with delusions of
nobility. Maybe Westchester. Maybe Great Neck."

Mike grabbed the telephone directory off my
bookshelf. "These 'guys listed under the *D*'s or the
R's? We haven't got a lot of them in Ireland."

"Start with *D.*"

"DuBock. DuBose." He ran his forefinger down a
long list of names. "DuQuade. Now we're getting
close. DuRaine, DuReese, DuRoque . . ."

"I don't want to put a damper on your enthusiasm,
but something as old as this," I said, fingering the
worn cuff of the once-glamorous coat, "you've got to
figure that since the furrier closed so long ago, and
with all the PC attitudes towards animal skins lately,
this may have been through thrift shops or second-
hand-clothing places."

"You need a more positive attitude, Coop. Some
folks have still got the first fancy outfit they ever wore
to church or work or a funeral parlor. Maybe it's the
difference between your relatives and mine."

"Suit yourself. Then don't forget that most women
store their furs for the summer. Better check and make
sure there wasn't a heist on Seventh Avenue," I suggested, directing Mike to the fur district between
Twenty-fifth and Thirty-fourth Streets.

Laura was out on her lunch break, so when my

phone rang I answered it myself. It was the security officer in the lobby of the building. "Thanks for letting me know. It's okay, I realize it's not your fault."

I looked up at Mike. "Maybe you could shut my door. There's a screamer on her way upstairs. Tiffany's mother just blasted past the guard's desk when they tried to stop her at the metal detector."

"I had a pet water buffalo once had a better disposition than Mrs. Gatts. He was smaller than she is, too." Mike walked toward the door but he was a few seconds too late.

All 280 pounds of Etta Gatts blocked the doorway of my office.

"Where do I find Alexander Cooper? Where is he?"

The three of us spoke at once. As I identified myself to her and corrected my name, Mike was saying that he wasn't here just now, and Mercer was doing his best to step between the woman and me to diffuse the situation, telling her to calm down and back off.

"Where you got my baby at?" She was breathing fire.

I hadn't even asked Mike that question. I assumed they had the sixteen-year-old in custody, but I didn't know for what.

"Take it easy, Mrs. Gatts," Mercer said, towering over the large woman. He explained to her how important it was to stay quiet so she didn't get thrown out of the building.

While he tried to soothe her I talked to Mike. "I've got a case to try. What the hell is going on here? Where's the girl?"

"Downstairs, in the holding pens."

"Charged with?"

"Criminal possession of stolen prop—"

I interrupted him before he could finish. "You can't make out felony value with this old thing," I said, pointing to the fur coat. "It's not worth twenty-five hundred dollars at this point."

"And aiding a fugitive—"

"Better."

"And felony-weight possession of crack cocaine. A white patent leather bag full of little vials."

I turned back to Mrs. Gatts. "I think the best place to wait for your daughter would be downstairs, inside the entrance to One Hundred Centre Street, where the judge will see her later this evening and set some bail."

"What you mean 'this evening'? It's not even two o'clock yet. What you mean 'bail'? Tiffany's just a baby. You got no right to hold her where I can't see her."

Mercer reached out his hand to steady Mrs. Gatts's flailing arms. She took a step back and kicked at my door with all her considerable might.

I tried to follow Mercer's lead and be diplomatic. I took a step toward the woman but Mike blocked me with an outstretched arm. "You could make things much easier for Tiffany, ma'am. We just need her to help us. She's been keeping some dangerous company."

"Like who?"

"Kevin Bessemer."

"Bessie? That man in jail. He old enough to be her

father. What she doing with him?" Etta Gatts clucked her tongue in disbelief, and I let Mercer try to explain why Tiffany was in trouble.

"Don't mean a damn thing. The lieutenant told me my baby was too young to have sex with a thirty-two-year-old man. That it's rape. Well, in this state she too young to vote and too young to drink. That makes her too young to go to jail."

"Three out of four ain't bad, Mrs. Gatts. Sixteen years old and she gets treated like an adult in criminal court. You oughta do like Ms. Cooper says and have a serious talk with Tiffany. She's the only one," Mike said, pointing at me, "who can give your daughter a break."

"I don't want no break from you," the woman said, kicking the metal door again. Mercer reached for her elbow but she raised her voice a few decibels as she twisted loose and kept hollering.

"Take it easy."

"Don't touch me," she screamed at Mercer. "And you, you skinny-ass bitch, you watch yourself. My hand to the heavens, my people ain't through with you yet."

6

"Look on the bright side, Coop. At least she called your tail part 'skinny,'" Mike said, tossing his napkin across the room into the wastebasket. "I'm going to take this coat over to the photo unit to get it shot, along with some close-ups of the label and monogram."

"First you could escort Alex up to the courtroom," Mercer said. "She needs you to eyeball a couple of funny-looking feds, get a make on them. I can't go because the jury panel will be hanging out, and I'm going to testify next week."

"Guard my pelts, pal." Mike picked up my case file and followed me out the door.

We weaved our way around and between the potential jurors, who waited impatiently outside the courtroom in the airless corridor. One of the court officers saw us coming and opened the door to admit us.

Five minutes later, at two-fifteen sharp, the group of sixty was allowed in. Twelve resumed their seats in the box and the others obeyed directions to fill the benches in front.

The two men in dark glasses parked themselves in the back row.

I walked to the rear of the courtroom with Mike to try to get an overheard. As we neared the pair, Mike looked up and broke into a smile, surprised to spot an old acquaintance.

"Hey, good to see you. I'm Mike Chapman." He extended his hand to the guy farther away from the aisle, who shook it but didn't say a word. "Sheehan's bar, right? Didn't I catch you there just before the summer? You bought the last round."

The man shook his head. "I think you got that wrong."

"No, no, I didn't. Must have been another watering hole, but I'm sure you're the guy I was talking to. You're a G-man, aren't you? Used to work out of Langley."

The second guy looked at his partner to see whether he blinked.

"Good try, but you're wrong. Must have been talking to my twin brother."

"The better-looking one, yeah. Probably so. You here to testify?"

"Nope."

"Look," Mike said, "I'm a cop, a detec—"

"No kidding. And last I knew these were public courtrooms, so I hope you don't mind that my buddy and I just sit and watch."

Mike just shrugged. "Suit yourself. But you're in the wrong seats. The judge has a couple of places saved for you two."

Again the younger one, closer to me, furrowed his

eyes and checked his partner while Mike pointed and spoke. "Right over there. First two behind the dark-haired little broad with the dandruff on her shoulders, there's a label that says 'Reserved for assholes.' Must be a really top level assignment to be baby-sitting one of your former whackjobs at his trial. Next time you guys oughta ask for a clothing allowance. That polyester is so flammable. C'mon, Coop, get to work. I'll split."

"I didn't invite you here to stir up a hornet's nest," I said as we walked away. "Moffett is barely tolerating me as it is. Now you have to go and mouth off to these characters."

"Those two are completely useless. What's the difference if I agitate them a little bit? You needed a pro to tell you those guys are CIA? Check your peepers with an eye doctor." Mike turned away and let the courtroom door swing shut behind him, and I walked back up to the well just as Harlan Moffett stepped into the courtroom.

"All rise. Hear ye, hear ye," the clerk droned on, announcing the entrance of the judge and reading the case into the record.

Moffett explained the procedure. In the old days, most of the questioning of the panel was done by the lawyers. In high-profile cases, or matters with sensitive issues, it could drag on for days. More recently the state courts had adopted the federal procedures, in which the judge controlled what was asked. We would have our jury sworn by the end of the afternoon.

He began with general information, reading the names of all the participants and witnesses in the case.

"You know anybody, recognize any of these names? Just raise your hand and I'll call on you." Jurors took the opportunity to look each of us over but none responded.

"You're going to hear from three police officers during the trial. Anybody here have cops in the family?" Six hands went up around the room. "No reason to make you believe them any more or any less than other witnesses, is there? You'll evaluate their testimony the same way you would any other person, isn't that right?"

Robelon and I were making notes next to those names we had of people already sitting in the jury box, how they responded to the inquiries, whether aloud or with facial expressions and physical gestures. We would probe them on personal information that seemed relevant to either side. In this case, Paige Vallis carried far more weight than the few police officers, who would be subject to more intense scrutiny as witnesses in drug sales or gun possession cases. They had nothing to offer that would shed light on the events in Andrew Tripping's apartment.

Moffett had reached the point at which he talked about the crimes with which the defendant was charged. "You got any problems with any of these?" he asked, trying to get past the word "rape" without raising any red flags. In my dozen years at the prosecution table, I wagered this would be a first if he succeeded.

Two hands went up in the jury box. I looked over my shoulder and saw more scattered through the rows.

"Your Honor," I said, getting to my feet, "may we take these at the bench?"

Moffett wasn't pleased with my suggestion. It would waste precious minutes, and would result in more people being excused than he wanted. He knew that if he denied my request to approach him and hear the personal revelations one by one, fewer women would discuss their concerns in the open courtroom, among strangers. Both Robelon and I would have less opportunity to make challenges for cause.

He was about to deny my request when my adversary rose to agree with me. Always better for the defense to let the jurors think they were truly sensitive to the issue.

Number three stood between Robelon and me, at the front of the courtroom, telling Moffett she could not possibly serve at this trial. "I was a victim of rape myself, Judge."

"When was that?"

"Five years ago. Raped and beaten."

"Was it here, in New York? Miss Cooper or one of her colleagues handle your investigation?"

"No, sir. No one was ever caught."

"And Mr. Tripping didn't commit the crime, did he?"

She stared at her shoes and tears filled her eyes. "No, sir."

"And you know he's presumed innocent and has the right to a fair trial?"

She was choking up and couldn't talk. She nodded her head in the affirmative.

"So what's your problem?"

Robelon got the point and was eager to have the judge let her go. He had no desire to waste one of his limited number of peremptory challenges on someone who was clearly not going to be sympathetic to his client, or anyone else charged with this offense.

"All I'm asking is why you can't give this defendant a fair shake. Tell me."

"Judge, I think she's—"

"Don't tell me what you think, Ms. Cooper. I'm trying to move this along."

The juror looked at me, obviously hoping I would intervene again so that she could regain control of her emotions.

"Let me get you a cup of water," I said, stepping back to counsel table.

"I'm afraid I'm the wrong person for this kind of trial, sir. You may not think it's rational, but I can't sit here and listen to another woman describe a forcible assault. It's—it's still too raw for me. I'm sorry, I'm just not able to do it."

The judge had heard enough. "Report back to the central jury room tomorrow morning. Tell 'em to mark your ticket for civil court next time."

In all, seven women approached the bench to talk about their personal experiences. Four asked to be excused, and three felt they could not honestly know how they would react to sitting through the emotionally charged testimony of another survivor.

"Nobody says she's a victim yet," the judge growled at the last one on line. "That's what the jury's got to decide."

I checked my watch. Moffett would keep us till seven or eight in the evening to complete our selection. Nothing would move him from his schedule.

When he finished the general questioning, he passed the long green seating chart over to me so I could continue on with the more personal inquiries. I placed it on the small podium in front of the box and took a few seconds to match the jurors' faces to the names and addresses on the small printed summons representing each person before me.

By five-fifteen we had agreed on eleven jurors. I had bounced the butcher whose two teenaged sons had been arrested for a variety of crimes they didn't commit, the department store customer-complaint representative who thought it was impossible for women to be raped by men they knew and dated, and the acting student who thought O. J. Simpson was misunderstood by the media.

Peter Robelon made the classic mistake that defense attorneys often did while handling their first rape cases. He struggled for ways to get rid of all the women on the jury, figuring that men would place themselves in Andrew Tripping's shoes, find them too close a fit, and walk him out the courtroom door.

Little did he know the sad lesson I had learned over the years, that women were far more likely to criticize the conduct of others of their sex and blame them for their own victimization. I used to knock myself out trying to stack the box with a dozen intelligent women, until a small delegation of men told me, after a trial, that the ladies had been far too judgmental about the victim's conduct.

I watched my adversary knock off the avowed feminist with three unmarried sons in college and graduate school—not likely to vote with me when it came time to reach a verdict—and get rid of five or six young women whom he didn't happen to notice were making eye contact across the room with Andrew Tripping or Robelon himself, almost flirtatiously.

I didn't see my paralegal, Maxine, enter and walk up to the clerk's desk on the front side of the room opposite the jury box. She was distracting Moffett, and he called her on it. "You got something you need to disturb us for, missy?"

"She's got to talk to Ms. Cooper, pronto, Judge," the clerk said.

He stood behind his chair and waved me in Maxine's direction. I was no happier than Moffett and my expression must have showed that.

"Sorry, Alex. Mercer told me to get to you immediately. He wants to know if you can ask the judge to revoke the defendant's bail and remand him overnight."

"What possible reason would I have to do that?" I asked.

"A woman called your office a little while ago, looking for you. She claims to be the foster mother of Dulles Tripping. She says the principal sent the boy home with a note this afternoon, telling her that there was a man hanging out in front of the school yard at seven-thirty this morning, asking other kids if they knew where Dulles was."

"Did the woman leave her name and number? Did the teacher describe the guy?"

I was snapping at Maxine for answers that I knew I should not expect her to have.

"From what she said to me, it sounds kind of like the defendant," Maxine said.

"If it happened first thing this morning, why did the principal wait so long to tell her?"

I was trying to recall what time Tripping had gotten to the courthouse.

"He didn't wait. The woman had some medical appointments in the morning, after she dropped Dulles off at school. They'd been looking for her all day but she never went back to the house until after she picked up the boy."

I was over a barrel again. I couldn't make a bail application alleging that the defendant might have violated the order of protection without at least a first-hand ability to assess the foster mother's credibility. One more player I hadn't yet met. I needed to get the details from the principal. If the request for remand backfired, I would have aggravated the judge unnecessarily. If I erred on the side of caution, I might be giving Tripping one more opportunity to intercept— or even to harm—his young son.

"I'll ask for ten minutes so I can call her. Give me the woman's number," I said to Maxine.

"That's just it. She was spooked. Said you didn't know her name and she wasn't about to leave it with Mercer or anyone else who could track her down. She just wanted you to know that she was taking Dulles and leaving town with him. She'll be in touch."

7

We finished picking our jury shortly after seven.

"Ten o'clock sharp, ladies and gentlemen," Moffett said, dismissing the twelve we had selected, along with two alternates.

"Tell you what I'm gonna do with regard to the boy," he announced to Robelon and me after the courtroom was cleared of the group. "I'll tell Ms. Taggart to have Dulles produced in my chambers after school tomorrow. Miss Cooper can try to talk to him and that other lawyer, what's his name?"

"Hoyt. Graham Hoyt."

"Yeah. He can sit in on it, too, on the boy's behalf. I'll hang around to iron out any problems that come up. How's that sound?"

I couldn't concentrate on the conversation. My mind was spinning, wondering whether the child was in any actual danger, where the foster mother might have taken him, how Nancy Taggart would respond when I told her about the call from the school, and why everyone in this case—except the victim—seemed to have his or her own agenda.

Robelon spewed out some form of objection and tried to make up for lack of case law to support his position by the sheer volume of his rhetoric.

"Alexandra," Moffett said, "I'm talking to you. We'll stop with your witness at five o'clock tomorrow and then I'll give you a chance to see if the kid'll cooperate."

"Fine, Your Honor." I had a better chance of winning the lottery than sitting in a room with Dulles Tripping by the end of the next day.

"Anything else?" he asked, unhooking the clasp of his robe and handing it to the court officer to hang until the morning.

"Judge, I'd just ask you to remind the defendant, now that proceedings have started, that the order of protection is in full force. He is not to attempt or have any contact with his son, whether in this courthouse, at his school, or—"

"That's really unnecessary, Alex," Robelon objected. "We don't even know what school the kid goes to or where he's living."

"I have no idea what you or your client know at this point. I'm in the rather unorthodox position of not having access to my own witnesses. It's quite clear that the family court, by allowing telephone calls and several meetings between Mr. Tripping and his son, undercut the order of one of the criminal court judges—"

I knew how to get under Moffett's collar. "Which she had no business doing. Alex is right about that. Be a good boy, Mr. Tripping, understood?"

"Yes, sir." The defendant seemed to be smirking at me as he answered Moffett.

The elevators stopped on the seventh floor and I ran my security badge through the scanner, walked down the quiet corridor and up to my eighth-floor office.

Ryan Blackmer, one of my favorite young lawyers, was keeping Mercer company in my office when I dragged in. "You need me?" I asked.

"Just a heads-up. Mind if I work on an investigation at Bayview?"

The prison facility on Manhattan's West Side was the only place in the county where female inmates were housed. "Be my guest. What is it?"

"Prisoner claims one of the guards—he's a captain, actually—has been having sex with her."

"Wouldn't be the first time. But those can be awfully hard to prove."

"She's doing seven years on a robbery with physical injury. Her lawyer claims she hasn't had a single visitor since Christmas, when her husband left her for her younger sister. Now she's four months pregnant. Might be as easy as a fetal DNA test."

"Go for it," I said as the phone rang.

Mercer answered it. "I don't think she's in the mood," he said, holding out the receiver to me.

"Chapman?"

"I'm running out of steam, Coop. Never shut my eyes for a minute last night and I'm just about to go lights-out."

"I'm too busy to tuck you in."

"I need a favor."

It was hard to refuse Mike. He had saved my neck on more occasions than I could count. "Shoot."

He laughed. "But first, what do you give for 'Famous Funerals'?" I glanced down at my watch. The "Final Jeopardy" question.

"Nothing. The subject's too close to home at the moment."

"Laid to rest in London's Highgate, his orator described him as the 'best hated and most calumniated man of his times.'"

From the days when I was immersed in my major in English literature, I knew that one of my favorite authors was interred there. "George Eliot's buried in Highgate. But she doesn't fit. And Bram Stoker's notorious vampire, Miss Lucy. Otherwise, not a clue. Skip the education and tell me what the favor is."

"That was Engels describing his buddy Karl Marx to the eight mourners who gathered at the graveside. Only eight. Imagine that. So can you stop at the morgue on the way home?"

"Sure. I didn't want to eat any dinner or polish up my opening statement."

"I know your style. You had your opening in the can a month ago. You've already written the summation."

Mike was right. I had learned from the old school, the guys who had mastered the art of criminal trial work under great prosecutors. Start your preparation with the closing argument. That way you could make a coherent presentation from the outset, building your case with a sound structure and layering in any new information that you gathered during the testimony of the witnesses. I had outlined those arguments weeks ago.

"What do you need?"

"You told me you were going to assign last night's homicide to someone."

"I forgot about it completely." I had promised Mike that I would tell Sarah Brenner, my deputy, to make one of the unit assistants available on the murder of the elderly woman.

"I know. I just tried to reach Sarah so I wouldn't bother you. She didn't know what I was talking about. I could hear her kids in the background—"

"She's got her hands full at this hour."

"I think I can make it easy for you. Just a quick detour. Dr. Kirschner thinks I'm wrong about the rape. Autopsy shows no sign of sexual assault."

"Nothing?" I asked.

"Not a single thing with a foreign profile. No semen, no loose pubic hair—"

"Bruising?" I would expect, in a woman as old as Mike's victim, that the vaginal vault would exhibit lacerations and swelling, because of the atrophy that accompanied the lack of sexual activity.

"Not internal. Not even on her thighs."

"Sounds like a blessing to me if she wasn't subjected to rape as a final indignity."

"Kirschner thinks the scene was staged to look like a sexual assault. He just finished up and if you can get there within the hour, he'd go over the results with you and show you the crime scene photos. Brainstorm and see what you think. That way I can get started in a new direction when I go in tomorrow morning."

"Okay."

"And Coop? Say good night to Queenie for me?"

"Is that her name?"

"McQueen Ransome. Known to her neighbors as Queenie. Lived in that same little apartment for the last fifty years. Never hurt a fly."

"Family? Next of kin?"

"Not a soul. Had one son who died before he got to high school. No sign that she was ever married, but there are pictures of the boy on the wall in the living room."

"Sounds like a stupid question to ask about an eighty-two-year-old lady, but did she have any enemies?"

"Not that I heard about today. Kids were hanging out all over the stoop. They loved her. Did all the errands for her in exchange for candy, and some entertainment."

"What do you mean?"

"She'd sing and dance for the kids, that's what they say. Put on her old vinyl records and cut a rug. I got a whole children's crusade working on the case with me. Told 'em all they could be my deputies if they catch the killer. Anyway, leave a message on my cell and I'll speak to you at the end of the day tomorrow."

"Last thing, Mike. You make any progress on Tiffany Gatts?"

"She won't be arraigned before morning. There was a labor demonstration over in the garment district, and the backup cause of all the extra arrests for dis con is cramming the system. Have Mercer walk you to your car. Mama Gatts'll be looking for blood."

"Thanks for the reminder."

"We may have a lead on the mink. Found an open squeal in the Seventeenth Precinct. UN delegate from France named du Rosier. Reported a theft six months back. He and his wife thought it was an inside job. His chauffeur had access to the apartment, even when the couple was back in Europe. A bunch of jewelry, two furs, and some pricey antique silver service."

"Any description?"

"The du Rosiers are traveling at the moment. I'll try and get something more detailed from their insurance company tomorrow. Speak to you then."

Mercer waited while I closed up and we headed out the door together. My car was parked near the intersection of Centre Street and Hogan Place, at the corner of the courthouse. The laminated NYPD plate displayed in the windshield was one of the privileges of rank in the office, and I was pleased that no one had double-parked me in place, as often happened when cops delivered prisoners to the courthouse.

The dump sticker from the town of Chilmark, where my home on Martha's Vineyard was located, and the Squibnocket beach pass on the rear window, were the only things that personalized my winter-green SUV. It was even more heartwarming to see that the Vineyard stickers had not seemed to draw the attention or wrath of Etta Gatts, who might have noticed the Vineyard posters in my office. The windows were intact.

I stepped off the curb at the rear of the car, keys in

hand. Mercer went around in front to open the door for me.

"Looks like I'm your transportation for the evening," he said, taking the keys out of my hand. "Your car's in dry dock, Alex. Someone slashed your two front tires."

8

hand, Mercer went around in front to open the door for me.

"McQueen has my undivided admiration for the crowd," she said, picking up a newspaper at my stand. "You can't sit at the Oak Room when one started your two-bit crew."

There is a cruel invasion of privacy that attends a death by violence.

Mercer and I sat in a small cubicle adjacent to the autopsy theater in the office of the chief medical examiner, Chet Kirschner. The brilliant pathologist had finished his work for the day, and was taking us through the Queenie Ransome homicide findings.

The strong odor of formalin was exaggerated by the closeness of the room. I coughed to clear my dry throat, listening to Kirschner's voice, which was so oddly comforting in these starkly clinical circumstances.

I stared at close-ups of the nude corpse, taken in her home by a Crime Scene Unit detective, shuffling them around on the table in front of me.

"There are two different scenarios you want to think about here," he told us, after describing what McQueen Ransome's body had revealed to him. "You remember the old Park Plaza cases?"

Both Mercer and I recognized the name. The building had been a flophouse on the West Side of Manhattan, a dilapidated single-room-occupancy hotel that was home to dozens of senior citizens living on welfare. Throughout a two-year period, several of the octogenarians had died without any suspicion of foul play.

"The first five women had no relatives in the city to raise any concerns, no property of any value, and histories of illness that allowed their physicians to certify their deaths as occurring from natural causes."

"They weren't even autopsied?" I asked.

Kirschner shook his head. "The sixth one was slightly different. Mildred Vargas. She owned a television set, and it was missing from her room when her body was found. We did a postmortem, even though there were no signs of a struggle, and we wound up with unexpected evidence that there had been a sexual assault."

"What killed her?" Mercer wanted to know.

"She was suffocated. Smothered with a pillow."

Exactly what Mike said had happened to Queenie.

"I got an order to exhume the other bodies and autopsy them," Kirschner said.

Mercer remembered the outcome. "All five had been raped."

"And smothered. No external signs of injury. Just the internal bruising, and the minute petechial hemorrhages in their eyes that the physicians missed in each case."

Hallmarks of an asphyxial death, the tiny red pinpoint markers were quiet indicators of strangulation and suffocation, blood vessels bursting in eyes as they were deprived of oxygen.

Kirschner straightened his lean body and rested an elbow atop a file cabinet. "That killer made a specialty of getting in and out of apartments with no visible signs of forced entry. He even took the time to re-dress three of his victims, so the sexual assault was not the least bit obvious. Chapman's looking to link McQueen Ransome's death to those cases."

"Do you have DNA in any of those?"

"In all of them, actually. Our own databank linked them to each other after the exhumation and examination."

"Has the profile been uploaded to Albany and CODIS?"

The medical examiner's local databank could match unsolved cases to each other because of evidence taken from a crime scene or victim's body. The profile would be sent on to Albany, and a computer would scan the results against convicted offenders in the New York State databank, who were mandated, according to category of criminal offense, to submit blood or saliva samples for the profiling of their DNA. CODIS, the Combined DNA Identification System, was capable of linking unsolved cases in one jurisdiction to a burglar, rapist, or killer anywhere in the entire country.

"Four months ago. We're still waiting for a cold hit."

"But there's no DNA in this case?"

"Not on the body. I told Chapman to go back and swab the doorknobs and some of the surfaces the killer may have touched."

The technology of this science had become so sophisticated that a serologist could develop a genetic fingerprint from the mere sloughing off of skin cells onto most objects that had been handled during the crime, called touch evidence.

"But you don't think this is your senior citizen serial killer?"

"Too many distinctions, Alex. The pillow was undoubtedly the weapon. That's certainly a similarity. We'll work it up for amylase," Kirschner said, referring to an enzyme found in saliva that might tell us whether the fabric had been held over Ransome's mouth to kill her.

"You're bothered by the fact there's no sexual assault, I guess," Mercer said. "What if he was interrupted? What if he meant to do that, but got distracted because, unlike the others, there really were so many possessions here that he ransacked the place. Maybe he thought someone heard noise and was coming to check on Queenie."

Kirschner removed a pipe from his rear pants pocket and raised it to his mouth.

He tamped tobacco in, lit the match, and filled the tiny room with the welcome aroma of a sweet, smooth blend that temporarily masked the smell of death.

"Possible, of course," he said. "But all the other crime scenes were in such perfect order. Chapman left these here for you two to study. Look again. Take your time."

The eight-by-ten color crime scene shots of the Ransome apartment had been developed immediately and hand-delivered to Kirschner.

"You've really got juice," I said. "I'd be lucky to get these in a week."

"Don't be jealous. It's not a full set. I just get a few body shots to get me started."

There was McQueen Ransome, lying on her back on the bed. Her housecoat was pulled up to expose her genitals, with panties and what appeared to be thick support hose rolled up in a ball beside her. Her head was turned to the side, faded hazel eyes fixed in a vacant gaze.

"Somebody sure wants to make the point about the sexual aspect of this," Mercer said. "Nothing like this in the Park Plaza cases?"

Kirschner shook his head. "No. Unless your killer read about the exhumations in the tabloids and decided to change his signature."

Queenie's legs were spread apart, twisted slightly, with one knee bent beneath the other in what seemed to be almost an obscene pose.

Next to the bed was a metal walker, and I remembered Mike telling me the woman had suffered a stroke several years ago.

I strained to study her head and hands more closely.

"Are those scratches on her face?"

"Yes, Alex. By her own hand. Typical in asphyxia. She was trying to clear the airways of the obstruction, so she could breathe. Free her mouth from whatever was covering it. Probably the pillow."

"And the killer?" I asked.

"Several of her nails are broken. We might get lucky and come up with something other than her own blood in the cuttings. He might have some marks on his face or hands, if she had the strength to swipe at him."

The six photographs Kirschner had were all of Queenie's body, taken from every position in the room. I thought of the indignity of this kind of death, in which dozens of strangers had entered her home to catalog and ferret through her meager accumulation of possessions. A young medical examiner on duty and his assistant, cops in uniform to secure the scene, a crew from the Crime Scene Unit to take photographs and dust for fingerprints, and a team of detectives who would try to find a motive for this murder—and a killer.

I thought ahead to the scores more who would pore over these photographs in the months to come. Colleagues of mine would study them as they worked up the case for trial, forensic consultants would enlarge them to look again for any kind of trace material or significant detail, and psychologists would struggle with them as they searched for an understanding of the murderer's mind. Eventually, when Chapman and his team caught the man—and I needed, now, to believe that they would—a defense attorney would be entitled to a complete set of pictures, too, and even the killer himself could revisit the scene of his pathetic triumph in the privacy of his jail cell.

"The person who did this wants you to think 'sadistic sex murderer,' Alex," Kirschner said to me. "I suggest you broaden the search. Some other motive."

Mercer and I had handled cases in which the appearance of a rape had been staged. Once we'd recognized that fact we'd had to find another reason—the real reason—for the crime to have occurred. Here was an elderly woman, partially disabled, living on welfare in a Harlem tenement. Her death was not a matter of academic rivalry, professional jealousy, domestic rage, or a fancy jewel heist gone violent.

"It'll be interesting to see what the rest of the photos show," said Mercer. "Everything within sight has been turned topsy-turvy."

On the side of the bed was a nightstand. The shallow bowl with the victim's dental plate had been overturned. Both shelves had been emptied and their contents spilled on the floor. The edge of the dresser was in view, and each of the three drawers had been dumped out and spread across the floor.

"Is she wearing any rings or bracelets?" I picked up another photo and looked again at McQueen Ransome's wrinkled hands.

"She wasn't admitted with anything," Kirschner said.

Mercer checked the pictures taken from other angles and agreed there was not even a wedding band on her finger.

"I'll have to ask Mike whether she had any items of value in the apartment, but it sure doesn't look like it, from these shots," I said.

"Dr. K, have you got a magnifying glass?" Mercer asked.

Kirschner left the room for thirty seconds and returned with one.

"Looks like we have some homework to do. She doesn't seem to have much here except junk, but maybe some of her acquaintances know things about her background that can help us," Mercer said.

"What do you see?" I asked.

"Ever hear of James Van Derzee?"

Both Kirschner and I nodded. "Harlem Renaissance," the medical examiner said. "One of the great African-American photographers."

"Look at that," Mercer said, passing the magnifier over to me. "Check out the photograph over the headboard of the bed, the words at the bottom."

I picked up the glossy image that Mercer had been studying. The photo had been taken by a cop standing at the foot of the bed, so it provided a lengthwise view of the victim's body. Directly above her head was a black-and-white portrait that hung on the wall. Only two-thirds of it was captured in the crime scene shot. The model's head was out of range.

In the lower right corner was an inscription, which I squinted to read: *For Queenie—from her royal subject, James Van Derzee. 1938.*

"Now look up," Mercer said.

I didn't need the magnifying glass to see the chilling irony. The exquisitely voluptuous nude body of the young McQueen Ransome was hanging above her corpse, which had been positioned to mimic an identical pose.

9

Mercer left me at my apartment at nine-thirty. I dropped my mail and files on the table in my entryway and fished Nancy Taggart's home number out of my pocketbook.

I had waited to call her, certain she would know about the disappearance of Dulles Tripping and his foster mother.

"Ms. Taggart? It's Alex Cooper."

"Yes?" It was more of a question than an acknowledgment.

"I know that Judge Moffett asked his law secretary to call you about having Dulles in his chambers late tomorrow afternoon."

"She did."

"It's not going to be a problem, is it?" I asked.

Taggart hesitated. "I don't expect so."

"Do you know where the boy is tonight?"

"Look, Ms. Cooper. I don't have to answer any of your questions. You know that."

"That's certainly true. I just wanted to make sure you knew that the foster mother called me today, to—"

Taggart snapped at me, "When? What did she want?"

"It would be awfully juvenile of me," I said, "to tell you that I didn't have to answer any of *your* questions, wouldn't it? I assume you have the same concerns for Dulles's well-being that I do."

There was silence. Taggart obviously wasn't willing to concede that I was interested in anything but a prosecutorial victory.

I tried again. "I don't know the foster mother's name," I said, thinking that would reassure Taggart. "But she sounded frantic when she spoke with my assistant, telling us she was taking the boy to 'a safer place.'"

"I think she panicked for no good reason at all," said the foundling hospital's lawyer. "There's nothing distinctive-looking about Andrew Tripping. I think this is much ado about nonsense."

"Is that what you'd like me to put on the record in the morning?"

"I'd advise you not to bring this up with the judge until I get to court, Ms. Cooper. His secretary told me to come at four o'clock, after school. I intend for us to be there."

"But now you know Dulles won't even be going to school."

"I have every reason to believe the foster mother—who is very reliable—will contact me first thing tomorrow and we can follow the plan that Judge Moffett wants."

"Look," I said, trying to reassure the woman. "All you need to do is say the word and the police will help you find them. We can trace the phone call, we can work with the principal. I promise I won't use that opportunity to talk to the boy. If there's a chance he's in more danger, then the police should be the ones—"

"Don't you think there's been enough damage done with the police dragging the child's father out of their apartment in handcuffs? In keeping the father on Rikers for more than a week? For splitting up the family? Let's leave the police out of it this time," Taggart said.

"Then I'll see you tomorrow afternoon, unless you need help from my assistant during the day."

I hung up the phone and walked into the kitchen, turning on the light to see just how bare the cupboard was. There was a delicious slab of a smooth pâté, *mousse de canard,* in the refrigerator, left over from my weekend purchases. I scrounged for some crackers and a few cornichons for garnish, poured a Diet Coke, and headed to the den to try to unwind before my last review of the morning's presentation.

The phone rang before I sat down on the sofa. "I was about to give up on you," Jake said. "Thought you'd be home early. I've already left three messages."

"I haven't even been in the bedroom to pick them up. I'm just sitting down to dinner," I said, describing my meal to him.

"Doesn't sound like enough to keep body and soul together. I'll have to make up for that tomorrow night."

"What's all the noise in the background?" I asked.

"It's the party at the British embassy I told you about. They've got all the Washington correspondents here, sort of an annual meet-the-press deal. Dinner and dancing, but it's about to break up."

Who's your date? is what I really wanted to ask Jake, but under our new arrangement, we were both free to spend time with other people if we were not available, since our jobs interfered with our personal lives so frequently. Instead, I told him I couldn't wait to see him and tried to believe it when he whispered that he loved me into the telephone.

I dialed my best friend and former college roommate, Nina Baum, who lived in California. "Great timing. You just got me coming in the door."

I could hear her four-year-old son screeching in delight at her arrival. "I'll let you go. Call me over the weekend."

"You sound flat, Alex. What's going on?"

No one on earth knew me better than Nina. We had leaned on each other through every good time and bad in each other's lives. I told her what had happened to my case, how depressing it was to see the photos of Queenie at the morgue, and how jealous I was to think of Jake at a party with someone else.

"You've heard me on this subject, Alex." Nina was not keen on Jake Tyler. She had adored Adam Nyman, the medical student I'd met during my law school days at Virginia. She had mourned with me when he had been killed in a car wreck on his way to our wedding on Martha's Vineyard, and she had helped me throughout my slow emergence from the black hole into which I sunk after absorbing the news of Adam's death.

In the years since that tragedy, I had never let myself get as close to anyone as I had to Jake, only to find that my dearest friend, whom I trusted implicitly, thought he was too superficial and self-involved for me.

"Try your damn case, will you?" Nina said. "You want to know what time Jake gets home tonight? Forget it. You want to know what whoever she is he settled for in your absence was wearing to the party? Trust me, you would never have bought the rag in the first place. You want to know how much she knows about you? If she isn't sticking pins in a tall, blonde, mud-wrestling voodoo doll who thrives on competition by this time, she ought to go out and buy one immediately. Speak to you on Saturday. I've got to go feed Little Precious."

I laughed at Nina's nickname for her son and put down the phone.

When I finished my snack, I spread all the case papers out on my desk. I had outlined an opening statement, and now took half an hour to reduce it to an abbreviated list of bullet points. I smiled as I thought back to my first felony trial, when I'd stood before the jurors with a painstakingly detailed speech, written in essay form, of which I'd read every word. Midway through, the judge interrupted and wiggled his finger at me, asking me to approach. "Miss Cooper, this isn't a book report. Put down those pages and *talk* to the people before you lose them."

I had learned to abandon the crutch of too many notes and simply sketch out the main points I needed to make. The advantage of vertical prosecution—of working a case from the moment of the first police report up to the verdict—was that we knew the facts cold and could proceed without any notes or outlines.

In the morning I would spend one last hour with Paige Vallis, steadying her before her difficult day on the witness stand. I arranged all the questions I would ask her and made a list of the items I would ask the court to premark for identification, to avoid delay in the presence of the jury.

By midnight I had undressed and turned out the light, but the adrenaline that fueled my courtroom rhythm made a good night's sleep impossible. At six o'clock I got up and showered. Blow-drying my hair, I looked at my reflection in the mirror and wondered how long it would be before the dark circles that frequently took up residence beneath my eyes during a trial would reappear.

I finished dressing and dabbed some perfume on my wrists and behind my ears. I called a car service and went down to the lobby to wait for the sedan to take me to the office, and I was at the coffee cart at the building entrance before seven-thirty.

My car was still there, so the first call was to AAA, to tow it to my repair shop and replace the two tires. Then I settled down to the business on my desk until Mercer arrived with Paige Vallis almost an hour later.

I closed my door to give us more privacy. She didn't need to go over the facts again. The events of March 6 were indelibly etched in her mind's eye. I knew that if I questioned her about them now, it would heighten her state of nervousness, as well as take the emotional edge off the presentation she would make to the jury.

Instead, we talked about what I thought the pace of the trial would be and when we might expect to go to verdict.

"Andrew's lawyer?" Paige asked.

"Robelon. Peter Robelon. What about him?"

"Do you have any better sense of what he's going to do to me?"

We had been over this countless times, and Paige didn't like it better than any other witness. When the assailant in a sexual assault case was a stranger, the defense did not have to attack the victim. They could acknowledge that a vicious crime had occurred, and suggest that the woman was tragically mistaken in her identification of the defendant. Poor lighting, little opportunity to see his face clearly, and general hysteria were the traditional arguments against a reliable identification by a rape victim. All of that changed when DNA technology replaced the survivor's visual memory as the means of confirming who her attacker had been.

But it was terribly different when a woman was assaulted by someone known to her—a friend, a coworker, a lover, or an ex-boyfriend. More than 80 percent of sexual assaults occurred between people who knew each other, so identification was not the issue at trial. Yet these victims were far more likely to have their credibility attacked in the courtroom.

Mercer was standing beside his witness, removing the lids on the cardboard coffee containers he had brought for each of us. "It's like Alex has been telling you all along, Paige. Robelon can only go one way in this case. He can't say it never happened and that you're making this whole thing up. The presence of Tripping's DNA makes that impossible."

"So it's that I consented? That I'm lying about this, right?"

I nodded my head.

"Will the jury already know that when I walk into the room and take the stand? I mean, does he just say that when he addresses them the first time?"

"I'm sure he'll plant that seed in their minds," I said. Robelon was a good lawyer and likely to be more subtle than most. I didn't think he would out-right accuse Paige Vallis of being a liar. Rather, he would paint the jury a picture in very broad strokes, setting them up to believe that she had been hungry for this relationship, pursuing Andrew Tripping and unhappy when something went wrong during the night in question.

I hated this moment in the process. I hated being the person who had to deliver the victim into the hands of my adversary, in public view, to tell this story of trust and betrayal to a courtroom full of strangers. In the months since Paige reported the crime, I had struggled with Mercer to gain her confidence, to ask about intimacies that most people never discuss outside of their bedrooms. Now that I had gained that acceptance, I could not give her a victory without first exposing her to public humiliation and dissection.

"Will there be newspaper reporters at the trial?" she asked.

"I don't expect any. So far they haven't expressed interest in the case, and I can't imagine why that would change. Did you end up asking a friend to come with you? Anyone to sit in the courtroom for moral support?"

Paige gnawed at the corner of her lip and twisted a handkerchief in her hands. "No. I haven't got much family. Distant relatives are all. And my closest girl-friend told me to forget about going through a trial, to walk away from the whole thing."

My paralegal, Maxine, would be her anchor dur-ing the trial. They had worked together since Paige's first interview here, and I had encouraged them to talk to each other regularly. Maxine would be the vir-tual handholder for her through these next difficult hours.

"Do you think Andrew will take the stand?"

"I haven't a clue at this point, Paige." So much of that will depend on how you do, I thought to myself. Robelon did not have to make that decision until I had completed my case and rested. If Paige held up well throughout cross-examination, then he might gauge it necessary to let Andrew Tripping speak to the jurors. It could be a real problem for the defense, since the "bad acts" that had been ruled inadmissible on my direct case were things I could question him about if he chose to testify on his own behalf.

She could see that I was frustrated by my inability to give her definite answers about so much of what we were facing. "It seems so unbalanced," she said, forcing a wan smile. "You have to tell them every-thing about your case, and about me, but they don't have any obligation to do the same."

I returned the smile. "You've got to relax a bit and

let me worry about that. It's a very uneven playing field, but Mercer and I are used to it."

I stood up to move Paige into the adjacent conference room and give her a newspaper to read for the time remaining before we went to court. "Alex, one more thing. Did you get a ruling about my sexual history? I mean, can Mr. Robelon ask about other men I've had intercourse with?" She colored deeply as she spoke to me.

We had talked about this issue before. "I thought I explained this to you," I said, sitting down again so I could look Paige directly in the eye. "That's why I gave you such a hard time about exactly what went on between you and Andrew on the three occasions you were together."

Like every witness I interviewed, I had pressed her aggressively about whether there was any kind of sexual overture or foreplay before the rape. It was common for many women to minimize or omit that fact from their narratives, fearful that a prosecutor would refuse to entertain a case in which there had been any sort of consensual conduct leading up to the crime.

"I've told you the truth about that, Alex."

"Then why are you worried? Nothing else is relevant."

"I went on-line last night," she said, now wringing the handkerchief between her hands. "I started to look up articles about cases that had been written up in the newspapers. Sort of to see what to expect."

I guess everything I had told her had not provided enough reassurance.

"I found a long feature in the *Times* that quoted

you last year, talking about how bad the laws used to be. It kept me up all night."

"That's old news, Paige. That's all changed now." Rape shield laws had passed in every state in America in the last quarter of the twentieth century, protecting victims from questioning about their sexual activity with men other than the defendant. But until that time, a woman who had ever had intercourse prior to the rape—who was "unchaste"—was assumed to have consented to the act with the man on trial. The courts defined the ideal victim as a "virgin of uncontaminated purity."

"But that case you cited in the article?" she asked.

"It was decided before I got to law school. It's history, Paige."

At the time I studied the case, I had been stunned and disgusted that in my lifetime there was still a court in this country that threw out a man's rape conviction because the accuser had not been a virgin. Using the flowery rhetoric that referenced ancient Roman history, the court had asked: "Will you not more readily infer assent in the practiced Messalina, in loose attire, than in the reserved and virtuous Lucretia?" The unfaithful wife of Claudius was the Eighth Judicial Circuit's vision of an unfit victim, just as they held up to the world the virtuous Lucretia, who killed herself rather than see her rapist brought to justice.

"There'd have to be some direct relevance to Andrew's case," I told her. "They just can't go fishing into your private life anymore."

"C'mon, Paige," Mercer said, leading her out to

the conference room. "Alex'll rip the throat out of anybody who tries to go after you that way. Won't happen."

They were almost at my door when she turned to look at me. "There's something else I need to tell you, Alex."

My fingers froze on the sheaf of papers in my hand. I was less than an hour away from addressing the jury. If Paige had not been honest with me about some fact in the case, this was my last chance to make that discovery.

"I had a phone call last night from a man I was— well—was involved with."

"Sexually?" Mercer asked. There wasn't enough time to be subtle.

"Socially, first. Then, yes, sexually."

Now I was standing, too. "Let's cut to the chase. Does it have anything to do with Andrew Tripping? With this trial?"

"It might." Paige's teeth were practically biting through her lip as she hesitated.

"The reason he called was to try to persuade me not to testify today."

"Someone threatened you?" I asked, as Mercer spoke over me, trying to get the man's name at the same time.

Her head swung back and forth between the two of us. "I can't exactly call it a threat. But it seems he talked to Andrew yesterday. He actually came to the courtroom and met with him."

I slapped my hand on the desk as I looked at Mercer. There hadn't been many people in Moffett's trial part, and I thought immediately of the lawyer who was the young boy's legal guardian. "Graham Hoyt," I said aloud. "The kid's lawyer."

"No, no. I don't know who that is. That's not his name," Paige protested. "It's Harry Strait, the one I'm talking about. He's a government agent, like Andrew Tripping claims to have been. He's with the CIA, I think."

10

"And at the conclusion of the case, ladies and gentle-men, I will again have the opportunity to stand before you," I said, walking to the defense table and stop-ping directly in front of Andrew Tripping. If I wanted the twelve good people in the box to look him in the eye and declare him guilty, I needed to show them that I was not afraid to do that myself. "At that time, I will ask you to consider the testimony of the wit-nesses who appeared before you, discuss the evidence that has been presented, and find this defendant guilty of the crimes with which he is charged."

Thorough, calm, understated. I had given them the basic elements of the crime, read the indictment, and previewed Paige Vallis's story. That way, when she gave them more, they would be surprised and some-what pleased that I had not promised anything I could not deliver. Dulles Tripping, though essential to this case, was practically a footnote, so uncertain was I of the role he would be allowed to play.

Robelon was cool. He started his presentation at the podium, but then stood behind his client's seat, placing his hands on Tripping's shoulders. He was embracing the falsely accused man, as it were, just as Emily Frith leaned in to pat the defendant on the forearm.

He was staying away from specifics, laying in the general picture of the struggling single-parent father, trying to put bread on the table and care for a rambunctious child.

He didn't make my witness out to be a monster, but the undercurrent was set in motion.

The foundation he was building on would lead him to sum up, I assumed, with a description of Paige Vallis as emotionally unstable, socially insecure, confused by Andrew's mixed signals, and insensitive to his personal travails.

"Don't be taken in by Ms. Cooper, sitting here all alone at counsel table, while the three of us do our job with her witnesses," Robelon said, with a wink at the panel. I always liked that dynamic, assuming some jurors would cast me in the role of the underdog going against the triad of the defense team. In this instance, I thought, glancing across at them, they looked like corporate travelers sitting abreast in the business-class section of a New York to Chicago flight.

"She's got all the enormous resources of law enforcement available at her fingertips," he went on. "Believe me, if there was evidence to be found against my client, she had the means to gather every bit of that."

It may have been bullshit, but juries believed that argument. There was nothing the NYPD could do to enhance this case. We take our witnesses as we find them. Give us your tired, your poor, your hungry—

and then, while you're at it, might as well throw in your psychos, junkies, liars, whackjobs, and hookers. I didn't believe in dressing any of them up or polishing their performance before the jury in any case I had ever tried. It was a technique that was bound to backfire. Whatever the point of weakness that would be apparent in the courtroom—whether drug addiction, mental illness, or any alternative lifestyle—that was the vulnerability that the perpetrator had identified and attacked on the street.

Robelon closed with the routine keep-an-open-mind pitch. He made no promises about whether his client would testify, insisting instead that he would hold my feet to the fire and dare me to prove my case.

"Let's have your first witness, Ms. Cooper," Moffett said.

"The People call Paige Vallis."

One of the court officers walked to the side door in the middle of the courtroom, which led to the corridor that housed the bare, dingy witness room. I stared at the group we had selected—eight men and four women—as every head followed him.

Fifteen pairs of eyes—twelve jurors, two alternates, and a curious judge—scrutinized Vallis as she walked in front of the first row of benches, alongside my table, and stepped up to her place on the stand. The officer asked her to put one hand on the Bible and raise the other to take the oath. She was trembling as she complied with his direction.

There was not a single spectator in the room, except for my paralegal, who was there to help steady Paige with eye contact and a reassuring smile.

"Good morning," I said to her, as I rose to begin my questioning. "Would you please tell the jury your name?"

Vallis reached for the paper cup filled with water before she spoke. It shook as she lifted it, and water splashed over its edge. "My name is Paige Vallis."

I took her through a series of pedigree questions, which I had told her I would use to try to calm her down, and get the jury to relate to her. If she could describe her background and her work to them, it would settle her in before moving into the more highly charged testimony about the crime. I wanted to humanize her for the people who would judge her credibility, so that they could understand she had no reason to fabricate the story she was about to tell.

"Where do you live?"

"Here in Manhattan, in TriBeCa." The judge had agreed with me that she did not need to put an exact street address into the public record.

"How old are you?"

"I'm thirty-six." We were exactly the same age, I thought, looking at the young woman whose life had become unraveled on the evening of March 6.

"Were you raised in New York?"

"No, I was not." I had prepped her to look at the jurors and talk directly to them, and she was trying to do that as she answered. She was dressed in a navy blue suit with a pale yellow blouse, and her naturally curly brown hair was swept back away from her plain-featured face. "I was born here, in the city. My father was in the diplomatic corps, so I spent most of my childhood abroad."

"Would you tell us about your educational background?"

"I attended the American schools wherever my father was posted. I returned to this country to go to college, and received my bachelor's degree from Georgetown University, in Washington, D.C. I worked for a few years after graduating," she said, describing a number of entry-level jobs. "Then I decided to go to business school, and got my master's from Columbia five years ago."

Vallis had impressive academic credentials. So did a lot of crazy people I knew.

"Where are you employed, and what specific duties does your job involve?"

"Before my graduation, I was recruited by an investment banking firm, where I had done a summer internship," Vallis said, clearly comfortable discussing the work she did. "The company is called Dibingham Partners. I'm a research analyst there, and I specialize in foreign equities."

Vallis went on to describe to the jury exactly what she did to investigate overseas companies in order to make recommendations about whether to purchase stocks for her customers' portfolios.

I flushed out the promotions she had been given and the number of people she supervised, establishing the stability of her professional performance.

"Are you single, Ms. Vallis?"

"Yes, I am. I've never been married."

"Do you know the defendant in this case, Andrew Tripping?"

Vallis cleared her throat and glanced quickly at the

defense table. The few moments of relaxed testimony she had given came to an abrupt end, as she visibly tensed as she answered the question. "Yes, I do."

"For how long have you known him?"

"I met him in February of this year. February twentieth, to be exact."

"Your Honor, may we approach?" Robelon got to his feet. This was his style. Just as my victim was about to get her narrative going, he would interrupt as frequently as he could. It served the dual purpose of rattling the witness and distracting the jury from her story.

Moffett shrugged and reluctantly waved us up. He made Paige step down to the side as we huddled before the bench. "What is it?"

"I'm having trouble hearing Ms. Vallis. I'd like permission to move my chair over there." Robelon pointed to a spot behind my seat, directly in front of the jury panel.

"Sure. Go—"

"I'll just ask the witness to keep her voice up. Peter can sit exactly where he's supposed to."

"What's your beef, Alex?" Robelon asked.

"You ought to use one of your client's bayonets to clean the wax out of your ears. The only time you develop a problem is when a witness is testifying and the prosecutor's back is turned. The last time you repositioned yourself between me and the twelve angry men in the box, you spent the entire time rolling your eyes at them in disbelief and mumbling under your breath just loud enough so they could hear your comments."

"Cut it out, you two," Moffett said, turning to

Paige. "Do you think you can speak any louder, young lady? Mr. Robelon needs to hear everything you say."

"I can try, Your Honor."

He waved us back to our seats and I picked up my questioning.

"I'm going to direct your attention, Ms. Vallis, to the evening of February twentieth. Would you tell us where you were and how you met the defendant?"

"Certainly. I attended a lecture at the Council on Foreign Relations, at their building on Park Avenue. I'm a member of that organization, and I had arranged to meet a girlfriend at the event, which started at seven o'clock. Then we were going to go to dinner together."

"Did you keep that plan?" I asked.

"No. I mean, I did go to the lecture, but my friend's plane was held on the runway in Boston because of snow. She called on my cell phone to tell me she wouldn't be able to make it."

Paige Vallis paused. "There was a cocktail reception after the lecture. I knew a number of the people there, so I decided to stay and chat for a while."

"Did you have anything to drink or eat at the reception?" Bring it out on the direct case, so that it didn't look like I was trying to hide any alcohol that was involved.

"Wine. I had a couple of glasses of white wine. Two. Nothing to eat."

"Did Mr. Tripping approach you that evening?"

"Objection. Leading."

"Overruled. Ms. Cooper's just trying to set some background up here."

Paige waited for the judge to tell her to proceed. "Three of us were standing together, talking about the situation in the Middle East, and what our own personal experiences had been there. Andrew must have heard me—"

"Objection as to what he might have heard."

"Sustained. Just tell us what he said or did."

The objections had their desired effect. Paige Vallis was shaken each time Robelon called out the word, as though she had done something wrong.

"Andrew Tripping asked me about Cairo," she said. "He wanted to know when I had lived there and for what reason."

Tripping started fidgeting as she spoke, trying to get his lawyer's attention. Robelon brushed him off, continuing to take notes on the details in Vallis's testimony that he had not heard before. The defendant put his head together with Emily Frith, whispering to her, distracting several jurors from the flow of the testimony.

"What did you tell him, exactly?"

"I talked about my father's career and told him what I remembered of his tour of duty in Egypt. I hadn't been back there since finishing high school."

"For how long did you talk?" I asked.

"Probably half an hour."

"Did you leave the council alone?"

Paige Vallis blushed and picked up her water cup again. "No, no, I didn't. Andrew told me he knew a nice restaurant in the neighborhood and invited me to go to dinner."

"Did anyone else—"

I started to ask the next question but Paige Vallis

wanted to explain her decision to the jury. "I don't normally do that. I mean, go off somewhere with a man I don't know. But I can't imagine a safer place to meet a guy than a political policy discussion with the members of the council," she said, giggling a bit.

Laughter didn't work in the middle of a rape trial. I knew it was just a nervous reaction, but she would need to get beyond it. Don't apologize for anything you did, I had told Paige for weeks. Just tell the jury the facts. In my summation I would have lots of opportunity to talk about her judgment calls.

"Did anyone else go with you to dinner?"

"No. I said good night to the people I knew, got my coat from the checkroom, and we walked three or four blocks to a small bistro on a side street."

She took us through the dinner and conversation. Yes, there was another glass of wine for each of them. Yes, they both discussed their personal lives. Andrew told her that he was widowed, and that his mother had raised his son until her recent death. No, she certainly could not remember everything that they had talked about.

I would argue that was because there was no significance to most of the conversation at this first meeting. Robelon would attribute her lack of specifics to the third glass of wine.

"What time did you leave the restaurant, and where did you go?"

"I saw that it was getting late—after ten o'clock. I told Andrew that I had to be in my office before eight the next morning. He put me in a cab outside the restaurant and we said good night."

"Who paid for the meal?"

She looked at me and reddened again. "We split the check. I paid for my dinner and he paid for his."

"Did you kiss each other?"

"No."

"Was there any kind of physical contact—touching each other or holding hands as you walked on the street?"

"None."

"Did he ask for your phone number?"

"No."

"Did he say—"

"Hey, Ms. Cooper," Judge Moffett said, "whatever happened to woman's lib? Ms. Vallis, did you ask him for his number?"

"No, sir."

"Was there any discussion about seeing each other again?" I asked.

"No, there wasn't. I got in the cab, closed the door, and went on my way home. I thought it was a pleasant evening, but that was the end of it."

"When was the next time you had any contact with Andrew Tripping?"

"About three or four days later, when he called me."

"Where were you when he called?"

"At my office. Dibingham Partners," Vallis said, looking over at the jurors. "My personal phone isn't listed. I had told Andrew where I worked, and I guess—"

"Objection."

"Sustained. You can't guess in my courtroom, Ms.

Vallis," the judge barked at the young woman from his elevated position over her head, and she recoiled, shaken again. "I'm sorry, Your Honor."

"Would you please tell us what the defendant said in that conversation?"

"It was a very short discussion. I told him I was about to go into a meeting. He asked if I wanted to have dinner with him the following night, and I said, 'Sure.' We arranged to meet at the Odeon. That's a restaurant near my apartment. That's all."

"Did you keep that date?"

"Yes, we did. I got there first. When Andrew arrived, we each ordered a glass of wine and chatted for a while before we ate dinner."

"What did this conversation concern?"

Paige Vallis described a coolly impersonal meeting, in which her companion spent most of the time talking about himself or questioning her about her political views. She only had one drink and again she paid her own way. There were no sexual overtures when he walked her back to her building at ten o'clock.

"Did you invite the defendant up to your apartment?" I asked.

"There was no reason to. I thought—"

"Objection as to what she thought, Your Honor," Robelon said.

"Sustained."

The heavy oak door creaked open behind me. I kept my attention on Paige Vallis, but she picked her head up at the sound and stared off in the distance.

"Ms. Vallis, what did you say or do when you reached your building?"

Her mouth twitched and she answered softly, "Andrew asked if he could come in for a cup of coffee. I told him that would be impossible. I—uh—I had a friend in from out of town who was staying in the apartment. Actually, I'm just remembering that now, as I try to recall the details of our dinner," she said, looking back at me.

I squeezed the pen I was holding so tightly I thought it would break in half and spurt ink all over the jurors. I had never heard that explanation in all the weeks of preparing Paige to testify. The truth, the whole truth, and nothing but the truth. Better late than never. What friend, I wondered to myself, and what relevance did this have to her story?

Paige Vallis was trembling visibly now, as I tried to direct her attention to the night of the crime. "I'm going to ask you some questions about the day and evening of March sixth of this year."

She licked her lips to moisten them and reached for the water. Her hand missed and knocked the cup off the railing in front of her; water began dripping onto the court stenographer, who shoved her machine out of the way and reached for tissues to wipe up the mess. Paige stood and leaned over as though to reach for the fallen cup, bursting into tears as she tried to apologize to the judge for the disturbance.

Moffett banged his gavel on the bench. "Brief recess. We'll take ten minutes."

Paige spoke to him before the jurors could be led out of the box. "I'm so sorry, Judge. I can't testify about this in front of him. Does he have to be here?"

She was pointing a finger, while Moffett answered

her, and I moved forward to calm her and bring tissues to wipe her face. "Of course he has to be here. The Constitution gives him that right, young—"

"Not Andrew, Your Honor. Him." Paige lifted her head and I turned around to look.

The older of the two men whom Chapman had tried to identify in the courtroom the day before was seated alone now in the back row. He must have been the person who came in just as Paige had fallen apart a few questions back. He rose as my witness waved her hand in his direction, and he pushed the swinging door to exit.

"That's Harry Strait, Alexandra," Paige said, grabbing my hand as I extended the tissue to her. "That's the man I told you about."

Andrew Tripping smiled broadly, put his arm on his lawyer's shoulder, and broke away to follow Harry Strait out into the corridor.

11

I had less than six minutes to corner Paige Vallis in the witness room and read her the riot act. "I can pull the plug on this entire proceeding right this minute. Do you want to explain to me what just happened on the witness stand? I told you from the moment we first met that there was only one thing you could do wrong and that was to lie to me about even the most seemingly insignificant question I've asked you. I don't give a damn about your judgment or your lifestyle or your morals. I need to know the truth."

"I've never lied to you, Alex."

"I'll walk into that courtroom and ask the judge to dismiss the charges if a single thing you have told me is not true. Now's the time—"

"I swear to you, every word I've told you is the truth."

"But you've left things out, is that what you mean? An omission is the same as a lie, if it has something to do with your case. What haven't you told me?"

"Nothing important that involves Andrew Tripping or these charges."

"Whether a fact is important or not isn't your decision, Paige. I need to know every single detail. Everything. I'll be the judge of what's important. Get it? Who was the 'friend' in the apartment that night?"

She returned my stare with a pitiful expression on her face.

"Don't give me that helpless, pathetic look. It was this—this Harry Strait guy, right?" I asked.

"What difference does that make? Andrew didn't know that at the time."

"This isn't a goddamn game, Paige. Do you understand that?" I was furious now. Maxine tapped on the glass panel of the door, reminding me to keep my voice down. "Why is it that when people go to doctors to ask for help, you tell them every symptom, every fact, every ache and pain, so they can make a precise diagnosis. With lawyers, people leave out whatever they want—things that make them look stupid or evil or crazy or thoughtless—then they expect the lawyer to be smart enough to cover their asses without knowing the full picture. Well, you've come to the wrong place, Paige."

"I'm sorry, Alex. It's, it's so . . . embarrassing."

"Well, it's damn embarrassing to be charged with first-degree rape, too. Especially if you didn't commit the crime."

"Andrew Tripping raped me." She was angry now, and I liked that. It was appropriate that she could still be outraged by the fact of her victimization.

"So what is it you neglected to tell me?" I pounded my index finger against the tabletop in the small, hot room. "Did Andrew and Harry know each other?"

"No," Paige answered quickly. She thought for a minute and then said, "Not that I was aware. I mean, neither had any reason to know about each other, so I had no way of thinking they were acquaintances. Why does it matter?"

"Because everything that went on matters, whether you think so or not. I need to know as much as Andrew's lawyer knows. I need to know every detail that he can provide to Robelon, because Robelon will use them to blow your ass—and mine—out of the courtroom. That's the only way I can protect you. If you had been raped by a stranger who climbed through your window, attacked you, and walked away, then he wouldn't know a thing about you to tell his lawyer."

She nodded her head in understanding.

"But this man spent three evenings with you, talking to you for hours each time. And you talked to him. You said things to him that I would never expect you to remember—little things, personal things that would have seemed of no import before the rape occurred. Yet I can't possibly reconstruct what they were, and I can't ever know what Andrew has told Peter Robelon. Worst-case scenario, want to play that out?" I asked.

Paige was puzzled. She didn't answer me.

"I'll help you. The night of March sixth, you go out with Andrew. Was Harry waiting back at your apartment that night?"

"No. By then—"

"Because all Mr. Robelon has to do is plant that seed with the jury. All he needs is a motive for you to lie."

"But I'm not—"

"Listen to me, Paige. All he has to do is convince them that Andrew seduced you, convinced you to spend the night with him at his place. You wake up early in the morning, realize you have to explain why you didn't come home to an angry boyfriend—"

"Harry wasn't my boyfriend by then. I'd ended it weeks earlier. I just couldn't get rid of him. He wouldn't leave me alone," she said, pleading with me to understand.

"That's all Robelon needs to work with. Harry's pissed off because you spent the night with another man. So you tell Harry it wasn't your choice. He doesn't believe you so you beef up the story a bit. Make it sound like Andrew forced you. He held you against your will and raped you."

"Whose side are you on, anyway?" she asked me. It was not the first time a victim had been pushed to that question. "Andrew *did* rape me. I swear it. And Harry wasn't in my apartment the night of March sixth. Why would anyone lie about something as serious as rape?"

"To save her own neck. To get back at someone who hurt her in another way. I don't have time to give you all the reasons."

Maxine knocked again and stuck her head in. "The judge is ready."

"Last chance, Paige." I was face-to-face with her now, as close as I could get. "Screw around with me and I'll see that you're indicted for perjury. For filing a false report. Am I missing anything else?"

"No, I promise you, Alex. Harry Strait used to

scare me to death, he was so jealous, so demanding. I didn't want his name brought into this. I had no idea that he had any contact with Andrew Tripping. I still don't know how or when they met, or why he's here today."

"Will you tell me about Harry this weekend? Either come in to my office on Sunday afternoon for a few hours or give me some time on the phone."

Paige nodded.

I went on. "I need you to think back about everything you remember, some way we can connect Strait and Tripping. Who is Harry Strait and what do you know about him? Why he scared you and what you mean by 'demanding'?" I was still hoping that my four o'clock interview with Tripping's son would take place, but I wanted to know why Paige was so fearful of Strait.

Reluctantly, Paige Vallis whispered, "Yes. Yes, I will tell you."

"And if he's back in the courtroom now, you're just going to have to suck it up and carry on. Trials are public. Judge Moffett hasn't got a basis to exclude him."

I opened the door, leading the way back inside. There were no spectators in the gallery. Moffett let the witness resume her seat before bringing in the jurors.

The smooth flow of the narrative that I had counted on was hopeless. On top of that, I worried that the jurors would now view Paige Vallis as hysterical and flighty. The tears, the trembling, and the freaked-out reaction to the reserved-looking man who had walked into court would be all three or four of them would need to discount her reliability.

"You may continue, Ms. Cooper."

"Thank you, Your Honor," I said, rising once again to stand at the podium. "I'm going to direct your attention to March sixth. Do you recall what day of the week that was?"

"It was a Wednesday. I had just come out of our regular staff luncheon meeting when Andrew telephoned."

"What was the purpose of his call?"

"He asked to see me again, for dinner."

"Had you heard from him since the last time you saw him, the night of your dinner at the Odeon?"

She shook her head back and forth.

"Words," Judge Moffett said to her. "You gotta answer in words. The court reporter can't take down your head movements."

"Yes, sir."

"Yes, you heard from him?" the judge asked.

"No, I meant no to that." Now she sounded confused as well as slightly hysterical.

"Did you have dinner with the defendant?"

"Yes, I met him at seven-thirty, at a restaurant he suggested, near Grand Central Station." Paige Vallis described the meal, the bottle of red wine they split, and the conversation, which was mostly about the boy, Dulles Tripping.

"How was the dinner paid for this time?"

"Andrew took the check," she said.

Robelon called out, "What'd she say, Judge? I couldn't hear it."

It was hard for him to hear the answers that were helpful to his arguments, and those he would ask Paige Vallis to repeat. I could tell how he would work this fact. Now that Andrew Tripping had paid for the food and wine, of course his date was willing to put out for him. Robelon wanted to underscore that for the jury.

Paige had accounted for most of their time together in the restaurant. Then Andrew asked her if she wanted to come to his apartment to meet his son, Dulles.

"Yes, I said that I did. Andrew hadn't told me until that moment that he had left the boy alone for the evening. I was surprised, considering how young he was. So I agreed to go with him."

There was no touching, no hand-holding, no suggestion of intimacy as they walked to the building on East Thirty-sixth Street.

"Andrew opened the apartment door with a key. It was completely dark inside, so I thought perhaps—"

"Objection."

"Sustained."

"What happened when you entered the apartment?" I asked.

"Andrew turned on the light. Dulles wasn't asleep—I figured he might have been, because it was almost ten o'clock, and because it was so strange that he would be waiting in total darkness," Vallis said, slipping in her "thought" by the back door. "He was sitting on a chair, a straight-backed wooden chair, in a corner of the living room."

"Who spoke first?"

"Andrew did. He told the boy my name and asked him to introduce himself."

"And did he?"

"No. He didn't say a word. He didn't move a muscle. Andrew spoke again, and like a military commander, ordered Dulles to stand up and come shake my hand."

"What did you observe as the boy approached you?"

"Tears were streaming down his cheeks. That's the first thing I noticed. As he got closer, I could see that his left eye was bruised, and there seemed to be some scratches on his face, too."

"Did you say anything to him?"

"I dropped to my knees and grabbed hold of his elbows. I started to ask if he was all right, and as I was doing that, his father began shouting at him, telling him to grow up and act like a man."

"What did you do next?"

"I tried to embrace the boy, telling him that he would be okay. But he stepped away from me and wiped his face with the backs of his hands. I stood up to get closer, so I could try to examine his eye. 'What happened to you?' I asked him."

Paige Vallis explained that Dulles resumed his seat while his father answered her question. "'He made mistakes,' is what Andrew told me. 'He's going to get things right this time. Aren't you, Dulles?'"

Then she described how Andrew pulled up two chairs, facing the boy, and ordered Paige to sit down in one of them.

"Did you sit?"

"Yes."

"Did you make any effort to leave?"

"No. Not then. I didn't think that—"

"Objection," Robelon said.

"Sustained. Don't tell us what you were thinking, tell us what you did," Moffett told the witness.

"Yes, Your Honor." She turned back to the jury. "Andrew began drilling the boy, talking to him like a soldier. He made him stand up at attention, and then fired a series of questions at him."

"Do you remember any of them?"

"I remember the first thing Andrew asked about. 'The lion's brood,' he said. 'Tell us their names.' Dulles answered him. He named Hannibal and his three brothers—they were weird names like Hasdrubal and Mago—I can't think of the others. He got it right, apparently. Then Andrew told him to list the winning battles of Aetius, who was some kind of Roman general. Dulles did that right, too. He knew all the places and the dates."

Paige continued with a litany of quizzes, all of them about military figures. Mike Chapman could have answered them without missing a beat, but the ten-year-old child had been force-fed the list in the few months he had taken up residence with his schizophrenic father.

She got through five subjects that she was able to recall and estimated that there was a handful more that she could not. She tensed visibly as she moved to a more difficult part of the scene.

"Then Andrew started peppering the child with questions about Benedict Arnold. 'Death to traitors,' he kept saying. 'You know what happens to traitors, don't you, boy?' Dulles knew about the betrayal of West Point and the Quebec campaign, but Andrew asked him something about the Battle of Valcour Island and the boy simply froze."

"What did Andrew say to him next?"

"He pointed at the closet door. 'The gun, Dulles, don't make me take out the gun again.'"

Paige Vallis described how the boy's body shook in response to the threat. She got up from her chair and went to grab him by the hand, begging Andrew to stop and let her take the boy with her.

"Did you attempt to leave the apartment?"

"Objection."

"Overruled. I'll hear this. Go on, Ms. Vallis."

"Of course I did. I told Andrew I was going and I was taking Dulles with me. He stood in front of the door and told me the boy couldn't leave. He said that if I went to the police, he had people who would take care of me. Those were his exact words. I swore I wouldn't go to the police, that I just wanted Dulles to see a doctor. I wasn't worried about myself—this was all about the poor little boy."

"Did Andrew Tripping step away from the door?"

"No, no, he did not. He put his hand on the child's shoulder and asked him if he had forgotten about the gun. 'Death to traitors,' he repeated. 'Benedict Arnold was the scum of the earth.'"

Paige Vallis lowered her head. 'That's when he stepped away from the door."

"Did you open it?"

"No, Miss Cooper. Not then."

The logical thing to ask her was why, but the law wasn't always logical. She was not allowed to talk about the workings of her mind, just what she did and what she observed. "What happened next?"

"Dulles broke loose from me and ran back to the chair. His father followed him."

"What did you do?"

"I stayed. I couldn't bear to leave the child in those circumstances."

This was one of the biggest problems we faced with the jury. I might have proved the misdemeanor charge of Tripping's endangering the welfare of his own child, but not much more. At that moment on March 6, Paige Vallis had the clear opportunity to get herself out of harm's way. She had not witnessed any assault on Dulles Tripping and had no clear understanding of how he had been bruised. She heard Andrew refer to a gun, but had not seen any weapon nor been threatened with the use of one.

"Objection," Peter Robelon said. "Move to strike."

"Motion granted," Moffett said, tapping on the railing in front of him, telling the reporter to strike the comment about Paige not being able to bear leaving Dulles behind.

But the jury had heard the words, and it was impossible to erase them from their minds.

"What did the defendant do next?"

"He took something out of his pocket. Something small. At first I couldn't see what it was. Dulles started to whimper. 'Please don't,' he said, over and over."

"Did there come a time when you could tell what the object was?"

"Tweezers. It was a small pair of metal tweezers. He leaned the child's head back, and inserted the tweezers in his nose."

Juror number four slinked down in her seat and closed her eyes. Squeamish, I guessed. An appropriate reaction. Number eight leaned forward and seemed to enjoy the detail. Too much television, no doubt.

"What did you do?"

"I ran to stop him. But I couldn't. He had already placed them in the child's nostril, and I was afraid I'd cause more damage if I shook his arm. In seconds, he pulled a bloody piece of cotton out of the boy's nose."

"Was there any discussion about that?"

"Yes, Andrew told me he had packed Dulles's nose to stop some earlier bleeding, before he came out to meet me for dinner. It looked to me as if the stuffing must have caused as much pain as the initial blow."

"Objection, Judge."

"Sustained."

Jurors were listening intently, some of them occasionally glancing over at the defense table to see whether Andrew Tripping was reacting to Paige Vallis's testimony. I desperately needed the testimony of Dulles himself. Without him, there was only this hint of what his father's nightly torture routine had been.

The luncheon recess interrupted the narrative's drama once again. Neither Paige nor I felt like eating. She noshed on a sandwich and I played with a salad, knowing how likely I was to develop a crushing headache by midafternoon with the combination of the stress level escalating during the proceedings and my failure to eat.

Back on the stand, Paige took us through the rest of the bizarre evening. Eventually, at some point after midnight, Andrew allowed Dulles to change into pajamas and go to sleep on the narrow cot that had been placed in the alcove off the kitchen.

Then, Vallis said, Andrew spent more than two hours telling her about the terrible pressures of raising the boy alone.

"It must have been two o'clock in the morning," she went on. "Andrew stood up in front of me. 'You're going to come inside,' he said. 'I want you to come in and take off your clothes.'"

"What did you do?"

"'No,' I said to him." Vallis tried to stay composed as she looked at me, instead of at the jurors. "'Don't do this, Andrew.' That's what I said."

"Did Andrew respond?"

"Yes. He said, 'Don't make me hurt you. Don't make me hurt my son.'"

"What did you do, Paige?" I asked.

"I had no choice. I, I—"

"Objection, Your Honor. The jury will decide that," Robelon said, smirking at the panel.

"Sustained."

"I went into the bedroom and did exactly what Andrew Tripping told me to do," Paige said, finally getting angry with Robelon. "I was afraid he'd kill his son, and I was afraid he would do something to hurt me."

"From the time that Dulles went to sleep, did Andrew ever mention his gun again?"

Vallis answered softly. "No."

"Did you ever see a gun in the apartment?"

"No."

"Did you see any other weapons?"

"Lots of them. Odd things, hanging on his walls and on tabletops. Machetes and swords and arcane-looking things with blades. I wouldn't even know what to call some of them."

"Did he threaten you with any of them?"

"No. Not explicitly."

Robelon and I would both try to use this fact to our advantage. He would argue that Tripping had the means to scare his companion into submission, if he had needed to threaten her into sex. I would say that a sign of her credibility was that despite the presence of so many sharp objects, she had never exaggerated the kinds of threats that the defendant made.

Paige Vallis went on to describe the sexual assault, which occurred for the next hour in Tripping's stark bedroom. Not a word was exchanged between them after he demanded that she undress and get onto the bed. He moved and positioned her as he desired, subjecting her to a variety of sexual acts that I made her detail for the jurors. She cried, she told them, from the moment she crossed the threshold into the room until her tormentor fell asleep beside her.

"What time was that?"

"Four o'clock in the morning, roughly."

"Did you leave then?"

"No. I just lay still in the bed until I could see daylight through the crack in the blinds. I got up and dressed myself. Quietly, very quietly. I awakened Dulles and helped him to put his clothes on. That's when I saw even more bruises, on his forearms and thighs. Andrew must have heard—"

"Objection."

"There was a noise in Andrew's bedroom, so I hurried the boy along. When the two of us got to the front door, Andrew was in the hallway near the living room. I told him I was walking Dulles to school, and that I had written my home phone number on the telephone pad in case I could help in the future."

"What did he say?"

"He asked again if I was going to the police, and started to walk towards us. I turned to face him, putting the boy behind me, nearer the stairwell that led to the building's exit."

"Did you answer him?" I asked.

"Yes, I did. I told him not to worry, not to come any closer, either. 'I can't go to the police,' is what I said to Andrew Tripping. 'I killed a man last year.'"

12

We take our witnesses as we find them, as I had told the jury in my opening statement. Now they would hear for themselves what had happened to Paige Vallis several months before she met Andrew Tripping.

"Is that statement you made to the defendant about killing a man true?"

Paige was strangely calmer now, as she told the story. "Yes, it is." She shifted her body in the chair and faced them squarely. "I mean, not on purpose. Shortly after last Thanksgiving, my father died. He was almost eighty-eight years old and passed away in his sleep.

"He had lived alone, in a small house in Virginia, since he retired more than twenty years ago. I was the only child—he had married late, and never really wanted a large family because of all the moving around his professional life entailed."

Robelon was on his feet, objecting again. "Your Honor, this would be a lovely retrospective for the Biography Channel," he said snidely, drawing a few smiles from the jury box, "but I think that all we need to know is that Ms. Vallis killed a man. Period."

"May we approach?" I asked.

Moffett waved my witness off the stand and away from the bench, while we conferenced the issue. "Where are you going with this, Alexandra?"

"If Peter doesn't intend to cross-examine my witness about how and why she—uh, she got into the situation she did, I'll leave it alone. But if he plans to ask a single question about the man's death, I'm going to bring out the facts on my direct. Ms. Vallis has got nothing to hide."

"How about it, Pete?"

"I've got a couple of questions for her, sure. But I'd rather give them up and move this along."

"You're telling me you're not going to touch the subject in summation, either?" I asked. I knew that when Robelon heard all the facts, he would be eager to remind the jury that Vallis had once defended herself when she was in mortal danger. He would say she was just as capable of defending herself against Tripping. I wanted to compare and contrast the circumstances, acknowledging—as she did—that it was the boy's life, not her own safety, that had concerned her on the night of March 6.

"I won't concede that."

Moffett was ready to think like Solomon and split the baby. "Alex, what are you trying to bring out here? That Ms. Vallis killed a man in self-defense? She have a weapon?"

"She didn't, Your Honor. There was an intruder— he's the one who had a knife. He held it to her throat and they struggled over it, and when they fell to the floor, he landed on the knife."

"Okay. So I'll allow you to ask that much. Skip over 'This is your life, Ms. Vallis.' You," Moffett said, addressing Peter Robelon. "I'm gonna limit you, too. Nothing beyond the scope of Cooper's direct, then short and sweet in summation."

That meant Moffett was reading the jury as already being in Robelon's favor. He was trying not to prolong my agony.

Paige recounted the short version of the event. I took her back to the night of the crime, letting her tell the panel that Tripping allowed her to walk out with his son after hearing that statement. I would later argue that the reason the defendant stayed in the apartment, the reason he didn't flee before the police arrived, is that he believed what Paige Vallis told him and thought she would not go to the police.

"What did you do when you left the apartment?"

"I got out on the sidewalk with Dulles. I needed to explain to him what I was going to do. I wanted him to understand that he wouldn't get hurt any more if I told the police, to know that he was entitled to be safe in his home. The first thing I did was take him to a coffee shop. I bought him breakfast—I don't think—excuse me, sir. He didn't look as though he'd had a real meal in months—and talked to him for almost an hour. Then, on our way out, I found the first uniformed policeman around, and asked him to drive us to the station house."

I could anticipate Robelon's cross now. So, Ms. Vallis, I expected him to say to her, after you were raped—*before* you went to the police, *before* you talked to a doctor—you had two eggs over easy with a side order of bacon? Or were they scrambled? Did you back up your coffee with a mimosa or a Bloody Mary?

"And when you finished making your statement at the police station, where did you go?" I asked.

"To the hospital. They took me to Bellevue Hospital."

"Were you examined there?"

"Yes, by a nurse. I think they call them forensic nurse examiners. She did a very thorough physical exam."

I started to take Paige through the many steps of the painstaking procedure necessary to complete a rape evidence collection kit, everything from swabs for DNA to pubic hair combings to fingernail scrapings.

"We'll stipulate to the medical findings," Robelon said.

Of course he would. None of them was harmful to his client.

"Did you sustain any injuries, Ms. Vallis?"

"No, no, I did not."

Physical injury was not an element of the crime of rape. In fact, fewer than a third of women reporting sexual assault have any external signs of injury or abuse. I couldn't go into that with Paige, but the nurse examiner would be qualified as an expert next week and take us through those facts.

"Did you ever see or speak with Dulles Tripping again?"

"No, I did not."

"Until you walked into this courtroom this morning, did you ever see or speak with the defendant again?"

"Never."

I finished all the steps of my direct examination, cleaned up the loose ends, and told the court that I had no further questions of this witness. It was shortly before four o'clock in the afternoon, and a quick look over my shoulder confirmed that the spectator seats were still completely empty.

Robelon stood to begin his cross, but the judge wiggled the pinky ring in his direction and we both approached the bench. "That woman ought to be here with the kid any minute. Why don't we hold this until Monday morning?"

"I'm ready to go, Your Honor."

I knew that Robelon wanted to ask his first few questions. If he started with Paige Vallis, she would then be directed to have no conversation with me about the case throughout the weekend. The strategy was obvious, and though I objected, I really had no grounds, nor any reason to discuss the evidence with her. My curiosity about Harry Strait, who had not reappeared, would have to wait until she was off the stand.

It was also clear that Robelon didn't want the jurors to linger over her previous testimony with any sympathetic thoughts during the two-day hiatus. He wanted to score a few points about Paige's lack of injury that would sink in their minds over the weekend, so that they would be receptive to his consent defense.

"Good afternoon, Ms. Vallis, I'm Peter Robelon," he said, communicating the fact that in contrast to my easy familiarity with the witness, he had never met her before. "I see from your hospital records that there were no signs of trauma in your physical exam, is that correct?"

"It is."

"Any bleeding?"

"No."

"Redness or swelling, internally?"

"I—uh, I wouldn't know."

"Well, no discomfort that you complained of, was there?"

"Not once I left your client's bedroom."

"No lacerations that needed stitching or sutures?"

"No."

"No follow-up treatment necessary, was there?"

"Yes, actually, there was. I had to be tested for sexually transmitted disease," Paige told defense counsel, now looking at him instead of the jury. "I was quite worried about being forced to have unprotected sex." Robelon had made the same slip that many lawyers did, failing to get someone to interpret the seemingly illegible notes in the body of the medical record.

He bluffed his way through a few more questions and must have decided to give them a more careful review before going on. Within ten minutes, he told the court he was ready to suspend the proceedings for the day.

Moffett excused the jurors for the weekend, told the court officers to escort Paige Vallis to the witness room until I made arrangements for her to leave, and asked his clerk to call Ms. Taggart's office to see why she and Dulles were delayed.

Mercer Wallace had come up at three-thirty, as we had arranged earlier, so that he could wait for Paige and drive her home. He was sitting with her when I went to the witness room.

"Alex," she said, getting to her feet as I walked in, "I want to apologize again for what happened this morning. For—for leaving out that stuff about Harry Strait. I'd like to explain—"

"I'd like it, too, Paige. But it's got to wait until next week. Months ago you told me straightaway you had killed a man during a struggle for your life, but you couldn't even own up about a former lover who's somehow entangled in this mess?"

Mercer shook his head from side to side, wanting me to back off, cut Paige some slack.

"I'm trying to tell you I'm sorry. I had no idea it would be relevant."

"Okay, okay. Look, I can only talk to you about administrative things while you're Robelon's witness," I said, squaring away when Mercer would deliver her back here on Monday.

Maxine had followed me in and handed back Paige's pocketbook. Mercer picked up her briefcase, which she had left in my office.

"I don't know what to do with this, Alex, other than give it to you," Paige said, opening the clasp and removing a brown paper bag. "The hospital mailed this to me because they didn't have a home address for Dulles, once he was put in foster care."

I reached in and pulled out a blue baseball jacket. The word YANKEES was written across the back of the windbreaker in white lettering, and the team logo was on the front breast. I smiled. At least the boy and I had one thing in common.

"I thought I'd see him here today, and be able to give it to him myself," she went on. "That's why I hung on to it. I'd like to talk to him, to see how—"

"Forget that one, Paige," I said. "Maybe when this is all over. I couldn't let you do that now, even if I wanted to. But this is going to be very useful to me, when I actually get to meet Dulles. It'll be a great ice-breaker. Maybe I'll get him a cap to go with it."

"You'll give it to him then, for me?"

"You bet."

"We've got tickets for the play-off games at the end of the month," Mercer told her. "Maybe I'll just leave Alex home and take the kid."

"I think it was like a security blanket for that child. The one constant in his young life. His grandmother gave it to him before she died, and he wouldn't leave the house without it, the morning I took him," she said, shaking her head.

I folded it over and replaced it in the bag, glad to have some connection to happier days with which to begin my eventual conversation with Dulles.

"Anything else you need before you go home?" I asked. "You'll call or beep Mercer if Harry Strait shows up on your doorstep this weekend? Or if you get any other calls connected to the case, right?"

"Of course."

I thanked her for her fortitude and patience with

THE KILLS 135

the process, and sent her off with Mercer, walking down the corridor to the main hallway so that Maxine and I could reenter the courtroom through the front door.

Mike Chapman was leaning against a column close to the entrance to the trial part. He was holding a red-and-white Marlboro box—odd, since he never smoked cigarettes—and it looked like it had a thin metal strip extended for an inch above its edge. He was speaking into the piece of wire as I approached, and Andrew Tripping was pacing frenetically just three feet away from Mike.

"What's going on?" I asked, as he waved at Mercer over my head.

"Agent four-two to command central," Mike said, doing an obvious stage whisper into the wire. "Subject is agitated. Blonde persecutor is approaching and subject is twitching and tweaking—"

"Would you please cut it out before I get called on the carpet for this?"

"Works like a charm on a paranoid schizophrenic. Another few minutes of my talking into this paper clip and your man Tripping will flip out big-time. I've been telling command central that I thought the perp was ready for a secret assignment inside Attica, like going undercover as the girlfriend of the biggest, baddest inmate in the joint."

"Put your toy away," I said, pushing in the double doors.

"Mercer said you might need help carrying your files downstairs after he left."

I handed him the paper bag with the Yankees

jacket. "Hold on to this for me. I don't have enough evidence in this case to overburden myself."

"I'm also here to tell you that we might get lucky. Those lifts we got from Queenie's apartment?"

"Yeah?"

Mike was referring to the latent fingerprints for which the Crime Scene Unit had dusted.

"Well, they got prints of value."

"Fresh? I mean, it sounds like there were kids in and out all the time, doing errands for her."

"These should be good. You know those raised seats, the plastic ones, that have to be on top of the toilet if you've got injuries or health problems and you can't lower yourself down all the way?"

"Sure." Queenie Ransome had suffered a stroke, and I thought again of how every aspect of her privacy, every shred of dignity left to her, had been invaded and abused by this investigation.

"The killer must have stopped to relieve himself, and picked up the seat to place it on the floor. Lifted some good prints right off the sides. Both hands, four fingers each. Clean and clear."

"Have you run them through NCIC?"

"Jeez, Ms. Cooper, how did I make it this far without you?"

"So there's no match?"

"Nope, not yet. But it gives us something to work with."

"See you downstairs. I've got to finish up here," I said, letting the doors swing shut behind me.

Within minutes, Nancy Taggart and Dulles's

lawyer, Graham Hoyt, pushed through the same doorway, and marched together, grim-faced, down the aisle toward us.

"I don't like to be kept waiting, Ms. Taggart. You're holding up the works here. And that's the second time today for you, Mr. Hoyt," Moffett said, stepping down from the bench, unhooking the clasps of his black robe and heading for his chambers. "You, Robelon. You and your client are excused until Monday. We'll start up at nine-thirty sharp."

Hoyt shook hands with both Andrew Tripping and Peter Robelon as they passed him, with Emily Frith trailing behind them. He spoke quietly into Robelon's ear.

"Follow me," the judge said, when the others had left the room. "You wanna get the kid? And the foster mother?"

"We've come to tell you we can't do that, Your Honor. There's a problem," Taggart said, unable even to look in my direction.

"Now what?"

Nancy Taggart began to explain to the judge. I rose to my feet, tapping the cap of my pen against my file, anxious to tell Moffett that this was predictable from the mother's phone call to me last evening. Now we had lost a whole day because Taggart had demanded that I leave this in her capable hands.

"Judge, Ms. Taggart isn't being entirely candid with you. Let me tell you what happened yesterday afternoon, and about my conversation with Ms.

Taggart thereafter. I offered to provide all the help she needed to find this foster mother, whoever she is—"

Taggart pointed to the hallway behind her. "I've got Mrs. Wykoff here—the foster mother. She's not the problem. It's Dulles who's gone missing, sir. He's run away."

13

Six o'clock on Friday afternoon, I was sitting in Battaglia's office with Mike Chapman, Mercer Wallace, and Brenda Whitney, who was in charge of the district attorney's press relations.

"You think kidnap or you think runaway?" the DA asked. The smoke from his cigar mingled with the smoke of the cheaper brands he had given to Mike and Mercer.

Brenda coughed as I answered. "The foster mother thinks the kid just bolted from her car and took off, while she went into the high school to pick up her older child. But I've never laid eyes on her before," I said of Cicely Wykoff, "so it's impossible for me to gauge her credibility."

"What's the department doing to find him?" Battaglia asked of the cops.

"I called headquarters from the courtroom. Chief of D's put a couple of guys from Major Case on it. We're dumping phones, doing a background on the foster mother and everybody in her orbit, and checking with the crossing guards near the school to see if they can ID the kid," Mike answered.

"Where's Mrs. Wykoff now?"

"Pat McKinney assigned the investigation to the Child Abuse Unit. I'm not sure who's interviewing her. He figures they'll get a lot more information if she isn't worried about me using it in the case. The child welfare agency had drilled that into her."

"He's right, you know," Battaglia said, chewing on the cigar end as he talked. "Besides, you're in the middle of a trial. You can't possibly handle this."

"I know it," I said. "But the kid's life is a hell of a lot more important than the Vallis rape. I hate to say that, but the reason she was attacked was because she wanted to make the boy safe. I'm ready to walk away from this case if it's freaked out the child so much."

"And let him go back to that lunatic father?" Mercer asked. "No way."

"Boss, I know I won't be able to concentrate on the testimony if we haven't found the boy by Monday."

"Don't jump the gun, Alex. Do what you've got to do and trust the PD to do their bit. Can't you buy a little time from Moffett?"

"He looks ready to tank the whole thing. We'll finish the Vallis cross on Monday. Then I've got a waitress from the coffee shop, the cops, and the nurse. Without the boy, the judge is likely to dismiss for failure to make out a prima facie case if Robelon is persuasive when he makes his motion."

"Brenda, how do we handle this? I'm sure DCPI gave it to the press," Battaglia said. He knew how to spin the media better than most people knew how to spell their names.

The NYPD's deputy commissioner for public information would have already released a photograph of Dulles Tripping, asking for help in locating him.

"They're faxing over a copy of their press release. They don't want to connect it to the trial at all. They're just sticking with the missing child approach. The chief was hoping to make it in time for coverage on the six o'clock news. It'll probably be the lead story by eleven."

Mercer had dropped off Paige Vallis at her apartment in TriBeCa and returned to my office before Battaglia had called me in. "You'd better get back on the phone with Paige and explain it to her before she hears it on television," I told him.

"This is going to hit her hard. She'll blame herself for his disappearance," he said.

"There goes my jury," I said, practically groaning. So wrapped up in worry about the boy, I hadn't thought about the need for press announcements to mobilize the public to help find Dulles. My jurors would see the weekend news on television and in print. There had been so much testimony about Dulles, through Paige, that they would certainly connect the fact that he had vanished to our trial.

"Didn't the judge instruct them not to listen to media accounts involving your case?" Battaglia asked.

Chapman blew a smoke ring and stood up, helping himself to another cigar from the DA's humidor. "Yeah. The jurors won't dare read the page-one headlines about the case, just like I'm about to slither into a hot tub tonight for a ménage with Sharon Stone and blondie, here, and like you won't be sitting behind that desk when you're eighty-five years old. Get a grip, Mr. B—they'll devour the story."

"I'll keep you both posted over the weekend," I said to Battaglia and Whitney.

We walked back to my office. Mercer said good night to us, heading over to the sixth floor across the street, which housed the Child Abuse Unit. He was going to bring the detectives up to speed on everything he knew about Dulles Tripping. Nancy Taggart was probably already there, being debriefed.

"So much for bonding with my witness," I said, taking the paper bag from Mike and locking the Yankees jacket in a filing cabinet. "You got anything else for me?"

"Well, before your weekend was ruined, I was going to ask you to come with me for a couple of hours tomorrow morning. Just wanted an extra pair of eyes going over Queenie's apartment one more time."

"What about Sarah?" I asked.

"Somehow, I don't feature going over a crime scene with Sarah's toddler and infant in tow behind her. Too much drool minimizes the potential to pick up DNA."

"Why is it that everybody is so sympathetic to motherhood?" I asked, smiling. "I haven't got any excuses that stack up against breast-feeding, Saturday-morning soccer games, runny noses, or a trip to Costco to stockpile Pampers."

"Hey, if the choice is encouraging you to stay in bed or come with me to Harlem, it's not even a close call. Pick you up after your ballet class?"

Mike knew the drill. I had studied dance since childhood, and used my weekly lesson now not only as a form of exercise, but as a way to relieve some of the tension of this all-consuming job.

"Ten o'clock, in front of William's studio."

"And do me a favor this time. Shower before you get dressed. Last time I met you after class, you smelled like a goat."

"Last time," I reminded him, "you appeared in the middle of class to drag me out because you found a dead rapist Mercer and I'd been after for two years. Trust me, I'll even put perfume on."

"I'll up the ante for you. Remember I told you the kids claimed that Queenie danced for them?"

"Yeah."

"Well, apparently before she had the stroke, she could really shake it up." Mike removed some photographs from the Redweld he carried as his case folder. "You'd have gotten along well with Queenie. She was a dancer, too."

I reached for the faded black-and-white pictures that Mike handed to me.

"See what I mean?" he asked. "Just a bit more exotic than you. Think of the money she saved on costumes."

In most of the images, there was nothing between the body of McQueen Ransome and the lens of the camera. A rhinestone tiara on her head, long black satin gloves up over her elbows, and some high-heeled strappy sandals—her exquisite figure was displayed with great confidence and pride. She appeared to be onstage, dancing for an audience. No wonder great photographers like Van Derzee had worked with her.

I turned over a few of the photos looking for anything that identified the time or place. On the back of several was a handwritten notation of the year, 1942.

"Where did you find these?" I asked.

"In one of the piles of stuff that had been dumped out of the drawers."

"Any more up there?"

"There are lots of photos. I just grabbed a couple of these to lure you in. I'm wondering if someone found all this old kinky stuff and it turned him on."

"Let's hope not. Queenie could hardly be confused with the nineteen- or twenty-year-old in these pictures. But you're right, I'm in for your morning trip," I said, gathering up my files to head for home.

"Aren't you going to stay for *Jeopardy!*?" Mike asked.

"Jake's back in town. Dinner at home. Why don't you scoot and take Val out someplace for a change?"

"Still here?" Lee Rudden asked, standing in the doorway with a bottle in each hand. He was one of the best young lawyers in the unit. "Want a cold brew, Alex?"

"I'm out of here, thanks." By the end of the business day on Friday, most of the bureau chiefs brought in some six-packs to end the week with a collegial get-together.

"Let me take that off your hands," Mike said, taking the offered beer from Lee.

"Got a minute? Can I run something by you real quick?"

I took the brass hourglass from my desk and turned it over. "I'll give you three, and the meter is running." One of my favorite law school professors had amused us with a similar response. Every time a student asked for a minute, it inevitably had turned into no less than ten, and now it was the same with the members of my unit.

"You know that case you assigned me on Monday?" Lee asked.

I nodded at him, but the beginning of the week seemed like a lifetime ago.

"The girl who came in from Long Island for the Marilyn Manson concert, remember?"

"Yeah. Someone spotted her standing alone on the train platform at Penn Station, crying her eyes out. Called the police."

"Right. Well, I finally got her in for the interview today. Twelve earrings in her left ear, a pierced tongue and a navel to match. Eighteen years old. She came in to Madison Square Garden with her friends, but they all got separated before the concert. The others went to buy some dope."

"And your girl?"

"She just waited for them near the stage door, holding up a poster she made at home to get the attention of the bassist."

"I'll bite. What'd it say?" I asked.

"'Fuck me, Twiggy!'"

Chapman laughed as he swigged his beer. "Don't tell me she's complaining that he actually did?"

"Nope," Lee continued. "Along came an enterprising young man who said he was part of the band's stage crew. He offered to get Alicia front-row tickets in the mosh pit, in exchange for a blowjob. So Twiggy could see the sign real good."

"This guy's taking scalping to a new level," Mike said.

"Alicia didn't mind the price a bit. They went into an alley around the corner, on Thirty-third Street, and she did the deed. The mook didn't come up with the tickets, though. She never reconnected with her buddies, and she ended up using the money for her train ride home to buy a cheap seat in the peanut gallery to hear the band and hold up her sign hoping Twiggy could see it."

"So the tears?"

"Tears for Twiggy and the lost opportunity. Says she lied to the cop and told him she was raped 'cause she once had a friend who was assaulted in the city, and those cops drove her little buddy all the way home to Syosset, free of charge."

I shooed both Mike and Lee out the door. "Doesn't sound like you need me at all."

"Just want to know whether you want me to charge her for filing a false report."

"Who'd the cops lock up? The guy she had oral sex with?"

"Yeah. Originally she claimed he forced her. Now she admits it was consensual. But he's been in jail for five days."

"How much time did the cop put in on this?" Mike asked.

"Spent half the night with the kid at the hospital, then schlepping her home to Mom and Dad and explaining the whole situation. The parents broke his balls, even though he was just the messenger."

"Book 'er," Mike said. "Whaddaya say, Coop?"

"I'm with Mike. Let's go, guys."

We turned the corner into the main hallway, which was dark and quiet. A figure was sitting at the security desk opposite the elevators, talking on a cell phone, his back to us. It was long past the hour the guards remained on duty anyplace in the building except the entrance lobby.

As we passed the desk, the man in the chair spun around and spoke. I recognized Graham Hoyt just as he said my name. "Ms. Cooper? Alex? Could I speak with you?"

I took Mike by the arm, knowing that he would recognize that as a signal to stay with me. I wanted him there as a witness to any conversation I had with Dulles's lawyer. "Sure. How'd you get in here at this hour?"

"Oh, I dropped by to see one of my law school classmates, and had this idea I wanted to talk to you about. I went by your office on my way out, and when I heard voices, I decided to wait for you."

"Who's that?" Mike asked, with an edge in his voice. "Your law school classmate?"

"Jack Kliger, in the Rackets Bureau. Took him a bottle of champagne. He and his wife just had a baby."

Jack was a bit older than I, and had gone to Columbia. It was true that his wife had recently given birth to their third child. I could check Hoyt out with him next week, but it seemed obvious he knew Kliger.

"What did you want to see me about? I've got an appointment I'd like to keep this evening."

He looked at Chapman, and then back to me.

"Mike Chapman," I said to Hoyt. "Homicide. He stays."

"I'm in the middle of a difficult situation," Hoyt said, with some hesitation. "Peter Robelon doesn't know I'm here. I think he—and Andrew Tripping—would take my head off if they thought I was talking to you about Dulles. But I think you and I ought to find a way to agree on some kind of solution that would be in the best interest of the child."

"I smell a setup here, Mr. Hoyt." I walked to the elevator and pressed the button. "Aren't you the same guy who told the court just yesterday that Dulles's injuries came from playing lacrosse? I don't think we're likely to agree on anything."

"You've got the detective here as a witness. What if I told you I think I can find a way for the boy to talk to you?"

I turned to face him.

"I'm very willing to do that, Ms. Cooper."

"Then why the hell did you say that to Judge Moffett about his bruises?"

"Because I was standing in court next to Peter Robelon and Andrew Tripping. That's been the party line, the defense to that portion of the case. You knew that."

"First things first. Do you know anything about where the boy is right this minute?" I pointed to the window that faced my colleagues' offices in the Child Abuse Unit. "There's a massive manhunt to find the child. If there's something you know, that's our first obligation."

"I'm well aware of that. I haven't a clue at the moment, but I'm here to see you because I believe that *if* Dulles ran away from the Wykoff home—and that's what I'm hoping, as opposed to someone snatching him—*if* he ran away, he's very likely to try to contact my wife or me before he calls Robelon."

"Because you're the legal guardian?" I asked.

"Because we've known him since he was born."

"What's the connection?"

"Andrew, Peter, and I all were at Yale together. I met Peter first, freshman year. We were both in a lot of the same classes all the way through, we were both heading for law school."

"And Andrew?"

Hoyt was quite direct. "I never liked Andrew very much. I was madly in love with the woman he married. Dulles's mother, Sally Tripping. I dated her for a couple of years. She was also a classmate of ours. Sally left me for Andrew."

"Doesn't say much for you, pal," Chapman said.

"Andrew's illness wasn't really in evidence then. He's quite smart. Brilliant, maybe. He didn't spin out of control until after we left school. I think he was diagnosed with schizophrenia when he was in the military."

"Were you still in touch with Sally until her death—I mean, when she killed herself?" I asked.

"No, sad to say. That's one of the reasons I wanted to involve myself in helping the boy. It's a bit of guilt, that perhaps she'd be alive today if I had been a better friend. Of course," Hoyt said, "I still don't believe she took her own life. Maybe things would have been different if you were on that investigation, Mr. Chapman."

I was interested in Hoyt's relationship with Dulles. "Maybe we should arrange for you to talk to the Major Case detectives. Would you mind if we put a recording device on your home phone, in case the boy calls?"

"Not at all."

"Can you take him over to the guys in Child Abuse?" I asked Mike.

"Sure."

"I probably have more sophisticated caller ID equipment than the NYPD, but do what you can."

"What's in it for you?" I asked, puzzled by this offer to help. "I mean, trying to arrange a meeting with me and Dulles."

"I want a good life for this child, Ms. Cooper. I want him to have a life without his father, to be absolutely honest with you. Now that puts me in a sticky situation legally, which is why I hope this visit can be off-the-record. I've made a lot of money in the last ten years."

"Practicing law?" Chapman asked. "All Coop gets is a city paycheck every two weeks and a shitload of aggravation."

"Investments. Clients who've put me into lucrative deals. A bit of good advice and a lot of luck. Bottom line? I've got a wife I adore, an apartment on Central Park West, a beach house on Nantucket, and a ninety-two-foot yacht to sail me there. What I don't have,"

Graham Hoyt said to both of us, "is a child. My wife and I would like to adopt Dulles Tripping. We can give him a good life, a stable one—maybe even a joyous one."

"And Andrew knows this?"

"Of course not. It's why I'd be thrilled to see you put his ass in jail. The best that happens is that he might step out of the way and clear a path for us to file for adoption. The worst would be that he's out of the child's life, behind bars, until Dulles reaches his majority and can make decisions for himself."

"How about Peter Robelon?" Battaglia didn't trust him, but I assumed part of that stemmed from Robelon's plans to run against him in the next primary. "Does he have any idea what you're interested in doing?"

"Look, Ms. Cooper. Why don't both of you sit down with me for an hour or two tomorrow? I'll lay out everything for you. Hopefully, by then, Dulles will have come to his senses and returned to Mrs. Wykoff—or called me. You tell me exactly what it is you want to get from the child, and I'll give you all the family history I can muster. We have the same basic goal, after all. Fair?"

The day was shot anyway. "In the afternoon?" I asked. "Want to come here?"

"I'll tell you what. Meet me at my club at two o'clock. It's right in Midtown. We can have lunch and figure out a plan."

He reached for another business card and wrote out the address.

"I was asking you about Robelon. Don't you think

he'd have something to say about this? Tripping must be paying him a good piece of change to defend him."

"Tripping's got no money," Hoyt said.

"But," I answered, "I thought he inherited some when his mother died last fall."

"He inherited a run-down cottage on a half-acre of land in Tonawanda County, a pantry full of his mother's homemade preserves, and his late father's gene for madness."

"And his business?"

"There are enough legitimate former feds to do all the security consulting the government or private enterprises need. Nobody wants to hire someone with Andrew's psych background. He pulls in next to nothing from that. We all throw him some odd jobs now and then, and help him with money to live—and make bail."

"So what's in it for Robelon?"

"Tell Paul Battaglia not to lean on me until after the adoption procedure is completed, and he'll be thrilled to know that Tripping can give him whatever he wants on Robelon. That's the real reason I stopped in to see Jack Kliger tonight. Tripping claims he's got information on several insider trading deals that Peter Robelon engineered."

I was incredulous. "He's blackmailed Peter into representing him for this trial?"

Hoyt picked up his briefcase and walked me to the elevator. "Peter Robelon would kill to keep Andrew Tripping out of jail."

14

Mike put me into a Yellow Cab and said good night, turning back from well-trafficked Centre Street onto Hogan Place, to take Graham Hoyt up to meet the detectives investigating Dulles's disappearance.

The ride uptown took more than half an hour, city streets clogged with bridge-and-tunnel suburbanites who made the Friday-night drive into Manhattan for restaurants, theaters, clubs, and bars.

I put my key in the lock and opened my apartment door. It was good to be home, and I felt happy with the anticipation of an intimate evening. I removed the jacket of my suit, slipped out of my heels, and tiptoed into the kitchen in my bare feet. Jake was thoroughly engrossed in the preparation of what smelled like a divine *fettuccine alle vongole,* clam knife in hand, struggling over the sink to open a dozen extra cherrystones for an appetizer. I came up behind him and wrapped my arms around his neck, biting his earlobe as I did.

"Can't you wait until dinner?" he asked, swiveling to meet my lips with his.

"I'm starving. I didn't take much out of you. How about a squeeze?"

"I'm covered in clam juice," he said, holding his arms out away from his side.

"I really don't care, dammit." I lifted the silk shell of my suit over my head and started undressing in the kitchen. "It's been a long week."

"You must have kicked ass in court today. You're awfully frisky."

"On the contrary, I barely got out with my case intact. I may not be in such a good mood when Peter Robelon finishes cross-examining my witness on Monday, so if you want some affection, this is the night to get it." I was standing naked in the middle of the kitchen. "Here, you can't get food stains on anything I'm wearing. How about it?"

"These aren't even oysters and look at the effect they have on you," Jake said, putting down the knife and taking me in his arms.

We embraced and kissed each other for several minutes before I took Jake's hand and led him into the bedroom, where we slowly made love.

I almost succeeded at forcing the day's dark thoughts from my mind as I responded to his touch. Too many times in the past months I had allowed the sad business of my work to encroach on the private emotions so essential to our relationship, and it had made my time with Jake much more difficult than it needed to be.

I rolled onto my side and let him caress me, fitting in tightly against his body with my head on his outstretched arm. "Did you hear any news tonight?" I asked.

"I haven't had the television on. I picked up the food at Grace's Marketplace and just started to cook. Why?"

"The little boy in my case is missing. The police are putting out his picture and description tonight. I just wondered how it played."

Jake stroked my hair with his free hand. "We'll have a nice, relaxed dinner, and then we can check out the local news at eleven. How come you're so calm about it?"

"Major Case has the assignment. Battaglia agrees I shouldn't be the one to work it. The kid's lawyer stopped by to see me after court. He's known Dulles since he was born, and he told Mike and me that he's a very resourceful boy. That he's run away many times before, when he lived upstate, and that he always comes back in a day or two."

"Where does he go?" Jake asked.

Riding down in the elevator, Graham Hoyt had told Mike and me that Dulles usually showed up at a school friend's home before bedtime. When he was living with his elderly grandmother, he fantasized about being part of a real family. He'd settle on a classmate whose parents were warm and loving, and where there were other children in the household, sisters and brothers with whom to laugh and play and argue. I explained that to Jake.

"How long do I have until dinner's on the table?" I asked, slipping out of the bed.

"As long as you like. Everything's ready to go."

I went into the bathroom and turned on the water in the tub, filling it with scented crystals. When the steam had clouded the mirrors and the bubbles reached to the rim, I switched on the jets and climbed in for a relaxing soak. Jake appeared with two glasses of a chilled Corton-Charlemagne, and I reached out an arm from within the bubbles to sip it. He knelt beside the tub, took the washcloth, and gently ran it across my neck and shoulders, while I described my day in court.

It was nine-thirty by the time we sat down at the dinner table, and eleven when we settled in to go to sleep. "Want to see the news?" he asked me.

"Guess it's wiser if I don't. Mercer would have called me the minute Dulles showed up somewhere."

I slept fitfully, thinking of the child and his whereabouts, and was out of bed by 6 A.M. I let Jake sleep while I made the first pot of coffee, struggled with the *Times* Saturday-morning crossword puzzle, and dressed in my leotard and tights to go to class.

I kissed Jake good-bye, went downstairs, and hailed a taxi to take me to my instructor's West Side studio. For the next hour I lost myself in the discipline of the ballet warm-up and exercises. I concentrated on the movements: stretches and pliés at the barre, floor exercises, and choreographed routines to classic Tchaikovsky.

As we changed clothes in the dressing room, my friends and I chatted about the past week's events. I declined an invitation to join two of them for a spontaneous shopping spree to fill in their fall wardrobes, and passed up an opportunity for brunch at an outdoor café on Madison Avenue. I didn't often envy them their daily routines, but when my plate was

filled with people whose lives were disrupted by violence, my mind drifted to thoughts of what it would
be like to be as unburdened by tragedy as most of
them were.

Mike Chapman's department car, a beat-up old
black Crown Vic, was double-parked in front of
William's building when I came out shortly after ten.
He was eating a fried egg sandwich on a hard roll and
had an extra coffee container in the cup holder on the
passenger side for me. "Want half?"

"No, thanks. I ate before class."

"But you must have worked up an appetite in
there. Have some," he said, extending his arm in
front of my face.

I pushed him away. "Hear anything about Dulles
Tripping?"

"All quiet. Mercer says everyone's being very cooperative. Mrs. Wykoff, your buddy Hoyt, the school
authorities. Everybody's optimistic. You know the
agency records show he ran away more than a dozen
times in the last two years?"

"It's a lot different to spend an overnight at a
friend's house in a small town than it is to try and find
your way around New York City when you've only
lived here for a year, and you're just ten."

"Hey, there are no signs of a kidnapping, and no
reports at any hospitals of an injured child. So don't
fill that twisted head of yours with evil thoughts,"
Mike said. He was eating with one hand and steering
the car uptown on Amsterdam Avenue with the
other.

He parked at a hydrant near McQueen Ransome's

tenement building. A uniformed cop had been sent by the precinct commander to meet Mike at the stoop and let us into the apartment. Half a dozen curious adolescents followed us up the steps and asked what we were doing at "Miss Queenie's" place. I closed the door behind us and then opened a window to let some air into the musty rooms, which had been closed tight since her death.

The whole apartment was in disarray. I could see more here than the crime scene photographs had captured. "Was this the way you found it, or is this a result of all the cops being in here?" I asked. Sometimes the investigators made more of a mess than the perps.

"This place was turned upside down by the killer. The landlord was going to give us another week before he boxed everything up and threw it out. The lady who did her banking thought there were a couple of nieces down in Georgia who might come close out the account—there's nothing to speak of in it—and take some of the furniture and the family photo albums."

The small parlor inside the front door had a sofa, two armchairs, a television set, and an old-fashioned record player on a side table, with a stack of 33 RPMs next to it. Mike turned it on, placing a needle on the vinyl disk that must have been the last music Queenie heard.

"Edward Kennedy Ellington. The Duke," said Mike. "Only fitting for Queenie."

The piece was called "Night Creatures." The distinctly American jazz sound filled the room and lightened the pall that the old woman's death cast over us.

The living room walls had a collection of photographs more sedate than that over Queenie's bed. Most of them featured Queenie. Several looked to be posed with family and friends.

"This must be her son," I said to Mike. She was dressed in a light-colored suit, the slim skirt covering her calves, and a Mamie Eisenhower–style hat and handbag complementing the outfit. She had her arm around the boy's shoulder, and he looked even younger than Dulles Tripping. They were standing at the base of the Washington Monument.

"You think this kid is African-American?" Mike asked, looking at the fair-skinned child with the sandy blond hair.

"Well, Queenie Ransome was pretty light-skinned herself. Maybe his father was Caucasian."

"Check this one out," Mike said. "She's in uniform."

It was another picture of Ransome on a stage, dressed in khakis designed to look like an army uniform. She was tap-dancing, it appeared, and her hand was about to salute someone with a touch of her cap. A USO flag hung from the bunting behind her. I took the photo off the wall and turned it over.

"Same year as those nightclub photos you brought to the office yesterday, 1942. This one looks like she was entertaining the troops."

"Here's another James Van Derzee portrait," Mike said. "Pretty spectacular."

It was a studio shot of the stunning young woman,

again signed by the photographer, and probably
taken after the Second World War, when she was still
in her twenties.

Set against the faux backdrop typical of the period,
she was dressed in a satin evening gown, her hair
coiffed in a large bun atop her head, reclining against
a marble column.

The gallery stopped at the far wall, which had a
small bookcase across its end. Every book had been
pulled off the shelf and strewn on the floor. I stooped
to pick up a few—popular novels of the fifties and
sixties—flipped through their pages but found nothing loose or stuck inside.

"What do you give me for a first-edition Hemingway?" Mike asked. *"For Whom the Bell Tolls."*

"Nineteen forty. That fetches a sweet number today." He knew I collected rare books. "I think the last
one went at auction for about twenty-five thousand."

"Does his signature add value?"

"You're joking. Let me see." I took the book from
his hand. The dust jacket was pristine, but whoever
dumped it on the floor had cracked its spine by throwing it there. "'For Queenie—who is, herself, a move-
able feast—Papa.' Take this one with you and voucher
it. Let's look over all the books before we're done."

"Guess she didn't only kick up her heels for the
boys in the 'hood. Don't you wish you'd had a chance
to meet her?" said Mike, changing the record. "Just
sit in this room and listen to her stories? She must
have been something."

I turned the corner into the bedroom, flipping on
the light. "Any reason I can't touch things in here?"

"Everything's been processed," Mike said, following me in.

The dresser drawers were all ajar, contents spilled out, as Mike had told me. The black fingerprint powder covered Queenie's old pink leather jewelry case. "Was there anything in this when you found it?"

"Just what you see."

There was a long strand of fake pearls, knotted the way that flappers once wore them. There were several large brooches that seemed to be made of colored glass, and lots of dangling earrings in bright colors, made of Bakelite or plastic. Some flea market vendor would relish this stuff, but none of it had any street value, and even the pettiest of thieves would have left it behind.

I opened the closet doors and separated the hangers.

"So much for those gowns and tiaras. Wear 'em while you can, Coop. This is what it all comes down to in the end," Mike said. There was an assortment of checked and flowered housedresses, and a couple of outfits that looked suitable for church—or burial. "The ME asked me to have you pick out a dress for Queenie to be buried in."

"Is there actually a funeral?"

"The squad's doing one. Nobody's been able to locate the nieces in Georgia, and all the guys want to arrange something for her. It'll be next week—I'll let you know what day."

It was an unspoken tradition among the elite homicide detectives that if there was no family to put a victim to rest with dignity, they often did it themselves. Queenie would go in a plot near the still-unidentified toddler known to the squad as Baby Hope, and the homeless man dubbed Elvis who played his guitar in the 125th Street subway station, slain for the few bucks he had picked up panhandling.

"What's on the floor?" I asked.

"Bastards even dumped out all her shoe and hat-boxes. Took whatever cash she had left. That's just the pocket change you're playing with."

The dark closet floor was littered with silver coins, which gleamed against the wooden background. I kneeled again and scooped up a handful. "This must be the stash she used to tip the kids who bought her groceries."

I let the coins run through my fingers and clink against each other as they fell. Both Mike and I knew victims who had been killed for far less money than was sitting on the floor of Queenie's closet.

"I want you to promise me that someone's going to do a careful inventory of all these things," I said. "It may not look like much of value to you, but there's a lot of memorabilia here that shouldn't be thrown away."

"What I wanted you to do is look at these photos," he said, sweeping the bedroom walls with his hand. "You ever see anything like this? It's like a shrine to herself. I mean, it's a damn good body she had, but could these photos—could her own personal history—have anything to do with her murder?"

I recognized the bed on which her body had been found from the crime scene photos. The detectives believed that's where she had been killed. In addition to the Van Derzee portrait that had been above her head, there were seven other shots—all taken in different locations—which were erotic in nature. They weren't pictures of Queenie dancing, nor were they posed on a stage or in a studio. They were, pure and simple, pornographic.

This was not a situation I had seen before in a criminal case. Although the images' purpose may have been to arouse sexual interest sixty years ago, I couldn't imagine anyone responding to the partially paralyzed octogenarian in the same way today.

There was a dressing table opposite the bed's footboard. To the right of the mirror was another photo of the young Ransome, dancing as Scheherazade, wearing gauzelike harem pants and clasping tiny cymbals above her veiled head.

"Beats me," I said. "Can't rule it out."

To the left of the looking glass was a photo of two women facing each other in profile, both in strapless satin dresses, with trains hanging to the floor and pooling behind them. "Here's one more you've got to see. It's Queenie, nose to nose with Josephine Baker," I said, recognizing the American dancer who had lived much of her life in Paris and was considered to be one of the most sensual performers of all times.

"Later for the talent show, Coop. Are you getting anything in here?"

"Like what?"

"Vibes," Mike said, sitting on the stool at the dressing table and leaning on Queenie's metal walker. "Sometimes, when I just sit here alone, in the middle of the victim's world, with all his or her belongings around me, I get a sense of who might have come here to hurt them, or what it is they were looking for."

"How about if it's just random?" I asked.

"Doesn't matter. Sometimes the place and its people speak to me," he said softly. "This one's so incongruous. I wanna feel like she's my own grandmother, but this—this scene—"

"The photos bother you?"

"Don't they bother you?" he asked me.

"They're quite beautiful, actually," I said, tousling his hair. "It's your parochial school upbringing, Mikey."

The ringing of my cell phone interrupted the quiet, with only Ellington's tunes playing their scratchy sounds in the background on the old Victrola from the other room.

"Hello?"

"Alex, it's Mercer."

"Any news?"

"No sightings. But a ray of hope. I just got into work—we had a late night trying to interview everyone who saw the boy yesterday, before he disappeared. Did you hear from Paige?" Mercer asked me.

"No. But she's in the middle of cross. You know she's been instructed not to talk to me."

"She left a voice mail for me at the office, at about ten o'clock last night. I didn't pick it up until this morning. Dulles Tripping called her after I dropped her off from court. She had given him a slip of paper with her phone number on it, that first morning in the coffee shop. Paige said he sounded fine, just scared and lonely. Have you got a cell number for her?"

"For Paige? No. I've always found her at her office, or at home. Does she know where he is?"

"No. That's the point. There's no answer at Paige's apartment and I thought you'd know how to reach her. She called to say she's trying to bring the boy in herself."

15

The three-dimensional building, set back in tiers like a giant birthday cake, has the most distinctive windows in New York. They were modeled to look like the bulbous aft end of old Dutch sailing ships, and as we drove up to the front of 37 West Forty-fourth Street—the New York Yacht Club—its century-old limestone facade seemed like a throwback to another era.

I was a few minutes late for my meeting with Graham Hoyt. Mike had decided to work with Mercer, figuring I needed no help in bartering a deal with Dulles's lawyer.

"Beep us if he knows anything," Mike said to me.

"Of course. You do the same."

"Sure they'll let you through the front door? The lieutenant says it's tougher to get into this yacht club than into your pants."

"For certain I'm a cheaper date than trying to pay the dues here," I said, slamming the car door. "Speak to you later."

I had spent a lot of time in the building across the street from the club—the Association of the Bar of the

City of New York—and I'd downed my share of cocktails in the sleek lobby of the Royalton Hotel. But this architectural beauty, with its galleon-styled windows, was one of Manhattan's great mysteries. Its elite membership, its fabled pedigree, and its prohibitive fees had long made it an object of curiosity. One couldn't buy his way in with money—it took a real knowledge of boating to penetrate the ranks. Despite myself, I was impressed that Graham Hoyt was a member.

Hoyt was waiting for me inside the lobby, so the doorman just nodded and let me pass through the grand salon.

"Shall we talk in the Model Room?"

"Whatever you like. I've never been here before," I said.

It was clear that the room was the centerpiece of the club. The entire history of yachting seemed to be displayed in its cavernous space, with hundreds of models of members' ships, with globes and astrolabes, and with braids of seaweed draping its huge mantel and wall trim.

"Is Chapman joining us?" Hoyt asked as we settled into a pair of corner seats.

"No. He's actually working on another case. Have you heard anything from Dulles?"

"Afraid not. I've got Jenna—my wife—sitting by the phone. I'm determined not to panic either one of us until another day goes by."

He leaned forward and cupped his hands over his knees. "Alex, why don't you just lay out what you've got, and tell me what you think the solution is? Perhaps we can fashion something that I can sell to Andrew, to convince him that pleading guilty would be in the boy's best interest."

"I think he's pretty well aware of the strengths of my case—and its weaknesses." I didn't trust anyone enough to reveal my personal thoughts about the witnesses.

"I knew from the discovery material you had turned over to Peter Robelon before the trial that Paige Vallis had accidentally killed a man. What's that about? Don't you think Peter's going to rip her to shreds on cross-examination?"

"Look, Graham, I'm sure you can understand why I'm reluctant—"

"I'm not a litigator, Alex. Strictly corporate law. Forgive me if you think I'm stepping on your toes. I'd just hate to see the jury find her less than credible, and throw out Dulles's case with hers."

I let Graham tell me about how he and his wife had bonded with the boy over the past years, how they wanted to help him—maybe even have him as a member of their own family. It seemed clear they had better expectations for his future.

"When we've got him safely back," Hoyt said, "I can probably persuade the people at the child welfare agency to let him sit down with you, as long as we can find a noninstitutional setting in which to do it—I don't want him subjected to another police station or courtroom. And on the condition, of course, that I can be present."

"I assume there's some quid pro quo for this, something you want from me," I said.

Hoyt straightened up. "I want you to offer Andrew Tripping a deal. A plea bargain. Something that will speed this along and have him sentenced so that he's in jail—immediately—and Dulles can breathe more easily. You can't imagine how this hangs over the child's head—this love-hate thing with his own father that the shrinks will testify about."

All the psychiatrists spoke of the same findings. The boy had a natural filial love for Andrew, but his fear was even greater. He knew that telling the truth could make him safe, but if the judge or jury didn't believe him, he would be back at his father's mercy and in more danger than before.

"Tripping's been offered a deal from the get-go," I said. "I talked to Peter about a charge of third-degree rape instead of first."

"Sorry. I don't know the criminal law. What's the difference?"

"The amount of time he'd have to serve. It's still a felony, but he wouldn't be exposed to as many years in state prison," I said. The case was complicated. The top charges in the indictment related to the rape of Paige Vallis. I had added misdemeanor counts of physical assault and endangering the welfare of a child—counts that involved Dulles's abuse—knowing that they might be taken more seriously in the higher-court forum where the rape trial would be heard. It was an unorthodox way to proceed, but I thought it was worth the chance.

"Can't we still—?"

"It's too late for that, Graham. I told the defense team that once Paige gave sworn testimony, once she had to go through the experience of telling her story publicly, the offer was withdrawn. The ball was in Andrew's court for months and he didn't want to play."

"But you'd save her the embarrassment of cross-examination. She can't be looking forward to Monday."

"You know something that I don't?" I asked. "You want to tell me what other surprises Peter has to hit her with?"

Was he bluffing now, I wondered, or did Robelon have more dirt on Paige Vallis, something else she had omitted from her narrative of events?

Graham Hoyt cocked his head and thought for a moment. For too long to make me comfortable. Why was it the prosecutor was so often the last to know?

"I've got a four-thirty appointment across town," I said. "I think we both agree there's nothing more important than Dulles's mental health. For that, I'll make almost any deal you want. But we've got to find him quickly or there's no point negotiating."

"Finding him, and finding him safe, is our first concern, of course."

We talked for a few minutes more about the police efforts and the fact that there had been no bad news as of yet. "It actually helps me to hear how optimistic you are about Dulles," I said, smiling as I stood up to leave.

"I have to be. Jenna is set on doing the right thing for this boy. It's broken her heart to be childless, and this seems like such a chance to solve both sets of problems," Hoyt said. His somber expression passed in seconds. "Want to have a look around before you go? J. P. Morgan's folly."

Maybe I could do some reconnaissance for Paul Battaglia on his future political opponent. It would behoove me to be sociable for fifteen minutes, especially if I could bring home some information about Peter Robelon, follow up on the hint Hoyt had dropped last evening. It never hurt to have some professional gossip for the Boss. "Sure. I didn't realize Morgan was responsible for this place."

"Not for the club, initially. That was started in 1844, on a yacht anchored in New York Harbor. But he was responsible for the acquisition of this great building. That's his portrait over the stairwell. And those are some of his yachts."

The painting of the Commodore was of minor interest compared with the models of his boats. "The *Corsair II*," Graham said. "Two hundred forty-one feet."

"That's not a yacht," I said, "that's a—"

"A behemoth. Precisely. Do you know that when the Spanish-American War broke out, the government asked Morgan to turn over the *Corsair* to be converted into a gunboat, to blockade the Spanish at Santiago Harbor?"

I might not only get some scoops for Battaglia, but some trivia for Chapman. "Did he get the yacht back?"

"No, he simply built a bigger one. *Corsair III.* Three hundred and four feet. Faster and stronger, more than six hundred tons and twenty-five hundred horsepower. 'You can do business with anyone,' Morgan liked to say, 'but you can only sail with a gentleman.' I look at what's happened in boardrooms across the country these last few years, and I have to admit that he wasn't wrong. Do you enjoy sailing, Alex?"

"I like anything on the water. I've got a house on the Vineyard," I said, remembering Hoyt's reference to nearby Nantucket. I thought of Adam Nyman, and how, when we were engaged, he loved to take me out on his sloop. "I used to sail quite a bit."

"When this is all behind us," Hoyt said, talking about the trial, "I'll make it a point for Jenna to put a date together with you, on the islands. There are a few hurricanes kicking around in the Caribbean, so let's hope they blow past northeast without any damage."

"Well, this is the season for them. Is there a model of your boat in here?"

Hoyt walked me to a point on the far wall, below an ornate balcony, and pointed at a black-hulled vessel that looked as though it would have put him back a couple of million.

"The *Pirate*?" I asked. Not a very original name, but an exact translation of *corsair*.

"J. P. Morgan's my personal hero."

"A robber baron as role model. Is that the part of him you admire?" I asked, with a smile.

"No, no. The greatest collector of all times. That's what I love about the man. One of those passions you either have or you don't understand."

"I've got a similar taste for rare books—just a different budget." The Pierpont Morgan Library housed one of the most exquisite collections in the world.

"He had brilliant accumulations of paintings and sculptures, manuscripts, Steinway pianos, Limoges

THE KILLS 173

enamels, Chinese porcelains, snuffboxes, Gothic ivories. Imagine being able to indulge every one of your fantasies."

"And yours?" I asked. "What do you like to collect?"

"Several things. Pretty eclectic. Contemporary art, watches, medieval prints, stamps. Nothing out of my range. I imagine, when you're ready to leave the district attorney's office, that half the law firms in the city will be clamoring to take you on board, and pay you what you deserve to be earning. How *do* you manage to keep up a house on the Vineyard on a prosecutor's salary?"

"I get a lot of help from my family," I said. His question put me in my place. I hated being asked that kind of thing, and knew what great good fortune it was that my father's invention had provided me with such extraordinary rewards. I had been on the verge of questioning Graham Hoyt about how he'd amassed the money for such high living from a couple of lucky investments and the ordinary practice of law, but now—on the defensive—I thought better of it.

"Well, I don't know how Battaglia continues to attract the best and the brightest. My father used to say, 'Pay people peanuts, you get monkeys to work for you.'"

I swallowed the urge to respond to his backhanded compliment. The young lawyers with whom I worked shoulder to shoulder every day had chosen public service as a career path, as I had, out of a desire to give back to society. Their starting salaries were less than one-quarter of the money that associates going to corporate law firms were paid, and the only bonus they received was the psychic satisfaction of their work. They didn't need yachts or art collections to make them happy.

I stopped beneath the oil painting of a tall black-skinned man in a loincloth, carrying a long staff with the flag of the New York Yacht Club aloft. I doubted he was a member.

"The Nubian?" Hoyt asked.

"It's a curious sight."

"It was James Gordon Bennett—you know, the publisher of the *New York Herald*—who paid for one of his reporters, Henry Stanley, to go to Africa and find the great Dr. Livingstone, who'd been missing for months. Bennett was our commodore, of course, back then, in the 1870s. When Stanley rode out of the jungle on the back of a mule, this fellow emerged first, carrying our club burgee. Quite a crew of intrepid sportsmen."

"A lot of history in here," I said, scanning the portraits and plaques stretching from floor to ceiling. "Thanks for suggesting we meet. Do I have to worry about Peter Robelon being indicted before I finish my case? The last thing I need, after all this, is a mistrial because we lost the defense attorney."

"Not a chance. They're just in the early stages of gathering all the information and building a case."

"Is there anything I can offer to Paul Battaglia as an olive branch? He'd love me to get rid of the Tripping case," I said.

"You mean something that his own Jack Kliger doesn't know about Peter Robelon yet?" Hoyt asked.

"That would be a good place to start."

He put both hands in his pants pockets and shuffled his coins. I smiled at him and assured him that anything he told me could only help soften Battaglia to back me on any decisions that had to be made.

"Remember what happened with ImClone a few years back? Sam Waksal started dumping the stock when he got word that the FDA was not going to approve the drug the company was testing."

"Sure. Classic insider trading. Even his father and daughter were involved, not to mention catching up Martha Stewart in the whole thing."

"Tell your boss that Robelon's been drawn in by the same kind of net. The SEC's computerized alert system picked up his brother's company on the radar screen. Small business that normally traded five hundred thousand shares was spiking to three million a day. Peter's cell phone was more active than the One Hundred and First Airborne during a shock-and-awe campaign."

"And Jack Kliger knows . . . ?"

"He's only aware of the tip of the iceberg, Alex," Hoyt said, cutting me off as he sensed my instinct to press further. "I'll call you Monday morning, before you head up to court."

I turned left on Forty-fourth Street and walked up Fifth Avenue. It was a spectacular fall afternoon, but despite the clear skies and mild temperature, I made a mental note to call my Vineyard caretaker and remind him to batten down the house. If the prediction of approaching hurricanes Hoyt had mentioned was accurate, I'd be glad I did it.

By four-thirty I was comfortably settled into the chair at my hair salon, so that my friend Elsa could refresh my blonde highlights and Nana could give me an elegant "do" for tonight's theater date.

There were no messages on the machine when I got home at half past six, no update from anyone. Jake came in from a late-afternoon run in the park shortly after I arrived.

"Is there a plan?" he asked.

"We're meeting Joan and Jim at the theater, just before eight. Would you be sure to take the tickets?" I said, pointing to the dresser, as I pulled a black silk sheath out of my closet and began to dress. "Dinner after the play, at '21.' Can you hold out?"

"Yeah. I went into the office to research a story. Grabbed some lunch while I was there."

We took a cab to the Barrymore Theater, where our friends were waiting below the marquee. Ralph Fiennes was starring in *Othello*, and the reviews from London's West End had been smashing. We settled into our seats, and Joan and I caught up on gossip until the lights dimmed and the curtain rose. I had turned my beeper to the vibrate mode and put it in my evening bag on my lap so that I could slip out of my aisle seat in case anyone tried to communicate with me about Dulles in the next few hours.

At the intermission after the second act, the four of us stretched our legs and went to the lobby for a drink. When we reached the bar, I saw Mike Chapman standing against one of the pillars, cocktail in hand, flipping through the Playbill.

There had been so much tension with Jake lately

that I hoped Mike had only chosen to interrupt one of our few social evenings for good news about the missing child. Jake followed me over to where Mike was standing, and I tried not to show my disappointment at his arrival.

"'To be, or not to be: that is the question.'"

"Wrong play," I said. "Look, is there—"

"'There's the rub—that sleep of death—the shuffling off of this mortal coil,'" Mike said, doing his Hamlet with a vodka gimlet in one hand. "Hate to do this to you, Jake, but the next dance is mine. It's the kills again. Always the kills."

"What? Make sense for a change, Mike. Stop joking with me," I said.

"There's been another homicide."

He downed his drink and stepped to the bar to replace his glass.

"Not Dulles?" I covered my hand with my mouth, relieved to see Mike shaking his head as he swallowed.

"This one's going to hit you hard, Coop. C'mon with me—I'm on my way to the First Precinct," he said, reaching out and taking me by the hand. "Paige Vallis has been murdered."

16

I couldn't grasp the fact that Paige Vallis was dead. And I couldn't stop thinking that Andrew Tripping had the best reason to kill her.

Mike led me up the two flights of stairs to the squad room. I assumed from the somber-faced team of detectives who greeted me that they knew how personally shattered I would be by the death of my own witness.

Over and over again, I played in my mind the words that Judge Moffett had said at the start of Andrew Tripping's trial: *"Murder. You should have charged the defendant with murder."*

He hasn't killed anyone, I had thought. Not that I could prove.

The questions I had thrown at Mike on the long ride down to the southernmost station house on the island of Manhattan, none of which he could answer, were the things we started with now.

"Do we have a time of death on this?" I asked, after saying hello to some of the guys I recognized and had worked with before. No one answered.

"Who's in charge here?" Mike asked.

We were out of his territory now, on the turf of the Manhattan South Homicide Squad. There wasn't a man in the room who took pleasure in being second-guessed by a colleague from the north, or a prosecutor in a black couture dress and peau-de-soie shoes with three-inch heels.

"Yo, Squeeks. You the man?" Mike said, pointing to a guy who was hanging up a phone on a desk in the rear of the room.

Will Squeekist had been a detective in Narcotics for five years before a recent promotion to Homicide. The nickname that Mike had given him when they were in the academy years earlier had stuck, and fit the small-framed man with a high-pitched voice.

"Come on back here. Let's get started," Squeeks called out to us. "Hey, Alex, how you been?"

"Doing fine until this news."

"Sit down," he said, stepping away from his desk chair and turning it over to me. Space was at a premium in the outdated old squad rooms of most precincts.

"No, thanks. Stay where you are," I said, refusing the offer.

"I need to have my back to the guys while I say a couple of things to you. Get something off my chest. Do me a favor and sit down."

Squeeks went around the desk so that he could talk directly into my face. "Sorry about the frigid greeting, Alex. A couple of them have a problem with this."

"With what?" What I had thought was empathy was something else altogether.

"We understand the deceased was a witness of yours. Paige Vallis. That right?"

"Yes. What's the problem?"

Squeeks paused. "I mean, they want to know why she didn't have any kind of protection, any—"

Mike jumped to my defense. "What are you, nuts? This broad's a complaining witness in a garden-variety sexual assault case. She was—"

I was steamed, too. "There's no such thing as a 'garden-variety' rape, Mike. Let me handle this myself. What do you guys think this is—Hollywood? When's the last time you know a witness who's been guarded during a trial in Manhattan Supreme Court? We've got forty felony cases going every day, and witnesses walk in and out of the place like it's an ordinary office building. This isn't a mob case, there's no drug cartel connection, Tripping wasn't a gunrunner or a Mafia kingpin. Who's the asshole who's blaming *me* for this murder?" I stood up. "Let's clear the air about this right now."

I came around from behind the desk and started for the group of detectives huddled between the coffee machine and the door to the lieutenant's office. Mike grabbed me by the arm and tried to hold me in place, but I shook loose.

"She feels like shit already, Squeeks," Mike said. "The broad is dead. What was Coop supposed to do different?"

"Could have let the Terrorist Task Force know what was going on," he answered.

I stopped in my tracks and turned back. "What?"

"A couple of the guys are just saying you could

have told the task force your witness was at risk because of her background," Squeeks said.

"Well, I'd have to know about it first in order to tell them, wouldn't I? The defendant claimed a lot of things that turned out not to be true. There's no middle ground with you guys. I ask you to go to the mats in order to get me evidence for my cases and you tell me there's no manpower to do it, or that no one will authorize the overtime. Now you're accusing me of not seeing conspiracies where I don't believe they exist—like the task force would have taken this schizophrenic wanna-be spy seriously if I had thought to call them? That's a load of crap."

"Not Andrew Tripping. I don't mean him."

"Exactly who do you mean, Squeeks? I'm running clean out of guesses."

"The terrorist. The guy she killed down in Virginia."

Mike was sitting on the edge of the desk. "Who'd she kill?"

"Let's back up a few steps," I said. "I know she accidentally killed a man, and I thought she had told me everything I needed to know. You obviously know more about that incident than I do."

"That's unusual, Alex. The guys who've worked with you," Squeeks said, cocking his thumb over his shoulder to point behind him, "they say you know more about your victims than they know about themselves. Say you don't go to trial until you've pulled every last ounce of information out of them."

"That's the truth," Mike said. "Get your hands off your hips, blondie, and lighten up. That's a good thing."

"They figure you're aware of all this, Alex."

I raised both arms in bewilderment and shook my head at Squeeks.

He went on. "After we found the body, we ran her. Just a name check, not even fingerprints. That's routine. Never expected to get anything—and bingo—came back with a homicide arrest down in Fairfax."

"I know that. I spoke to the DA there myself," I said. "He gave me the whole file. There was nothing in it about a terrorist."

"Maybe someone sanitized the file," Mike said. "Can you show them what you've got, Coop?"

"Drive me over to my office and I'll get the whole thing. What I thought I had was a copy of the original court papers. You can see the entire record," I said to Squeeks.

I picked up the phone on the desk and dialed Battaglia's home number. "Paul? Sorry to wake you. I've got some very tough news," I said, telling him about the murder of Paige Vallis, which would certainly be Sunday morning's headlines in a few hours.

"And I need a couple of things from you. Right now, if you can. There's a prosecutor in Virginia who gave me information on an old case. There's a chance his boss made him purge some details from it," I said, asking him to place an emergency call to the district attorney in Fairfax, to grease the wheels to get the real story.

"One more thing. Your contact at the CIA? Would you call and ask them for information on an agent called Harry Strait? He may have something to do with this."

I paused and waited for a response. "I know it's the middle of the night, Paul, but they're not going to give this stuff to anyone else."

Squeeks was waiting for me to get off the phone. "Why don't you tell me what you did know about Vallis's case."

Mike listened as I laid out the facts for both of them.

Paige's eighty-eight-year-old father had died, of natural causes, at his home in Virginia. Paige had gone down there to organize the funeral service and arrange for his personal belongings to be moved or sold.

"The prosecutor told me it was a part of a pattern, a scam that a burglary team was operating," I said. "The obituary listed the date and time of the funeral, as they always do. That's when the burglars check out the address of the deceased, figure that anyone who knew and loved him would be in church at the ceremony, and they break into the house because they figure it will be unattended."

I went on, "Paige said she came home from the cemetery and went in via the back door, surprising the burglar. He lunged at her with a knife, they struggled, and when they fell to the floor, he landed on it."

"Hoist on his own petard," Mike said.

"Exactly. The case went to the grand jury, Paige told her story, and if I remember correctly, the jurors actually stood up and applauded her."

Squeeks opened his case folder and looked at his notes. "You got the guy's name?"

"In my office. I want to say it's something like Nassan. Abraham Nassan."

"Close. It's Ibrahim."

"What's your point?" Mike asked.

"That it's clearly an Arabic name. That Cooper should have known—"

"I'm telling you that the court papers I have say Abraham. I even have a photograph of the guy. What should I have known?"

"They didn't tell you he was part of a cell? An arm of al Qaeda?" Squeeks asked.

"They told me he was Abie the burglar. Abie the second-story man," I said, slamming my hand on the desktop. "A rash of funeral-related thefts. Close this case out, close them all."

"Coop thought he was one of her boys, not Abie the Arab," Mike said.

I fished in my evening bag for my set of keys. "Send one of the guys over to Hogan Place. Here's the key to my office. The folder's in the third cabinet from the bookcase. Bring the whole goddamn case and look at it for yourself. Why the hell is any prosecutor going to purge a file to give to me?"

Squeeks answered me. "The police chief thinks the district attorney in Fairfax had orders from the feds. There was a major investigation in progress, a follow-up to the Pentagon plane crash, and the feds were running a pretty tight ship. They didn't want the public to panic. Figured if one of the terrorists was dead and the death was justifiable, no need to alarm the good citizens of the Commonwealth. Still can't believe they didn't tell *you* the truth."

"Well, start believing it. And let's send out for some coffee. Black for both of us. We've got lots of other people to talk about," I said.

"You know what Victor Vallis did for a living?" Squeeks asked.

"Paige's father? I know he was in the diplomatic corps."

"Posted in Egypt, actually. Paige testified about that."

Squeeks gave Chapman a look, again suggesting I should have divined a connection to some kind of international intrigue, rather than a simple break-and-enter.

"And he was also posted in France, Senegal, Hong Kong, Lebanon, and Ghana," I said, ticking off the countries I could remember on my fingers. "Maybe I should have polled the United Nations on what kind of danger that put Paige in."

"You know that he came out of retirement after the Persian Gulf War?"

"Hey, Squeeks," Chapman said, jabbing the shorter man's chest with his finger. "If you're such a frigging fountain of knowledge, why didn't you give blondie a call?"

"'Cause I just found this stuff out while they got Paige Vallis on ice up at the morgue."

"Yeah, well, it's amazing how people start to regurgitate the truth after somebody winds up dead."

"They knew Victor Vallis was an expert on Middle Eastern affairs," Squeeks said. "They paid him to be a CIA consultant, right up to the end. He knew all the players, what caves they were cribbing in, how the money moved around the region."

"Was Paige aware of it?" I asked. "I swear she never mentioned anything about this to me."

"I have no idea whether the old man told her he was still involved."

"This Ibrahim guy get anything from the Vallis house? I mean, was there an accomplice waiting outside?" Mike asked.

"He seemed to be there on his own. Chief says there was nothing much in the place to take, and he must have only got started minutes before the girl came home. Like Alex says, Mr. Vallis died of natural causes, so that didn't seem to be related to the break-in, either."

"Can we talk about the murder, Squeeks?" I asked. "Mike says you wouldn't even answer his questions when you called. Isn't it time we get some of the details?"

Squeekist leaned against the desk and scratched his ear.

"Did you guys find anything at the scene that's got you going in a direction related to what happened at her father's house?"

He shook his head.

"Because I gotta tell you, it seems insane to me to overlook the obvious. She's the only witness against my defendant, Andrew Tripping. Anybody figure out yet where he was when she got killed? He was keenly interested in her Egyptian connections, too. He's also got some kind of Middle Eastern expertise and experience. Supposedly worked there briefly in his CIA days."

"Calm down, Coop. C'mon, Squeeks. Give us what you got. I don't even know when and how she died," Mike said.

Squeekist was reluctant to let us into his investigation, but knew we had information that might ultimately be useful. "This probably happened sometime during last night, going into Saturday morning. In her building."

"You know about her call to Mercer Wallace? You know about the boy?"

Squeeks said he did not, and asked me to explain. "Mercer said she left that message in his office at around ten. And her records might tell us where the kid was calling from."

Mike was making a list of things that needed to get done.

"Forced entry?"

"No. It wasn't actually inside her apartment. Happened on the stairwell from the first floor, going down to the laundry room in the basement."

"Doorman?" Mike asked.

"No. The building doesn't have one," I said. "Just a buzzer and intercom system."

"No security camera?"

"Nope."

"How'd she die?" I asked.

"Strangled. Marks and discoloration on her neck," Squeeks said.

"Manual?"

"No. Some kind of ligature. I'm expecting the ME will tell us it's a piece of rope. Thin, like a laundry cord. There were a few of 'em hanging in the basement."

"Was she down there doing laundry in the middle of the night?" Mike asked.

"No sign of that."

"You think—"

"We've got guys over there now, canvassing the neighbors. Maybe she buzzed in someone she knew, maybe she got followed in from the street, maybe—"

"Maybe it was a random push-in," Mike suggested.

"She couldn't be that coincidentally unlucky," I said.

"So tell me about your case." Squeeks had his notepad out and was ready to get more information from me.

We sat for almost two hours, as I tried to recall everything that Paige Vallis had told me about herself, and everything I could think of that might be important about Andrew Tripping. I had no appetite for the doughnuts and cupcakes that were serving as dinner for the other detectives, but I went through three cups of coffee and let the caffeine get to work on my already jangled nerves.

"Don't forget to tell him about Harry Strait," Mike reminded me.

"Who's he?" Squeeks said, jotting down the name.

"CIA agent. Paige had a relationship with him. Not a very long one. Tried to break up but he didn't take it very well. I don't know whether he was actually stalking her or not."

"What do you mean you don't know?" the detective asked me.

"Look, she never mentioned him to me at all until yesterday. I didn't know he existed until he walked into the courtroom."

"You didn't even ask her about him?" Squeeks was looking me in the eye, shaking his head back and forth.

"How the hell can I ask about someone before I know he exists?"

"Cut her a break, Squeeks. She's a head taller than you and her balls make yours look like marbles."

"She was hiding things from me, that's for sure. Just the usual stuff—at least, that's what I thought. Embarrassment about a relationship, that kind of thing. It was only yesterday morning that she confided in me that this guy Strait had called her the night before to convince her not to testify."

"He threatened her?" Squeeks asked.

"She denied that. Just told me he scared her because he used to be so demanding when they were dating." "Scared her to death" were the exact words Paige had used. "She had promised to tell me more about it, but I wasn't allowed to talk to her after she got off the witness stand. That's why she called Mercer to tell him something about trying to find Dulles, Tripping's son. She wasn't supposed to call me."

"Tell him about the glut of lawyers, Coop."

I let out a sigh. "I suppose you should know about everybody involved. There's a guy called Graham Hoyt," I said, spelling his name for Squeeks. "He's the boy's legal representative. Claims to be very interested in adopting Dulles. Says he and his wife, Jenna Hoyt, have a relationship with the kid, and thinks he'll be the one to win his confidence.

"And he's helping one of my colleagues at the DA's office with an investigation into a deal that the defense attorney for Tripping is caught up in. Robelon. Peter Robelon." I gave him the name of the firm at which he worked. "Hoyt claims Robelon's got his hands dirty in some kind of securities fraud."

"You got more on that?"

"Check with Jack Kliger in the investigations division." I paused. "There are several other lawyers, too. One from the foundling hospital and another from the child welfare bureau. Their names and numbers are in my files."

"And the snitch. Don't forget about the snitch."

"Mike's right," I said. "Seems like it happened so long ago it must have been another trial. I was thinking of using an informant on my case. His name's Bessemer."

"Heard about him," Squeeks said, smiling for the first time since we arrived at the station house. "Guess some guys got flopped for that one. He was in this mess, too?"

"I hadn't met with him yet. He was being brought in to talk to me when he skipped. He had been Tripping's cellmate in Rikers."

"You think Bessemer knows anything about Paige Vallis?" Squeeks asked.

"Only what Tripping might have told him. No sign that he ever had any contact with my witness. But he's on the loose and I have no idea what his agenda is."

Detectives had come and gone all through the hours between midnight and two, as we talked about Paige Vallis and these other characters. It had been quiet for quite a while, and the ringing phone on the front desk jarred all of us.

Mike walked over to answer it. "First PDU," he said, expecting the call to be for an officer in the First Precinct detective unit. "Yeah, Mr. B. She's still here. We got her in the hot seat." He listened to a message then hung up the phone to relay it to me.

"That was Battaglia. Got through to Langley and they called him back with the information you wanted," Mike said to me. "Harry Strait? He's ex-CIA. No longer with the Agency. Here's the contact guy who'll give you his background facts."

"He must get a pension check or some kind of retirement benefit. They still have to have some way to find him," I said, taking the paper from Mike's hand.

"Hard to do, blondie. Even for a crackerjack operation like the CIA. Harry Strait died almost twenty years ago."

17

I crawled into bed next to Jake at about four o'clock in the morning. He didn't move when I slipped in beside him, and I couldn't tell whether he was feigning sleep in order not to engage me in a self-pitying dialogue about my victim's death. I ran my finger down the length of his spine and kissed the small of his back, but got no response.

When I opened my eyes at seven, the other half of the bed was empty. I picked Jake's shirt up from the back of the chair, where he had draped it when he'd undressed last night, and put it on.

I found him in the den with a cup of coffee, reading the first section of the Sunday *Times*. I stood in the doorway, waiting for him to look up from the paper. "Good morning," I said. "Sorry about last night."

"Not your fault."

"How was dinner?"

"I wasn't in the mood to go with them. I just came back here when the show ended. Did you get anything to eat?"

"My stomach was too roiled up," I said. "I'm going to pour myself a cup of coffee. Want some more?"

"No, thanks. I'm fine."

I walked into the kitchen and filled a mug. I was starving, and put an English muffin in the toaster oven. While it was cooking, I went back into the den. Now he was fixed on the Style section. "Those weddings must be riveting."

"Some sweet stories, actually," Jake said.

"The bride majored in classics at Columbia and is writing her doctoral thesis on sexual mores in ancient Rome. The groom is getting an on-line degree from the University of Paducah. They both like beagles, hang gliding, and pepperoni pizza," I said, mocking what had become of the marriage announcements in the Old Gray Lady. "The bride, who is Catholic, and the groom, who is Jewish, were married on the beach in Southampton by a Buddhist priest. More than I need to know."

"I'm just trying to see what obstacles some of these couples overcome on their way to the altar. Maybe it'll inspire me."

"I didn't know you were short on inspiration."

Jake put the paper down and looked at me. "Most of the time I'm not, Alex. But I'm at a loss right now. I know how devastated you were last night, and I understand why you had to go downtown with Chapman. Now what am I supposed to do to pick up the pieces? I get tired of asking you about a case and being told you don't want to talk about it. Or worse than that, having your boss tell you not to discuss it with me because I'm a reporter. I'm damned if I don't and I'm damned if I do."

I stood up to go back to the kitchen. "I've been very open with you about the Tripping case. Friday night I told you everything that had happened in court. I don't want to exclude you from anything that's important to me."

I called back to him over my shoulder, "You ready to tell me who Deep Throat is?"

Jake followed me into the kitchen. "What are you talking about?"

"You know you're not about to reveal any of your sources on a big story. Obviously there are times I'm not going to be free to tell you everything I know."

"That's not what I mean, Alex. I want what you keep bottled up inside. I want what you're thinking and feeling when this stuff is chewing your guts apart and keeping you up at night like you had toothpicks stuck in your eyelids."

The muffin had burned to a crisp. I tossed it in the garbage and opened the package for another one. Jake took it from my hand and started the process over.

"There was a call last night. Right about midnight. Peter Robelon."

"Shit," I said, sitting at the dining room table. The body wasn't even cold yet and the vultures were beginning to pick at it. "Did he know about Paige?"

"He said he heard a late news story on one of the local stations. They didn't give her name, but he recognized the address and Peter said he knew it was a loft building with only a few residential tenants."

"Of course he knew exactly what the setup was.

He'd hired a private investigator to snoop around the neighbors looking for dirt on Vallis. Don't tell me he was unctuous enough to be calling with his condolences?"

"He sounded perfectly appropriate. Thought it was tragic, wanted to make sure you knew about it—that kind of thing."

"You make it sound like a pleasant conversation."

"It was, actually. I guess he knew we're a couple. Said he recognized my voice from the tube. We talked for a couple of minutes. Did the six-degrees-of-separation thing. Friends of mine who are friends of his."

I didn't say what I was thinking.

"Whoops, did I screw up again? You've got that Cooper pout on your face. Peter Robelon isn't your enemy, even if his client is guilty."

"I know he's not my enemy. You want to chat with him, do it from your office. I don't trust the guy for a minute. You shouldn't either."

"So I'll cancel my lunch date with him."

"Keep it. Fine. Don't let me interfere with your endless efforts at intelligence gathering. When he gets indicted by one of my colleagues, Jake, I sure as hell don't want fifteen-minute phone calls showing up on the records from my place to his and vice versa."

"What do you mean, indicted?" he called after me as I headed into the bathroom to shower and dress.

"He's a sleaze," I said, closing the door behind me.

When I got back to the kitchen twenty minutes later, Jake had eaten the muffin and returned to the den. I fixed myself a bowl of cereal instead, and ate it alone at the table.

"What are you going to do today?" I asked when I finished eating.

"Read the paper. Go to the gym. Find someone who wants to have brunch at a charming sidewalk café like Swifty's and enjoy this beautiful day. Any takers?"

"If you can hold off brunch until two and let me go down to the precinct for a few hours to see what they've got, I promise to come back in a better mood."

"I don't care if your disposition is better or worse, as long as you explain it to me. Help me understand it."

"And you'll make an early-morning shuttle to D.C. tomorrow?" I asked.

"No. I'll go back on the six tonight. There's a White House briefing at nine and I can't take the chance of missing it."

It was a subtle way of pressuring me. No chance for a bedtime reconciliation, so I had better get back uptown in time for brunch. I was disappointed, but also relieved. It was easier to have Jake out of town while all this mayhem was swirling around me. That, in itself, told me something about our relationship that I had been slow to acknowledge.

Nothing had developed at the First Precinct in the few hours since I left the squad room. Squeeks and his partner had slept on cots in the locker room and were already back at the crime scene, scouring for clues and tips.

I drafted a bunch of subpoenas for telephone records, even though no results would be available until the business offices opened again on Monday. I used numbers Paige had given me that were in my trial folder to call several of her coworkers at the investment bank—her supervisor and two friends—to notify them about the murder before they read about it in the newspapers. Mostly, I sat at a desk feeling useless and unhappy.

At one-thirty I went downstairs and hailed a cab, calling Jake to tell him I would meet him on Lexington Avenue, at the restaurant.

"A bit of good news for you, Alex. Peter Robelon just called again. He said to tell you that both he and Graham Hoyt had calls from Dulles Tripping today. The boy sounded fine. Said he had saved his allowance and taken a bus back upstate to the town he had lived in with his grandmother. Quite a mature ten-year-old. He was going to a friend's house. And yes, darling, he did have caller ID on the phone. The operator confirms he was calling from a pay phone upstate. I'll bring the number with me."

"Thank God he's all right," I said. "I've got my cell phone with me. You could have told Robelon to call me."

"After you said you didn't want phone records showing up between the two of you? I was trying to do the right thing, Alex. Sorry if I made another mistake."

"No, no, no. You're right. I'm just so anxious to resolve this with the kid. I don't want him spinning further out of control when he finds out that Paige was killed."

I took a Post-it out of my checkbook. "Read me the number of the pay phone. I'll call it in to the detectives and they can pinpoint exactly what town it's in." I wanted to get the business out of the way before I met him for lunch.

Jake was seated at a small, round table for two, surrounded by a chic-looking assortment of Upper East Side regulars.

"Did you take care of that message?"

"Yes, I did. The cops had actually tried to find the principal of the school in Tonawanda, to get a list of kids' names and addresses. Can't be done until tomorrow. The school's shut down completely for the weekend."

I paused while the waiter took my order of a chopped Cobb salad and a Virgin Mary. It wasn't worth drinking in case we got lucky with a break in the case. Jake got the twinburgers with a vodka and tonic.

"Shall we start the day over? Aren't you going to ask me how I feel?" I asked.

"Sure," Jake said, smiling. "As long as you want to talk about it."

I described how painful it was to learn about Paige's murder, and how much more it hurt to have some of the detectives think that I had failed to protect her in her final hours. I explained her complexities and how much she had chosen to keep hidden from me, despite my best efforts to elicit her trust. I talked about her willingness to tell me she had accidentally killed the burglar, without any probing, but that she had withheld information about one of her sexual partners.

"Do you think you know everything there is to know?"

"I don't believe that ever happens," I answered. "Subconsciously or not, we always filter what we tell other people."

"Always?"

I looked up at him. "Most of the time. And certainly to those with whom we're not intimate. People like Paige wanted me to think better of her, not be judgmental, not second-guess her choices."

"So what do the cops make of this Harry Strait character?"

"A classic case of identity theft. The real Strait died of a heart attack while sitting at his desk at Langley. No controversy, no scandal, no crime. Someone plucked his date of birth and death out of the records or off his tombstone, no doubt forged a set of documents to accompany the name, and is walking around pretending to be Strait."

"Any idea why?"

"Not a clue. And if he throws the stuff in a garbage pail tomorrow and decides to be somebody else, they may never figure out who he is. They'll go through everything in Paige's apartment and office pretty carefully. Maybe he left some contact information or something else that will reveal him to us."

We walked back to the apartment and spent a few quiet hours together before Jake left for the airport. Everything about being with him soothed me and made me happy, if I kept it in the present tense. It was only when I thought about our future, and the barriers that had presented themselves in the past, that I made myself anxious.

I closed the door behind him and settled down on

the sofa for the evening with Thomas Hardy and the D'Urbervilles. The bleak Dorset landscape and the workings of the malevolent forces of the universe suited me beautifully.

Monday morning, I left the house early for the dreaded trip to my office, to prepare for the fallout when news of Vallis's death spread, and to go before Judge Moffett.

I kept my door closed until I went to the courtroom, researching the law on-line. I didn't find what I needed. When I got upstairs, the scene was not what I expected. Tripping, Robelon, and Frith were again seated at counsel table. They all looked relaxed and calm. Behind them was Graham Hoyt, and next to him were the lawyers for the hospital and child welfare agency.

Now, however, the two rows behind them were filled with courthouse reporters. I knew that the tabloids had connected the TriBeCa murder with the fact that Paige Vallis had been on the witness stand in the case, but my guess was that Robelon had invited them to come and watch him secure a dismissal of the charges against his client. I had hoped to put this matter to rest out of the glare of press coverage.

Judge Moffett was the last to arrive. The media had always been fair to him, and he would play with them to get himself some favorable ink. He took the bench and began by making a statement in open court about Paige Vallis's murder and the great coincidence that she had spent her last day testifying before him.

"Do you have an application, Mr. Robelon?" Moffett asked.

"Yes, Your Honor. At this time, on behalf of my client, I move to dismiss all the charges against him. We are, obviously, entitled to a mistrial. I had been looking forward to the now-impossible opportunity of cross-examining Ms. Vallis. Not only do we mourn her death, but we regret that this deprives Mr. Tripping of the chance to completely exonerate himself."

Robelon's grandstanding went on for ten minutes. The judge asked me to respond. I rambled more than I intended, talking about the rape charge first, disagreeing—most respectfully—with the court's conclusion that Vallis's death was coincidental to the trial, and making the point that she was not the sole victim in this matter. There were still counts in the indictment—assault and endangerment—that referred to the missing boy.

"What's the solution, Ms. Cooper?" Moffett asked facetiously. "I'm supposed to move to strike an entire direct exam? Just ask the jury to forget what they heard and move on to your other witnesses? You got law on it?"

"No, sir. I haven't been able to find a single case on point. I'd like some time to—"

"You don't need time. You need a miracle," Moffett said, looking to see how many of the reporters were taking down his repartee.

"We had open issues on the table. Dulles Tripping is still missing—"

Robelon stood and interrupted me. "Mr. Hoyt and I can give you an update on that. The boy is fine. He's upstate with friends. We're happy to arrange a meet-

ing with Ms. Cooper so she can speak with him herself as soon as we get him back here."

Graham Hoyt was standing behind Robelon and
winked at me, as though to confirm he had brokered
that deal for me to see Dulles.

"May I have a few hours to consult with the head
of our Appeals Bureau?" I asked. The most brilliant
legal scholar in our office was John Bryer. Whenever
our shoot-from-the-hip trial dogs got into trouble in
court, the fastest solution was to call Bryer. If anyone
could fashion a creative solution to keep my case
alive, it would be he. "I might want to submit papers—to write on this, Your Honor."

"Write, schmite. Knock yourself out, Ms. Cooper.
I'll give you two days. We'll be back here Wednesday
morning. Call my clerk if there's any law on your side.
Bring the jury in, Mac."

The court officer opened the door and the jurors
straggled in. From the way most of them glanced at
me, I knew they had heard the news about Paige. I
couldn't fault them, despite the court's instructions.
Several were holding folded newspapers. One of the
tabloid headlines was written in bold-faced type
above a photograph of the earnest young woman
from the Dibingham Partners annual report: WITNESS
FOR THE PROSECUTION—SLAIN.

The judge apologized to the panel for the inconve-
nience, reminded them of the now ridiculous admonition not to read press accounts involving the case and
its witnesses, and excused them until Wednesday
morning. I looked straight ahead to avoid making eye
contact with any of them as they filed out of the room.

Mike Chapman was sitting in my chair, feet up on my desk, gnawing on a bagel, when I dragged back downstairs to my office.

"Good morning, sunshine. You look like you're in need of a turn in your luck. Ah, the wonders of the automated fingerprint identification system," he said.

"Fingerprints? Where?"

"Queenie's apartment. The lifts we got off the plastic toilet seat. This one'll please you."

"Just give me his name. I'm too whipped to guess."

"Little Miss Sweet Sixteen. Your snitch Kevin Bessemer's child bride, carrying her old mink coat."

"What?"

"Tiffany Gatts herself was inside Queenie Ransome's apartment."

18

"In case you were searching for the lowest common denominator between the two women who were killed—Queenie Ransome and Paige Vallis—looks like the computer found it for you. And I do mean the lowest," Mike said. "Killing that old lady for a long-dead rodent? Kevin Bessemer and Tiffany Gatts."

I remembered the initials on the lining of Queenie's coat: *R du R*. "Why didn't it cross my mind that the mink could have been hers? *R* as in Ransome."

"*R* as in Robelon," Mike answered me. "Her initials still don't fit the monogram. Why would you think someone living on social security in a Harlem tenement was likely to be the owner of a Parisian-made fur coat, I don't know. We need to talk to that kid."

"Did you check with Corrections? Is Tiffany Gatts still in jail?"

"Yep."

"Who's got her case?"

"Nedim. Will Nedim. Trial Bureau Thirty."

"Call him for me. Tell him to get the girl's lawyer

over here as soon as possible. We need to put in an order to produce Tiffany this afternoon, if he can do it that fast. Let's see whether she rolls over and gives us Kevin Bessemer when we tell her she's a suspect in a murder case," I said.

"Usually I'm not so dense. I get lost in the forest, I can follow the trail of bread crumbs to get me out of the woods," Mike said. "Tripping's in Rikers for raping Paige Vallis and beating his own son. Kevin Bessemer's his cellmate. Bessemer waits until the eve of trial and decides to be a snitch against Tripping. On his way to see you, Bessemer stops for some nooky with Gatts, and they're both gone with the wind. Ransome is found dead. Gatts is locked up. Paige Vallis testifies. The Tripping kid disappears. Vallis is killed. But for the life of me I can't think of anything to connect Queenie Ransome to the Vallis girl. You got any bread crumbs to put on my path?"

"Sure. That's why we're going to lean on the weakest link. Get me Gatts. Kevin Bessemer is the only person linked to both cases."

By two o'clock, Mike Chapman, Will Nedim, and I were sitting in my conference room with Helena Lisi, counsel for Tiffany Gatts. I had laid out the new evidence that placed Gatts in the apartment of Mc-Queen Ransome. Lisi had given permission for her client to be picked up from the Women's House of Detention and brought to my office so the two of them could talk about what we had discovered.

When detectives arrived with the handcuffed

Gatts, we stepped out of the room so Lisi and the teenager could confer privately.

"Lisi's your vintage, no? Same age?"

She had started at the Legal Aid Society, defending indigent prisoners, shortly before I joined Battaglia's staff more than a decade ago. "Yeah. She and her husband opened their own firm a few years back. Remember him? Jimmy Lisi? They handle mostly low-level crimes, here and the Bronx."

"Hookers and humps?"

"Yeah. Not exactly who you'd hire if Battaglia had you in his sights in a major investigation. Fine for a few nickel bags of dope and a stolen fur that should have been in mothballs," I said.

"Give me a pair of sharp scissors and some elocution lessons, I could make Helena Lisi a contender."

Lisi was short, squat, and pushing forty. She had drab brown hair that hung in straggly clumps below her buttocks, pinned in place from the front by a black velvet headband. Her accent called up some remote part of Brooklyn, and was aggravated by a dreadful, constant whine that cut through me like a saw.

"I'll take her just the way she is," I said. "If she had any more serious clientele than she's got, and she couldn't plead them out before trial like she does ninety-nine percent of the time, I couldn't make it through from opening to summation. The voice just wears me down."

"You think Helena is pelican division?" Mike asked. He'd had a running gag for years, creating something he called the CPD—Chapman's Perpetrators' Dictionary—filled with street lingo for criminal justice situations. Lawyers appointed by the court were selected from a panel monitored by the Appellate Division of New York's Supreme Court, and the word "appellate" had become universally bastardized by defendants, who referred to it as the "pelican division."

"An arraignment and criminal-court plea with Helena Lisi would probably fit fine in Mrs. Gatts's budget. Check with Nedim. I'd guess the mother paid for a private lawyer for her little girl."

We were interrupted by Laura, my secretary, who told me that the judge's clerk wanted to speak with me. I picked up the phone on a nearby desk and punched the extension. "Hello? This is Alex Cooper."

"Judge Moffett asked me to give you a call. Dulles Tripping's foster mother just phoned. The boy is back at home, safe and sound."

"What a relief," I said, resting my forehead in my hand. "Thank God that's been resolved successfully. Any idea where he's been?"

"Upstate with friends is all we've been told. Moffett's going to give you a few more days. He's putting the case over until next Monday—a week from today. He wants the boy to settle in at home, and then you can arrange your interview for the end of this week, when he's had a chance to calm down."

"Thanks so much. Has the judge told Peter Robelon yet that he's going to allow me to interview Dulles? And the boy's lawyers?"

"Hey, Alex. Between the two of us—are we off the record?"

"Sure."

"Well, don't get your hopes up. I overheard him talking to Robelon about the kid."

"When?"

"Just now. Peter Robelon called to make sure that Mrs. Wykoff got through to Moffett with the news. I heard him say that the mistrial was a lock. He's giving you the extra time to humor you, and to get some kind of transition set up for Dulles, so that he's not returned to his father without controls and some kind of monitoring in place. But don't knock yourself out on your research, Alex, 'cause there's not a prayer in hell that Moffett is letting you go forward with your case."

"Thanks for the heads-up," I said. Good news, bad news.

Helena Lisi stood in the doorway. "May I come in?"

Chapman stood and pulled up another chair. "Take a number."

"I don't need to sit, Alex. I've advised Tiffany not to cooperate with you." Lisi's voice scratched like fingernails on a chalkboard.

"I'm really surprised. You've explained the new evidence to her? You told her she's looking at a murder charge?"

"D'you tell her that if Coop sends her up the river for slaughtering an eighty-two-year-old woman, P. Diddy'll be Puff Great-Granddaddy by the time she sees daylight?"

"I don't look at it that way, Detective. You don't have anything on Tiffany. She and her mother used to live on the same block as the deceased. Any of the kids will tell you she was in and out of Ms. Ransome's apartment all the time, just like the rest of them. Tiffany carried her groceries, helped her with laundry—"

"I'm talking a fresh set of prints, Ms. Lisi. Not old, not smudged."

She ignored Chapman and kept talking to me. "Actuarially, Alex, McQueen Ransome's life expectancy wouldn't have been—"

"What did you just say?" Mike asked.

"I said that if you look at an actuarial table for African-American women in the United States, living below the poverty level, you'll find that the average life span—"

"That is the single most stupid remark I've ever heard in my life," Mike said. "You're gonna stand in front of a judge at Tiffany Gatt's arraignment and ask for bail because Queenie would have dropped dead someday anyway? I'd like to take that hideous hank of hair you use for toilet paper and wrap it around your throat for about ten minutes, nice and tight so you can't breathe too good. Maybe when I let go it'll open up some of the arteries that are supposed to be feeding your brain."

"You want me to advise my client to cooperate with someone who talks to me like this?" Helena asked. "Her mother already thinks you're railroading her daughter, Alex."

"Fingerprints in the deceased's apartment and Ms. Ransome's coat on her back. It's a compelling combination," I said.

"What about the coat? The lady was hardly aristocracy. Explain to me how Ransome's name matches up to the monogram in the coat."

I couldn't.

"Maybe she bought it at a secondhand shop," Mike offered.

Helena Lisi ignored him. "I told Tiffany everything. She doesn't want to talk to you and that's all there is to it. Can you get her back to Rikers before dinnertime so she doesn't miss a meal?"

I followed Helena across the hallway and into the conference room, where a female detective and her partner were guarding the teenager. As I entered the room to give them instructions to return the prisoner for lodging, Tiffany clicked her tongue against the roof of her mouth, letting out an audible "tssssh" at the sight of me. She murmured to her keepers, "What the bitch want?"

I told the team to get started back to the jail. As they directed Tiffany to stand up and placed the cuffs on her, she kicked against the table leg with the toe of her sneaker.

"I ain't got nothing to say to you, so don't be bothering my lawyer again, you hear?"

"Tiffany," Helena said, flicking her hair off her shoulder, "don't speak another word."

"I can say whatever I want. She don't control me. I don't want to be in her office, I don't want her to be in my face—"

"Stop talking, Tiffany," Helena said. "I want you to be quiet right now."

"Shit. My mother paying you, lady. Don't you tell me to shut up. You working for *us* now."

"I'm asking you to be quiet, Tiffany, because I know what's best for you. I'm your lawyer."

"Yeah, but that bitch ain't," the girl said, jerking her head toward me.

"There's no reason to be saying anything," Helena again cautioned her agitated client.

Tiffany looked up at me as the detectives tried to pull her along. "You can't prove no murder case on me, sweetheart. By the time I got to that ol' lady's house, she was already dead."

19

"How many times have you heard that one before? 'I was counting on killing Queenie, but she was already dead when I got there,'" Mike said, mocking the girl.

I didn't dismiss Tiffany Gatts's denial as easily as he did. "It's one thing when you get that kind of statement thrown at you from somebody who's been through the system a few times. This kid's just flailing around like she's been hung out to dry. Maybe it's the truth."

"Don't go all soft on me, blondie."

"No danger of that. But she must have convinced Helena in just those ten minutes in the conference room that there was nothing to worry about on a murder charge. Helena didn't even try to cut a deal or offer to flip the kid."

"So maybe Tiffany waited outside on the stoop while Kevin Bessemer went into the apartment and killed Queenie. That still fits with the old lady already being dead when she got inside. She's playing with you, Coop."

Laura opened the door. "Were you expecting anyone from the FBI?"

"No."

"Two agents here. Say they need to interview you."

I waved them in. An attractive young woman in a smart gray pinstriped suit was accompanied by an older man. He looked like a central casting hire for a federal agent, while she looked like she had stepped out of the pages of a fashion magazine.

"Claire Chesnutt," she said, extending a hand to each of us and palming her identification for us to examine. "This is my partner, Art Bandor."

Chesnutt explained that they were assigned to try to identify the man impersonating the late Harry Strait, and needed to interview me about him.

"I don't know very much."

"We understand that. If you don't mind, it would be important if we separate you two for this conversation. You saw him, too, didn't you?" she said to Chapman.

"Let's go into the conference room," I said to her. "Mike can use my phone while he's waiting his turn."

I walked Chesnutt and her silent partner back across the hall and told them everything I could remember about my conversation with Paige Vallis.

"Did she tell you how she met the man who called himself Strait?"

"No."

"Did he ever show her any ID?"

"I have no idea. Not that she mentioned to me."

"Why did she believe he was CIA?"

"I'm sorry," I said to Chesnutt. "I never had the opportunity to explore these questions with her."

What the agent wanted most was a physical description. I closed my eyes to try to re-create the visual of the man I had seen in the rear of the courtroom. I was giving a description of the generic white male of average height and build. "Again, I apologize. Somehow it's always so embarrassing to be on the reverse side of this process."

Chesnutt had a nice manner. "I know you didn't have much of an opportunity to make an observation. You don't need to explain."

"How much of a problem is this identify-theft stuff?"

"It's becoming a bigger and bigger issue for us, since the Internet has made it so much easier to do, but it's been around forever. Used to be, people checked cemetery headstones for birth and death information, then created documents to go with the name of someone who was dead and buried. Now we get guys hacking into files or accounts on-line, getting everything from social security numbers to credit card information. They don't even have to leave home to do it."

"Why Harry Strait?" I asked. "What kind of work did he do for the CIA?"

Chesnutt smiled at me. "Frankly, I don't know."

Even if she did, she certainly would not have told me.

"Has someone tried to impersonate him before this?"

"Unfortunately, Ms. Cooper, I'm here to ask questions. Not answer them."

I took her card, in case I remembered any other details, and switched places with Mike Chapman.

"Don't get comfortable," Laura said. "Battaglia wants you." Scooping up the phone messages from her desk, I kept on walking, into the executive wing. Rose Malone signaled me straight in to the Boss.

"Sit down," he said, removing the cigar from his mouth. "First thing I want to know is how you're handling this. The girl's death, I mean."

Battaglia's exterior was ironclad. It was rare he engaged in a conversation about emotions, but he was keenly aware of the personal toll this job could take when a tragedy hit close to home. Occasionally, when I needed it most, he responded with a question or piece of advice that suggested he knew exactly the depth of my own turmoil.

"Maybe I'll stop second-guessing myself in a couple of weeks. Right now it's tearing my guts out. Paige Vallis's death, the prospects of the boy's future—it's all ugly. You get anything for me?"

"Promise me you'll watch out for yourself, Alex. When this is resolved in a week or two, take some real time off and—"

"I've just had a two-week vacation, Paul."

"Hardly. Prepping for trial. Why don't you and Jake get out of town for a while?"

I nodded my head. Battaglia had such a sixth sense about people, and now I knew he was fishing to see whether our relationship had stabilized, to check on whether I was getting the appropriate support on the home front. "Good idea, Boss. You hear back from the DA in Virginia?"

The cigar was wedged back in place, and the conversation was carried on out of the other side of Battaglia's mouth. "No question that case file his assistant sent you was whitewashed. National security and all that bullshit. You wonder how some of these guys get elected in the first place."

He looked down at notes he had scribbled during a telephone conversation with the prosecutor about the burglary case during which Paige Vallis had confronted the intruder in her father's house.

"Let's see," he went on. "The man who was killed was named Ibrahim Nassan."

"The cops told me that Saturday night."

"Egyptian-born. Twenty-eight years old. Been in the States less than two years."

"Was he really al Qaeda?"

"He spent some time in one of the training camps. Only way they know is that they searched his apartment after his death. Rented a single room in a boardinghouse in Washington. Pretty bare, except for a computer. Found some e-mails that connected him to some other known terrorists, but nothing to indicate active involvement in any trouble here in the States."

"Any family?"

"No," Battaglia said. "One of those kids who came from an upper-class background. Parents were merchants, father was educated at Oxford. Rebelled somewhere along the way, for no obvious reason."

"So, this intrusion into Paige's father's house is really linked to the work Mr. Vallis was doing for the CIA?"

"Well, they never established that, either. An educated guess. You know nothing was taken during the burglary, right?"

"Yeah, 'cause the perp never got out of the house," I said. "Do they know what he was looking for?"

"They claim not to have any idea." Battaglia shuf-
fled his notes and kept reading. "Victor Vallis. Career
Foreign Service. Sounds like he'd been posted all over
Europe and the Middle East."

"He was in Cairo, right? I know Paige had talked
about that."

"Yes. Twice, actually."

"Any connection to the CIA?" I asked.

"They haven't made any so far."

"When was Vallis there? In Egypt, I mean."

"Where's Chapman? His military history might
come in handy for this," Battaglia said, referring to
his papers.

"I'll be sure to tell him you said so. He's in my
office."

"The second time Victor Vallis was in Cairo was
from 1950 to 1954. That covers the period of the
coup, when the king was deposed and General Nasser
took control of the Egyptian government."

"The king?"

"Farouk. The last king of Egypt."

"What was Vallis's position at the time?" I asked.

"Political advisor to the American delegation. Still
pretty junior."

"How about the first time he was stationed there?"

"In the mid 1930s. Probably his entry-level job after college," Battaglia said. "But he wasn't working
for the government then."

"What did he do?"

"He was a tutor. The royal tutor. You're too young
to know anything about Farouk," the district attorney told me. "He was the playboy pasha—a spoiled

prince who grew up to be a corrupt monarch and a Nazi sympathizer. I hated his politics."

"And Victor Vallis taught him?"

"For almost three years, when young Farouk was living in the palace in Alexandria, and later in Cairo; Vallis made his home with the family and taught the prince all his studies. Foreign languages, world history, geography."

"So did the district attorney ever get any closer to figuring out what the feds thought this burglary was about?" I asked. "Foreign intrigue? Terrorism?"

"He says the file was still an open case. Nobody knows. They looked for connections between Victor Vallis and the Nassan family, but if the CIA knew of any, they sure didn't tell the local prosecutor."

"Thanks for making the call," I said, as he handed me his notes of the conversation. "I'll have Laura type these up."

I headed back across the main corridor to my office, where Chapman was talking with my assistant, Sarah Brenner. "Are the FBI agents gone?"

"Yeah," Mike answered.

"Talk about feeling stupid. Were you able to give Ms. Chesnutt a 'scrip of Harry Strait?"

"Not a very good one," he said, repeating it to me.

"Doesn't sound any better than mine."

Sarah had a different perspective. "Sounded to me like you were describing Peter Robelon."

"Or the defendant, Andrew Tripping," I said. "Totally fungible white men. They're not going to get very far on what I told them."

"Well, forget about Harry Strait for the moment

and come on down to my office. I was just telling Mike that uniformed cops brought in an acquaintance of Queenie Ransome's you need to talk to."

"Kevin Bessemer?" I asked.

"Not quite so lucky as that. But I think you'll want to question this guy."

"Where'd they find him?"

"Inside Ransome's apartment earlier today."

"A break-in?" Mike asked.

"No. That's what makes it so interesting. He let himself in with a key."

20

"Is he under arrest?" I asked the cop who was standing outside the door of Sarah's office, guarding the wiry young man who sat inside.

"Not exactly. We didn't know what to charge him with."

"Burglary?"

"He's got a key, ma'am. Says he knows the tenant."

"The tenant's dead."

"Yeah, but he claims she gave him permission to be in the apartment."

"Not lately, I don't imagine," I said.

"That's why we brought him down here. You guys can decide whether or not to charge him."

"Was the crime scene tape still over the door?"

"Yes, ma'am. He just lifted it and went inside, apparently."

"Didn't your sergeant think that's enough for a trespass?"

"He says the city don't pay him to think. That's why they got lawyers."

I waited for Chapman and then entered Sarah's

small office. "My name is Alexandra Cooper," I said. "This is Mike Chapman. He's a detective and I'm an assistant district attorney."

"I'm Spike Logan." He had been resting his head on his crossed arms, on a corner of Sarah's desk. He stretched and yawned. "Wanna tell me what this is about?"

"Happy to," Mike said. "Then we got a few questions for you."

"Am I in custody?"

Mike looked to me for a decision.

"No," I said.

"Or do you mean not yet?" Logan said. "I'm free to leave?" He stood up, as though to challenge my response.

I stepped back to let him pass.

"That's fair," he said, reseating himself.

"We'd like to talk to you about McQueen Ransome," I said, "maybe starting with what you were doing in her apartment this morning."

"She invited me there. I had an appointment with her. Eleven o'clock."

"What kind of appointment and when did you make it?"

"Every third Monday of the month. Been doing it since the beginning of the year. Look, these cops told me Queenie's dead. Somebody killed her. I've probably got more questions for you than you've got for me."

Mike pulled two chairs from the anteroom outside Sarah's office and we settled in for our conversation with Spike Logan. I couldn't fathom why Queenie would have any standing engagements to meet with young men in her home, but Mike was ready to take over the questioning from me.

"You saying you didn't know Ms. Ransome was dead when you went in there today?"

"Uh-uh. Nope. I haven't been in town since last month. Just drove in last night. You gotta tell me what happened to her, man."

"Didn't you see the tape outside her door?" I asked.

"Lady, crime scene tape on a stoop in Harlem ain't quite the odd thing it might be on the front steps in Beverly Hills."

"Let's back up a bit," Mike said. "Why don't you tell us about yourself? Who you are, how you know Ms. Ransome, what the purpose of these meetings were."

Logan leaned back and stretched his legs in front of him. Lean and slight, he was dressed in jeans and a sweatshirt. He was a dark-skinned black man, with a mustache and goatee, dark-framed eyeglasses, and several piercings in both ears.

"Me? I'm thirty years old. Born here in the city, went to Martin Luther King High School. College at NYU. I'm in graduate school now."

"Where?"

"Harvard. African-American studies program."

"You got any ID on you?"

"It's in my car, uptown. In the glove compartment. Just my driver's license."

"No student ID?"

"I'm not enrolled this semester. I'm on leave."

"Where do you live? Where'd you come in from last night?"

"Massachusetts. Oak Bluffs."

Logan must have noticed my reaction. I looked over at Mike to see whether the name had registered with him. Oak Bluffs was one of the six towns on Martha's Vineyard. It had an unusual history, and for more than a century had been a summer community and home to an African-American population of professionals, scholars, and intellectuals.

"Who do you live with?"

"Alone. It's my uncle's home. I'm house-sitting for the winter."

"Ever been arrested?"

Logan hesitated for a moment, looking back and forth between Mike and me. "Couple of times."

"What for?"

"Protests, demonstrations on campus. You're gonna run me anyway, right?"

"Bank on it."

"Once for robbery. But it was mistaken identity. The prosecutor in Boston dismissed the case. My lawyer told me I was allowed to answer no if cops ever asked whether I was arrested for that charge, 'cause it was supposedly wiped off my record. I'm just telling you in case it shows up, so you know I didn't try to lie."

"How long ago?"

"Five, six years. No trouble since then."

"How do you support yourself?"

"I've got a fellowship for grad school."

"You just told me you're not there this semester."

"Yeah, well, my mother helps me out. I've got no rent to pay and some money I've saved up from my last job. Don't be getting hostile now, bro. I may be the only friend Queenie had," Logan said, pointing a finger at Mike and pushing himself up in his chair.

"How'd you meet her?"

Logan folded his arms across his chest and looked at the ceiling. "It was sometime late last fall. I'd been doing a research project up at school. My father was killed in a car accident about twenty years ago, and I always had this idea to go back and trace the history of his family. How his grandfather came up North, got educated, started his own business. Just find out everything I could about the man and the people I came from.

"So I'm doing all this stuff in the archives at the Schomburg Center," Logan said, referring to the research facility for black culture on Malcolm X Boulevard. "They had lots of documents about my grandparents, and photographs from the schools and clubs and professional societies in Harlem, with my father and some of his kin in 'em."

"You related to Queenie?"

"I kind of wished I was after I met her. I tried to find people who used to know my dad. My mom had all these pictures of him as a little boy, before they hooked up. In a lot of the shots he was with another kid she said was his best friend. Looked like a little white boy. On the back of the pictures was the other kid's name, Fabian Ransome."

I thought of the photo we had seen in Queenie's apartment, in which she had posed with her child. Mike had learned from neighborhood talk that her son had died before his tenth birthday.

"I always wanted to meet the boy in the photographs—Fabian. Find out about my dad's childhood from him. So at the Schomburg, I came across these clippings from the 1940s and 1950s, with pictures of McQueen Ransome. Her name caught my attention, and four or five of her photographs had Fabian in them, too. I recognized him from my dad's album."

"How'd you locate her?"

"Pounding the pavement," he said. "She wasn't listed in the book, and there weren't many people around who remembered her from her glory days, but I eventually got word of the old lady who liked to dance for the kids who ran her errands."

"What'd she do when you showed up at her door?"

Logan smiled and stroked at his goatee with his hand. "Man, she just came alive. I think she was so hungry for a bit of family, so happy to have a connection to her son, she just embraced me like I was her own blood."

"She remembered your father?"

"Told me the best stories about him. Things I never would have known if I hadn't come across her. I'd drive down here from the Vineyard once a month, she'd put the music on—wouldn't have none of my tapes or CDs, just her old vinyl. I'd bring her favorite things—gumbo, rice and beans, monkey bread, key lime pie. We'd go on talking for hours, then she'd heat up the food and we'd have a long meal with more conversating, as she liked to call it."

"You write your paper? Your family history?" Mike asked. "Is it something we can get a copy of?"

"The one about my father? I never finished it. Queenie got me off on a tangent."

"About what?"

Logan looked at Mike. "I fell in love."

"With?"

"With her, man," Logan said, sitting back and slapping his knees with both hands. "These meetings? I convinced her to do a history with me. An oral history for the Schomburg, and then I could use some of it for my dissertation at school. Not her personal stuff—but things I learned that related to my own family—"

"Why? What about her did you like?" Mike asked, while I thought of the photographs in Queenie Ransome's bedroom, those of her in costume as well as the nudes.

"Queenie? Now that girl had a life." Logan became animated, gesturing with his hands as he told us what he knew about her childhood in Alabama, and how she ran away from home to come to New York City to become a dancer.

"In the legitimate theater?" Mike asked.

"That was her dream. But it didn't happen, Detective. There weren't a whole lot of roles on Broadway for colored girls in the forties."

"She knew Josephine Baker, though."

"Yeah, you've checked out those pictures in her apartment? I've never seen a more beautiful woman in my life. Somebody brought her to the attention of Baker, right at the beginning of the Second World War. Josephine was staging a revival of *Chocolate Dandies*, the revue that made her famous in the 1920s. She came to New York for auditions. Queenie tried out just hoping to be part of the chorus line, but she had real star quality. Rose right to the top."

Mike remembered the photographs that we had seen together. "She performed for the troops during the war?"

"Yeah. Went everywhere that Josephine Baker did at first, till she spread her own wings a little later on. You know about De Gaulle giving them each the Legion of Honor?"

"Nope. I'd like to hear it."

"I got it all on tape, the stories she told me. Queenie and Baker both worked as intelligence agents during the war. Celebrities were able to move around much more freely than anybody else. Claims she even carried secret military reports from England to Portugal that were written on her sheet music in invisible ink. She was a hot ticket."

"What did you say about De Gaulle?"

"Baker worked with the French Red Cross. She was very active in the Resistance. She got Queenie involved, too. They were especially good at using their various—let me say, 'charms'—to convince foreign dignitaries to issue visas to some of the young women who needed to get out of Eastern Europe. Between the two of them, they saved a lot of lives."

"That sounds fairly dangerous," Mike said.

"She seemed to thrive on hazardous duty. There wasn't much that scared her. That was probably the second most dangerous thing Queenie did."

"I'll bite. What was the first?"

"Gathering intelligence for the American government."

"Spying?"

"You got it."

"On whom?"

"The king of Egypt."

"Farouk?" I asked, sitting bolt upright.

"Yes, ma'am, Farouk. The Night Crawler—that's what she called him. McQueen Ransome was King Farouk's mistress, Ms. Cooper."

Josephine Baker, the Revue Nègre, the French Resistance, and General Charles de Gaulle. I thought of the letters *R du R*, the old Parisian label in the mink coat that Tiffany Gatts had stolen from the apartment, and I traced them with my fingertip against the green desk blotter.

"*Ransome du Roi*," I said to Mike Chapman. "The King's Ransome."

21

Less than half an hour had elapsed since Battaglia had mentioned Farouk's name. Paige Vallis's father had tutored the playboy prince in the mid-1930s. Then Vallis had also been posted in Egypt later on, when Farouk's monarchy was deposed. I had not even had the chance to tell Mike about my talk with Battaglia before walking into the room to meet Spike Logan.

"These tape recordings you made with Queenie, where are they now?" Mike asked.

"In a bank vault on Martha's Vineyard."

Dozens of questions raced through my mind, and I needed to break in on Mike's interrogation. But I didn't want to interrupt the flow of Logan's answers by stepping out of the room and bringing Mike up to speed. I didn't want Logan to know that he might have hit on something of consequence.

"You mind turning them over to us?" Mike asked.

Logan hesitated.

"Ms. Cooper can give you a subpoena."

The slip of paper would have no authority in the Commonwealth of Massachusetts, and it might take me a few days to secure one via the local prosecutor, but Logan didn't know that.

"Let me think about it," Logan said.

"Why, what's on 'em that concerns you?"

"That's all the lady's private thoughts, Mr. Chapman. I signed a contract with her, through the Schomburg, that none of the stories of her intimate relationships would be made public until twenty-five years after her death. You know, it's got anecdotes about lots of famous people—some of them still alive today."

I stepped on Mike's toe, signaling him to lay off the issue of the tapes. I'd find a legal way to get them produced so we could explore them for any information of value.

"What can we tell you about Ms. Ransome?" I asked. Perhaps by making this process a two-way street, we could soften Spike Logan to give us more facts.

He asked questions about how she died, whether anyone had appeared to claim her body or her possessions, and what point we had reached in the investigation.

When we had satisfied his interest, I turned the tables again. "I'm fascinated about this relationship with the Egyptian king. Do you know how all that started?"

Mike Chapman stood and opened the door. "You and your girlfriends eat up all this crap about the royals. A commoner like me couldn't get lucky in your crowd if I was hung like a stallion. Either of you guys want coffee?"

"Yes, please. Get me two. Spike?"

THE KILLS 231

"Could I have a sandwich and some soda?"

"Sure. Be back in ten."

It was obvious that Logan liked talking about Mc-Queen Ransome. "So Josephine Baker was responsible for taking Queenie to Europe to perform. There was never quite the color barrier there that there was for entertainers in this country."

"Paris?"

"That's where it all started, dancing in the Folies-Bergère. But once they got involved with Resistance work, Queenie was sent on missions all over Europe. Farouk had become king of Egypt in 1936, but by 1939, the British had taken over control of the country. Rommel was in the desert, ready to pounce, so the Allied troops packed the Egyptians off to guard the Suez Canal, and took over the government, basically."

"And what became of Farouk when the British took charge?" I asked.

"Just left to be a figurehead. He was barely in his twenties, with a net worth of one hundred fifty million dollars. He had the full run of a five-hundred-room palace, freedom to play with all his toys—yachts, airplanes, racing cars, breeding horses—and to chase broads."

"Was he married?"

"Not very happily."

"How did Queenie meet him?"

"She'd been sent to Egypt supposedly to entertain the troops. It was much later in the war—about forty-four. And she performed at the king's favorite night-club in Cairo—Auberge des Pyramides."

"Farouk went to clubs during the war?"

"That's how he got the nickname the Night Crawler."

Chapman had used the same phrase himself, but he referred to the vermin who crept around the city streets from dark to daybreak, looking for trouble.

"Every night he was out carousing—belly dancers, jazz bands, caviar and champagne. Next to Mussolini and Goebbels, who got private tours of the pyramids, his favorite people were showgirls."

"So Queenie was really ordered there for the purpose of seducing Farouk?"

"She took the assignment as kind of a dare. She didn't believe he'd go for her."

"Looking at those pictures, it would be hard to imagine why not."

"'Cause he liked them blonde, Ms. Cooper, and he liked them no older than sixteen. She was the same age as the king, and a bit more mocha than he usually fell for."

"What happened?"

"Queenie Ransome danced. She came out onstage and moved that magnificent body like no one else could."

I thought of her photograph in the Scheherazade costume and imagined her dancing in it for Farouk.

"After the performance, one of his bodyguards came backstage and invited her to join the king's party. King Farouk stood up to greet Queenie, and when she curtsied to him, he took a necklace out of his pocket and draped it around her neck. 'This is your passport to my palace,' he said. 'The guards will bring you to me later tonight.'"

Logan stopped to laugh. "Queenie told me she un-hooked it and took a look at it. Sapphires all around it the size of quail eggs. She dropped it into his soup bowl and told him, 'I think you have me confused with the next act, Your Highness. She's the whore. I'm just a dancer.'"

"She walked away?"

"Right out the door and back to the Red Cross headquarters, where she was staying. Night after night Farouk came to the club to ply her with gifts but she refused to see him. When he finally showed up empty-handed, and came backstage to apologize, it was the first time Queenie agreed to speak with him." Logan paused. "She played hard-to-get for a few more weeks. Demanded a real courtship."

"And then?"

"The royal affair. Nights in the palace, cruises up the Nile, mingling with all the high society in Cairo and Alexandria, which were quite sophisticated places at the time. There was a big American colony in Egypt. Queenie said Farouk used to invite dozens of Americans in to see Hollywood's latest propa-ganda—movies like *Casablanca,* musical scores from brand-new Broadway shows like *Oklahoma!*"

"Was she on duty or in love?" I asked.

"It started as an assignment. Hell, she was picking up whatever intelligence she could from within the bedroom. She was there when President Roosevelt and Winston Churchill stopped to meet Farouk on their way back from the Yalta Conference. Farouk's wife even moved out of the palace—"

"Because of his affair with Queenie?"

"Not entirely. Because she had failed in her efforts to produce an heir to the throne. Three daughters, but not the son that Farouk needed to guarantee succession for the Egyptian monarchy. It just meant that Queenie had his full attention at the time, and his complete confidence. And yes, she fell in love with him."

"Did she tell you why?"

Logan thought for a minute. "He wasn't the pathetic old exile the world got to know later on, when he had worked himself up into a three-hundred-fifty-pound glutton. Queenie showed me the photo of him that was on the cover of *Time* magazine when he was crowned, sort of the great white hope of the Middle East. Prince Charming in the land of the pharaohs. He was smart, spoke seven languages, was a high-liver, and he loved women."

"I guess the sapphires didn't hurt, either."

"Queenie had a good laugh about that one," Logan said. "The necklace he tried to give her the first night? A total fake. He carried costume jewelry with him every night that he went out on the town to give away to the showgirls and hookers. He had millions, but he was a real cheapskate with the ladies. I think it fascinated him that Queenie didn't care about his possessions—the jewels, the cars, all the other things."

"What do you mean, 'things'?"

"The king was a collector. Of things, loads of things. Weird things, expensive things. He just had to own whatever he could get his hands on."

"What exactly did he collect?"

"The way Queenie talked, to me it sounded like everything. You know about the pornography, right?"

"No, no. I don't."

"Hasn't anyone told you about those pictures in Queenie's bedroom?" Logan asked.

"The ones by James Van Derzee?"

"Not them. Those are great photos. Really classy. The Schomburg has his whole collection of those— very artistic, very elegant."

I didn't want to tell Logan that the killer had stopped to pose his victim the same way the great photographer had memorialized her. Maybe he already knew that.

"What pornography do you mean?"

"King Farouk had the world's most extensive pornography collection. Erotic art, objects and devices of every kind, timepieces with fornicating couples gyrating on the watch face as the hands moved around. Pornographic neckties, playing cards, calendars, corkscrews. Then he got the bright idea to make Queenie pose for photographs."

"And she did?"

"She did at first. She never minded displaying that body of hers. It was only after the king wanted her to perform sexual acts with other men, so that they could be photographed for his collection, that she objected. She refused to do that. It was the beginning of the end of their relationship."

"The pornography—what became of all of it?"

"Queenie took whatever pictures she could with her when she left Egypt in 1946. When Sotheby's auctioned the rest of Farouk's collections after he was deposed, she contacted them to see whether she could buy some of the photographs, so they wouldn't become public. But at the last minute Sotheby's withdrew the pornography from the auction, along with some other royal loot. She never knew what happened to the stuff. Didn't much matter, though. Her spirit was already broken."

"Because?"

"Fabian, her son."

"Had he died?"

"Yeah. He had contracted polio. Infantile paralysis. Nineteen fifty-five, a few months before the vaccine was approved for use in the States. Shortly before the auction."

I did the math in my head. "Fabian was—"

"King Farouk's son. The prince of Egypt, heir to the throne."

We were both silent.

"That blond child with fair skin looked exactly like his old man," Logan said. "I'll show you the pictures."

"She must have been devastated."

"Still couldn't talk about it without breaking up, Ms. Cooper. I mean, she knew long before she became pregnant that she wasn't much more than one in a long line of royal concubines. There were belly dancers and British diplomats' wives in the same club as Queenie. Two of the king's favorite mistresses were Jewish—it was a different Egypt in those days—but none of them was likely to become the queen."

"Did he know she was pregnant when she left him?"

He nodded his head. "She was too proud to tell him. But after she gave birth to their son here in the States, she sent him some photographs, knowing how badly he wanted a male heir, and seeing how closely the child resembled the young Farouk. She did the *F* thing, too."

"What?"

"Farouk's father, King Fuad, had once consulted a seer, who told him that all his good fortune derived from the letter *F*. Fuad then demanded that everyone in the royal family be named based on that prophecy—Farouk himself, and his sisters Fawzia, Faiza, Faika. Like that. He had even made his wife change her name. Queenie thought she'd get his attention that way. 'Here's your prince, Fabian, just look at him.'"

"Did Farouk respond to her?"

"She never heard from him again. He divorced his wife and married a sixteen-year-old girl, who finally gave birth to an heir—the next Fuad."

"Did he ever contact Fabian? Support him?"

"Queenie didn't want money from him. She just wanted him to acknowledge the boy, to know that she had done what the royal princess failed to do until that time."

"But how did she live? Did she continue to dance?"

"Not for very long," Logan said, stopping to open his mouth wide and stroke his goatee. He seemed to be thinking about whether to go on. Then he leaned back and reached into the pocket of his jeans.

"Queenie gave this to me in June, for my birthday," he said, handing me a pocket watch.

It was in a solid-gold case, and on the back were the initials *F.R.* "Farouk Rex," Logan said. "Given to him by his pal, the Duke of Windsor."

"And Farouk, he gave things like this to Queenie?"

"Not exactly," Spike Logan said, smiling. "My girl got a few kicks in before she left town to come back to Harlem. She stole this from the king."

22

McQueen Ransome stole a gold watch from the King of Egypt. What else of value might she have taken in a fit of pique, out of favor and heading for home?

"Did she tell you," I asked Spike Logan, "whether she took any of Farouk's other 'things' when she left?"

"Hey, it all started as a prank. There was a well-known story at the time about Farouk pardoning a famous pickpocket from one of Alexandria's penitentiaries. In return, the king wanted lessons from the guy. So the thief agreed, and taught His Majesty how to steal by sewing tiny bells into each of his own pockets, like little alarms, before filling them with objects. By the end of his lessons, Farouk had mastered the art of light-fingered lifting. You never heard the story about Churchill's watch?"

"No."

"Churchill was visiting the troops and stopped to have dinner with Farouk, who lifted his watch from the prime minister's waistcoat during cocktails, without the great statesman having a clue. Only after the meal, when Churchill asked the time, did the king pull out the old guy's watch from his pocket and tell him."

I laughed at the image.

"Farouk thought it would be fun to teach Queenie, too. She got a platinum cigarette case off Noël Coward one night, and the money clip that Jack Benny carried in the inner pocket of his dinner jacket when he came to perform for the troops."

"But she carried it farther than that, I take it."

Logan got serious. "She could see what was coming, Ms. Cooper. The king was losing interest in her, she knew she couldn't make a living dancing while she was pregnant, and she didn't know what kind of hard times she was facing back in the States, going home to Harlem after the war."

"What did she admit to you that she took with her?"

Logan's fingers tapped on the desktop. "I don't remember, exactly." He seemed to recognize that he was displaying Queenie in a negative way.

"I'm sure you can give me a general idea." I needed to get those interview audiotapes before he altered or destroyed them. "We're beyond the statute of limitations for theft, Mr. Logan," I said, smiling at him. "It's quite fascinating."

"I'm not the only one who knows," he said, as if he were justifying his reasons for telling me. "Some jewelry. I mean, Farouk actually gave her stuff during the time they were together. But I guess, in the end, she got her hands on some uncut gems he had stashed away. Sold 'em off or pawned them from time to time over the years. Farouk also collected rare stamps and valuable coins, odd things that she really didn't know the value of," Spike said.

Then he looked at me, as if to gauge my reaction before going on. I didn't display any.

"Queenie was able to survive for about ten years on one of the treasures she scored."

My raised eyebrows gave away my interest. Spike went on. "You know what a Fabergé egg is, Ms. Cooper?"

The brilliantly jeweled objects had been made by Carl Fabergé for the Russian czars, and the ones that survived the revolution had been collected and traded by the richest men in the world. "Sure I do. Farouk had those, too? Queenie took a Fabergé egg? My admiration for her taste keeps growing."

Spike Logan didn't care whether I approved of Queenie's methods or not. "Some antiques dealer in London bought it from her. I looked him up on the Internet but couldn't find any recent trace of him. She joked that Farouk was better than the goose that laid the golden egg—he mislaid it and she took it. That single egg kept her and Fabian going for the next ten years, till the boy died. Queenie realized she got stiffed when she sold some of these objects 'cause she didn't have any proof of ownership. The dealers knew she had stolen goods, otherwise she would have made enough money to live in style the rest of a very long life."

"Didn't Farouk miss any of these things? Didn't he send people out to the States to try to find her and get them back?"

"You speak any French?" Spike asked.

I nodded my head.

"*Touche pas!* Know what that means?"

"Don't touch," I answered.

He leaned forward and lowered his voice for dramatic effect. "When the king wanted to play with his toys, he'd go into the rooms in his palace where everything was stored, taking Queenie with him. I'm talking dozens of enormous rooms. They'd sit on silk cushions, laid out on the floor, for hours and hours. He'd let her try on tiaras and necklaces, run gold pieces through her fingers, and place Fabergé goblets in her hands. But when it came to the pieces he prized dearly, the things that were most rare, most valuable, he'd scream at her, '*Touche pas! Touche pas!*' She wasn't even allowed to hold them. Fabergé goblets, yes, but the jeweled eggs—no."

"So it was easy for her to tell what the best treasures were, I guess."

"That's what she thought. Queenie told me that when she was packing her bags to leave the palace, she made one last sweep of the joint. She figured Farouk had so many collections, so many toys, that if she was careful, he wouldn't begin to know what was missing. She headed right for the things that she had never been allowed to touch. Instead of taking all his precious eggs, she just took one. Same for the gemstones and the other valuables. When he opened his closets and vaults, he'd still see dozens of sparkling objects—he'd never stop to count. The most obscene thing is that he probably never knew any of the things she took was even missing."

"She had no trouble smuggling these things out of Egypt?"

"Farouk had turned his sights to a younger girl, the war was over, and everyone around the king was delighted to get Queenie out of the palace. She put her finest prizes right in her handbag, took her chances with what she'd concealed in the luggage, and got on the next plane to Portugal, then home."

"What became of all the other valuables?" I asked.

"She spent some of the money she raised by selling them. But after Fabian's death, and because Farouk had never responded to the boy's photographs, she went into a profound depression. Spent five years institutionalized in a private sanitarium—mental hospital in Connecticut. That chewed up most of what she was able to hock."

"And the rest?"

"She didn't have legitimate title to these things, so she found herself selling to some pretty shady characters. There was no way to prove—what do you call it?"

"Provenance," I said.

"Yeah. She had some rare stamps that don't go for much on the open market. And some foreign coins that might have been worth something as part of a larger collection, but she never got more than face value. And then she just ran out of juice, Ms. Cooper."

Why, I wondered, did Spike Logan ask us about what had become of McQueen Ransome's possessions? Why had he let himself into the empty apartment, and had he been looking for anything in particular when the police arrived?

"Do you think, Spike, that she still had any of Farouk's valuables that she kept in the apartment? Objects she had mentioned to you? Or possibly something that she didn't even know had current worth?"

He stretched his legs again and crossed his arms. "I think she would have told me. Queenie trusted me, Ms. Cooper. I think this watch was about all she had left to give."

She may have trusted him, but could we?

"Did you ever see a fur coat?" I asked.

He shook his head. "In her crib? Nope. But I never had reason to look in her closets, and we never went outside together in the winter. We could look through the old photographs and I'm sure they would tell the story. It wouldn't surprise me at all. Queenie would have liked a nice fur coat in her prime."

Mike Chapman came back into the room with lunch for Spike Logan. "Would you excuse us for a few minutes?" I said, walking out with Mike before going upstairs to my office.

I filled Mike in on what Logan had told me. "The uniformed guys give you any sense of what Logan was doing in the apartment when they arrived?" I asked, opening the lid and sipping the hot coffee Mike had brought me.

"Sniffing around pretty good. You believe he didn't know Queenie was dead when he got there?"

"All I have to go on is what he says. We'll see if phone records tell a different story."

"You gonna honor your word?" Mike asked. "Let him go home?"

"All we got is a trespass. No judge is going to hold

him on that. Might as well get the goodwill by showing we trust him."

"You got enough Vineyard contacts to get the local
police to keep an eye on him."

"I'm not as worried about Logan as I am about
getting my hands on the tapes that he's got stored in
the bank before he does anything to them. Queenie
may have said things that would have no significance
to him, but would give us some direction. I gotta get
started on that. Would you be sure to get all his contact information before you let him go? And the key
to the apartment."

"You wanna hold on to that gold watch from the
Duke of Windsor, too?"

"Absolutely," I said.

Sarah Brenner offered to work on the interstate
subpoena, since she would be handling the grand jury
investigation of the Ransome homicide. I went to my
desk to phone the Oak Bluffs Police Department, to
give them a heads-up on Spike Logan.

As I hung up the phone, I noticed Laura standing
at the doorway between her desk and the hall. A man
was speaking to her, and she was keeping him out of
my way until she determined whether I wanted to see
him, guiding him to the conference room.

"It's one of those days," she said, coming back to
tell me about it. "Doesn't anybody call for an appointment anymore? It's Peter Robelon—and actually, he's with that other lawyer, Mr. Hoyt. They were
in the building and wanted to know whether you had
a few minutes for them."

I took my coffee down the hallway, curious to

know what delaying tactic they had in mind at this point.

They stood up when I walked in the room. "Alex, I'm so sorry about Paige Vallis. We both are."

I was stone-faced. "Let's not put your credibility on the line, guys. I've really been trying to take you seriously up to this point. I take it this isn't a condolence call."

"C'mon, Alex," Graham Hoyt said. "You can't take every one of these cases home with you. Don't blame yourself for—"

"I don't, thank you very much." Stay out of my personal life, I thought, looking daggers at him. "I blame the killer."

"Look, Alex, Graham's been working on me all weekend. I just spent the last couple of hours with Andrew Tripping. I think maybe we ought to revisit our discussion of a plea, especially now that the circumstances have changed so dramatically. Will you sit?"

I pulled out a chair and joined them at the table. "You've been jerking me around since the get-go, Peter. If that's what this is about, forget it. Why would Tripping possibly see the light of day at this point?"

"Because the girl was the sticking point. With all due respect, Alex, he wasn't ever going to jail because he did anything he would admit was wrong to Paige Vallis. She's dead now. Can you understand you've got nothing to go forward with in regard to the charge of rape? You're headed straight to a mistrial."

I hadn't finished the legal research to see whether it was possible to sustain that count if I was lucky enough to get Dulles to testify honestly about the events of the day and evening. The medical evidence and DNA results proved that sexual intercourse had occurred. Maybe Dulles could establish the fact that there had been threats. I knew the chances looked pretty bleak. I didn't answer.

"Suppose I move to dismiss the rape count of the indictment," Robelon said, Hoyt sitting patiently by his side. "I'm not asking *you* to do that. I'll make the motion—oppose it if you want. You'll be clean on the record, if that makes you feel any better about it, and Moffett will rule on it. My way."

"Guess you've already had that conversation with him. Ex parte." I was certain that out of my presence the judge had given Robelon the go-ahead on his plan.

"You're too emotional about this, Alex. Moffett's got no choice," Robelon said.

"You don't either, if we're talking realistically."

"And the assault charge on Dulles Tripping? Andrew will plead to that?"

"Graham and I think that if we work on him together, we can get you that plea. The misdemeanor—assault in the third degree."

"Jail time?" Just the abuse of his son should have earned him the better part of a year behind bars.

Robelon pursed his lips and stalled for a minute. "We're just starting that part of the discussion. When you were talking rape, he knew he was facing state prison. That was out of the question. This is just city jail. I think we can bend him."

"Why the change of heart? Besides Paige Vallis, I mean?"

Graham Hoyt spoke. "Andrew Tripping knows

he's not fit to have custody of his son. He loves him—
or at least he wants to love the boy, but he's totally
unequipped to take care of him. He's not going to say
that in open court, Alex, but I think—are we off the
record?"

"Of course."

"I think he'll admit that to Peter and me. He's like
any other parent—he simply wants what's best for the
boy. Among us, we'll figure out what that is."

"And the other lawyers," I said, referring to Nancy
Taggart and Jesse Irizarry, from the city child welfare
agency and the foundling hospital, "they'll go along
with whatever you propose?"

"We haven't talked with them yet. Not till you say
you're on board," Robelon said.

"Andrew Tripping will do a full allocution?" I
wanted a complete admission to the assault on
Dulles, no weasel words or excuses.

"We'll work on that with him."

"On Wednesday morning, when we report back to
Moffett?"

"Yes, but—" Robelon started to answer.

"Why doesn't it surprise me that there's a 'but'?
Why is it always an angle with you guys?" I asked.
"What's this one?"

"He pleads guilty on Wednesday morning. He admits to hitting the boy, causing the injuries. We'll give
you everything you want on that. But we put the sentence off for three weeks. Let him get his affairs in order, see the boy one more—"

"No way."

"No, what? It's a misdemeanor charge. A short adjournment to tie up loose ends, secure his belongings, make arrangements for his bills to be paid while he's in jail. Nobody in your office ever objected to that kind of thing."

"It's the boy, Peter. I don't want him seeing the boy."

"One time. Supervised. You've read all the reports. You know the kid loves him. Since when are you some kind of expert on child psychology, Alex? That Dr. Huang will be present to supervise. Andrew needs to have one face-to-face with the kid. Apologize to him, explain why it's better that he gets help before he thinks about asking to raise Dulles by himself. What the hell do *you* know about how this kid's gonna feel that his father's in jail for a complaint that the child himself made to the doctors?"

I couldn't respond to Peter's tirade. If there was a single visit, with close supervision, I suppose it might be a necessary part of the child's recovery process. "Let me talk to our shrinks," I said.

Graham tried to be the diplomat. "Look, Alex. It's late in the day, and we're hitting you with this by surprise. Think about it overnight, talk to your people tomorrow, and let's see if we can work this out by Wednesday. I really believe a plea would resolve this quite reasonably for everyone involved."

"Everyone except Paige Vallis," I said, thinking of how her death had taken her interests completely out of the criminal case. "And now I'm supposed to leave Andrew Tripping out of jail even longer, risking the possibility that he'll never surrender, but I don't have a clue whether he's responsible for the Vallis murder."

"Goddamnit, Alex," Robelon shouted at me. "If

you had a scintilla of evidence to point in his direction, then you and your goons should lock his ass up. Don't you dare think for a fraction of a second of walking into a courtroom and making that kind of allegation that you can't support. That's completely unprofessional."

Robelon was on his feet, and Hoyt was pressing the palm of his hand against the taller man's chest.

"We all need a break," Hoyt said. "Let's wrap it up before the weekend. Gretchen's on her way. You and I will be out of here."

"Gretchen?" I asked, completely distracted by his non sequitur.

"Hurricane Gretchen. She's headed for the Outer Banks tomorrow, and then supposed to roll up the coast, hitting us hard on the cape and islands. That's what this drizzle is about," Hoyt said, pointing to the gray clouds outside the window.

"I didn't even notice. I don't think I've looked out the window since I got here this morning."

"I've got to fly up to Nantucket to secure the boat before the weekend. Better check on your house," he reminded me.

Hoyt was giving me the chance to small-talk my way back into a conversation with Robelon. I'd be damned if I'd apologize for my crack about Tripping. His involvement in Vallis's death certainly hadn't been ruled out by the homicide detectives.

I tried to stay in neutral territory. Bouncing off my interview of Spike Logan, I remembered Hoyt's lively discussion about collectors when we had been at the New York Yacht Club.

We closed up the conference room and walked to the elevators. "I've got a question for you, Graham. You told me on Saturday that you're the maven of great collectors. Besides J. P. Morgan, who were the other well-known collectors of the twentieth century?"

Robelon walked behind us, brooding, as Hoyt answered me. "Nelson Rockefeller, Armand Hammer, William Randolph Hearst, Malcolm Forbes. Dozens more like them, just not as well known. You looking for a rich husband, Alex?"

"Skip the husband. Just a tiara. How about King Farouk? Would he be on that list?"

"What'd you say about Farouk?" Robelon asked.

Tell your client I'm on to him, I thought to myself. "I asked Graham what kind of collector he was."

"Something to do with Paige Vallis?" Hoyt wanted to know.

"No, no. Another matter altogether."

"One of the most bizarre collectors of all times. I mean," said Hoyt, "there were the usual high-end things. Famous jewels, postage stamps, rare coins—"

Robelon broke in. "Cars. Wasn't he the guy with the red cars?"

Hoyt nodded. "He had a passion for red cars. Bright, tomato red. Collected hundreds of them. Passed a law forbidding anyone else in Egypt from owning a red automobile, so when the soldiers saw a scarlet car speeding through town, they knew it was the king himself."

"Incredible."

"And antique weapons. Had a real thing for them."

"Like Andrew Tripping?" I said. Maybe Farouk was the inspiration for the scabbards, daggers, and scimitars that decorated his spare apartment.

"A little finer than Andrew's. And quite a cache. If you're really curious, you can check the old auction books. I think there were more than a thousand pages of cataloged items that Sotheby's put together, and those were only the things that Farouk couldn't get out of the country with him when he fled in fifty-two."

"Pornography?" I asked. Was there any sex offender twisted enough to kill for an original collection of erotic art, part of which Spike Logan thought was still in Queenie's apartment at the time of her death?

"Loads of it. But for some reason, that was all removed from the auction offerings just days before the collection went under the gavel," Hoyt answered. "The odd thing was that Farouk had piles of junk, too. Paper clips and labels from ketchup bottles, walking sticks and aspirin bottles. He's not my model, Alex. I prefer the more discerning pack rats, like Morgan."

"Autographed pictures of Adolf Hitler," said Robelon from behind me. "The fat old bastard collected those, too."

"How come everyone knows about Farouk except me?" I asked.

"Peter comes by it naturally," Hoyt said. "I think that's what attracted Andrew to him in college."

"My father's English," Robelon said. "Worked abroad for the government."

"In Egypt?"

"No, no. In Rome, actually."

"What does that have to do with King Farouk?" I asked.

"That's where Farouk died, in exile, in 1965," Robelon said.

"Let's put this case to bed. Then I'll buy the first round of drinks, Alex. Maybe we can get the truth out of my classmate here. Peter claims his father was just an attaché at the embassy. But Andrew swears Robelon senior was the most important British spook in Europe."

23

"Where has this day gone?" I asked Mike, who had settled in behind my desk. It was after six-thirty and the corridors were quiet and dark.

"Fill me in over dinner."

"Another time. I'll give it to you quickly. But I'm running downtown. There's a seven-fifteen service for Paige Vallis."

"I thought she's from Virginia?"

"Her body's being shipped down tomorrow for burial. But her boss organized a memorial for her tonight, at a little church on the Battery, and he invited me to be there. Did you speak to Squeeks? Anything new on the death investigation?"

"All quiet. You want a ride?"

"I'll walk."

"It's wet out there."

"I won't melt. Mercer's invited, too. He said he was going to be late getting there, but he'll take me home."

I closed up my office, telling Mike about my conversations with Peter Robelon and Graham Hoyt before again walking to the elevator. "So all these connections to Farouk and people who worked in the Foreign Service; do you make anything of it?"

"Conspiracy or coincidence, huh? You're always seeing some dark intrigue behind things like this. Me? I'm a coincidence man. Odd things just happen sometimes. Ingrid Bergman happens to walk into Humphrey Bogart's Casablanca gin joint. Farley Granger happens to share a train compartment with a stranger who agrees to murder someone for him. Peter Lorre and Sydney Greenstreet happen to bump into Sam Spade while they're looking for—"

"Those aren't coincidences, Mike. They're plot devices. You're talking fiction and I'm talking real life."

"Hey, how many people do you need to have in a room to guarantee the chance that at least two of them would have the same birthday?"

"I don't know. Three hundred sixty-four."

"Ha! Twenty-three. At least two out of every twenty-three people will have exactly the same birthday. Statistical odds. A lot of life is coincidence."

We walked out the door and I turned right to go to Centre Street. "Wait a minute, blondie. I got a brolly in the car."

"I don't need it."

"Don't be stubborn."

I turned my collar up and crossed the street with Mike, waiting while he fished out his car keys and shuffled through the heavy assortment of police equipment that filled the trunk.

"So I'll give you a substitute *Jeopardy!* question, since you're standing me up tonight," he said. "Military history."

"I lose before we get started."

"The answer is from army basic training. Three things a soldier in uniform is instructed not to do," Mike said, finding an old black golf umbrella and trying to extricate it from beneath a fingerprint-dusting kit and orange jumper cables. "I'll spare you. Push a baby carriage, wear rubbers, and use an umbrella."

He pulled it out and opened it, straightening two of the bent metal spokes. "Ever go to an Army–Navy game on a rainy fall day?" he asked. "Sailors sit under their umbrellas, soldiers get soaked. Napoleon laughed at the British troops carrying umbrellas at Waterloo in 1815. Guess who won?"

I twirled it for him a few times and got back on course. "See you in the morning. Say hi to Valerie for me."

Office workers unprepared for the change in weather were scurrying toward the entrance to the subway station in Foley Square. I passed it by, cutting across City Hall Park to walk south on Broadway, which was better lighted than the less-trafficked and twisted side streets of the city's financial district.

The gaping hole behind the Trinity Church graveyard that has become known to the world as Ground Zero still took my breath away and turned my stomach whenever I thought about it or, as now, skirted its perimeter. I kept my head down, dodging pedestrians who moved northward as I sidestepped puddles to try to keep my feet moderately dry.

At Bowling Green, I took the fork to my left and trotted the last three blocks down Whitehall, as the showers fell more steadily.

I was at the very toe of Manhattan—the Battery—named for the row of guns that had once guarded this vulnerable tip of the early colonial settlement. The address Paige Vallis's boss had given to me, 7 State Street, was about the southernmost building on the entire island, but for the fortress of Castle Clinton.

It was hard to see numbers because of the dim street lighting, and I looked in vain for something that resembled a Catholic church. People raced by me on their way to the Staten Island ferry terminal and the express bus stop that would speed them to their homes in the outer boroughs. I doubled back to find a coffee shop and asked for more specific directions to the Rectory of the Shrine of St. Elizabeth Seton.

I climbed the staircase, fooled by the appearance of the original facade. The small chapel had been an early Federal mansion—a private home—built at the end of the eighteenth century. The slender Ionic columns and delicate interior detailing had survived two hundred years of commercial development all around it, and was now a small sanctuary named for America's first saint.

The service was already under way. I walked to the far side of the room and sat on a bench below a wrought-iron balcony, shaded by its overhang, and out of sight of the others who had come to pay their respects.

There were prayers and musical offerings, and a succession of Paige's business associates extolled her virtues and mourned her untimely and unnatural death. There were more men than women, all dressed in Wall Street blues and grays. Most of the older women dabbed at their eyes with handkerchiefs.

I didn't know who, besides her boss and two coworkers, had known of Paige's involvement in the criminal case. No one mentioned it in his or her remarks. I scanned the room for the man who had told Paige that he was Harry Strait, but saw no one resembling him here.

The last hymn was "Now the Day Is Over." Everyone rose to sing and remained standing as the organist played the recessional. By the time the crowd was filing out, most of them were talking about how the market had performed today and whether the Federal Reserve was likely to raise the interest rate in response to recent signs of economic recovery. Several of them were planning to gather to carry on their reminiscences of Paige over a few martinis at the nearest watering hole.

I stepped away from the group and sat in one of the last pews for a few minutes of quiet reflection. I had not seen Mercer enter the rectory, and I assumed it had been impossible for him to park in this crowded warren of narrow streets.

I closed my eyes and thought about the Paige Vallis I had known, about the parts of her life that she had let me enter, about the terrible distress she had been in during the days and hours before her death. I didn't have to be reminded that life isn't fair. That was something I encountered every day I went to work.

Shortly before nine o'clock, the janitor came into the room with a large broom. He asked if I would mind leaving, and I told him I was sorry to have stayed so long. I said another prayer for Paige, and picked the umbrella up from the seat next to me.

There was no sign of Mercer Wallace. I ducked under the stairwell of the old building for shelter from the rain, scanning the street in both directions to look for his car. I took out my cell phone and turned it on.

"*You have one unheard voice mail,*" the recording said. "*Message one. Eight-twelve P.M.* 'Hey, Alex. I'm stuck in the Thirty-fourth Street tunnel. Bad accident. I'll get there as fast as I can.'"

A tall figure in a hooded parka, umbrella over his head, ducked in beside me. He smelled of alcohol and was mumbling to himself. I didn't wait to get a look at him, but stepped forward again onto the quiet sidewalk.

The man followed me, and I glanced around in hopes of spotting a uniformed police officer. Traffic was still moderately heavy, cars going both to the northbound entrance of the FDR Drive and west to the Brooklyn–Battery Tunnel. I jogged across State Street to stand on the open median that divided the roadway, trying in vain to hail a cab.

The man loped after me. I could hear my own breathing now, as I tried to assure myself he was just a bum, hoping to get close enough to snatch my bag. I saw a break in the traffic and bolted back to the sidewalk, heading over to Broad Street.

I looked over my shoulder and saw the man still coming behind me. The umbrella blocked any view of his face, and the visor of the black rain jacket was pulled low over his forehead. Where were all the yuppies who worked late in the skyscrapers of these canyons below Wall Street? The driving rain seemed to have kept everyone indoors.

I turned the corner and saw the faded lettering on the old wooden sign outside Fraunces Tavern, with its historic plaque noting the spot where General Washington bade farewell to his troops. I pulled at the door handle with all my strength for eight or ten seconds, until I noticed the small block lettering on the window: CLOSED ON MONDAY.

The cell phone was still clasped in my hand. These streets behind the main thoroughfares were too small and winding to use as a sensible retreat. I dialed 911 and moved through the shadows around the corner onto Coenties Slip. Behind me I heard the crashing sound of a metal garbage bin rolling on the ground. I glanced back and stepped out of the way as it rolled toward me. My pursuer was not in sight, but three enormous rats were scrambling over the remains in the barrel as its lid flew off.

The operator asked what the emergency was. "There's a man after me," I said, breathless from the combination of fear and running.

"You'll have to speak more slowly, ma'am. I can't understand you."

"It's a man—"

"Did you say asthma, ma'am? I know you're breathin' hard. Is this a medical emergency?"

I could see the figure again, as I approached the intersection of Water and Broad streets. "No, it isn't. I want a police car."

"You say you're in a police car? I don't understand your problem, ma'am."

I dashed across the street again, splashing in a large puddle that had pooled at the edge of the curb. I had listened to thousands of these 911 tape recordings. Some of the operators had lost their jobs as a result of their responses—telling a rape victim whose lungs had been collapsed by stab wounds in her chest that she damn well better speak up loud enough to be heard and stop that stupid gasping—along with wonderfully compassionate responses that had saved lives with their ingenuity. This communication problem was clearly my own fault.

I stopped and tried to speak more clearly into the phone. "I'm being followed by a man. I need the police."

"What has the man done to you, ma'am?"

Nothing, I thought to myself. Absolutely nothing.

"Ma'am?" she asked once more.

I looked again and watched as he dodged between cars whose windshield wipers were throwing off pints of water. I still couldn't see his face, so I focused on his lower body. His pants looked like the navy blue of a police officer's issue, and his shoes were the shiny black brogans that went with that kind of uniform.

"I—I think he's trying to attack me."

"Where you at?"

"The intersection of State Street and Whitehall."

"Stay on the line with me, okay? I'm gonna get you someone."

I ran again, crossing the last section of highway and climbing over the barrier that separated it from the pavement near the entrance to the Staten Island ferry terminal, dropping the umbrella as I slid off the divider to the ground. My long-legged pursuer vaulted the concrete block, his umbrella blown inside out by the biting wind that kicked up off the harbor.

The boat whistle blasted and caught my attention, buoy bells clanging in the water beyond it and gulls screeching overhead. I had not been on the ferry in more than twenty years. I didn't know the part of the island at which it docked nor whether its fifty-cent fare had doubled or tripled.

In the distance, at the mouth of the drab-looking double-ended boat, I could see clusters of drenched commuters gathering past the turnstile, trying to get inside the dry cabin for the ride home. I started to run in that direction.

Something crashed down on my right shoulder and I dropped onto one knee. Lightning flashes streaked through my eyes and I extended my left hand to push back up to a standing position. The man in the black rain gear lifted the closed umbrella over his head and brought it down toward my back again. I rolled as I saw it coming, swirling in a puddle of cold water.

I was screaming now, hoping to get the attention of someone on his or her way to the departing ferry. The honking car horns, the foghorns, the far-off sirens of what I hoped was an approaching police cruiser all masked my cries.

The heavy black shoe swung at me as I got to my feet and started to run directly for the boat. The arms of the giant iron turnstiles stood in front of me. There was not enough room to pass beneath one, so I turned around and hoisted myself atop the stanchion to swivel around and get to the other side. Again he came at me, and this time, before dropping down, I bent my right leg and kicked hard, landing a blow with my foot against his chest. He yelled out and fell back a step or two.

Now people stopped. I must have looked deranged. My hair was hanging in wet clumps and my clothes were mud-soaked from that last roll on the ground. I had jumped the turnstile and I had kicked a stranger in his gut for no apparent reason.

I ran past the onlookers. Another man in a brown uniform with a Department of Transportation logo on his jacket reached out a hand to slow me down and collect the fare. I screamed at him to get out of my way, shoved him against a column with both hands, and jumped onto the ferry as the boarding ramp was being pulled out of place. A police car stopped thirty feet away, at the point I had crossed the road in my run to make the boat.

Another DOT guard clamped his hand on my shoulder and I grimaced in pain.

"Take it easy, lady. Calm yourself down," he said to me. "The kicking and shoving is over. You're under arrest."

24

I was probably the happiest prisoner in history.

"I've got the money to pay the fare," I told the officer, knowing it was a story he had probably heard every day that he was on duty.

"It's a free ride, lady. That's not the problem."

"No, no. I mean I realize that I jumped the—"

"Guess you haven't been on board since ninety-seven. The token's been eliminated. You're not in trouble for beating the fare."

I didn't even mind that there was no reason for me to be in cuffs, in the safe hands of PO Guido Cappetti.

"Assault on a peace officer," he said to me. "I saw you shove that guy right out of the way."

"I'm not going to argue with you," I said. "That's exactly what I did. But it's only because I was being chased by a man who attacked me."

"I didn't see nobody doing nothin' to you."

"I kicked the guy after he smacked me with an umbrella. He'd been chasing me up and down White-hall."

Cappetti got on his radio and called ahead for a patrol car. "Possible 730."

"You're gonna psycho me?"

He was surprised I recognized the designation. "You been before?"

"No. Actually, I'm a prosecutor. Manhattan DA's office."

"Here we go, sweetheart. And I'm the commissioner."

"Do I get a phone call?"

"Back at the house."

"I was waiting for a New York City detective when I was attacked. I can give you my cell phone. If you call him, he can come meet me. Verify what I'm saying."

Cappetti listened to me for a few minutes, took the phone from my pocket, and dialed the number I gave him. "You Mercer Wallace?" he paused, then asked a few more questions, establishing to his satisfaction the fact that Mercer was, in fact, on the job, a real New York City cop. "I'm with Alexandra Cooper. She tells me she's an assistant DA." Another pause. "Really?" And then, "Is that right?"

Mercer told Cappetti to keep me with him when the boat landed at the St. George Terminal on Staten Island. For the next fifteen minutes, I sat side by side with Cappetti, who had liberated me from my restraints, leaving me to stare back at the sweeping vista of the great New York Harbor gleaming through the mist. The burning torch in the outstretched arm of Lady Liberty, the wide mouth of the Hudson River, the office towers of Lower Manhattan, and the spidery, weblike cables of the Brooklyn Bridge occupied my imagination while I kneaded my shoulder and tried to figure out who my assailant had been.

Together, Cappetti and I waited almost an hour until Mercer made his way out through Bay Ridge and across the Verrazano Bridge.

Mercer found us in the terminal police station, wrapping me in an embrace.

"Let go before you get yourself covered in this filth," I warned him.

"Your prisoner free to leave, Cappetti?"

"Yeah."

"Did I hurt the ferry guy when I shoved him? I'd like to apologize to him."

"Nah," Cappetti answered. "We get loonies all the time. Maybe you had a good reason tonight."

"Why don't you go inside the rest room and wash up?" Mercer said.

It was stupid of me to be nervous about it, but I had handled too many assaults that had occurred in public bathrooms. He picked up on my hesitation.

"C'mon. I'll check it out and stand at the door."

I went into the grim ladies' room, with its faded yellow tiles, exposed lightbulbs, and paperless towel holders. I avoided the mirror, stooping to wash my face and hands, letting them drip dry. I knew Mercer needed five minutes alone with Cappetti, to see whether there was anyone to corroborate my strange encounter.

It was almost eleven o'clock when we got in the car to drive back over the Verrazano, one of the longest suspension bridges in the world. The fog was now so

thick that the skyline had been lost from sight altogether, and the immense tower at the far end of the
span was barely visible.

"Buy you a drink?" Mercer asked.

I nodded my head.

"Mike's sitting at the bar at Lumi's," Mercer said,
referring to one of my favorite restaurants, just a
block from home. Warm and quiet, with a superb
kitchen, the restaurant owner would have a fire burning in the small hearth right inside the front door.

"You've told him already?"

"You know how he hates surprises, Alex. Might as
well get his thoughts on it, too."

While we drove to Manhattan's Upper East Side, I
told Mercer exactly what had happened. We parked
at the fire hydrant in front of the restaurant.

Lumi was entertaining Mike when we came in.
"Holy shit," Mike said, getting off the stool, holding
up two fingers in the sign of the cross, as though
warding off a vampire. "You're really rushing the season on Halloween, aren't you, kid?"

Lumi kissed me on both cheeks and took me into
her office, handing me a pullover sweater of hers, a
hairbrush, and a tube of lipstick, closing the door so
that I could repair some of the water damage.

"You're still shivering, Alex," she said when I returned to the bar. "Are you hungry, too?"

I warmed my hands in front of the fire. "It's gotten
so raw out there. No thanks. Maybe when I defrost."

"I'll nibble on some osso buco," Mike said. "And
an artichoke dip to start. Mercer?"

"Vickee fed me at home. It's all yours."

Lumi went into the kitchen to place the order while we talked.

"So what did he look like?"

"I can't say."

"Didn't you see him?"

"His face? Never."

"Well, was he white or black or—"

"I don't know."

"Don't give me that color-blind crap," Mike said. "I hate when my victims do that."

Mercer laughed. "She never saw his face."

"How about his hands?"

"Gloves."

"I gave you a damn umbrella. Why the hell didn't you hit him first?"

"Because I thought that he was just a drunken bum who had gotten too close to me by accident. Or that he was going to ask me for money."

"You should have taken the point of it, shoved it in his butt, pressed the button to open it, and sent him flying like Mary Poppins. What a waste of a weapon."

"Tell him about the pants and shoes," Mercer said, prompting me.

"That's when I realized he wasn't a bum. Navy wool gabardine, nicely center pleated uniform pants. And department-issue shoes."

"You're talking cop?"

"Or fireman. Or any uniform force in the city, except the Brownies."

"You do anything lately to piss anybody off? You're like our poster girl, Coop."

"I feel more like a poster girl for the Salvation

Army. The only thing I can think of is that I just gave the go-ahead to lock up a sergeant in Correction. Impregnated a female prisoner over at Bayview."

"Give us his name and we'll get on it."

"The victim says at least five of the guards are involved. They take turns looking out for each other, divvying up the new inmates, charging for protection."

Mercer had another thought. "Mrs. Gatts got any relatives on the job?"

I shrugged my shoulders and shook my head. "I don't know anything about her."

"Well, let's do a little digging."

"You got a lot of balls in the air, Coop, and some of them are loaded with dynamite."

"I'll tell you what," I said. "If the Tripping plea actually goes down on Wednesday, I'm going up to the Vineyard to sit out the storm. Roaring fire, lobster dinner—"

"Jake?" Mike asked.

"Or no Jake. You're all invited."

"You'd fly in this weather?" Mike asked, revealing one of his few phobias.

"If the pilots go, I go with them. When they know enough to stop, I'm grounded. I've got to close up the house. My caretaker's going off-island, to his brother's wedding, and I can make sure the house is all tight. Think about it, guys. We could start off the fall season with a country weekend together." It would relax me to be there even in foul weather.

"Talk among yourselves," Mike said, digging into the veal.

"First," said Mercer, "we've got to figure whether this little encounter of yours is related to Paige Vallis—"

"Or Queenie," Mike said.

"Or one of my endless stream of attractive miscreants. It's a big fan club."

"Did you notice whether the guy was in the church during Paige's service?"

"No. I didn't see him until I came out onto the street. Actually, all I can say is that I didn't see anyone dressed like him."

Mike was picking at the marrow in the bone shank with a tiny fork. "Maybe he followed you downtown from the courthouse."

"She would have noticed."

"Coop? She wouldn't have had a clue if some mope was walking behind her on a rainy night while she's got her head stuck under a big fat golf umbrella. If he followed her from Centre Street, it explains the uniform pants, and why someone would have known where to wait for her," Mike said.

I chewed on a breadstick and sipped my scotch. Lumi had brought out a small bowl of risotto and I was making a dent in it, giving in to my emerging hunger pangs. "You know what I'm going to do tomorrow? I'm going to get Battaglia to sign off on a FOIA request to the CIA."

"Don't you love it when she thinks, Mercer?" Mike stopped eating and sniffed the air. "Hot little brain waves firing on all cylinders beneath those peroxide streaks while I just sit here enjoying a good meal. What are you talking about?"

"Freedom of Information Act request. There's got to be some connection among all these players that has to do with the CIA and the Middle East. We ask for the files of Victor Vallis and Harry Strait. Who knows? They might even have one on McQueen Ransome."

It made such a difference to have some kind of paper history of an individual, some written record of what he or she did to create a picture for us and retrace old paths.

"Don't think J. Edgar didn't keep Queenie's file at home. He probably had a hankering to try on some of her snazzy costumes—satin gowns, harem pants, over-the-elbow gloves," Mike said.

"And King Farouk," I said to Mercer. "You know the government must have kept some kind of dossier on him. There's got to be a way to find a nexis between these two murders."

"What other themes have come up more than once?" Mercer asked.

"Pornography. Queenie had it, Farouk collected it. And antique weapons," I said. "Farouk collected them. So does Andrew Tripping. And rare coins. Both Spike Logan and Graham Hoyt mentioned them."

"What were all those coins that we saw on the floor of Queenie's closet?" Mike asked.

"Just miscellaneous change, I think. I didn't look closely."

"Are they still there?" Mercer asked.

"After Mike and I found the inscribed first-edition Hemingway, we asked them to seal everything so the place could be inventoried."

"Yeah, well, that didn't stop Spike Logan from climbing inside."

"Tell you what," Mercer said. "Mike'll make sure you don't get re-arrested for anything before you get snug in your apartment tonight. I'll pick you up at seven, and we'll make another sweep up at Queenie's to see about those coins and anything else we might have overlooked."

We said good night to Mercer and finished our drinks. Mike's car was parked down the block, closer to my building, so we walked home and into my lobby. There was no point objecting to his plan to make sure I got safely inside and that there were no weird or threatening messages waiting for me on my machine.

I flipped on the lights and we walked in. It was obvious I had come home to an empty nest. "Nightcap?" I asked.

"Nah. You got an early wake-up call and I got somebody keeping the bed warm back at my place. You got any unhappy campers on the line?"

I checked the phone next to the bed and returned to the living room. There had not been a single caller. I dropped onto the sofa and stretched out, hoping Mike would stay and talk to me. Something about the dynamic of our relationship was changing, and I wanted to recapture the friendship that had always been so natural.

"Let me hear you turn that dead bolt when I walk out, Coop," Mike said, kissing the top of my head and walking to the door.

I got up and followed him, locking the door and putting the safety chain across. I took a long bath, then massaged my shoulder with Tiger Balm before climbing into bed, too exhausted to read or even relive the evening's chase.

The next morning Mercer and I rode up to Mc-Queen Ransome's apartment and let ourselves in. It looked pretty much as it had when I was last there. The closet door was still ajar, wire hangers still displayed a few cotton housedresses, and dozens of silver coins were spread out over the floor.

Mercer and I put on rubber gloves. He had a pack of plastic evidence envelopes that he stacked next to us, and we both kneeled to gather the coins.

"Anything unusual about these?" I asked.

"So far, they all look American," he said, examining them front and back before bagging them. "Different denominations, but nothing too unusual, it seems to me."

"I don't know about your pile, but everything I've got is old," I said. "There's nothing here minted after 1930."

"I see what you mean. There's about ten of them here from 1907."

"We'd better take them to an expert, who can give us an idea of their value."

Mercer scooped up a handful and reached back to the floor to retrieve a small white piece of paper that looked like some kind of ticket stub. He examined it before speaking. "I know he had an appointment here with McQueen Ransome, but I hardly think that would have required him to crawl around on her closet floor—especially if it was after he'd found out she'd been killed."

"What are you talking about?" I asked.

Mercer held out the piece of paper to me. "Spike Logan said he drove here from Martha's Vineyard, didn't he? Well, he must have dropped his ferry ticket stub when he was in here yesterday. Guess he wasn't too despondent to be searching for something that belonged to Queenie."

25

"Get me Monica Cortellesi on the line," I said to Laura, as I unlocked the door to my office. I had explained to Mercer that she was in charge of our frauds bureau and would know who the best experts were for evaluating any unusual artifacts.

"Who's your contact in the Oak Bluffs Police Department?" he asked.

"What's the point in tipping off Spike Logan that we realize he wasn't entirely candid with us? As long as we know where he is, let's hold the calls until we decide what to do with the information we get."

"Alex," Laura said. "That's Cortellesi on your backup line."

"Monica? Quick question. Who do I want to talk to about rare coins?"

"I can give you the head of the American Numismatic Association. It's in Colorado Springs. They do a lot of—"

"Too far to go. Today. Closer to home."

"How's Fifty-seventh Street?" she asked.

"Perfect."

"Stark's. Probably the preeminent firm in the nation for private dealers."

"Reliable?"

"Like Fort Knox. Family business, started by two brothers in the 1930s. There probably isn't much they can't help you with."

"Thanks, Monica," I said, handing Mercer a piece of paper with the name on it. "Want to call and get us an appointment while I work on those FOIA requests for the CIA?"

Laura came in with a handful of messages. "Call Christine Kiernan. She's been up all night on a new case. The others can wait."

"Would you see if you can book me on a flight to the Vineyard tomorrow?" I asked.

"Don't you have to be in front of Judge Moffett in the morning?"

"Yes. A mercifully short appearance, I hope. Something late in the day. If I can wrap up the Tripping case early, I may take a long weekend."

I sat at the computer working on the requests for the old CIA files while I talked with Christine, the phone propped between my shoulder and ear. "What'd you get?"

"Rape—robbery in Hell's Kitchen. Can I come up?"

"Sure. You got a victim?"

"Nope. She's still at the hospital. Took a bad beating when she resisted the guy."

By the time I had completed the boilerplate applications for the information I wanted and sent Laura to get Battaglia's signature for the cover sheet supporting the urgency of my request, Christine had appeared with her file.

"I got the call at three A.M.," she said, handing me copies of the detective's scratch sheet.

"This all the paperwork you have?"

"Yeah. The cops haven't had time to type up the police reports yet."

"What's the story?" I asked.

"My complainant is in her twenties. She's a medical student at NYU. Just moved into a renovated brownstone in the west Forties. Dicey block."

Every time a run-down section of Manhattan was gentrified, there was a period of increased violence before the neighborhood reinvented itself. Thirty years earlier, when TriBeCa was transformed from an area of commercial buildings and warehouses to residential lofts, the first tenants were exposed to muggings and assaults on a regular basis. There were no streetlights, no local merchants with familiar faces, no grocery stores to duck into when being followed, and many marginal transients who squatted in abandoned spaces. A similar fate befell the residents of Alphabet Town—Avenues A through D—when they reclaimed their streets from the drug dealers and prostitutes who had made the neighborhood so unsavory for so long.

"Coming home from the hospital?"

"You got it. Twenty-four-hour shift, she was exhausted and completely oblivious to her surroundings. She had the hood of her anorak pulled up over her head because it was raining so hard."

"Tell me about it."

"Never heard the guy coming. Got her as she was going into the vestibule of her building."

"A push-in?"

"Yeah. He held something against the small of her back, sharp and pointed. She thinks it was a box cutter. Told her to get under the stairwell and keep her mouth shut or he'd slit her throat."

"I hope she obeyed," I said quietly. I had seen too many autopsies of victims who had unsuccessfully tried to resist an armed attacker.

"She did exactly what he told her to do. Took off her clothes and laid down on the floor. He was about to penetrate when a hypodermic needle fell out of his jacket pocket. She freaked and started to scream."

"AIDS?"

"That was her first thought. She was sobbing to me at the hospital, asking me what the point of surviving the attack was if the rapist transmitted a terminal illness."

"So he beat her to shut her up."

"Broke several bones in the orbital socket of the right eye. Knocked out a tooth."

"And raped her anyway?" I asked.

Christine nodded her head.

"Have they offered her the prophylactic to prevent HIV transmission?" There were powerful drugs that physicians believed would block the virus, but they were only effective if taken within twenty-four hours of the assault.

"Yes. She's probably going to start them this morning."

"What did he take?"

"Her briefcase."

"Was she wearing scrubs when he attacked her?"

"Yeah, he figured out she was a doc. Kept asking if she had drugs in her bag, or any blank prescriptions."

"Did she?"

"No. Just books. A ton of medical texts, a wallet, a cell phone."

I looked up at Christine. "You do a trap-and-trace yet?"

"I haven't done anything. I just got down here from Roosevelt Hospital and knew I had to give you the details."

"Ever done one?"

"Nope," she said, with obvious hesitation in her voice. "What is it?"

"It's a triangulated cell phone call. It works like GPS—global positioning satellites. If the perp is using the stolen phone to make calls, the cell company can tell us exactly where he's standing when he's on the line. Just one catch. You've got to get it done before the battery charge runs down and he tosses the phone away."

Most thieves who took victims' cell phones, even as an afterthought, used them until the batteries ran out, for sport if not necessity. Before the recent successes of the GPS technology, we could often connect them to the crime weeks or months after it was committed by tracking calls on the stolen phone to long-lost relatives and friends. This gave us the chance to find the assailant before he attacked again.

"You need to call TARU," I said, referring to the NYPD's high-tech-equipment unit. If there was any way to eavesdrop surreptitiously or use electronic surveillance of any kind, these teams were the leaders in the field. "Get started with a court order and they'll have tracking devices up and running within the hour."

I could smell Battaglia coming. The cigar smoke wafted into my room before the district attorney turned the corner. I sent Christine on her way and offered him a chair.

"Let me guess," I said. "Judge Moffett called. Wants you to convince me to let Tripping take the misdemeanor plea without any further complaining—or research."

"Can you tell me this weekend's Yankees–Red Sox scores, too?"

"Hardly clairvoyant, Paul."

"Put this whole thing to bed, Alex. You got bigger fish to fry. While I have your ear, got a piece of advice for a friend of mine?"

"Sure."

"What do you do with an employee—single mother, law degree, supervises young attorneys—goes on an office business trip paid for by the government and gets herself featured in a glossy woman's magazine headlining an article called 'Romance on the Tracks'?"

"Meaning what?"

"Gives them an actual photo of herself to run with the article. Describes meeting a guy on a train ride from Albany, having a few drinks with him, and then going back to his apartment for a one-night stand."

"If she admitted it was job-related? I'd can her.

That's a stupid and dangerous message to send to the public in my line of work, not to mention to your own troops. But then, not everyone's a sex crimes prosecutor."

"Well, the woman I'm talking about is. DA's office in another borough. Can you imagine what a role model she must be?"

"Don't tell me—"

Battaglia chomped on the cigar and stood up. "Yeah, your friend Olivia. Do me a favor, Alex; if you decide to go public with your sex life, no illustrations, please. Check the October issue of that sex-and-the-single-girl's magazine. The DA's wife saw it in the dentist's office."

"Sorry to interrupt, Mr. Battaglia. Alex, Will Nedim says it's pretty important."

"Hold on a minute, Paul. This might be of interest. The Nedim kid is handling the female defendant who was caught with McQueen Ransome's mink coat. We've been trying to flip her."

I picked up Nedim's call. "Will? I've got the boss here with me. Any developments?"

"We may have a change of heart on Tiffany Gatts."

"Way to go. Helena Lisi call you?" I said, referring to Tiffany's lawyer.

"Nope. Tiffany herself just called. Left a message that she wants to talk to me after all."

"You have a plan?"

"I thought I'd have her produced in my office to-morrow."

"With the lawyer, of course."

"Certainly. I thought you might want to be there."

"No way," I said. "You'll never get anything out of her in my presence. I'm like a lightning rod for Tiffany Gatts. If she's getting along with you, let's leave it at that."

I cut Nedim short, realizing that I was holding up Battaglia. "Nothing to report yet, Paul. This girl could give us a big break on Kevin Bessemer, if we're lucky."

He waved his cigar in the air as he left, a sign that I was to carry on with whatever I had been doing before he came in the room. I sorted out the usual problems of the day and ordered in lunch for Mercer and me.

"Bernard Stark will see us at four o'clock," he reported to me. "He's the patriarch of the firm. Happy to help. Mike's going to meet us in their offices on West Fifty-seventh Street. That's the good news."

I smiled at him. "What's the bad?"

"The phone company in Massachusetts confirms that a call came in to Spike Logan's house on the Vineyard the afternoon before he drove into the city."

"You think he wasn't as surprised about Queenie's death as he told us he was?"

"The records show the caller's address—the deceased's next-door neighbor. I've checked with the squad. The guy had already been interviewed by the time he called Logan, no doubt to give him the sad news. No way that jerk didn't know she was dead."

We were eating our sandwiches at my desk at two-thirty when Laura came in with a sheaf of papers she had pulled out of the fax machine. "I got a call from an administrative assistant at the CIA," she said. "There will be a hard copy of these in the mail, with all the formal signatures and seals, but that's going to take another month. The agent said he was told to comply with Mr. Battaglia's requests as soon as possible."

"Must be nice to have a name so big you can throw your weight around gracefully and get answers the same day," Mercer said. "Maybe these papers will resolve some questions about our odd group of players."

I thumbed through the photocopied documents, knowing that the pile wasn't thick enough to contain anything of value. The answers for the file requests of Victor Vallis, Harry Strait, and McQueen Ransome had exactly the same explanation as the one for the late King Farouk.

> As the agency's coordinator of information and privacy, I must advise you that the CIA can neither confirm nor deny the existence or non-existence of any CIA records responsive to your request. The fact of the existence or non-existence of records containing such information would be classified for reasons of national security under Section 1.3 (a)(5)—Foreign Relations—of Executive Order 12368.

Mercer listened to me read him the response before speaking aloud what both of us were thinking. "The King of Egypt was sent into exile almost half a century ago, and he's been dead more than thirty years. What the hell does he have to do with our national security now?"

26

I was as captivated by the sparkling gold and silver coins in the window outside the entrance to the Stark brothers' offices as Holly Golightly had been while staring at the diamonds on show at Tiffany. Each was displayed against a deep blue velvet cushion, a setting that was more like a museum's than a retail operation's.

Mike was the last to arrive, and we announced ourselves to the receptionist in the waiting area. He took a quick inventory of the cases of coins. "Some piggy bank these boys have, huh?"

"You do anything useful today?" Mercer asked.

"Just a tidbit here and there. Spent a bit of time trying to figure out who might have smacked Miss Cooper here upside the shoulder last night."

"You check with the First Precinct to see if they've had other cases?" I asked.

Mike turned to Mercer. "I guess I'm just fortunate she doesn't stop by the apartment in the morning to make sure I put underwear on."

"And they haven't had anything like it?"

"There are a few hot spots downtown. But that area between the entrance to the ferry terminal and the promenade where all the buses stop is kept pretty well patrolled. Too many Wall Street high rollers to complain about bums and hustlers."

"You check on that Correction Department crew she's investigating?"

"We're getting information on all of them in the perp's team. What their work schedules are, and even though you can't make a facial ID, I want photos along with descriptions of their height and weight. Got one other piece of info."

"What's that?" Mercer asked.

"Throw in court officers. Guys in the area with blue uniform pants. Somebody who could have waited for Coop to leave the building, follow her to the church, and be waiting for a chance when she came outside."

"I've got no enemies in that department, I'd be willing to swear," I said, laughing. "My unit's probably responsible for more hours of overtime than any group of prosecutors in the office. And Laura bakes cookies for them every time I'm on trial."

"Well, your friend Etta Gatts? She's got a brother-in-law who's a court officer. Little Tiffany's favorite uncle, the brother of her late father."

"Criminal court?" I asked, racking my brain to think of an officer named Gatts.

"Uh-uh. Supreme Court, civil term. Sixty Centre Street."

"But I never—"

"She told you her people weren't through with you yet. Remember that moment?"

"Yeah, but Tiffany just called Will Nedim today. He thinks she's ready to roll over and give up Kevin Bessemer."

"Well, maybe her mama doesn't know that yet. Think of it, you had to walk directly past the front steps of his courthouse when you walked downtown last night."

"How could he know who I was?"

"Don't be naive, Coop. He could have been in the building with Etta Gatts the first day she came down here, after Tiffany was arrested. He's got the right uniform, the right ID—makes sense she would have called him to ask for help. Anybody could have pointed you out to him then. Might even have been the guy who slashed your tires that first night."

Mercer chimed in. "Motive, opportunity—"

"Pretty soon, the only joint it'll be safe for me to go is P. J. Bernstein's." My corner deli, fifty feet from the entrance to my building, was the best place for peace, quiet, and chicken noodle soup when I didn't want to stir far from home.

"Worst that can happen there is the latkes give you a little agita," Mike said.

"Mr. Stark will see you now," the receptionist said, pressing a button on her desk to open the first locked door leading to the offices. Once the three of us entered the small space, she buzzed again. The metal grating, like the kind in safe deposit vaults, swung open to admit us further, security cameras monitoring our progress.

Bernard Stark stood behind his desk, in front of a window that gave a sweeping view of Central Park crowned by a ceiling of rain clouds. He was in his late sixties, I thought, and seemed quite robust. He had thinning gray hair, a deep tan, a very warm smile, and was dressed in a nicely tailored suit.

"I've actually done a lot of work with the federal government, Mr. Wallace—the National Mint, the Federal Reserve Bank, the Treasury Department. It's not that often I'm called in to help you people. What can I do for you today?"

Mercer began the conversation. "We're struggling with an investigation. We thought maybe you could give us a little guidance, before we take a wrong turn and get too far off the scent."

"We're quite willing to pay for your time, your expertise, Mr. Stark," I added.

"Let me get an idea of what you need. Perhaps I can just point you in the right direction." He winked at me. "I don't charge for that."

"I'm afraid there isn't that much to tell right now," Mercer said. "We're trying to solve a murder case. It appears that someone—or maybe several people— thought the deceased had some property of significant worth."

"Was this person a collector?" Stark asked. "Is that why you've come to me?"

"No, she wasn't a collector. We found a few things of some value in her home, but they were gifts given to her many years ago."

"I see. Was she from a prominent family? Perhaps someone who was a client of my firm, or an obituary I read about in the newspaper."

Not unless you subscribe to the *Amsterdam News,*

I thought to myself. "No, her murder didn't even merit a mention."

Mercer reached into his pocket and took out one of his plastic evidence bags, which he had labeled with information about where and when he had retrieved its contents. He handed the package to Bernard Stark.

"May I empty this onto my desk to look them over?"

"Certainly."

Stark turned the bag upside down and gently slid the twenty coins onto his exquisitely tooled leather blotter. He spread them out with his forefinger, moving them around like checkers on a board, ordering them by size and color.

"What do you see?" Mike asked.

The dealer was slow to speak. "Most of these have some age on them. That's obvious from their dates."

"But their value," the impatient detective asked, "are they worth anything?"

"These over here," he said, pointing to a series of small coins that all appeared to be the same. "They're just proofs. Never actually put into circulation. Three-cent nickels are what they're called."

"Can you give me an idea of what they'd bring in at an auction?" Mike asked.

"This group, dated 1871, you might get a hundred dollars for each of them. Those from a decade later, maybe two hundred."

Not exactly a king's ransom, but then we'd each had cases in which people had been murdered for pocket change, or for parking in the wrong space on the street.

Mercer removed another bag of coins from his pocket.

"Ah," Stark said, taking a jeweler's loop out of his drawer and holding it up to his eye.

"I see you've got some foreign pieces, too. Romania, Sweden, Greece—none terribly valuable, but certainly interesting. You say these belonged to an amateur, not a collector?"

I didn't need to tell him they were the property of a thief who had pilfered from a world-class collector. Bernard Stark was already intrigued.

"My impression is that the deceased . . . well," I stalled momentarily, "she sort of inherited some of these from an old friend. Something like that, but we're not entirely sure yet."

"Someone had a good eye here, Ms. Cooper. Transylvania, 1764."

The three of us leaned in to look at the piece he was holding up to us.

"A two-ducat piece. Last time I saw something like this," he said, "it went for almost a thousand dollars."

Most of the local bodegas in Queenie's neighborhood didn't deal in two-ducat Transylvanian coins. She probably hadn't been able to tip her errand boys with it.

"No offense, Mr. Stark, but can you tell just by eyeballing these things that they're real?" Mike asked.

"You're not going to cut in on my business, are you, Detective?" the older man said, laughing. "That's why people come to me with their gold and silver. That's what I *do,* Mr. Chapman, the way you solve crime. And if my eye isn't good enough, there are, of course, ways to prove the contents of the coins."

We watched him handle each piece, turning it over and examining both sides.

"See this little fellow?" Stark asked. He seemed delighted to be poring over the dregs of Queenie's purloined collection. "Quite unusual. Don't come across these very often."

"What is it?" Mike asked.

"An 1844 dime. But Liberty's seated in this one. It's got its nice natural silver surface with what we like to call champagne toning. Come, come, Mr. Wallace—any more bags?"

Mercer handed over the third plastic envelope. This one had several more proofs of little value, and then Stark's broad smile reappeared as he lifted a large silver medallion and studied its pale green patina. "Very choice, this. Very, very choice. Look at the date on this beauty."

He held out the coin in his hand for each of us to study. The Latin inscription on the top border translated as "American Liberty." "July Fourth, 1776," I said.

Mike kept looking for the bottom line. "It doesn't have any number on it. What kind of coin is it?"

"It's a medal, actually, not a coin. On the rear you see the infant Hercules—that's the symbol for the American colonies—defending himself against the cowardly British leopard. Can you read the Latin on the back?"

"Sorry, no."

"'Not without divine aid is the infant bold.' From the Roman poet Horace," Stark said. "One of these silver medals was given to every member of the Continental Congress after the battles of Saratoga and Yorktown."

Now Mike was thoroughly engaged. Warfare did it for him every time. "You've seen these before?"

"Very few exist, Mr. Chapman. It was quite a magnificent strike, but small in quantity."

"What would you expect to get for it on the street?"

"Wrong question, Detective. It's got no street value at all—that's my point. It wasn't issued as a coin. But it's got major value in the auction market. The last of these fetched many thousands of dollars."

Stark's secretary entered the room with a large tray. It was decoupaged, covered with coins of every size and color. On it she carried a coffeepot and an assortment of sodas.

We each helped ourselves to something to drink.

Stark held his cup and saucer, standing at the window now as rain slapped against it. "I don't mind giving you a hand with whatever you're doing, but I hope you plan to let me in on your little secret."

"Secret?" Mike asked.

"My family has been in this business for almost a century, and we know where most of the rarest coins in the world have been bought and sold over the years. The minute you walk out my door," Stark said, "I can check our records for *Libertas Americana* and probably figure out where this very piece has been hiding for the past half century."

I wasn't planning to test him, but Queenie had been holding on to it for longer than that.

"I can be much more useful to you if I know what I'm dealing with," Stark went on, turning his back to stare out at the view, and giving us the opportunity to signal each other in agreement. I nodded at Mike—Queenie's homicide was his case.

"We don't know what we should be looking for, Mr. Stark. We don't know what the bad guys were looking for, either, and we have no idea whether they've found it. The woman who died," he said, after some deliberation, "was an eighty-two-year-old invalid who lived alone in an apartment in Harlem."

"With these coins? Unsecured, in her home?"

"Strewn about the floor of her closet and over-looked by whoever burglarized her place—and that person may, or may not, have been her killer."

Mike paused before going on. "Nobody would have known it to see her now, but back when she was a kid, my victim had an affair with one of the richest men in the world. He was the collector—he was the one she got these babies from," he said, playing the coins back and forth on the green blotter.

Stark was ready for the chase. He sat down at his desk and swiveled his chair to face his computer screen. "I'm sure I can check him in our database. There hasn't been an American in this game—auctions or private acquisitions—since the Starks have been in business that didn't get some of his coins from us."

"That's part of the problem," Mike said. "This guy wasn't here in the States. He wasn't American."

Mike looked to Mercer one more time, and got the

nod to tell the dealer. "In fact, he was the King of Egypt."

Bernard Stark pushed back from the keyboard and looked Mike Chapman in the eye. "This woman kept part of Farouk's collection in her bedroom closet? I'm not the least bit surprised that she's dead."

27

Bernard Stark pushed the pile of coins away and stood again, walking to close the door of his office. "No good has befallen anyone who's come into contact with Farouk's treasures. It's quite surprising the government never knocked on your victim's door, demanding a full accounting."

Mike was ready to take Stark into his confidence. "Let's say Queenie didn't come by these ducats in the most honorable way. Let's say she thought the old boy owed her a few quid, and she grabbed some fists full of gold and silver."

"That makes more sense. The feds wouldn't have known where to look, and a lot of this would have come back onto the market with your victim having no clue of the value of the things she had stolen," Stark said, thinking aloud.

"You think the feds have time to be interested in rusted old medals and coins that are only worth a few thousand dollars?" Mike asked.

"When you're talking about King Farouk, I'd say you'd have everyone from the Secret Service to the CIA on the hunt."

Stark had just ignited the spark that had been smoldering in our pockets. Whatever made him bring the CIA into this conversation?

Mercer took the lead, calm and easy, in his usual style. "I guess I'm just missing something, Mr. Stark. We're aware that the king collected royal jewels from monarchies all over the world, and that he had Fabergé eggs worth a good fortune. Ms. Ransome would have had to have carted off trunkloads of—of nickels and dimes, so to speak—to make it worth her while. We know that didn't happen."

"You'll have to talk to someone in the rare jewel business to find out how many Fabergé designs existed and what they're worth on the open market. When it comes to this kind of thing, I can assure myself that she need only have taken the right coin, Detective. Just one single piece that Farouk owned, and I'd say I know a lot of people who would have killed for it."

"Maybe she did take it," I said. "Maybe if you can describe—"

"Queenie—is that what you call her? Queenie didn't get the particular coin I'm talking about," Stark said, smiling at me again. "That one actually wound its tortuous way back into our very own hands. I just mean that with objects as rare as the things Farouk bought for himself, one of them alone might be worth a fortune."

"Well, go back to the piece you referred to—the one you wound up with. Maybe there was another just like it."

"Ah, Ms. Cooper. That is the stuff that dreams are made of—sort of like a dirty old black falcon that a private eye set out to find. This coin—*our* coin—was an eagle, and I know for a fact there was only one in the entire world."

"You mentioned the CIA and Secret Service, though," Mike said. "You want to explain what this is all about?"

"I think you should know the story, Detective. Perhaps it will suggest some comparable avenue of investigation. Have any of you ever heard of a Double Eagle?"

Stark walked to a glass display case that stood at the far end of the room. He took a small key out of his breast pocket and unlocked it, taking from the top shelf a black leather box with a hinged clasp.

He sat down and opened the box, staring at the large coin inside before passing it across to us. "Mind you, this is just a proof—a copy of the actual gold piece. But it might be the most magnificent coin ever struck."

I lifted the shining disk from its nest and rubbed my finger over its raised image.

"She's quite gorgeous," I said.

Stark took off a strip of paper that was affixed to the inner lid of the box. "This is a passage from the auction catalog when we sold the piece. It describes her better than I can."

He paraphrased the copy. "Lady Liberty, striding

forward in a loose gown, against the wind. Her left hand holds an olive branch while her right is extended with a lighted torch. There's a small representation of the Capitol Building on the bottom, with forty-eight stars circling the edge of the disc, and the rays of the sun emanating from beneath the feet of Liberty. The year of issue was 1933."

Mike took her from me and flipped her over. On the back were a finely etched profile of an eagle in flight, and the designation of the amount of the piece in United States value: twenty dollars.

"You sold one of these at auction?" Mike asked.

"Correction, Mr. Chapman. Don't get your hopes up. We sold the *only* one of these that existed at auction. July 2002. It was the one Farouk owned."

"You mean only one of these was ever made, that's how come you're so sure?"

"Many were made, in fact, but the government never issued them. They were all destroyed."

"I gotta ask you, sir, what this one went for. What price did you get for it?"

Stark was only too pleased to answer Mike's question. "It was in all the newspapers, Mr. Chapman. I've got nothing to hide." Stark reached over and reclaimed his proof, holding it up between his thumb and middle finger.

"The Double Eagle sold for more money than any other coin in history," Stark said proudly, puffing up as he gave the answer. "More than seven million dollars."

I looked at Mercer's three plastic bags of supposedly rare coins, which together would only fetch a few thousand. It was impossible to conceive that a single piece of gold with a face value of twenty dollars could eventually sell for seven million dollars.

Mike was incredulous, too. "So, just humor me, Mr. Stark. Suppose there was a second one. Just like that one you're holding, all solid and real. Suppose we found it mixed in with these others and brought it back to you. What'd you give me for it?"

"Nothing, Mr. Chapman. Not a dime."

Mike laughed. "At least I'd get twenty bucks' worth."

"No, that isn't true. Your hypothetical piece wouldn't even be worth the twenty dollars engraved on its back side. The coin was literally illegal the very day it was made."

Mike mimicked the position of Stark's fingers, which were still holding the coin. He had a goose egg instead of a gold proof. "Zilch. Zero. Bupkes."

"I suppose if you melted it down you'd get the price of the gold weight, but that's about it."

"How come?"

"Very simple, Detective. After the Mint creates the coins—all coins—they have to be 'monetized.' That's the process the Treasury Department has to go through with every kind of currency, or else—like the Double Eagle—it never becomes legitimate money. It's the process of monetizing the coins that makes them legal tender." Stark sighed. "This particular value is all in the history of this piece, the uniqueness of it."

"You wanna tell me about that?"

"Certainly. If I entertain you enough, perhaps I can

charm Ms. Cooper out of some of these other little treasures," Stark said, referring to Queenie's stash. "I'd like to see everything you found in the lady's closet."

He started after the Gold Rush of the 1840s, which placed the young American nation among the wealthiest in the world. "The United States Mint needed a new denomination for the growing economy, something more than the original one-dollar gold piece. The highest value of currency that had been available until then was the ten-dollar coin. So a bill was introduced in Congress to create a twenty-dollar piece, cast with nearly a full ounce of gold."

Stark went back to his glass étagère and brought several coins back to us. "Plenty of these twenty-dollar gold pieces to go around," he said. "They were minted almost every year between 1850 and 1933."

I looked at the older version that he handed to me. "This one isn't nearly as elegant as yours, is it?"

"You can thank Teddy Roosevelt for the improvement. While he was president, he had a chance encounter with the man most people considered America's greatest sculptor."

"Who was that?" Mercer asked.

"Saint-Gaudens. Augustus Saint-Gaudens. Roosevelt complained to him that the U.S. coins lacked artistic qualities. Old Teddy wanted something to rival the ancient Greeks, with brilliant design and high relief. He had found the man capable of designing it. This new golden Double Eagle became the symbol of American wealth and power, a very desirable object from the first moment it went into circulation."

"There's only one bird on this thing," Mike said. "Why call it a Double Eagle?"

"Because it was twice the amount of the old ten-dollar piece, which had been nicknamed the Eagle."

"What ended the Eagle's flight?" I asked.

"Another Roosevelt, Ms. Cooper. Teddy's cousin, Franklin. By the time he was inaugurated in 1933, the country was in the depths of the Great Depression. You could buy a daily paper for two cents and a pack of cigarettes for a quarter. The only thing that held its value during this crisis was gold itself."

"So there was a run on the banks, and people began to hoard gold coins," Mercer said.

"And two days after he was sworn in, President Roosevelt closed all the banks, embargoed the export of the very precious metal, and took America off the gold standard. After March of 1933, never again was the United States Mint to issue gold coinage."

"So Farouk's piece was made before FDR's proclamation?"

"Ah, the heart of the matter, Mr. Chapman. The Treasury Department prohibited the Mint from monetizing, or legitimatizing, any gold coins from that point on. But it neglected to forbid the actual *production* of the coins themselves."

"Farouk's Double Eagle was struck *after* we went off the gold standard?" I asked.

Stark nodded his head. "The Mint was just a factory, after all. The engraving for the coin had already been completed, the bullion was prepared, and within a month after the embargo, one hundred thousand 1933 Double Eagles had been cast. The Treasury realized the gaffe and immediately told the Mint not to license this particular coin."

"So the Double Eagles existed . . ."

"Yes, Mr. Chapman," said Stark. "But they had only the value of a small gold medallion. They were never legitimized."

Mike sat back in his chair. "That's an awful lot of gilded birds in the nest. How could anybody account for them all?"

"There are wonderfully arcane regulations that have been in existence since this country's birth," he answered. "Romans had their Trial of the Pyx, so our forefathers set up an assay commission. Samples of the strike were submitted in locked boxes to be weighed and tested—a laborious series of examinations—and while this was being done with just a few hundred coins, all the others were kept in storage at the Mint."

"What became of the one hundred thousand?"

"In 1937, the order finally came from the Treasury—right from the president—to melt down the entire strike. As far as the government knew, not a single coin was left."

"So when did the Eagle fly out of the cage?" Mike asked.

"I'm afraid that's the first time our company came into this mix," Stark said. "Nineteen forty-four. My father had been in business about ten years, doing quite well, when a great private collection came on the market which he bought for auction. The owner was a Colonel James Flanagan."

Stark took another sip of coffee. "Papa put an advertisement in all the papers, announcing the sale. And for the final lot, the biggest prize, the ad read, 'The Excessively Rare 1933 Double Eagle.' He was quite thrilled about his coup."

"I guess that let the cat out of the bag," Mike said.

"Needless to say, that wording caught the attention of a few giants in the numismatic field who were interested in bidding, one of whom took it upon himself to call the Mint and quite simply ask what made it so rare. How many coins had the government actually legalized and released was what he wanted to know."

"The answer was none?"

"Exactly. From there on, the feds moved in pretty quickly. The Mint brought in the Secret Service—"

I interrupted Stark and looked at Mike and Mercer. "I know the Secret Service is the law enforcement branch of the Treasury, but I can't for the life of me remember why. I just think of them as the presidential protection force."

Mike helped me with the history. "The Secret Service was created in 1865 especially to investigate and prevent the counterfeiting of U.S. currency, and enforce all laws related to coins and securities of the government. That's all that they were about at first. They didn't get into the protection business until President McKinley was assassinated."

Stark continued. "So there was my father in 1944, sitting at his desk during the second day of the actual auction. In burst a couple of agents who announce to him that the Flanagan coin had been stolen from the Mint, that it had absolutely no value, and that they were going to seize it from him before it went on the block."

Mike wanted the facts. "So whom had Flanagan bought the illegal Double Eagle from?"

"Precisely what the Secret Service wanted to know," he said, seeming a bit chagrined. "They also questioned my father about where he got the information in the catalog entry that said at least ten of the pieces had gotten into private hands."

"Did he have the answers?"

"Most certainly. He and my uncle were extremely cooperative," Stark said, starting to smile again. "After all, they had paid the enormous sum of sixteen hundred dollars for the coin. They had all the bills of sale, and took the agents directly to the jeweler, who was holding it in his safe."

"So the feds got that one back for sure," Mike said.

"I can promise you that, Detective. It was one of the first lessons I learned from my father. And then this lead agent spent the next few months tracking down the other Double Eagles my father told them about. He was like a bloodhound—Philadelphia, Baltimore, Memphis, London."

"How many were stolen from the Mint and avoided destruction?" I asked.

"Ten. That's what they figured when they went back to examine the assay samples I mentioned to you, which was the only group of coins that hadn't been melted when the orders first came down."

"And how many of them did the feds track down in 1944?"

"Nine. They got nine of them back. All except the one that went to King Farouk."

"Did they ever figure out who committed the theft from the Mint?"

"Seems to be nothing those investigators didn't figure out. There was a crook at the Mint—a man called George McCairn—who was in charge of the Weight Transfer Department the year the Double Eagles disappeared. After 1937, between the time of their theft and the date of the auction, McCairn was arrested for stealing some other valuable pieces from the Mint."

"So he was locked up?" Mike asked.

"For taking these later items. Never charged for the Eagles, because he never admitted being the thief. But the feds thought the method was the same. When the coins came in for assay—and mind you, he had sole control of the keys to the samples—he simply took ten of them out of the bag and replaced them with coins of the same weight and size, but no value."

"The old bait and switch," Mike said.

"Exactly. No one ever looked in the bags," Stark said. "Once it was realized the Double Eagles were not going to be declared legitimate legal tender— never monetized—they were just left to sit out their fate until the moment of meltdown. McCairn had exclusive access to the samples, and had helped himself to ten of the beautiful birds."

"How did they arrive at ten as the exact number?" Mercer asked.

Stark paused. "By the weight of what was recorded in the assay process. That's the best they could figure."

"That Secret Service agent worked damn fast," Mike said, making notes of the people and dates that Bernard Stark had mentioned. "What did you say his name was?"

"The man who tracked down the Double Eagles? It was Strait. Harry Strait."

28

"Did I say something wrong?" Stark asked, scanning our faces.

The three of us must have reacted to Strait's name with the same degree of surprise.

Mike made his notes and picked up the conversation. "No, no. Now this Double Eagle that made its way to Egypt, what can you tell us about how it got there?"

Stark pursed his lips. "Not very much. I think you'll have to get that story from the Secret Service."

He reached for his Rolodex and wrote down the name of the supervisor he'd dealt with when he auctioned the great coin for seven million dollars. "Harry Strait is dead," he said, "but I think you'll find this fellow most helpful."

"But the one you sold in 2002 was legal?"

"Oh, yes. We weren't about to walk into that mess again. I can't account for the half century that the coin was in Egypt, but a well-known British dealer brought it back into the States in 1996. What do you call those, um, shall we say 'rats'?"

"Confidential informants?"

"Yes. One of them tipped off the Secret Service, who did some wiretaps and all that, and intercepted the poor bird on his way home. Lawsuits and depositions and lots of haggling, but finally the government admitted a great mistake had been made."

"Worse than McCairn's theft?"

"A good deal so. When Farouk bought his Double Eagle, FDR's Treasury secretary—I can't recall his name—"

"Morgenthau," I said. "Henry Morgenthau."

"Yes, of course. Morgenthau actually issued an export license to the royal legation of Egypt, making that one lonely coin legitimate."

"Why?"

"No one is quite sure. To avoid government embarrassment, probably. He knew it was going out of the country to a king we were trying to keep as an ally, and there wouldn't be much harm in letting the twenty dollars that had been promised to Farouk before the error was caught go to the royal collection."

"So when the Double Eagle was finally sold, you and your firm got the seven million big ones, Mr. Stark?" Mike asked.

"In a very agreeable split with Uncle Sam, Detective. Perfectly reasonable."

"Play with me for a minute, sir. What if I were to turn up another stolen coin? Say everybody guessed wrong back in the forties, say McCairn reached in the bag and pulled out a dozen Eagles instead of ten," Mike said. "Tomorrow I walk in your door with one more plastic evidence bag, Liberty holding her torch aloft, 1933 and all that?"

"Without the certificate that monetizes her—and Morgenthau very likely didn't sign two of them—it's just one more lovely piece of gold. Carry it in your pocket for good luck or melt it down and turn it into a ring for your sweetheart."

"So it's the piece of paper that makes the coin worth its weight in gold?"

"Now you've got it."

"But how did this Englishman get the coin—the one you sold—from Farouk?" Mercer wanted to know.

"The depositions are all sealed. Perhaps you can convince the agents to tell you. And then, Ms. Cooper," Stark said, standing to usher us out of his office, "maybe when you bring me some of Ms. Ransome's coins to inventory, you all can let me in on the full story that you get from the feds. I've been curious for years myself."

We thanked him for his help and waited for the assorted security devices to let us make our way back to the reception area and downstairs to the lobby.

My cell phone was vibrating. As we stepped out of the elevator, I took it out of my pocket. "You call the Secret Service and make an appointment for noon tomorrow," I said to Mike. "Let me get this."

"Alex?"

"Yes."

"Christine Kiernan. Your trap-and-trace with the cell phone came through with the goods."

"You got the rapist?" I turned to Mercer and gave him a thumbs-up. "Where?"

"Just like you said, he was standing on the corner of One Hundred and Second and Madison, talking to his grandmother down in the Dominican Republic."

"Reach out and touch someone. Works every time. Fit the 'scrip?"

"As much as she could give, including a surgical scar on his groin area. Had the doc's cell phone and two of her ID cards."

"Track marks?"

"Yeah, he's a junkie. Stone-cold."

"Priors?"

"Depends which name you run him under." She laughed. "Once the fingerprints tell us what his real name is, we'll know more. But he's been through the system before. He's greeting everyone in the station house like he's a regular."

"Want me to come up and help with a statement?"

"He's not talking. Ponied up for a lawyer right away. Found the phone on the street, found the doc's ID in a garbage pail. That's all he gave us and now he's not saying a word. I'll do a court order to get a saliva swab for his DNA, and I'll draft a complaint. I don't think I'll need to bother you till tomorrow."

"Good job, Christine."

"Thanks. See you in the morning."

I snapped the lid of the phone closed.

"Where do you get a drink around here?" Mike asked.

I looked at my watch and saw that it was six-thirty. "Let's try Michael's, over on Fifty-fifth Street. We can sit quietly and figure out where we are in this maze."

"Has the rain let up?" he said, opening the door to look outside. "Where's your car?"

Mercer pointed up the street to where we had parked. Mike's was closer by, so we crossed Fifty-seventh Street in the light drizzle and squared the block on Fifth Avenue to get to West Fifty-fifth Street.

We had almost made it through dinner when Mercer's beeper went off. He left the table to return the call.

"You still going to the country tomorrow?" Mike asked.

"Absolutely. Any chance you and Val can join me? I'd love the company."

He ran his finger around the rim of the glass, which he'd almost emptied of his first vodka. "Val's having a bad time of it, Alex."

Mike had met Valerie Jacobsen after she had undergone a mastectomy. She had completed an intensive course of chemotherapy, but the doctors warned her that it was such a virulent strain of cancer that she had to be watched for every minor health change.

"Want to tell me?"

"Maybe it's nothing. I just know how it frightens her, even when she doesn't want to worry me about it. Mostly she's run-down, exhausted, listless. They're working up a whole slew of tests this week. Maybe you could give her a call, cheer her up."

"I'm mortified that you have to ask me to do it. I haven't spoken to her in a couple of weeks, between my vacation and the trial. Of course I'll call her. Don't you think a few days on the Vineyard would—"

"She can't do it right now, Alex."

"Look at me, Mike," I said, lifting his chin to make his eyes meet mine. "Trust me, will you? You've got to talk to me about these things. I can't read your mind."

Mercer stood behind me, resting his hand on my sore shoulder. "Finish your cocktails, folks. Have to make a stop at the ER."

I assumed that meant a sexual assault victim had been admitted and Mercer was tagged for the interview. "A rape?"

"Nope. Our friend Andrew Tripping is being treated for multiple stab wounds."

"Is he—?"

"He's going to live. Out of danger, just a few holes in his back."

"Bellevue?"

"Nope. New York Hospital."

York Avenue and Sixty-eighth Street. My neighborhood, not Tripping's.

We each threw some bills on the table to cover the drinks and dinner. The rain had stopped but the wet pavement still glistened against the headlights of the oncoming traffic as we weaved our way north and east to the hospital entrance.

The triage nurse was surprised to see us, particularly once we displayed our identification shields to her. She tipped her head in the direction of a small cubicle that was separated from her station by a green curtain. "He's been sedated. Let me check. I'm not sure it's a good idea to try to talk to him now."

She walked away and I whispered to Mercer, "I'm not sure it's a good idea for us to talk to him at all.

He's represented by counsel and he's supposed to show up in Moffett's part tomorrow morning to take a plea."

"I can ask him about the stabbing, can't I? This time, he's in as a victim."

"Check with the nurse. Wouldn't you think he's already been interviewed? I assume he came in here by ambulance after a 911 call."

I walked out to the waiting area while Mike and Mercer entered the cubicle. They were with the patient almost fifteen minutes before they came back to me.

Mike was shaking his head. "I don't know what to make of him. He's a nutcase to begin with, isn't he?"

"Diagnosed paranoid schizophrenic."

"So people are always after him, right?"

"Most of the time."

"In case you didn't have enough to worry about, Mr. Tripping was on his way to try to find where you live, Coop."

"But, why?"

"Guess he just couldn't wait until tomorrow morning. I didn't throw him any questions about your case, I just asked what happened this evening."

"What'd he say?"

"He's a little incoherent. I don't know if that's him or the drugs. Mumbling all kinds of conspiracy theories. The lawyers are out to get him, there are terrorists after him, the CIA wants him dead, and he's never gonna see his kid again. Now which of those make sense?" Mike asked.

"Don't I wish I knew. Why me?" I said. "That's the only thing I'm concentrating on at the moment."

"He's telling us he wants you to put him in jail. That's why he's looking for you."

"Happy to help," I said. "But all he needs to do is show up in court to get that done. I don't like this one bit. And who's following him while he's looking for me? Who does he say attacked him?"

Mercer waved his hand in a circle. "Wasn't sure, couldn't see, can't describe—"

"Well, that's ridiculous. He claims he used to be a CIA agent, for chrissakes."

"You didn't do any better last night with your attacker," Mike said.

I flapped around for an answer but had none. "What does the doctor say? How serious is it?"

"Not very," said Mercer. "In fact, the resident's got the chart all marked up for psych observation. He won't rule out that the stab wounds may be self-inflicted."

"Why?"

"There are a lot of small jabs in the upper back. Nothing life-threatening, nothing terribly lethal, and all are high enough that you could reach them yourself with a knife."

"Great. This is a surefire way for him to buy a little more time before he bites the bullet and takes the guilty plea. There must be a reason he wants to stay out of jail."

"That's not what he's saying tonight, Alex. He's telling us that jail is the only place he thinks his life is safe."

29

"How did it get to be ten-thirty?" I asked Mike and Mercer, as they followed me into my apartment after we left the hospital. "Somebody fix me a drink while I check my messages."

They went to the kitchen while I went to the bedroom to put on jeans and check the answering machine. There were a few personal calls, Jake among them, and a rather cool voice mail from Peter Robelon.

"It's Peter, Alex. Just had a call from the emergency department at New York Hospital. Andrew Tripping was assaulted tonight. They're going to treat and release him, but I don't think he's going to be in any shape for court tomorrow. I'm going to ask for an adjournment," he said, explaining the reasons why. "And Alex, keep your cops away from Andrew. This has nothing to do with your case, okay?"

By the time I got to the den, the guys had poured the drinks, made themselves comfortable, and turned on the Yankees game—which was only in the fifth inning because of an initial rain delay. I had lost my partners to the pennant race, so I stretched out on the sofa and enjoyed my scotch.

When I put the two of them out the door at midnight, Mercer arranged to pick me up and take me to the office, and to be there for the plea proceedings.

We walked into Judge Moffett's courtroom together at nine-thirty sharp. The lawyers for the child welfare agency and the foundling hospital had beaten us to the part, but everyone else was late. I didn't appreciate all my adversary's conversations with Moffett that had been conducted out of my presence, so I decided not to tell the judge about the stabbing incident ex parte.

Fifteen minutes later, the court officer held open the door and Peter Robelon walked in, pushing Andrew Tripping in a wheelchair. Graham Hoyt was a step or two behind, carrying Robelon's trial folders.

I rolled my eyes at Mercer and waited for the clerk to call the case into the calendar.

"What have we here, Mr. Robelon? A little accident?"

"I wish that were the case, Your Honor. Unfortunately, it's a lot more serious than that. My client was attacked last night—a vicious street crime—repeatedly stabbed in the back in a senseless act of violence."

"You know about this, Alexandra?" the judge asked.

"I don't think it's quite as serious as it looks, Your Honor."

"Now Ms. Cooper's a doctor, too," Robelon said. "Mr. Tripping was released from the hospital at two o'clock this morning. He's in great pain, and he's got a schedule of follow-up medical care that has to be kept. He—he can't even get out of this chair."

"That's ridiculous, Judge. He's got some superficial wounds in his upper back. I know all about this. If you'd just order him out of the chair, he's perfectly able to stand up and go forward with the plea that counsel and I have discussed."

Moffett pointed his gavel at me and shook it. "The last time I tried that, young lady, at the direction of one of your buddies, I was censured by the appellate court."

I had struck the wrong chord. Years ago, in an incident that had made tabloid headlines, cops had been pulling the leg of one of my rookie colleagues. The perp being arraigned was a notorious career criminal, who had frequently been a malingerer and faked diseases to avoid judicial proceedings. The night he was brought up on charges of homicide, the arresting officer insisted to the assistant district attorney that despite his protestations, the killer could get out of his wheelchair and stand before the court.

The prosecutor passed the message along to the judge, neither of them knowing that the victim's brother had just broken the defendant's kneecaps with a golf club. Moffett barked at the guy to stand up, five or six times, threatening to hold him in contempt if he refused. When the man tried to stand, he collapsed on the floor of the courtroom, and the Legal Aid Society brought a complaint against Moffett that almost caused him to be denied reappointment.

"Your Honor, there has actually been some

progress to report, if you'll give us some breathing space here. I've had a conversation with Ms. Cooper. My client has authorized me to accept an offer of a misdemeanor plea. We had every intention of going ahead with that this morning, but in light of Mr. Tripping's physical condition—his injuries—"

"Judge, this is ridiculous. Yes, we had plea discussions. And this—this sudden bunch of scratches on the defendant's back are nothing more than an insurance policy for the strategy planned by Mr. Robelon. Although he told me he thought there could be a disposition of the case, he wanted additional time out of jail for his client. When I told him I would not go along with that condition, this sham is apparently the solution they devised to buy some time out of Rikers."

"What does he need time for, Alexandra? He pleads guilty, so he gets a week or two to tie up loose ends. What's the big deal?"

"I have no idea why he wants it. Maybe he doesn't intend to surrender himself. Maybe he has plans to abscond. Maybe—"

Robelon was livid. "Stop with the fantasies, Ms. Cooper. Where do you come off throwing out these absurd ideas to prejudice the court against this defendant?"

"Look at him, Alexandra," Moffett said, pointing at Tripping. He had slumped down in his wheelchair and both arms were hanging over the sides. "He can't even hold himself together. They give you any medication, Mr. Tripping?"

Tripping looked dazed. He was nonresponsive.

Moffett tried again. "You, Mr. Tripping. You with me?"

"I'm sorry, Judge. I'm in terrible pain—"

Robelon interrupted. "I really don't want my client speaking on the record, Judge. Yes, he's been given MorphiDex. It's a morphine derivative, Judge. Obviously," he said, sneering at me, "someone believes he's in pain."

"Here's what we're gonna do. You lose, Ms. Cooper. I can't take a plea from somebody who's doped up on narcotics."

"You do it every day of the week, Judge. Just different narcotics."

"The boy, Dallas—"

"Dulles," I said.

"Dallas, Dulles, whatever—he's out of harm's way?"

"Doing very well," Robelon said. Hoyt, Taggart, and Irizzary all nodded up and down, like a row of bobble-head dolls.

"Let's put this over till the beginning of October. I try and allocute him today, and he'll come back wanting to withdraw the plea. It'll be a complete waste of time."

I didn't have a prayer in this skirmish, but there was one more fact for the court to know. "Your Honor, are you aware that this incident—this charade—happened less than two blocks away from my home?"

"You really are over the top, Alex," Robelon said quietly before standing up again to address the court. "Judge Moffett, this attack happened a block away from the Frick Museum, it happened a block away from the Ukrainian embassy, it happened a block away from the Nineteenth Precinct. Fortunately, none of the occupants of those buildings has any reason to be paranoid either. We don't have martial law in this city, do we? Mr. Tripping was enjoying an evening on the Upper East Side."

"He told the police, Your Honor, that he was coming to find *me*. I think you know I'm not an alarmist about these things, but it is quite disturbing to think the defendant believed he had any legitimate reason to be talking to me."

"Is that true, sir? You couldn't wait for this morning to see Ms. Cooper?"

Robelon leaned over and grabbed Tripping's arm, telling him not to answer. He straightened back up. "My client says that's absolutely ridiculous. That's a lie."

"October second, nine-thirty sharp. We'll take the plea and you can prepare to be sentenced the same day. Bring your toothpaste and pajamas, Mr. Tripping. No excuses next time." Moffett looked from the defendant to me. "You want an order of protection, Ms. Cooper?"

Little good that piece of paper would do if Tripping became unglued. "An admonition will do, sir. Make it clear if the defendant has anything to say to me, he can do it in the courtroom or through counsel."

"One last issue, if I may," Robelon said. "I had talked to Ms. Cooper about getting her agreement for a single visit between Mr. Tripping and his son. All the doctors believe it would be the healthiest way for them to separate, going forward."

"Fine," I said, giving up the fight. "As long as it's supervised and on the condition that it comes to an abrupt end if the defendant does anything at all to upset the child."

"Then the last order of business," Moffett said, "is for me to dismiss the charges of rape in the first degree against your client, isn't that right, Mr. Robelon."

"That's correct, Judge."

I left the courtroom amid the self-congratulatory backslapping of the defense team.

"Where'd Mercer go?" I asked Laura.

"He said to tell you that a Detective Squeeks—did I get that name right?—that Squeeks needed to see him down at the First Precinct on the Vallis murder. Just routine. Wanted to interview him about your original case. Said he'd meet you at Twenty-six Federal Plaza for your noon appointment."

The detectives on the Vallis case were certainly working hard to keep me out of the mix.

I took care of a pile of correspondence that had stacked up on my desk, returned a bunch of nonurgent phone calls, and gathered up some of the Tripping memos from my file cabinet so that I could write a closing report while I was in the country. I encouraged my assistants to cover their tails with paperwork. There were always bizarre defendants—like Andrew Tripping—who were bound to revisit the system at some future point in time, and it was smart to leave documentation of why an earlier case had been dismissed.

As I assembled a case folder to take with me, I came across Dulles's Yankees jacket in the rear of my file drawer. Returning it to me had been a last act of kindness by Paige Vallis that I had hoped to use to warm my introduction to the boy. I stuffed it in a folder to return to Robelon or Hoyt, now that I would not need to interview him.

"I'm probably going to go right from this meeting to the airport, Laura. I'll be on the Vineyard for the next couple of days, if anyone's looking for me. I'm hoping to clear my head. Sarah's in charge," I said, locking up behind me.

The Jacob Javits Federal Offices were just a few blocks south of our building, in the middle of Foley Square. A modern high-rise mix of granite and glass, it was home to a host of government agencies, and I had made frequent visits there for conferences, most of them with the FBI on cases involving joint investigations.

Security had always been tight at Federal Plaza. I readied my photo ID and headed for the queue that allowed government employees access. I was reclaiming my folder and cell phone from the metal detector when I looked up and saw a familiar face across the lobby. I was sure it was the man Paige Vallis had known as Harry Strait.

I grabbed my things and hurried across the tiled floors, slick from the water-soaked shoes that had traipsed through the corridors all morning. Dozens of people crisscrossed my path, coming into the building for work or appointments, leaving the area to go to lunch or run errands.

I didn't want to break into a run as long as I had Strait in my sights. I knew there were enough armed men around to pull me aside and see what my problem was if I looked hysterical or unstrung.

He seemed to be alone, heading for an exit on Duane Street, a narrow one-way road that cut across Broadway and ended in Foley Square, at the foot of the federal courthouse. He went out the door and stood at the top of the steps, looking about before trotting down to the sidewalk.

Strait's brief pause allowed me to get within twenty feet of him. My eyes swept the crowd for a sign of any other friendly face to help me try to corner and identify the guy. I was running a bit late for the meeting, and I hoped that Mike or Mercer would also be late.

I flashed my badge at a uniformed guard standing near the door. "You work here?"

"Yes, ma'am, I do."

"I've got to catch up with my old boss," I said, handing him my folder. "Could you hold on to this for me?"

He didn't know how to respond, but looked at the logo stamped on the label with the words: OFFICE OF THE DISTRICT ATTORNEY—HOMICIDE.

He took it from me and called after me, "I get relieved at two o'clock."

I turned and gave him a thumbs-up and continued on out the door. Strait was walking west now and I started after him. When I closed within five feet, I yelled out his name.

"Harry?"

There was no response to my tentative call.

"Harry Strait," I said, in a louder voice.

Without breaking his stride, the man turned his

head and looked directly at me. He said nothing but veered left into the street, past the African burial ground, and quickened his pace. Cars were stopped at the traffic light and I cut between them, keeping him in my sights.

Now he began to run, and I ran behind him, watching as the distance grew between us. He pushed people on the sidewalk out of his way, but was gone before they could express their annoyance at him. It was I at whom they hurled insults when I passed them. "Where the hell do you think you're going in such a hurry?" "Why don't you slow it down, lady?"

When he reached Broadway, he had the light in his favor and crossed with it. I couldn't make it in time, cars honking at me madly as I ventured too far into the roadway, waiting for traffic to let up. Then I got snarled in the line waiting outside McDonald's. I was sure I could see the top of Strait's head making for Church Street.

Another sharp turn and I followed him around the corner from Duane Street into the alleyway of Thimble Place. I was completely winded now, going too slowly to catch him. I had been a long-distance speed swimmer in high school, but had never sprinted well enough to make this effort worthwhile.

I caught my breath after I made the turn from Thimble onto Thomas Street. A black sedan pulled out of a parking space and stopped at an angle. I took a deep breath and rushed toward the car, as Strait—or whoever he really was—pulled at the door handle with his left hand. I heard him yell, "Unlock it, dammit!" at the driver.

I rushed toward him and he turned to face me, pointing a gun at me with his right hand. "Back up and get the hell out of here," he screamed.

He got into the passenger seat and the car sped off toward Broadway. I could have sworn Peter Robelon was driving.

30

"Of course he has a gun," Mike said. "He's an agent."

He, Mercer, and I were in the reception area of the Secret Service offices. "How the hell do you know he's an agent?" I asked. "We don't have a clue who he is. He pulled a gun on me a couple of hours ago and you're defending him already?"

"Yo, blondie. You saw him right here in this building, at high noon, where security's tighter than the inseam on your slacks. I assume he's legit. Maybe old Harry had a son. Maybe he's a junior—Little Mister Agent Strait the Second. He must have had some way to get in and out of this building without causing a stink. I truly doubt he pulled a gun on you. He must have had it drawn for a good reason."

"And I'm telling you that I was that very reason."

"Fine. So we made a report. You got a partial plate, and there'll be a make on the car by the end of the day. You're chasing the guy down the street like a banshee. Maybe he thought he had to defend himself."

"How do we figure out who he is? There must be photo IDs of everyone who works here in Federal Plaza."

"You weren't even able to describe him with any detail when the agents came to your office the other day. What are you gonna do now? Sit here and look at thousands of pictures of buzz-cut pasty-faced white men and hope for a match?"

"Yeah, I could do that. I didn't have any trouble picking him out of the crowd today."

It was going on two o'clock. My delay had taken us into the lunch hour, and the agent who had agreed to meet us had stepped away to keep another appointment.

A trim woman, younger than I, came through reception and directly over to the three of us. "Alvino. Lori Alvino. Sorry about your problem today. You ever get your man?" she asked, greeting me with a handshake.

"She never does, for very long. Don't you start worrying about that, too. I'm Mike Chapman. This is Mercer Wallace, and that's Alex Cooper."

She guided us into her suite, a good bit larger than most of the agent cubicles I had visited over the years, suggesting the importance of her position.

"You must have some juice, Lori," Mike said. "Big digs, glass partition, nice view of the Brooklyn Bridge."

"I show them the money," she said, grinning back at him. "That's why the feds love me. I'm the agent in charge of recovering all assets related to the National Mint, here and abroad. My boss says you need everything I can give you on the coin collection of King Farouk, is that right?"

"Yes, ma'am."

Alvino established what we knew of the story from Bernard Stark and picked it up from there. "The U.S. government worked with Farouk's people on a regular basis back then. We're talking 1944 and thereabouts, during World War Two. He had already become the king then—just twenty-four years old and richer than Croesus."

"Had he started collecting coins by that time?"

"Absolutely. He had dealers all over the States. They tripped over themselves whenever they had something unusual to unload, trying to get it under the royal nose. The more expensive, the better."

"How did they get the coins to Egypt? Did you just ship things as valuable and as small as that?"

"No way. Farouk used his royal legation to make purchases, which were sent to him regularly by diplomatic pouch. Just about every week. And his staff knew all the rules, believe me."

"What rules?"

"After FDR's Gold Reserve Act became law, it was illegal to export gold, unless the Treasury specifically issued you a license."

"Even a single piece of gold?" I asked. "A single coin?"

"You bet," Lori Alvino answered. "To get that license, you had to be able to establish that the coin being sent abroad had special, collector's value *before* 1933, before we went off the gold standard."

"How'd they prove that?"

"The keepers of the Castle, that was their territory."

"What castle?" I asked.

"Sorry. The old Smithsonian Institution—our guys always referred to it as the Castle. Experts at the Smithsonian decided on the uniqueness of whatever coin was in question."

"This happened often?" I asked.

"Pretty infrequently, actually," Alvino answered. "There weren't a lot of people during the war who were terribly concerned about their coin collections while the world was turned upside down. The entire European market was virtually shut down. It left the field wide-open for Farouk."

Mercer leaned in to speak. "This stuff doesn't quite qualify as ancient history, but it's a bit remote from what you're handling today. How come you know so much about all this? You had a refresher course recently?"

Alvino blushed. "I had a chance to look over the files a couple of weeks back. I had to pull all this paperwork together for someone else who came in for a briefing," she said, gesturing to the several folders full of documents related to the Farouk collection.

Chapman gave her his best trust-me-and-you-won't-know-I'm-working-you-over grin. "Anyone I know, Lori?"

She returned the smile and shrugged. "Can't help you there. My boss gave me orders to arrange all this for a presentation he had to make to some government officials. But I wasn't invited to the actual meeting, so I don't know who was involved."

Now he ran his fingers through his thick mane of black hair, moving on to his most serious mode. Mike was about to try to bluff her out of some information. "I've got a homicide to solve. The lieutenant told me those guys were a real threat," he said, flashing Mercer a glance. "Now I'm wasting precious time trying to catch up with what they already know."

Lori caught his sense of urgency. She wanted to be helpful. "Are—are we talking about the same people, do you think?"

"They were here to talk to your boss about Farouk, right?"

"Uh-huh."

"Let's make sure we're on the same wavelength. Which coins from his collection were you focusing on?" Mike asked, flipping through his notepad as though looking for specific names to match against things she said.

"I gave them a bunch of information—some silver pieces from the Civil War period, some gold ingots from San Francisco, circa 1849. The only kudos I got from my boss was for the research I came up with on the Double Eagle."

Mike slapped the pad against his knee. "Damn if I don't owe you for this one, Lori. I think we've already got all we need about his Civil War items. It's the other two we're after as well. Ever solve a murder before?"

"No, no, I haven't." She was grave as a stone now.

"Most satisfying thing you can ever be involved in. Give us what you got on the ingots and the big bird. I've always wanted a partner like you."

"Sure," Lori Alvino said. She spent the next ten minutes explaining the provenance and descriptions of some of the objects Farouk had purchased that had come out of the Gold Rush. Although handsome and somewhat unusual, they were far too plentiful—and probably too large—to have been part of McQueen Ransome's stash.

"Did you ever hear of Max Mehl?" Alvino asked.

The three of us shook our heads.

"He was a dealer. From Texas, I think. He's the one who first made contact with King Farouk about this fabulous twenty-dollar gold piece that he wanted to sell."

We listened carefully as she started to tell the story. "Mehl knew about the king's appetite for the rare and beautiful," she went on. "He not only convinced Farouk of the uniqueness of the coin, but also guaranteed that he could get it out of the country because of its special designation."

"How did he manage that?" I asked.

"Somehow, Mehl made a call to Treasury the very same day that Farouk expressed interest in the coin. The director of the Mint herself carried the Double Eagle to the Castle."

"Was that typical?" Mercer asked.

"Are you kidding? There was nothing routine about this bird's flight."

The more she talked about it, the more convinced I was that we were going in the right direction.

"The same day," Alvino said, "the curator examined the piece, declared it of special value dating back to before the presidential order of a decade earlier. To tell you the truth, he was under such pressure that my boss thinks he didn't even know what he was signing."

"But he agreed to request the licensing that made the coin valid?" I asked.

"Through ignorance, probably. No sign of a bribe, but that hasn't stopped some folks from believing there was one. Either way, he asked for the license—or the monetization—that turned the twenty-dollar piece into a small fortune."

"From the secretary of the treasury himself?"

"Exactly. Then the king's representatives took possession of the coin, packed it securely in the diplomatic pouch, and delivered it personally to Cairo, to Farouk's pleasure palace."

"What was the timing on all this?"

"That's what's so ironic. The coins were minted in 1933, as you know, and a bunch of them stolen a few years thereafter. Thousands more were melted down because we went off the gold standard."

"Sure."

"The royal legation picked Farouk's Double Eagle up from the Mint on March eleventh, 1944," Alvino said, looking down at her notes. "Exactly one week later is when the Secret Service found out about the plans that the Stark brothers had to auction another of the supposedly nonexistent treasures. They were furious."

"Did our government ever try to get the coin back from Farouk?"

"Yes, Detective. My predecessors knew that the license had been obtained from Morgenthau in error.

They tried diplomatic measures to get it back," Alvino said. "But think of the date. We were in the middle of the Second World War. Egypt was a pivotal piece of the map, controlling the Suez Canal and passage to the Indian Ocean. Nobody wanted to upset the applecart for a purloined Double Eagle."

How trivial a single piece of stolen gold, valued then at twenty dollars, would have seemed to diplomats in the middle of a raging war.

"And after the war ended?" Mercer asked.

She fingered papers on her desk. "I can show you the letter that the man who had my job drafted then, asking the king for the return of the Double Eagle. Unfortunately, protocol required that he send the document up to the State Department, to get approval to correspond with a foreign government. The powers-that-be at State denied his request to do that."

"Why so?"

"'Politically inadvisable' is the language they used. The Arab-Israeli war in 1948 was the next international hot spot, and Farouk was widely unpopular— at home and abroad—by then. And he was way too distracted to be interested in the return of the Eagle."

"You think anybody could have predicted its future worth in those days?"

She laughed. "Maybe to the tune of a few thousand dollars. Seven million was an astronomical figure back then. Nobody would have believed it possible."

"Seven million's still pretty far over the top, as far as I'm concerned," Mike said. "So the fat boy gets deposed in 1952. He's exiled to . . . ?"

"Rome," Alvino answered. "He loved *la dolce vita*. As a wild young man, he used to be called the Night Crawler."

"Yeah," Mike said, "so we've heard."

"Old habits die hard. He still spent his nights club hopping—the Hunt Club, the Piccolo Slam, the Boîte Pigalle, the Via Veneto. Flipped over to Monaco for Grace Kelly's wedding to his royal buddy, Prince Rainier. Ever the playboy."

Mike said. "So when he fled from Egypt, does anybody know whether that was with or without the bird?"

"Good question," Alvino answered. "And I'm not sure that anyone really does know the answer. The Egyptian revolutionaries—led by General Nasser—made Farouk leave most of his toys behind. But it's clear that in the months before his expulsion he got out enough money, enough jewels to sell, and some of his smaller treasures to allow him to live like a king, even in exile, for the rest of his life."

"The man without a country. But maybe *with* a Double Eagle," Mike said, thinking about the chronology. "So, he got the coin in 1944, left Egypt in 1952—and the coin finally surfaced when?"

"Not for almost fifty years, Mike. People assumed it had been left behind in Cairo when Sotheby's included it for sale in an auction catalog of Farouk's treasures in 1955. As soon as the Secret Service agents attached to the Mint saw that listing, they directed the American consul in Cairo to have the government remove the Double Eagle from the auction and return it to the U.S."

"So it never went on the block?"

"Correct. But we didn't get it back then either," Alvino said. "Nasser's aides claimed it was all a big mistake. That Farouk had taken it with him. That no one in Egypt had seen it in years. It disappeared completely—no explanation, no clue, no trace."

"The one the Stark brothers sold at auction in 2002—Farouk's seven-million-dollar Eagle—when did that get back into this country?" Mike asked.

"Not until 1996, fifty years after it was delivered to the king in Egypt."

"Who brought it in?" I asked, curious about its circuitous route home.

"There was a prominent coin dealer from England who flew in with it and arranged what he thought was going to be a private meeting with an American counterpart. Breakfast at the Waldorf-Astoria."

"You've got a shit-eating grin on your face, Lori," Mike said. "Must mean your boys were hiding under the table."

"You're not wrong. A few intercepted calls and wiretaps, and the Secret Service picked up the tab for the scrambled eggs and bacon."

"And landed the Double Eagle?"

"Exactly."

"Did the Brit tell you where he bought it?" Mercer asked.

"That's still a pretty murky story," she answered. "Gave us a lot of nonsense about one of the Egyptian colonels who sold it to a merchant after the coup. Couldn't name names or provide any documentary proof."

Lori Alvino hesitated. Her boss, she had said earlier, had told her to give us everything. "Besides, that wasn't what our intelligence picked up."

"What was the contradictory information?" Mike asked.

"I know you think all the federal agencies don't get along with each other very well," Lori said, looking back and forth among us to see if we agreed with her.

"We don't work with you guys often enough to know," Mike answered, in a less than candid fashion.

"Well, I don't want you to think this is one of those immature interagency rivalries. It's just the way business was."

"No quarrel from us."

"The CIA screwed this up," she said emphatically. "The Central Intelligence Agency made a mess of the whole thing."

"Of the Double Eagle?"

"That, too," Lori said. "I was talking about the political trouble they caused—with Farouk, with the rebels, with the coup. And as a side effect of those problems, the disappearance of that coin, among many other valuables."

The CIA had lurked on the outskirts of our case since the beginning. Andrew Tripping claimed to have been an agent. Victor Vallis may have been in their employ when he returned to Cairo in the early fifties. The faux Harry Strait had pretended to Paige Vallis that he was a CIA agent, when in fact the real Harry Strait had been a member of the Secret Service. What had linked these individuals together, to the government agencies, and to our case?

"The CIA," I asked, "was it actually involved with King Farouk?"

"In a very big way. Teddy Roosevelt's grandson—his name was Kermit—was the CIA's main man in Cairo in the early fifties. He made a fast friend of the king."

"That was easy to do?"

"Well, Farouk considered the Roosevelt family the royalty of the U.S. That was part of his access. And also Roosevelt had a guy on his staff who had an inside track."

"What do you mean?"

"Kermit Roosevelt brought with him as an aide a young Foreign Service officer who had served in the thirties as Farouk's tutor—a brilliant guy who spoke six or seven languages and knew more world history—"

Mike Chapman filled in the blanks, letting out a low whistle. "Victor Vallis."

"That's exactly right," said Lori. "I didn't realize the CIA would have been so cooperative and given you so much information."

Not to worry, I thought. You called that one right. The fact that we knew an occasional name or fact seemed to encourage her to trust us with more details.

"Apparently, the king was very fond of Victor from the old days—they were practically the same age, and he treated his old tutor like a brother. Gave him the run of the palace."

"Knowing he was CIA?"

"Oh, no. Believing that he just held some low-level post, the kind a tutor-cum-grad-student would land the first few times out. This Vallis fellow lived virtually inside the royal quarters, had an apartment of his own there."

"Talk about access and opportunity," Mercer said.

"So the CIA," I asked, "did they support Farouk's reign?"

Lori Alvino shook her head. "Not for long. FDR had two goals. He needed Egypt as a democratic stronghold in the Middle East, since the rest of the region was so susceptible to communism. And he was among the first to recognize the importance of Arab oil to fuel the American economy. Farouk? He was a loose cannon, and the Americans realized they couldn't control him."

"So the U.S. funded the Egyptian coup? We backed General Nasser and Anwar Sadat?"

She pursed her lips. "Not with guns and tanks and planes. Simply with the promise that if their coup was successful, the Americans would not step in to save the king."

"And when the time came?"

"Nasser's rebels took over the Egyptian army, closed the airfields so Farouk couldn't escape on one of his private planes, and held his royal yacht in dry dock. The king himself called the embassy to get Truman to intercede on his behalf—by then FDR was long dead—but the president refused to do it. His enemies sent him off into exile—with seventy pieces of luggage rumored to be packed with gold ingots and hidden jewels. The Americans never lifted a hand to help King Farouk."

"But the rebels let him live," Mike said.

"Nasser was no fool. He didn't want to risk a civil war, or make Farouk a martyr by killing him," Lori said.

"Do the math," Mike said. "Farouk had a five-hundred-room palace, chock-full of priceless treasures. Best guess is he beats it out of town with all those suitcases and pockets full of goodies. The rest that got left behind—maybe four hundred rooms' worth of stuff—who got it all?"

Lori shrugged. "Some of it was auctioned by Sotheby's. Some of it was taken by the rebel soldiers—all his great racehorses—and everything from his cigar collection to some of his pornography showed up at Nasser's headquarters."

"The CIA was in on that?" I asked.

"At some levels, sure. The stories were legendary. Somebody seen sipping a martini at Shepheard's Bar in Cairo, pulling out a cigarette lighter with Farouk's initials; or a young agent coming home to the States with a unique assortment of Confederate coins, which happened to have been a hallmark of the king's collection—that kind of thing."

"Nobody called on the carpet for any of it?"

"Hard to do. Most of them would just say the items had been a gift from the king. Awfully tough to prove otherwise, after time went by."

"And Victor Vallis, any stories about him, about what he took out of the palace?"

"Odd guy, the tutor. Didn't seem to be interested in all the glitz around him. He was a scholar. Nobody worried about what he took, because he asked first."

"Asked what?"

"He wanted letters, correspondence, government missives. He was a paper man. Probably could have filled his shoes with gold, too, but apparently he didn't. Said he was going to write a book about Farouk, but I'm not sure he ever did. He moved out of the palace days after the king went into exile, and Nasser let him take boxes of documents with him, assuming the CIA was glad to see the old boy out of the country, too."

Mercer was still puzzling over all the names involved. "Harry Strait," he asked, "was he with the CIA?"

"Oh, no. One of our own. The very best. I'm sure Mr. Stark told you what an amazing job Harry did getting back the stray Double Eagles. Pure Secret Service."

"Did he have a son?"

"Harry? Never married. One of those guys whose whole life was the service."

"You've been very gracious with your information, Lori," I said. I didn't want to reveal to her how tight the CIA had been in response to our efforts to get files on Vallis, Tripping, and Strait. But a deposed Egyptian king was a different story. "It's hard to imagine that half a century after this coup, the CIA still considers Farouk's files a matter of national security, isn't it? It's been hard to get the facts we need on all this."

"Ten years in exile, doin' as the Romans do," Mike said. "Wine, women, and song. Fat and happy. Has his last supper, smokes a big fat cigar, and then croaks at the dinner table. When you think of the fates of a lot of monarchs—from the guillotine to the firing squad—all in all, not a bad way for the king to die."

"That's just the official version, Mike," Lori Alvino told him. "That's the way the newspapers played it. The fact is, Mr. Homicide Detective, King Farouk was murdered."

31

"What the Romans needed, Mike, was a good homicide cop," Lori said. "They rolled over on this one, big-time."

He was standing at the window, looking at the traffic going eastbound over the Brooklyn Bridge. I knew what he was thinking, because I was trying to make the same kinds of connections. What was it that linked the unnatural death of an Egyptian king in Rome back in 1965 to the murders in New York City, in the last few days, of a Harlem dancer and the daughter of a former CIA operative? "How'd it happen?" Mike asked.

"Most of what you know from history books and old newspaper stories is true. The man weighed almost four hundred pounds. He smoked like a fiend, and took medication for high blood pressure. Went out for dinner at a fancy restaurant, in full view of a big crowd."

"Something on the menu he wasn't expecting?"

"Let me remember," she said. "I think he had a dozen oysters, a nice rich lobster Newburg, followed by roast baby lamb, with about six side dishes, and flaming crêpe suzettes for dessert. He lit up his Havana, and in front of a roomful of spectators, his head fell onto the table and he dropped dead."

"Cause of death at autopsy?"

"What autopsy?" Lori Alvino asked. "That's the whole point. Nobody ordered an autopsy. The king died of excess, they said at the time. A cerebral hemorrhage. It seemed so obvious that people didn't question it."

"But in fact?" Mercer asked.

Lori Alvino rested her chin in her hands, propped up by her elbows, telling us what she knew was in the official files. "There's a poison called alacontin. Ever hear of it?"

None of us had.

"Tasteless, odorless. Causes cardiac arrest immediately, but wouldn't show up in an autopsy."

"Why not?"

"Ask your docs how the drug works. I just read the reports, I don't do the forensics."

"No, I mean why no autopsy?" I asked.

"On the orders of the Italian Secret Service."

"There's an Italian Secret Service?" Mike asked. "That's got to be as effective as the Swiss navy."

"Easy, Detective," Lori said. "I've got paisans over there."

"Now we're talking 1965," Mercer said. "Who wanted Farouk dead at that point? He'd been in exile for more than ten years by then."

"Pick your leaders. Some say the poisoner was working for the Egyptians. In a decade, Nasser had gone from being a dashing rebel to a socialist dictator. Loyal Egyptians talked of restoring the monarchy, bringing home the exiled leader. Farouk's death would have been a gift to Nasser from his supporters."

"Who else?"

"The Americans, of course. And the English," Lori said. I reminded myself that Peter Robelon's father had also been a British agent in Europe during that period.

"Why them? Why us?"

"Because things had not gone as planned with Nasser. Our CIA and the British intelligence agency thought, quite wrongly, that the young general was going to be more malleable than Farouk had been. But he wasn't."

"Then why would *we* hurt Farouk?"

"A lot of government people thought, at the time, that Nasser would be ousted and the Egyptian monarchy would be restored. The Brits wanted their old outpost again in Cairo."

"So why not put a king back on the throne, and control him?" I asked.

"You got it. But Farouk hadn't worked the first time around. Now he was older, still very undisciplined, and totally unacceptable to the Western leaders. His son, however, was the perfect candidate."

Of course, I remembered. After Farouk had lost interest in Queenie, he had sired a son with his young second wife.

"The boy was only a teenager, so he would need guidance from the British and American delegations, they figured. And he'd be very appealing to the Egyptian masses as a return of the last ruling dynasty. The

U.S. could prop him up on the throne and we'd all be back in business."

"So Farouk's death could have been a first step in our Allied plan to regain control of the territory, rather than a gift to Nasser from his own followers?"

"It works either way," Lori said.

"So now, Farouk is killed, in Rome," Mercer said. "And what became of all the treasures he had taken there?"

Lori Alvino didn't answer.

"C'mon, Lori, too late to stop talking to us now," Mike said. "The CIA?"

"Or the British Secret Service. Or even the Italian Secret Service. There were enough slices of Farouk's pie for everyone to get a handful."

"I'm thinking," Mike said, "about how that Double Eagle got to Egypt in the first place."

"What do you mean?" I asked.

"In a diplomatic pouch. What could be a more foolproof way to move something valuable around the continent, or between continents? Who would know what's inside the little bag? What if the Double Eagle also left Italy in a government pouch?"

"I hate to remind you two," Mercer said. "But the coin that Mr. Stark sold in 2002 was the only one left like it in the entire world."

"That's the one I'm talking about, too," Mike said. "The one Farouk had since 1944—the one in Stark's auction in 2002. What are our choices? The king left it in Egypt when he was deposed, then someone found it and sold it to the British dealer. Lori here says that's not likely."

He looked to her for a sign of agreement and he got it.

"An American CIA agent sat on the nest in Cairo, after the fat man fled," Mike went on. "Someone who knew where to locate the coin, someone who had access to the palace. Other people forgot about the little piece of gold over time, because of all the turmoil in the region, and eventually our guy brought it out on the black market."

Lori picked up on the possibilities. "Maybe the Italian authorities who cleaned out his apartment in Rome found the coin. Maybe even the British agents, who continued to keep a close watch on him all his life. Lots of people have theories about the whereabouts of the precious little object for the fifty years it was missing, but the fact is that no one knows for sure."

I glanced at my watch, as the sky darkened over the East River. "I'm sorry to break this up. It's been most useful for us. I'm afraid I'm taking a couple of days off, and I've got a flight to catch out of La Guardia."

"Let me know what you need, Alex," Lori said. "Nobody's going to open those CIA files of Farouk's anytime soon. There was too much backstabbing and betrayal in play. None of the officials looks good, in hindsight."

We thanked her for the time and information, and I called a car service to meet me outside the building and drive me to the airport.

The three of us were talking over each other as we stepped into the elevator. Fortunately for us, no one else was aboard.

"McQueen Ransome, Paige Vallis, Andrew Tripping," I said, listing off some of the cast of characters. "They're all tied up with Farouk or the Middle East."

"You got Paige's father, Robelon's father, some nutcase calling himself Harry Strait," Mike added. "*Bam.* More Farouk."

I went on. "Graham Hoyt fancies himself a collector, on a smaller scale than Farouk, but with obvious delusions of grandeur. Spike Logan gained the confidence of Queenie—enough to wind up with a few expensive gifts that he knew came from Farouk, and a penchant to go hunting for more after she died."

"Nobody," I said softly, "nobody can really tell us how many Double Eagles were stolen. Ten? That's only the best guess. That's only the ones that were identified and recovered."

"You're dreaming big, blondie. And you're missing the point. Even so, even if you found a dozen of them on the floor of Queenie's closet, they were never monetized. Worthless. They're not legal. You heard Bernard Stark. You can't even get twenty bucks for them. Only the one that was auctioned in 2002 was monetized for Farouk."

"But the killer might not know that," I said.

"Yeah, but—"

"Just suppose, Mike. If I heard that a Double Eagle sold for seven million dollars, and I knew where to find another piece that was identical to it, it would never occur to me that it wasn't a legitimate coin. Maybe I'd still move heaven and earth to get my greedy little hands on one."

The car service driver was outside the building, flashers blinking, with the company name and car number displayed on a plate in the windshield.

"Why'd you call for this? I would have driven you to the airport," Mike said.

"I took you away from Val long enough last night. You don't need to chauffeur me around. Call me if anything breaks, guys, okay? I'll be home by the weekend."

I got in the car, slammed the door, and sat back for the slow trip over the bridge and out the BQE to La Guardia.

"U.S. Airways terminal, please."

"What time's your flight, lady?"

"Six-fifteen."

"You live dangerously. Cutting it mighty close. I'll do my best."

When I reached the check-in counter it was almost six o'clock. I showed my photo ID and e-ticket. "We've had some weather delays, ma'am. Your aircraft is coming in from Pittsburgh a bit late. We won't be boarding for another hour."

"How does it look on the Vineyard end?"

The small airfield on the Vineyard gets socked in regularly, subject to all the weather variables of an island surrounded by both cold ocean waters and warmer bays. You couldn't be a Vineyarder if you were unable to cope with the likelihood of getting stranded at an airport because of summer fog or winter storms.

"They've got a minimum ceiling now," she said. "If the visibility holds, you'll get in fine. Stick around the boarding area. They'll try to turn the plane around pretty quickly."

I went through security and down the concourse to the departure gate. There were only three other passengers waiting for the nineteen-seat Beechcraft. I looked for a quiet place from which to make a call and settled into a corner with my cell phone.

I checked my office for messages, and my home machine as well. Jake had called both places, trying to find out whether I was holding to my plan of flying to the country. Assistants had phoned in updates of the cases on which they were working, and friends had left snippets of social gossip to lighten my spirits. The last voice mail, only fifteen minutes earlier, was from Will Nedim. He had finished his first interview with Tiffany Gatts.

"Will? It's Alex. I'm calling from the airport, on my cell. Can you hear me?"

"So far, so good."

"Everything go as planned with Tiffany? You run into any problems?"

"She's a piece of work, Alex. But I guess you knew that."

"Happy to leave her in your lap. I've got all the aggravation I need right now. Did you get anything from her?"

"I think she's ready to roll over and give up the boyfriend, Kevin Bessemer."

"That's a huge step. How'd you get her there?" I asked.

"Don't give me any of the credit. She hates being in the slammer. She's only sixteen, remember? It doesn't exactly seem fair to her that it was Kevin's idea to go break into Queenie's apartment, and now he's running around free, while she's locked up behind bars."

"Does she know where Kevin is?"

"She's not sure. He hasn't signed up for visiting hours yet, so except for her mama's hand-holding, it's lonely in the jailhouse. There's a piece of Tiffany that wants to Tammy Wynette him," Will said. "Stand by her man and all that. But her resolve is definitely weakening, and it isn't helped any by the fact that two of the other prisoners beat the crap out of her the other day because she wanted to watch Oprah while they were tuned in to Judge Judy."

"How about specifics, Will? Did you try to squeeze her on what she and Kevin did to Queenie, and why they killed her?"

"I've seen you interrogate teenage girls, Alex, and maybe I'm just not as tough on them as you can be. But I'm leaning toward believing her."

"About what?" I asked.

"Tiffany is absolutely adamant that McQueen Ransome was already dead when they got to the apartment. I couldn't budge her from that story no matter which way I came at her. She describes exactly how the old lady looked when they went in, how the drawers were pulled out of the dressers and cabinets, with her belongings all messed up."

I didn't speak.

"Don't be pissed off at me, Alex. Doesn't what the kid says mean anything?"

"That's certainly the way Queenie's body—and the

apartment—looked when Tiffany left it. Whether
that's what she walked into, I guess time will tell. Did
she admit stealing anything?"

"Well, the fur coat."

Good job, Will. It would be hard to lose that larceny count at a trial. "Anything else?"

"She said Kevin found some things on the floor
that were silver and had initials on them. Like cigarette lighters and tie clips. There were a lot of old
snapshots—Tiffany said they were 'pictures of naked
ladies.' Kevin helped himself to those."

So much for the pornographic photos. "But she
didn't pick anything up?"

"Said she scooped up some coins from the closet
floor, but they all had foreign writing on them that
she couldn't understand, so she just dropped them
back on the floor where they had been. Didn't think
she could spend them on Adam Clayton Powell
Boulevard. And one other photograph she said that
must have fallen off the night table, right next to
Queenie's body."

"What did she do with that?" I asked.

"Tiffany thought she had it in her pocketbook
when she got locked up. Thinks the police gave the
bag to her mother when she came to the station house
after the arrest."

"Does it sound like a photo of anything we need?"

"Nah. She can't even explain why she took it. It's
the deceased—McQueen Ransome—and a young
boy. Like an adolescent. Tiffany called him 'a little
white boy.' She thought he looked real pretty."

"Could be Queenie and her son, Fabian. She had lots of pictures of him in the apartment. Guess we ought to get it if we can, to corroborate her story. And to make sure we didn't miss anything else in the handbag. Give Helena Lisi a call and ask her to have Mrs. Gatts bring it in," I said.

"I forgot to tell you yesterday. You know, when I was talking to you while Mr. Battaglia was in your office? I could tell you were trying to get me off the phone," Will said with a nervous giggle. "Helena Lisi doesn't represent Tiffany anymore."

"Well, lucky you. That should make your life easier. Who's her new lawyer?"

"Josh Braydon."

"Big step up. Maybe you'll get some real cooperation now. Did Lisi put up a fight when the family fired her?" I asked. "Hope she got her money up front. Mrs. Gatts is in for quite a struggle if she thinks Helena Lisi won't kick back and scream for her retainer."

"Helena's not exactly out of it yet, Alex."

"What do you mean?"

"I hope you don't mind what I did. I didn't want to get in a hassle with you while Battaglia was sitting in your office, so I just went ahead and used my judgment."

"To do what, Will?"

"When Tiffany Gatts called and asked to talk to me, I could tell she was really frightened. She thinks her life is in danger. Her mother's, too. She begged me not to tell Helena Lisi."

"So how'd you get to Josh Braydon?" I asked. "How'd he get into the case?"

"I had the court appoint him, Alex. I know you're not going to like this. Josh Braydon? He's shadow counsel."

32

"U.S. Airways announces the departure of flight 3709 to Martha's Vineyard. Boarding will begin in approximately ten minutes, through Gate Five."

I paused while the gate agent repeated the information, trying to control my temper.

"What the hell were you thinking, Will? Shadow counsel? How dare you jeopardize a homicide investigation with that kind of idea?"

"I read the leading case, Alex. *People Against Stewart*. I'm pretty sure—"

"Don't cite cases to me," I said, trying to keep my voice down as it resonated through the terminal's seating area. "*Stewart* only speaks to the dismissal of the indictment. The court never reached the issue of the propriety of shadow counsel. If you had bothered to read the dissent, Will, you would have seen that one of the jurists not only called the concept distasteful, but in violation of all ethical prosecutorial considerations."

Will Nedim was getting defensive. "Well, I'm sorry to disagree with you, Alex, but the appellate courts haven't—"

"This is no time to argue. That kind of ruse is not proper and it's not fair. I'd never think of doing anything like it."

"You weren't exactly available to check with and—"

"I've got to catch my plane now, and you've got to undo this. Where will you be tonight? I'll call you when I settle in at my house in a couple of hours, okay? I want to know who Tiffany Gatts claimed to be afraid of and everything else you told the judge to allow this sham to happen."

I scribbled his home number on the back of my ticket and trudged down the steps, out onto the tarmac, and up the steps of the small plane.

This was one more critical thing that Mike and Mercer would have to attend to. Who was funding Tiffany Gatts's defense? If her mother wasn't paying the bills, and if indeed she was fearful of letting her lawyer know her intentions, then we had to find out who was pulling the strings on this puppet.

I ducked my head to get through the entrance, which was several inches shorter than I was. I waited while the woman in front of me stowed her tennis racket in the overhead compartment, and then I sat in the second row, making notes about what I needed to do in response to Nedim's phone call.

"You writing a brief, Alex?"

I looked up and saw a familiar face. Justin Feldman, a prominent litigator in the city who also had a home on the Vineyard, sat opposite me across the narrow aisle.

"No, only a list," I answered. "I'm just letting off steam. I'm afraid I unloaded on one of the young lawyers in the office. Now I'm trying to repair the damage."

"Nothing terminal, I hope."

I respected Justin and had sought his advice in the past, especially on situations that involved ethical considerations, since he had chaired the bar association's prestigious committee. "Depends on your point of view. You know anything about shadow counsel?" I asked.

"Never heard the term."

"That's because you practice in a better place," I said, referring to the federal courts, where judges rarely tolerated the shenanigans that were commonplace stateside. "I'm only aware of one decision on point."

"What jurisdiction?" Justin asked.

"A Manhattan case a few years back. The perp was incarcerated, pending trial or plea. One day, he calls the prosecutor out of the blue. Claims he's ready to cooperate and give up his codefendants, but his lawyer has refused to let him do it."

"What was the lawyer's beef?"

"Turns out the defendant claims his lawyer was hired and paid for by somebody else—a major drug kingpin. When the defendant decides to accept the prosecutor's deal, he tells the judge that his lawyer actually said that the head of the drug ring would have him killed if he cooperated. That word would go back through the lawyer."

"What did the judge do?" Justin asked again.

"Set up this charade, this complete fiction. He made the defendant create a record in court saying that he feared for his life if he fired his lawyer and played ball with the prosecution. So the case actually went forward with two defense attorneys."

"Two? And the first one never knew the second one existed?"

"Exactly," I said. "There was the original lawyer, who was being paid by the kingpin and who told her own client that his life and the life of his family were in danger. The judge kept her on the case, but completely in the dark about the truth of the transactions. Then he went ahead and assigned someone new to do the deal with the prosecution."

"The so-called shadow counsel?"

"Yes. The judge used the lawyer he appointed to take the real plea, which was a deal with cooperation, all the while continuing to pretend that what happened in the presence of lawyer number one—a mock plea allocution, a sentence, and a resentence—was true."

"Creating a complete illusion. Violating all your disclosure obligations, derogating your ethical responsibilities, communicating with the court ex parte to set this up, and falsifying the judicial process all along the way." Justin ticked off every repugnant feature of the arrangement.

"I'm not totally crazy, am I, to tell my colleague I won't go along with something like that?" I asked, as the pilot started up the starboard engine.

"You'd be insane to do it," Justin said, shaking his head back and forth. "I wonder where some of these lawyers lose their senses," he said. "You know Marty London, don't you?"

He was referring to another giant of the New York bar. "Sure."

"I had lunch with him today. The very same kind of conversation about a bright young lawyer came up. Marty's representing a guy who's in over his head—runs the corporate department at a white-shoe law firm. Kept telling his partners that to keep high-rolling clients happy, he was making contributions to their favorite charities. Big bucks."

"Some kind of scam?"

"That's putting it mildly. He'd tell the managing partner he'd written a personal check for, say, fifty thousand dollars to some tug-at-your-heartstrings cause. Say it's children of some war-torn part of the world. Or a struggling dance company. Or an inner-city art museum. Had to be a personal check, so he'd get credit with the client for being a mensch. Who'd second-guess him for a good deed like that? Then, he asked the firm to reimburse him—and they did."

"I think I see this one coming," I said. "He never wrote the check to any such charity."

"How about that the charity never existed in the first place?" Justin said, shaking his head in disbelief. "Battaglia's going to make mincemeat out of this guy when he gets his hands on this case. Fifty thousand dollars of the firm's money in his own pocket every couple of months, on top of his draw of a few million a year. I don't understand these people, Alex."

Both propellers were geared up now, and it was impossible to hear over the din. He settled in with his newspaper and I continued making lists of things to do.

The small aircraft lifted up from the runway. Within minutes, we had flown into the enormous billow of cloud cover that had settled over the New York area. I pulled my seat belt tighter around my waist as the plane bucked in the rough currents. I tried to concentrate on organizing my evening calls, but the severe weather made any work effort impossible.

I stuck my pen in my pocket and stared out the window at the inner lining of the storm cloud. There were only five passengers on the flight, and all looked as gloomy as the skies around us. I watched as the woman in front of Justin's seat fumbled for the airsickness bag, hoping that she would not need to use it in the close confines of the still cabin.

The pilot broke in with a short message. "Sorry about the bumps in the road, ladies and gents. We've got that hurricane blowing in behind us, so we'll rock and roll like this all the way to the Vineyard. Be another thirty-five minutes till touchdown. Thanks for flying with us tonight."

I closed my eyes and tried to think about something pleasant. My lover was in Washington, altogether too pleased with the freedom of our new arrangement, my precious home was about to be battered by sixty-mile-an-hour winds, and the tangle of investigations on my professional plate seemed hopeless. I opened my eyes and stared off into the wild gray yonder.

I was as relieved as the woman clutching the paper bag against her chest when the pilot descended out of the clouds and I could see the lights on the landing strip glistening in the evening mist. We taxied to a stop and I trotted from the bottom of the steps into the shelter of the airport terminal. I walked to the parking lot, where my caretaker had left my car earlier in the week when he'd gone off-island. Soon I was heading up-island on the slick roadway that curved through the pastures and meadows of Chilmark.

It was close to nine o'clock. I was looking for something to eat, but there weren't many choices. I drove in the direction of Dutcher Dock, but both the Galley and the Homeport were dark.

I made a U-turn in front of the old red-roofed coast guard station, now the Chilmark Police Headquarters, going to the far end of the main road toward the gas station. Larsen's Fish Market had closed hours ago, so my last hope was the Bite, a two-hundred-square-foot gray-shingled kitchen from which the Quinn sisters put forth the best chowder and fried clams on the face of the earth.

There were two pickup trucks parked in front—drivers eating in their cabs—and I squeezed my little red convertible in between them. I ducked under the roof of the small porch to get out of the rain, and Karen spotted me when I picked my head up.

"Alex? That you? Haven't got a clam or oyster left. Wiped out."

"Just a cup of soup." My stomach was still settling down. "To go."

Her dialect was more Boston Southie than islander. "Better close your house up tight. Gonna be a wicked bad storm."

"That's what I came up to do."

She handed me a brown bag much larger than a

pint container of soup. "Take some with you for to-morrow. Extra chowder, some chicken wings, and my mother's brownies. You'll be glad you've got this goody bag if nobody opens up during the hurricane."

I thanked her and got back into the car and headed for the hilltop high above the water that surrounded my lovely old farmhouse on all sides, grateful for the placement the Mayhew farmers had given their home almost two centuries earlier, as the waves picked up steam on the shores below. I had expanded and rebuilt the sturdy structure, but it still retained the charm and character that came from its original bones.

My heart beat more rapidly as I made the turn off State Road. I thought of my friend Isabella Lascar, who had died on the very same path just a few years ago.

I was distracted by the movement of a large dark body in the bushes ahead of my car, just out of range of the high beams. My foot slammed on the brakes and the buck leaped directly in front of me, then up and over the ancient stone wall that ringed my property.

Seconds later, the doe and two small deer followed him, trailing off through the woods on my neighbor's land.

I drove on to my house and parked the car. Usually, my caretaker came ahead and lighted the entrance and living area for me, cutting flowers in summer to place around the rooms and stocking the refrigerator with basics. This time, because he had already left the island, I was faced with a dark, cold shell that seemed strangely unwelcoming.

I unlocked the side door and walked quickly into the kitchen and small parlor beyond, flipping on every light switch. I rested the bag of food on the countertop, opened the cabinet to grab a glass, and filled it with ice. In the living room, I pressed the CD player button for random select. By the time I poured some Dewar's, Simon and Garfunkel reminded me that I was fakin' it, and as I was well aware, not really makin' it. I clicked the remote, content to wind up on the bridge over troubled water.

Mike Chapman's home number was on my speed dial. I settled onto the sofa with my drink and waited for him to answer.

"Hello."

"Val? It's Alex. Is this a bad time?"

"No, no. It's fine. How've you been?"

"Good, thanks. Just came up to the country to prepare for the storm." I didn't know whether to mention that Mike had told me she hadn't felt well lately. Before I could decide what to ask, he had taken the phone from her hand.

"Etymology, blondie. Whaddaya know about it?"

I was too disinterested to answer fast enough.

"Me? I thought it was bugs. I'm fat on bugs—figured I would have cleaned up on you tonight. Who knew it was about words? O.K., you know, the initials? Know what they stand for?"

"Count me out, Mike. Look—"

"From the *Boston Morning Post*, 1839. Some cellist from Ottawa won fourteen grand on this. An editor who couldn't spell right used it back then to mean 'oll korrect.' Get it? 'All correct' gets muffed into *O.K.*"

"Riveting. I called to tell you the latest snag in the case."

"Can't you give it a rest, kid? Don't go snapping at me. I got my jammies on, about to have my night-cap—"

"Fine. Call me in the morning. The next dead body can be on your conscience."

Mike's tone changed and he snapped into business mode. "Whoa, whoa, whoa. What's up?"

"Funny stuff with Tiffany Gatts and her lawyer," I said.

"How funny? Laugh out loud?"

"Not exactly. She's willing to squeal on Kevin, but says if she does, her life's in danger. Someone's going to kill her mama, too."

"Better be bringing a cannon for that job."

"Helena Lisi's just a front," I said.

"For what?"

"For the brains behind the operation, I have to think. Somebody else is paying the legal bills, but doesn't want to be connected to the courtroom. You've got to find out who that is. Yesterday."

"You don't think Lisi will tell you, if you ask nice?"

"I can hear her start to whine before I even pose the question. I could try to subpoena her to the grand jury, on the theory that there's a criminal conspiracy, but she'll move to quash and we'll be arguing that one till doomsday."

"Lawyer-client privilege?"

"Even the Supremes let us get into some disclo-sures about fees in certain circumstances, but I'm counting on you to beat the clock. Maybe you start with Mrs. Gatts. See what she knows."

"So there's a new lawyer?"

"Shadow counsel. A stupid artifice that could undermine the whole case, and certainly toss a conviction, if we get anywhere close to one. If we nail Kevin—or someone else for Queenie's murder—this schmuck just becomes part of a fraud that greased the wheels for Tiffany to slide right into our laps, without any real representation."

"Got it."

"Thanks, Mike. We'll talk in the morning."

"Deal," he said, as I started to sign off. "Coop? You okay up there? You're not alone, are you?"

"We're fine," I said, misleading him with the plural pronoun. "Promise. Speak to you tomorrow."

I hung up and hit the number of Jake's cell phone. "Hey," I said as he came on the line. "Can't believe I got you on one ring."

I stretched out on the sofa and cradled the phone against my shoulder.

"Where are you?" he asked.

"Home. The Vineyard." Jake knew it was the one place in the world where I was most content. The tension sloughed off my shoulders within half an hour of my arrival here, even in the worst of circumstances. "And you?"

"Didn't Laura give you the message? I'm trying to get up there, too."

"I haven't even checked the machine. I—I just needed to hear your voice."

"I'm at Reagan National. Nothing's flying out at

the moment. The wind has increased and the first bit of the storm is about to hit."

The Vineyard weather was anywhere from twelve to eighteen hours behind D.C.'s, depending on the speed the system picked up along the way. I could expect Hurricane Gretchen to reach our shores by tomorrow afternoon.

"Go back to the hotel. The airport here has probably shut down already."

"That's not a problem. I was planning to fly to Logan and get down in the morning if I had to. Till I had a brainstorm."

"What's that?" I smiled, pulling a throw over my legs and stirring the ice cubes in the glass with my finger.

"I'm about a concourse away from the row of rental booths. I figure I'll get a car, turn the music up loud, drive up to Woods Hole—even if it takes the better part of the night—and be there in time for the first ferry. Nothing cozier than a great storm. We can stay the whole weekend and—"

I sat bolt upright and swung my legs to the floor, tangling myself in the mohair blanket. I shrieked into the receiver, "You can't do that, Jake. *Please* don't do that."

Didn't he remember what had happened to Adam Nyman, my fiancé, on the night before we were supposed to be married? Driving to the Vineyard from Manhattan, he'd been killed when his car had been sideswiped on the turnpike and had crashed down onto a riverbed below.

Jake clearly didn't connect the urgency in my voice to that tragedy. "Darling, either Mike's right about the fact that you're entirely too controlling," he joked, "or you're stowed away up there with some other foul-weather aficionado who doesn't want me in the neighborhood. C'mon, babe, the all-night drive'll make me feel like I'm in college again."

The static on his phone was masking the panic that had seized me.

"No, no, no, no, no," I kept repeating, until I could break into his response. "Don't you understand, Jake? It's—it's about Adam. It's too painful to bear. Ten hours of highway driving, half of it bound to be in a blinding storm?"

"It's not raining yet, Alex. The roads are—"

"You're missing the point. I'm begging you not to do this, Jake. I'd never forgive myself if anything happened to you on your way here. Wait till the front passes and fly up if you want, for the weekend. Just swear to me you won't try to drive it."

His tone chilled. "There's probably a good reason you don't want me up there with you. I'm sure you'll tell me when you're ready."

I tried again to make him see it from my perspective, but he was still clipped when we said our good nights.

I picked up my glass and wandered into the bedroom. I felt more alone than I had in a very long time. I turned the steam unit on in the shower and set the temperature at ninety-nine degrees, letting it warm up while I undressed.

The phone rang but I ignored it. There was no point in arguing with Jake, so I opted to let the machine record the message while I listened.

"You there, Coop? You outside baying at the moon?"

"Just screening, Mike," I said, grabbing the receiver from its dock. "You forget to tell me to have pleasant dreams?"

"Val's a whiz with the computer. Got me onto the website for Lisi and Lisi, the husband-and-wife law firm, so I'd have a head start in the morning."

"I didn't mean to get you riled up on Val's time, Mike. Tomorrow is fine."

"Forget Helena. What do you know about Jimmy Lisi?"

"Former Legal Aid. Pretty decent guy."

"Interesting bio, Coop. Born on the other side. Very proud of his roots."

"Why not?" I could see the steam misting on the glass door of the shower, and I ached to get inside and relax.

"Generalissimo Lisi, Jimmy's pop. Know anything about him?"

"Tell me."

"Jimmy was born in Rome. His old man rose through the ranks, wound up as head goombah in the Italian Secret Service. Puts him right near the kitchen where they cooked up some potent *pasta e fagiòli* for Farouk the night he croaked back in sixty-five."

"I like it," I said, putting down the scotch and picking up a pen and pad.

"So I did the same kind of check for the other lawyers in the case. Unfortunately, the law firms that those guys are with don't do the same kind of family sagas on-line, like the Lisis. Just have their fancy degrees and the alma maters listed."

"C'mon, Mike. I can tell you found something else that tweaked you."

"So Jimmy Lisi gets to college—Yale, by the way—and ends up in the same frat as a guy whose old man was also a spook in Rome, for the Brits, at the very same time Lisi's dad was doing spy work."

"I see where this is going. Forget about Josh Braydon and his shadow counsel role. We need to find out who's pulling the strings behind Helena Lisi."

"Maybe," Mike said, "the man Tiffany Gatts is afraid of is actually Peter Robelon."

33

The view from my bedroom's French doors out over the lawn that sloped down to the pond was a muted palette of grays and greens, moistened by a steady rainfall. Trees and tall grasses seemed colored by a dull assortment of Crayolas, and the pale sky hung heavily overhead. Only the whitecaps in the distance suggested that this calm before the storm would kick up and show its stuff within a few hours.

I drove to the Chilmark Store for coffee and the *Times,* and to reassure myself that there were plenty of people I knew who wouldn't be all that far away if Hurricane Gretchen packed her anticipated wallop.

"I'm running low on candles and flashlight batteries," Primo said. The owner was restocking his shelves with storm supplies. "Better take plenty while you're here, Alex. I'm closing early."

I picked up a fistful of C batteries, extra matches, boxes of candles, and rolls of masking tape and took them to the checkout counter. "Can you put this on my tab?"

"Sure. Need a hand with anything out your way?" Primo asked.

"I'm all set, thanks. This should do it. Would you save me a newspaper in the morning?"

"If they get to the island, Alex. Steamship Authority's gonna stop the ferries if the swells get real big."

"Of course," I said, embarrassed about forgetting how these self-sufficient islanders were cut off from all normal services whenever Mother Nature got angry.

I was back in the house at eight-thirty, and tried to find Jake, to apologize. Voice mail answered at his home, his cell phone, and the office. Maybe he was mimicking my habit of screening calls, or maybe he was paying me back for last night. Could he have really thought I was keeping him away because I was settled in here with someone else?

"Hey, it's me. Horatio Hornblower," I told his recorded message. Jake loved to make fun of my bright yellow foul-weather gear, and here I was pulling the rubberized hood back up over my head to go out and haul the deck furniture into the barn. "Call me when you get a chance, okay? I'm trying to hunker down for the storm. Miss you."

I went through the old summer kitchen, refitted as an office, and out the side entrance that led to the sheep barn, built more than a century ago. I pulled open the door and surveyed the space. The Gravely and mower took up a third of it, while the workbench and Adam's antique tool collection stretched along two complete walls. I shuffled around some of the gardening equipment to make room for everything that needed to come inside.

I spent the next two hours ferrying recliners, chairs, and tables from the rear decks around the building into the barn. I had been here for too many storms to risk chancing the results of Hurricane Gretchen's fury—chairs lifted and blown hundreds of yards away, and tables hurled against the side of the house, shattering windows and spreading glass all over the interior floors.

At eleven o'clock, I paused to make a cup of hot chocolate and sit at the kitchen table to dry out and listen to the radio. The marine forecast issued alerts for gale-force winds, and news bulletins tracked the eye of the storm as it buffeted the Connecticut coastline. Flooding and downed electrical lines had already caused five deaths in the New York area.

I put my slicker on again and circled the property for a last check. The wind was picking up, and I walked down to the edge of the wildflower field to recover the bird feeders. The last cosmos that stood amid the elephant grass were losing their heads to the elements, and the rain swept away small flecks of white and fuchsia petals.

My caretaker's cottage, beyond the rise at the foot of the hill, looked snug and tight. It was two small rooms, an old Menemsha fisherman's shack that once stood on the dock and had been moved up here in the sixties, before Adam and I bought the place. Now charmingly redecorated, it was home to an islander who maintained the property for me in exchange for a year-round residence.

Back inside, I hung up the rain jacket on a hook, stepped out of my boots, and changed into jeans and a sweatshirt. I tried again to find Jake, with no better luck, and decided against leaving more messages.

A fresh cord of dry firewood was stacked in the bin beside the rear door, and another neat pile was in the fireplace, ready to be lighted. I knelt on the granite hearth and placed a match against the thin pine starters beneath the sturdy logs, watching the flames take and spread. I was ready to give up rock and roll in favor of some Beethoven piano concerti, music that I hoped would soothe and calm me.

Now the wind howled at the top of the chimney, drawing up the smoke and carrying it away. I stood and looked outside, watching the tall evergreens bend and sway with the pounding gusts that swept the hilltop.

The rolls of tape were in the kitchen, and I made the rounds of the rooms, standing on a chair to place X's across the glass, corner to corner, on each of the enormous panes that afforded me such a glorious view.

As I balanced myself on my tiptoes in the bedroom, I heard a loud banging noise coming from the opposite side of the house. The tape dropped from my hand and rolled across the floor. I climbed down from the chair and followed after it. Retracing my steps through the kitchen and hallway, I found the front door open and swinging wildly as huge drafts of air pressed against it.

When I was at home, I rarely locked the doors. But the booming noise was so jarring that I pushed the door shut and turned the bolt. I circled the house, making sure the side entrance and the other two doors leading out onto the expansive rear deck were fastened as well, before going back to taping the glass.

Fierce weather spooked the animals. I was used to seeing that here in the country. Cottontail rabbits that usually didn't appear until dusk were skittering across the lawn. A family of skunks huddled against each other under the leeward side of a beach plum tree. Flocks of birds were fighting the wind in an effort to steer themselves south.

I was just as unsettled as the wild creatures. Somehow this old farmhouse had weathered scores and scores of storms, but now a cedar shingle ripped loose from the barn roof and flung itself against the window, reminding me that the glass was all that stood between me and the approaching squall.

Again, I paced around the house, checking windowsills for places that had leaked before, and laying old beach towels beneath them. When I returned to the living room, I fixed myself a spicy Bloody Mary, switched on the radio to track the storm, reached for an old copy of Sterne's *Tristram Shandy* in the bookshelf behind the fireplace, and settled onto the sofa to relax, read, and wait for Gretchen.

I must have fallen asleep, aided by the warm combination of the alcohol and fire. A loud thud right behind my head startled me awake. A large bird, some sort of grackle, had become disoriented and crashed against the pane. Dazed for a few seconds, it picked itself up and flew off with a few taunting squawks.

The day had changed. It was after three o'clock, and the sky had turned from a pastel gray to a deep black. Everything in the landscape was atilt, yielding to the power of the wind that was gusting at almost seventy miles an hour, according to the local newscaster.

For the next half hour, I felt as though I were on an amusement park ride that wouldn't stop to let me off. Objects swirled around outside and thumped against the roof and sides of the house. Tree branches snapped in half with a terrible cracking sound and slapped at my taped windows. I moved to sit on the floor in the middle of the room, fully expecting a limb or bough to hurtle itself through the glass and impale me against the sofa's cushion.

It was exactly 4:05 in the afternoon when the flickering lights went out and the electricity went dead. No radio, no music, no quiet hum of kitchen appliances. The interior darkness mirrored the weather, and I inched closer to the fireplace to add more logs to my only source of warmth and light.

I had flashlights at the ready in every room. I turned one on and tried to continue to read, but the drama outside the window made reading impossible.

The storm raged for more than an hour. The strange noises of nature's destructive forces had unnerved me. Old wooden floorboards creaked and groaned, damp drizzle seeped in through cracks in doors and window sashes, squalls pounded against every surface of the house.

And something moved up above me. Footsteps in the empty second-floor bedrooms? I took the flashlight and followed the beam up the staircase. Squirrels, probably, or field mice. Had to be some frisky critter that had found its way inside or burrowed under the attic eaves.

I checked from room to room, but all seemed fine. I shined the ray into the bathroom, and highlighted a spider on the outer window screen, clinging to an iridescent web as the wind tried to tear it from its hold. Standing at the top of the stairs, I could hear the pitter-patter of small-clawed feet echoing over my head. Whatever was in the attic could spend the night. I wasn't going up to investigate.

Now there seemed to be a distinct tapping coming from below me. I took three steps down and listened again. It was pitch-black, save for the narrow path of light leading from my hand. Lilac bushes stood outside the door. Their bare, hearty branches must have been scraping against the old six-over-six windows on the house's facade.

I returned to the living room and tried to settle down again.

Still there was something besides noise that was disturbing me. There were shadows, too. I hadn't put enough vodka in my drink three hours earlier to distort my vision, but ghostly shapes seemed to move back and forth along the length of the rear deck. I would have offered shelter to almost any form of animal life, but not to these weird, unwelcome dancing phantoms.

Maybe the bedroom was a better place to be. Careful not to trip over chair legs or stools, I made my way through the house. Too much glass, I told myself. I couldn't shake the eerie feeling that someone was looking in at me. Was I foolish to want to climb back upstairs to one of the guest rooms and snuggle under a quilt, out of range if someone wandered onto the property? How stupid to be afraid in my own home.

I pulled the chaise longue away from the foot of my bed into a corner of the room, flipped open my cell phone, and punched in Jake's number. A mechanical operator told me the call I wanted to place could not be completed as dialed. I tried Jake again before dialing Mike. The problem was clearly on my end, so I gave up.

I rested my head against a small pillow my mother had needlepointed for me, just as a violent spasm brought something crashing through what I thought must be one of the kitchen windows. I jumped to my feet and ran through my office to get to the large, open room, trying not to let my agitation overcome my wits. Why hadn't I gotten extra small batteries for the radio when I was at the store? Why had I wanted to ride out a hurricane in the first place?

One of the window boxes that hung outside beneath the sill had been thrown up through the glass and onto the floor with enormous force. Wet topsoil was everywhere, and blustery air charged into the room behind the wooden missile, which had overturned and landed beneath the dining table.

I looked up and thought I saw someone running on the slick lawn at the bottom of the steps that led down from the deck. Maybe it hadn't been the wind that had torn the flower box from its mooring and sailed it inside. Maybe I wasn't imagining the shapes and shadows around me after all.

Why wouldn't someone have knocked on the door

if he or she wanted to get inside? I picked up the land-line telephone to see whether it was working, but since the portable models were now run on electricity, too, the phone was dead. Back to the front door. I was nervous and edgy, checking to see whether someone had driven in from the road, looking for help. With the house looking so dark and quiet, it was possible that a person approaching it would think no one was at home.

A terrible rattling started again, now from the French doors in my bedroom. I slinked through the narrow hallway, clutching the banister to steady myself. There was a distinct outline of a body against the tall glass pane. Someone was trying desperately to get inside the house.

Should I call out to my unexpected visitor and let him know that I was indeed in residence? No. Not a good idea. I remembered the plume of smoke that must have been pouring out of the chimney. Forget the house's quiet and the darkness, of course an inter-loper would know I was in here. This was not some-one looking for my help. Whoever it was wanted to scare me to death before he showed himself.

The noise stopped. I turned off the flashlight and crouched in the area behind the staircase, not visible from any of the windows. All I could hear was the crackling of the logs shifting in the fireplace as they charred and burned.

Then another blast of broken glass. This time it sounded like it was coming from the living room. I had taped the giant picture window, but not the small panes in the door that opened onto the deck. Had the wind propelled something through the narrow space or was there really someone intent on breaking in? My gut told me it was the latter.

I crawled twelve feet to the front entrance, lifting my arm over my head to feel for the small brass lock and twisting it gently 180 degrees. I paused, and heard what I thought was a jiggling noise that might have been the door handle back in the bedroom. I wanted out.

Hoping that my visitor's attention was fixed on the house's rear side, I pulled at the knob and opened the door wide enough to slip through, still squatting, onto a patch of dirt between the lilac bushes as branches scratched at my cheeks and snagged my hair. The rain was pouring down, and within seconds I was soaked, my moccasins squishing in the cold mud.

I had choices now: I could try to run into the wooded area that ringed my property against the traditional stone walls, or go out the driveway and try to find cover in the yard of either of my neighbors, more than half an acre away at the closest point. Both were summer families whose houses were locked up for the winter months.

But if my burglar had arrived by car, and if there was an accomplice waiting to drive him away, that direction might prove disastrous.

There was only one way to go. The caretaker's cottage was down the steep hill, not even visible from the main house. It would be locked, I knew, but I also knew that there was a crawl space beneath it, rather than a real foundation. It rested on pilings and concrete since early house owners had moved it up from

Dutcher Dock. After Adam was killed, I had never gotten around to having it rebuilt, as we had once planned.

I ran to the far end of the main house but couldn't make out anyone from my position behind a stand of hydrangea bushes. Trees were blowing and bending with the wind, and everywhere the shadows danced and took on human form. I was wet and tired and scared. I wanted to click my heels so that the storm would end and I could wind up safely back in Kansas at Auntie Em's farm.

I heard the front door of the house banging furiously behind me. If my tracker could hear it, it would draw him around to see what was making such a racket. Now was my chance to sprint, running downhill, taking care not to fall and slide on the slippery grass. I reached the far side of the small shack and stopped again to catch my breath, fearing that he might hear my heaving gasps.

I lifted my head above the clothesline to see whether I could spot anyone, but I could barely make out the main house's shape through the fog and mist. I would be safe here if he didn't know the property well enough to realize that this little cottage existed.

On my hands and knees I crawled for the hole behind the three steps that bordered the deck railing. I found it and began to slither inside. If someone thought to search down here, I would be hidden completely beneath a sodden blanket of wet leaves. That was a trade-off, then, for bellying down with whatever spiders and snakes and rodents lived in this underground outpost.

I tried not to think about my possible companions and I covered myself as best I could. For more than fifteen minutes, I flattened myself against the ground, listening to my heartbeat, hearing nothing but fierce air currents whooshing over and around my head.

Then suddenly, I heard what sounded like padded footsteps on the thick, wet grass. I was lying on my stomach, my head turned to the side away from the house. I dared not move to look up at my intruder.

I stared straight ahead, frozen in place.

Suddenly the pattering sound stopped. Whoever was coming had put on brakes just a few feet from where I lay.

I smelled the creature before I saw it. Whoever had scared me had also frightened a mother skunk and her brood. She released her rank spray in the direction of the main house before creeping in with them to join me in my lair.

34

I waited for hours before I inched myself backward out of my flooded foxhole. I was soaked throughout, chilled and shivering, unable to control my tremors and too stiff to straighten myself completely.

The house was still dark, as was the sky, and there was no smoke coming from the chimney. I stayed as close as I could to the stone wall, as far away as possible from my home, until I reached a clearing and climbed over to the neighboring pasture.

The rain had stopped now and the wind had calmed to a mild breeze. I walked through open fields in the darkness, heading downhill, knowing that before too long I would reach the protected inlet at Quitsa Cove. Small boats were tied up there, and as soon as Gretchen cleared the southern shore, fishermen would be back out to check the damage, no matter what time of night. I didn't want to chance the roadway in case someone should be waiting for me, but the odds were good that I would find a familiar face here on the pond where I had so often moored my own day-sailer. I wasn't a runner, but I could outswim almost anything without fins.

Trees were down all over my path, and limbs dangled from overhead branches. I made my way slowly and carefully around the obstacles, sliding the last few feet as I came to a stop in front of the rickety wooden dock that stretched twenty feet out into the light chop of the water.

Again I waited, sitting and staring at the trail that came in from State Road, my arms encircling my knees, which were drawn against my chest as I tried to warm up. I knew that even in the dark, the shape of my body on the end of the dock against the watery backdrop would be apparent to anyone who approached. I wanted it that way. I was looking for help, not trying to scare whoever arrived.

Another hour went by before a pickup truck rattled down the path. Its headlights caught me straight on, and I got to my feet, waving broadly as the driver brought the car to a stop and stepped out, pointing a flashlight at me.

"You okay?" a man's voice called out as he raised his hand over his brow to peer out at me.

"Yes, I'm fine," I said. "It's Alex Cooper. Kenny—that you?"

"Yes'm. You tied up in here? You got a prob—? Jeez, Alex—you look like you been out in this storm all night."

Kenny Bainter's family had been on the island for six generations. He fished and farmed—swordfish and sheep—and had known me for a very long time.

He turned back to the truck and pulled a blanket out of the cab. I followed behind and let him wrap it around my shoulders while my teeth clacked and chattered against each other.

"You fall in the water or something?" he went on.

"No, no," I said, shaking my head. "Someone—someone broke into my house during the storm. I—uh—I ran down here to get away. I was hoping you could drive me to the Chilmark police."

"Who the hell was it, Alex? Some kids looking to give you a fright? I'll go back there with you and we'll—"

"Let's not do that. It wasn't kids, I promise you." Most of the islanders who knew me as a summer person couldn't connect me to the frontline prosecutorial position that carried with it all the attendant dangers of urban violence. I didn't think Kenny would understand that the intruder had been, in all probability, someone who wanted to kill me.

"Well, let's go get the son of—"

"Can you just drive me over to the station? That's really all I need."

"That and somethin' dry to put on, missy. I can't be driving you there. Storm knocked some power lines down and the Crossroads is all blocked off. Made a mess of it up here. Tell you what. Let me check on a few of the little stinkpots I get paid to baby-sit here, and then we can bail one if it's not dry and I'll zip you across the pond. How's that?"

"You think it's safe to go out?" I said, looking back at the surface of the water.

"Be calm as a bathtub in half an hour. Storm's way

out over the Atlantic by now. Get up there in the truck and turn on some heat."

"Let me help you, Kenny," I said lamely as I watched him step into the shallow water wearing hip-waders.

"I seen scarecrows be better help than you, Alex. Go on and dry off."

Several small powerboats were upended on the beach, large gashes cut into their hulls. There were lots of damaged craft, and some that had broken loose completely and were bobbing about farther out in the pond. Barrels and buoys, nets and rope, were all strewn around the ground. But Kenny was right about how gently the waves were now lapping against the rocky shoreline.

When he had finished checking everything, he unwrapped the tarpaulin cover off a small rubber Zodiac that he must have dragged to safety and tethered to a metal post on land before the storm hit. He led it back into the water and lowered the engine over the side.

"C'mon, missy. Have you there in five minutes."

I kept the blanket wrapped around me and stepped onto the dock, lowering myself over the bumpers and sitting on the edge of the little vessel, clinging to the handles on either side of me.

The night sky was still covered with clouds, but as we chugged along into the main body of the pond, I could make out the distinctive red-shingled roof of the old coast guard station, which now housed the local police. I knew they had a generator, and their lights were the only ones in town working, as far as I could see.

Kenny steered the small dinghy alongside the dock

at the Homeport restaurant and started to tie her up. I stood and climbed the ladder that reached down to the water as soon as we touched against it. "No need to come," I said. "I owe you, Kenny. I'll make it up to you."

"You don't owe me anything. Just dry that blanket off and get it back to me. It's what keeps my dog warm when he rides around with me all winter."

"Well, tell him I'm grateful for the loan." I blew him a kiss and made a beeline for the station, just a hundred yards away.

"Can I help you, ma'am?"

The clock on the wall behind the officer's head reminded me that it was one-thirty in the morning.

"Chip? It's me. Alex Cooper."

He did a double take. "What hit you?"

"I'll tell you everything as soon as I'm out of this gear. You got any women officers here? Someone who might have some dry civvies in a locker?" I spread my arms to unfold the blanket so he could see the condition of my clothes.

"Just a minute. Wait here." Chip Streeter went up to the second floor and came back a few minutes later with another tan-uniformed officer—a young woman who was shorter and heavier than I. She was carrying a pair of chinos and a plaid flannel shirt, which looked better to me at that moment than the entire spring couture line of Escada.

She led me to a bathroom, apologized for not having clean underwear to give me, but handed me paper toweling and a new toothbrush so I could clean myself up.

When I had finished the job, I went back out to sit at Streeter's desk. I described to him what had happened at the house a few hours earlier, during the storm.

"You sure you weren't imagining things?"

I bit my lip. "My imagination isn't that good. Have you got someone to take me home to check it out?"

"Like Kenny told you, we can't get through up that way by car. When the harbormaster gets on duty in the morning, he'll give us a boat to head on over. All my guys are out on calls on the North Road as it is. Hell of a lot of property damage, and we're checking on some of the seniors to make sure nobody's hurt or got any kind of medical emergency without power. Break-ins are taking a backseat right now. Anyone off-island you want to call?"

I shook my head. "Mind if I stay here till morning?"

"I'll brag about this for a long time to come. Only police officer in Dukes County to have a prosecutor in residence. Wouldn't have it any other way. We've got a couple of cots upstairs if you want to stretch out until daybreak."

I ached to close my eyes and be in a safe place. "Is it too much to ask for milk and cookies?"

Chip smiled at me and led me up to the small locker room. I thanked him and stretched out on the narrow bed, tucking Kenny's dog's blanket around my body.

I tossed fitfully for most of the remaining hours of the night, getting up to brush my teeth and try to give some direction to my hair a little after six-thirty in the morning. Sunlight was streaming in the window and reflecting off the water's bright blue surface. By the time I got downstairs, a fresh pot of coffee was brewing on the hot plate and two other cops had reported in for duty.

I introduced myself and asked for Chip.

"Gone up to your place to look around," one of the guys told me. "Somebody picking up lobster pots from the pond ran him over there. Asked to have you wait here for him."

I sat on a bench in front of the station, sipping my coffee. I could even make out my house on the hilltop across the way. Within the hour, Chip Streeter walked up the driveway, a clipboard swinging in his left hand, and what looked like a pair of my rain boots in the other. I stood to greet him.

"You find anything?"

"Sure looks like Bigfoot was roaming around up there."

"What do you mean?"

"I don't want to alarm you too much, but you weren't exaggerating the least bit. There's some impressions in front of the house, going off to the right, that must be your feet. Something with a soft bottom, no ridges?"

I stuck out my foot and showed him the plain sole of my suede moccasin. I nodded my head. That was the direction from which I'd left to go down to the cottage.

"But there's a set of footprints—I guess 'bootprints' is a better word—that circles the entire house. Firm and deep in the mud—"

"Did you take pictures? Can you make an impression of—"

"CSI, we ain't, Alex. Maybe the state police can do that kind of stuff. I'll give 'em a call."

"Could I go back over with you? Sometimes there's such a clear imprint that you can make out the brand and size of the footwear."

"Suit yourself. Road crew is out already, trying to clear the debris away. Somebody can drive over with you in an hour or two, if you're willing to hang around. You ought to know that whoever it was tracked inside the house, too. All over, like he was looking for you, or for something you had."

I sat back down on the bench, trying to think about who this could possibly have been.

"Alex, you got any ideas? You'll have to look the place over and tell us whether anything is missing. I checked the usual stuff—TV, CD player—all that's still there. I got no way of knowing about your personal things, cash or jewelry. Thought you might need these to get around, though."

Streeter handed me the boots. I removed the damp moccasins and pulled on the heavier gear.

"I'd like to ride over when you get the chance. I didn't have anything valuable with me." I didn't think my visitor was a petty thief, but there was no point pressing the issue with Streeter.

"Well, hang around and make yourself at home. They got some doughnuts down at the Texaco station. That's about all we got to offer so far today."

"Sounds perfect."

"Ever see those photographs of the thirty-eight

storm, the one that washed out half of Menemsha and killed scores of folk all over the area?"

"Yeah."

"Check out the beach parking lot. Doesn't exist anymore. It's covered with mounds of sand, rocks the size of my head, dead fish everywhere. Makes you understand that mean old hurricane and why so many people died back then. Puts your own bad night in perspective."

It was only a short walk from police headquarters, past the closed shops and fish stores, to the gas dock at the marina adjacent to the state beach and jetty. I was stunned by the amount of destruction that Gretchen had visited on this strip of land. This was the road I had driven down the night before last, and now it was clear that water had breached the beachfront and swamped the pavement, making it unrecognizable as the same ground.

I stepped in sandpiles that came up to the tops of my knee-high boots, bypassing crabs and shellfish that had been crushed by the waves. The *Unicorn* and *Quitsa Strider,* massive steel commercial-fishing boats, had weathered the storm just fine. But the old shacks that bordered the waterfront had thrown off shingles and shutters, pieces of wooden board sticking out from the sand all along the way that I walked.

The lone outpost at the end of the road was a small gray building just beyond the harbormaster. On the land side, the gas pumps that fueled our cars were half-covered with what had once been Menemsha's beach. The other side was known as Squid

Row, where boats gassed up before heading back out to sea, through the Bight, onto the corner at Devil's Bridge, where Vineyard Sound met the Atlantic Ocean. On a given morning, the old-timers filled the benches there, trading yarns and fish tales, while cabin cruisers vied for space at the dock with working boats that trolled the waters for blues and stripers.

Cassie, the sixteen-year-old girl who usually pumped my gas, held open the door for me when she saw me coming in. "Hey, Alex, wasn't that awesome last night?"

"Guess so. Hope you were home with your folks."

"Yep. Drove down here this morning but had to leave the car at the top of the hill and walk down 'cause of the sand and all. Picked up some stuff from Humphrey's," she said, lifting the lid on a box of pastries and baked goods. "Got a little generator, too, so we have some coffee brewed. Help yourself."

She turned away and walked to the door that opened onto the dock, pushing it and sticking her head out for a look at something. "Hey, Ozzie," she called out to one of the ancient mariners seated with their backs against the shop, "let me know when that big one pulls in. I don't want to miss her."

"She's next. Get yourself out here," came the reply.

"Wanna see a beauty?" she asked me. "Fancy yacht out here waiting to fill up."

I poured myself a cup of coffee and grabbed three sugared doughnut holes before stepping out onto the dock and saying hello to several of the regulars who had parked themselves at the water's edge for a bird's-eye view of the day's events. It was certain that there would be no traffic on the land side for the foreseeable future.

By the time I stepped out onto Squid Row, the gleaming black-hulled vessel had maneuvered its way into the harbor and turned around so that its rear end was against the dock, ready to start refueling.

The gold letters shined brightly as the sun glanced off them. *Pirate* was the name of the boat, and its home port was Nantucket. Graham Hoyt's yacht.

I closed my eyes and thought of last night's prowler. Could it possibly have been Graham Hoyt? How could I have forgotten that he was the one who first talked to me about coming to the Vineyard because of the storm?

The first mate and steward, dressed in crisp white sweatshirts with the yacht's name and outline emblazoned on the chest, were tying up along the pier. Cassie was asking them if they needed help and trying to make herself useful.

I started to make small talk with them, too, anxious to find out where they—and their skipper—had spent the previous evening. "She's a beauty. Hope you didn't have anyone on board during that blow last night."

"Had her all safe and sound, thanks, in the lee. No harm done."

"She'd hardly fit here in Menemsha," I said, aware that the marinas in Edgartown and Vineyard Haven would have had no problem docking a boat this size.

"No, no. Over in Nantucket," the mate shot back. "That's her home."

"You guys actually sit it out on the water in this?"

"Captain's orders," he said, looking over at the steward and laughing.

"Must have been rough."

"They don't make enough Dramamine to get you through one of these. And we were damn well sheltered."

Cassie was filling the fuel tanks and surveying the length of the yacht with great admiration.

I laughed, too. "Bet the owner doesn't hang out in the storm with you."

"Are you kidding? He wouldn't leave this baby for a minute. Rode the whole thing through with us. Only his wife got a pass to stay onshore."

"Is that you, Alexandra? I would never have recognized you."

I was startled by the sound of Hoyt's voice. Squinting and shielding my eyes from the sun, I raised my head and saw him in the cockpit on the flying bridge, one flight above the crew.

"I was just trying to call you," he said, waving the cell phone in his hand. "Thought seven A.M. was a respectable time to wake you up. We're heading for the city and needed to gas up. Don't know when the airport will reopen but thought you might want to hitch back with us."

"Way to go, Alex," Cassie said. "Totally cool."

"No thanks, Graham. Cell phones don't work in Menemsha." This sleepy little village was a black hole in the world of cell communications. "There's no tower."

"No tower, no power," he said, shrugging his shoulders. "How about the ride home?"

"Thanks. I may stay on the island for a while," I said, lying to him. I wasn't about to spend another night in the house until the broken glass was replaced and the locks and alarm system were changed. But that didn't mean I was ready to set out on the high seas with Graham Hoyt.

"I bet you won't say no to a hot breakfast. How about you, young lady? Want a tour?"

Cassie had stepped out of her boots and climbed on board without hesitating for a moment. From over my shoulder I heard one of the guys on the bench urging me to follow her. "What are you waitin' for, honey? Don't see one of these big guys pull into town every day. You afraid they's got Bluebeard hiding belowdeck or what?"

I forced a smile and kicked off my boots, winking at the grizzled old-timers. "If they pull out with Cassie and me on board, tell Chip to get the navy after them, okay?"

The men laughed but I wasn't entirely kidding.

Hoyt extended his hand to help me off the ladder, then turned to the steward. "Why don't you tell the chef to set a table on the aft deck for three? Some scrambled eggs and bacon, a fresh pot of coffee, and some juice."

The knots in my stomach were turning somersaults. Perhaps it was because I had not really eaten yesterday, but also because I worried about where Graham Hoyt had been during the storm. What if his crew were covering for him? They had no reason to be setting up a false alibi, I reassured myself. They couldn't possibly have thought that the bedraggled woman in the oversized flannel shirt and the Capri-length chinos was trying to cross-examine them.

"So this is my little folly, Alex. Let me show you two around."

I followed Hoyt and Cassie through the entrance into the yacht's main salon. The entire room was paneled in teakwood, with thick green leather sofas and wool sisal carpeting. Crystal wine goblets hung upside down over the wide bar, notched in place so they wouldn't fly off and break in the fiercest of storms.

"Come see the staterooms," he said, leading us down the aft staircase. The master had a queen-sized bed and full bathroom, and the two smaller rooms were just as exquisitely appointed, in the softest shade of sea foam.

"How big is she?" Cassie asked.

"Ninety-eight feet. A Palmer Johnson. Cruises at twelve and a half knots, holds five thousand gallons of fuel."

Cassie was more interested in the specs than I was, but the thought of the upkeep was overwhelming. It had to cost more than a million dollars a year to keep this toy afloat, with its crew of four and all that went with it.

Back on deck, I leaned over to check whether I could see how far below water the boat's bottom went. "What does she draw?"

"Six feet. We just make it in here."

I noticed a small motorboat tied up alongside us. A

twenty-foot Boston Whaler. For most people, that would have been more than enough of a vessel.

I looked at the gold lettering on the rear of the *Pirate*'s tender: *Rebecca*.

I turned to Hoyt. "Daphne du Maurier?"

"You mean *Rebecca*? Is that what I named her for? You really see murder in everything, don't you, Alex?" Hoyt shook his finger at me.

"Happens to be one of my favorite novels."

"Yes, but my wife would never go out on the water with me, if that was the inspiration for her name. James Gordon Bennett—the first commodore of the yacht club—that's what his boat was called. She's named in his honor."

The steward came back to whisper to Hoyt that our breakfast was about to be served.

"Is there another phone line? Other than the cell, I mean."

"Certainly. We've got satellite phones on board. Todd, will you show Ms. Cooper to the cockpit?"

I wanted to talk to Mike Chapman. I wanted him to know I was on Hoyt's yacht, and confirm his whereabouts last night. This might be the only working phone I would be near all day.

I reached voice mail at his apartment and on his cell. I dialed Mercer Wallace. The captain was working on his route chart right next to me, so I explained where I was without telling the story of the previous night.

"When are you coming back to the city?" Mercer asked.

"Uh—I'm still not quite sure." I wanted to tell him

as soon as the airport was open and I could find some way to get to it, but I couldn't trust the captain not to repeat that to Hoyt.

"You alone there on the *Titanic*?"

"No, no, no. Got one of my local friends here with me, and we're getting right off after breakfast. We won't even leave the dock."

"Well, hurry home, Alex. I'm trying to make progress. Seems that it most likely was Mrs. Gatts's brother-in-law who followed you down to the church last week. His supervisor says he signed out of court at five P.M., just up the street from you. Left the building in his uniform, without changing, which is not his usual pattern. Chief said he seemed in a hurry to go somewhere." That explained the navy blue pants. "And he called in sick the next day—just didn't come to work."

"Anybody keeping an eye on him?"

"They read him the riot act. If we can prove something, they'll suspend him."

"All circumstantial, but it's a start. Anything else before I lose you?"

"Yes, ma'am. Found out yesterday that Tiffany Gatts has some other family ties that might interest you," Mercer said.

"Like who?"

"Seems her boyfriend Kevin had good reason to know about Queenie Ransome and her collection of coins. Tiffany's cousin is the one who let the cat out of the bag, about valuables being in Queenie's apartment."

"I give up, Mercer. Who's her cousin?"

"Spike Logan. Know who I mean? The Harvard guy who lives up on the Vineyard."

I took another breath and thought about the intruder who had frightened me out of my home, into the wind and rain. Spike Logan lived up here. Where the hell was he during last night's storm?

35

Graham Hoyt went down the ladder to the dock ahead of Cassie and me, helping each of us off as we followed.

"When I stop by here next June, young lady," he said to Cassie, "I expect you to take the afternoon off for some waterskiing with the crew."

She gushed with delight and ran back into the mini-market to buy a disposable camera and snap some shots of the *Pirate,* while I thanked Hoyt for breakfast.

We shook hands and he held on to my left elbow, hesitating before he spoke. "You know, Jenna and I are spending the weekend with Dulles. Bringing him onto the boat, cruising up the Hudson and around New York Harbor to try to get him comfortable with us. Maybe, if you get back to town in time—I realize it's only a 'maybe'—but I'd like you to think about meeting us for lunch, to get a sense that Dulles is going to be okay with all this behind him."

The Hoyts were obviously intent on adopting the boy, and I was beginning to think it was hopeless for me to try to guess what would serve the child best in the long run.

"Help him understand that all this—this bad stuff—lawyers, courts, cops—that it's all behind him, Alex. Give him some closure. Give him back his childhood, his life. You represent the bridge between what's past and what kind of future he can have."

"It's a nice idea, but I'm not too optimistic we can end the emotional damage so quickly." I looked away from Hoyt, knowing that the judge wouldn't condone any further delays to dispose of the misdemeanor charges involving Tripping's son, now that the rape case had been tossed. "I may not be able to 'give' him those things any more readily than you can," I said, smiling at Hoyt, "but maybe I can return his baseball jacket. He's entitled to that."

"Yankees, I hope? They're the only thing in his life that provides pure joy. My wife already got some play-off tickets."

"Well, yes, he left his jacket at the hospital the night his father was arrested. We thought it might be his security blanket. Maybe that can be my peace offering, when I do see him."

Hoyt clasped his left hand on top of mine, shook again, and boarded the yacht. "Bet we beat you back to the city, Alex. Sure you don't want to try the high seas?"

"No thanks. Speak to you soon."

I trudged back to police headquarters through the mounds of damp sand. It was several hours until the island came to life again, as power was restored and the pavement cleared. When Chip Streeter got word that the Menemsha Crossroads had opened up, he offered to drive me home so that I could assess the damage and change my clothes.

The sunny fall day had everyone out picking up the debris around their houses. Several utility poles were still down and there were branches scattered everywhere. We pulled off State Road into my driveway, and as we came over the rise, things didn't look as bad as I had feared.

I got out of the car and kneeled to examine the tread marks that the intruder had left in the mud. An expert could easily match the marks to a shoe brand, which was likely to be all too common to be significant.

"Yup," Streeter said, "the state troopers took photos and measurements, and some kind of cast of the prints. Dusted around inside, too."

This wasn't the first time my home had been a crime scene. I knew that it wasn't going to be pretty. We went in and looked over the mess that had been tracked through. Once again, I felt shocked and unsettled at the sight of my belongings in such disarray. There was still no electricity or water, so the cleanup would be a job for my caretaker, when he returned to the island.

"Wanna see if anything's missing?"

"Sure," I said, walking from room to room, checking the obvious places and opening drawers and closets. Nothing seemed out of place. In the bedroom, I looked into my sail bag and purse. "Missing some cash. About a hundred and fifty dollars."

"See? Probably just an ordinary break-in, somebody looking for a quick score."

There was no point telling him about Spike Logan. I'd let Mike and Mercer work that angle, and allow Streeter to keep thinking this was just a petty theft. The island was so small, such an insular community, that there was no way of knowing who was connected to whom. In my book, taking the money was just a convenient way for my visitor to show me that he had been there, that he might come again.

"I figured I'd wait for you to change and drop you at the airport."

"That's too much trouble. I can get myself—"

"I got to go down-island to Shirley's Hardware to pick up some tools for repairs at the station. I'd rather not leave you here alone."

I was glad about that. "It will just take me a minute." I closed the bedroom door, pulled out a pair of jeans and a sweater from my closet, and folded the borrowed chinos and shirt for Streeter to return.

We drove to the airport, twisting our way around the assortment of storm-tossed things in the roadway. I thanked him when I got out of the car and joined the short line of impatient city folk waiting at the counter for word about air service to New York.

It looked like a special direct flight would leave for La Guardia at 6 P.M.

The day was a wash. My cell phone, uncharged for more than twenty-four hours, was dead. The telephone kiosks, which afforded no privacy, were in steady use by anxious travelers trying to find alternate ways to get to Providence, Boston, Hartford, and points west. I spun the paperback rack in the gift shop and found only the good books I had read in hardcover months earlier. There was a British thriller by a writer I'd never tried before, so I settled in a corner window seat and killed the time with crime fiction.

Somewhere in the northeast corridor, the airline had come up with a DC-3 to lug us home. It rolled to a stop outside the terminal, looking as if it had just come over the hump from Burma in a World War II flick. We boarded quickly, climbing up the sloping aisle to get into our seats. The normally short flight took almost ninety minutes, and it was close to 8 P.M. when I walked out of the New York terminal to hail a taxi.

Hot running water. I stripped down and turned on the shower full force. Mud was still caked between my toes and under each nail. I must have been a sight to all of the evening's air travelers. My matted hair looked several shades darker than before the storm, and I scrubbed for minutes until I could even get a lather going.

Dried off and snug in a long nightshirt, I sat on the bed and played back the eleven messages on the machine, hoping to hear one voice. I deleted Nina's news about her son's admission to a Beverly Hills pre-k; my mother's concern about the damage caused by the hurricane; three routine messages from Mike, who wasn't really sure where to find me; an assortment of nonurgent friendly calls; and found Jake on the ninth try.

"Hey, guess you decided to stay on after all." His voice sounded cool and clipped, and I had missed him by less than half an hour. "I'm off for supper with a friend. Be home for the weekend." Too much silence. "We need to talk, Alex."

The one thing I needed less than root canal was to talk. Whatever happened to action?

Good old action. Talk was going to expose every layer of difference between us, every nitpicking reason we weren't good for each other. His walking in the door and taking me in his arms and making me feel sexy and safe and adored was what I wanted more than anything at this very moment. Talk was as overrated as renewing marriage vows on top of a Hawaiian volcano to assuage a cheating husband's guilt.

No answer at Mike's place. I put on some music and sat at my desk, rereading the case files on Paige Vallis—the rape and the homicide—to see whether I could make sense of the directions things had taken in her life. No sense, no nothing. I moved to the mountain of bills growing beside me and took out my checkbook.

I crawled into bed before ten, hit with the exhaustion that follows shock and stress. Sleep helped, and I was up by 8 A.M. on Saturday, ready for a better day.

The first call was from Mercer Wallace. "Any trouble getting back into town?"

"The only easy thing that's happened in days. Look, I've got to—"

He and I were speaking over each other. I heard him say "I have news for—" but he stopped and asked me to finish what I had started.

"I've got to tell you what happened to me during the storm." I described the way my predator had circled the house trying to get in, and how I had escaped him. Unlike Chip Streeter, Mercer understood that this was no amateur, no coincidence, no joke.

"I'll get on the Spike Logan angle. Check out his car, his uncle. Make sure Hoyt was really in Nantucket on the boat. Speak to the troopers and see what they came up with."

"I'm sorry I jumped in over you. You had something to tell me?" I asked.

"Plate came back yesterday on that car you thought you saw Robelon driving when you chased the guy with the gun out of Federal Plaza. It's a rental."

"To Robelon?"

"Nope. Ever heard of a Lionel Webster?"

"No. Who is he?"

"I think he's the guy who's pretending to be Harry Strait. My lieutenant ran Webster last night and there's all kinds of info flooding back in this morning. He's ordered us to work overtime on it all weekend. Best I can tell, Webster is some kind of soldier of fortune. A mercenary. Services go to the highest bidder. Knows the caves of Tora Bora as well as he does Paris."

"Armed services?" I thought of Andrew Tripping and his fascination with all things military.

"West Point grad. Taught there for a while until he was kicked out. Stripped of his commission—"

"For?"

"You're thinking faster than I can read. I'm not sure it gives a reason in these papers. We'll get him checked out ASAP."

"Can you fax over a picture?"

"Hold your horses, Ms. Cooper. You might have to make an ID, you know. You're not getting any advance look at my mug shots."

"The buzz cut fits with the military background, Mercer. I wish we knew if the U.S. armed services had anything to do with King Farouk." The pieces of the puzzle were twisting in my mind.

"Only thing I know about is the Agency and its involvement in Cairo. Not the army. Although that lovely lady at Treasury we met with before you went to the country called me back with a nice little nugget of information."

"Lori Alvino? Don't hold out on me, Mercer."

"I don't know whether our military had anything to do with Farouk, but it did touch the wings of the Double Eagle."

"The coin? Are you talking about the coin?" Mercer knew his mention of new information was a teaser.

"Yes, ma'am, I am. That bird is mighty lucky she didn't have her wings clipped."

"What do you know?"

"Alvino had gotten us all as far as the Secret Service intercepting Farouk's coin when it was brought back into the U.S. in ninety-six."

"I was with you in her office. I heard that."

"She has tracked down its whereabouts after the ninety-six arrival here, and before the auction in 2002. Wanted to confirm it for us."

"Nice. And?"

"It was actually stored and safeguarded in the

Treasury Department vaults during the legal battles about who owned it."

"You mean Fort Knox?"

"Closer to home. For five years, the Double Eagle lived in a vault in the basement of the World Trade Center. Seven World Trade Center, to be exact."

I thought again of how often I had looked out my office window at those towers before September 11. So many lives lost in an instant of evil. The property losses mattered to me not at all.

Mercer went on. "A few months before the attacks, the coin was moved. Just a coincidence."

"To?"

"The bullion depository of the United States Mint."

"Where's that?"

"It's up at West Point, Ms. Cooper. You can't get any more militarily connected than that. The Double Eagle wound up quartered at the Point, in its bullion depository, overlooking the Hudson River."

"You put that upstate tour on the agenda for this week?"

"Mike wants to wait till the Army–Navy game next month to make that trip," he joked. "Anyway, he's going to pick you up in half an hour, if that's okay with you. I'm meeting you both at Peter Robelon's office. I reached him at home just now and told him it was urgent we see him this morning. We'll try to confront him about that encounter you had with Harry Strait."

"See you later."

The phone rang again as soon as I hung up. "Hello, Alex? You make it back all right?"

It was Chip Streeter, the Vineyard cop, checking on me. "Just fine. I appreciate all the time you gave me. Not to mention a dry place to sleep. I've got to run, but thanks for calling."

"I actually need your help for a minute. You know a guy on the island named Logan? Spike Logan?"

"Yeah. Yeah, I know who he is." Strange that Streeter should be asking about him.

"Was he up your way the other day?"

"No. But—why?"

"Found his car pulled off the road down by the Stonewall Bridge, coming from the direction of your house to Beetlebung Corner. Looks like it flooded out during the storm. Kinda abandoned."

"Anything in it? Any weapons, any—"

"Just a pair of boots, Alex. Fit the imprints in the mud around your house. Same size, same tread design, same maker logo. State troopers confirmed that for me."

"And Logan? Have you looked for him?" I asked more frantically than I meant to. "Have you been to the house he stays in? Have you asked—?"

"Made a lot of calls and visits last evening and stopped by again this morning. Just wanted to know whether he was an acquaintance of yours," Chip said. "Just wanted you to know that he's out there somewhere. Pretty sure he's gone off-island."

36

I was waiting inside the lobby of my apartment building when Mike's car drove up in front. "Yo, blondie," Mike shouted. "Let's hit the road."

Mercer had called to tell him about my Vineyard experience, and he was furious with me. "You lied to me, Coop. You let me think Jake was going to be there with you."

"It was true when I first told you that."

"He wimped out? Why doesn't that surprise me?"

"No, he didn't. The flights weren't going and I didn't want him to drive up. Adam," I said quietly. "You know."

"So you and Bigfoot played hide-and-seek instead, huh?"

"And now the police just called because they think my visitor might have been Spike Logan." I told Mike what Streeter had said about the washed-out car and the boots that were in it.

"Or his passenger. Coulda had somebody with him. Sounds too obvious to me to leave his car right where it was bound to be found. Maybe it's a setup,"

Mike said. He looked over at me as we headed uptown. "That won't stop you from scanning the horizon for the Spikester, right?"

I was staring off at the boats churning up water in the East River. "Tell me something good, then. Take my mind off mindless things. How's Val?"

He drew in breath before he answered. "That's a heartbreaker. She doesn't want me to tell anyone, but you gotta know. The docs found some more nodes. More—what do they call it?—involvement."

I looked over at him but he kept his focus straight ahead. "They doing chemo?"

"First surgery and then chemo. She's the toughest fighter I've ever met."

I reached over and put my hand on Mike's wrist, but when he made a left turn onto the Drive, his arm moved and I wasn't holding anything.

He continued to ask questions about the storm most of the way, and to cross-examine me about what had happened at the house. We parked around the corner and met Mercer in the lobby of the large commercial complex that housed Robelon's office.

Robelon was expecting us. "What's the posse here for?" he said, looking at me but pointing to the men on either side of me.

"This time I'm just the witness, not the prosecutor. They've got some questions for you."

"Like what?"

"Like who's your buddy?" Mike asked. "The guy who enjoys pretending he's the late great Strait."

"What?"

"The dude who sat in the back of the courtroom when Paige Vallis testified?"

"How would I know who was sitting behind me? I was looking at the witness."

"Let me—what do you say, Coop?—let me refresh your recollection, Counselor. The uptight guy who looks like he had his hair cut by Sergeant Bilko. The one whose rental car you were tooling around town in last week," Mike said.

Robelon pushed back from his desk and played with a pencil, tapping it against his left thumb. "I've got no idea what you mean. I thought you had something urgent to discuss, Mr. Wallace? Try not to act like you've picked up all your techniques on television, Detective." He raised his right leg and rested it on a desk drawer. His disdain for Chapman was palpable.

"Shit, you're probably right. I woulda been a bartender if it wasn't for *Law and Order*. Wouldn't have to put up with empty suits like you. There's the lovely Miss Cooper, running down the street last week in those ridiculous high heels she favors, trying to hail a cab, and you didn't even stop for her. Downright rude."

"I don't know what the hell you're talking about. Alex? Cab?"

"Thomas Street," I said, "you were—"

"Keep a lid on it, Coop. Think back to Wednesday, Counselor. A black sedan with rental plates. Parked on Thomas Street. Maybe it was a stranger who screamed at you to open the door and jumped inside holding a gun, is that it?"

Robelon kicked the desk drawer shut and crossed his legs. He yelled to his secretary, "Mrs. Kaye, you want to show these people the way out?"

She hadn't heard him clearly and came to the door of his office to look inside and ask him to repeat what he said.

"Lionel Webster, also known as Harry Strait. You got a second job as his limo driver?" Mike asked.

Mrs. Kaye looked confused. "Did you want me to get Mr. Webster on the phone?"

Robelon was fuming. He held up his hand and spun it around, motioning the secretary to back out of the room. Sorry, no doubt, he had made her come in for the impromptu weekend meeting.

Mike was on his feet, lifting the lid on the humidor and helping himself to a cigar.

"I'm so glad you weren't about to give me that 'I don't know any Lionel what-did-you-say-his-name-is?' Give that broad a raise. She saved your ass just now."

"Yeah, and I'd like to tell you what to stick up yours if there wasn't a lady present."

"Who, her?" Mike said, pointing the cigar at me. "That's no lady. Help yourself. She's just a louche broad masquerading behind a Wellesley degree and a fine pair of pins. Nothing you can say to me she hasn't said herself. So about Lionel Webster, what can you tell us?"

"Haven't seen him in a dog's age."

"Why don't you just talk to me about him? Everything you know."

"Whatever happened to attorney-client privilege, or don't you believe in that either?"

"Oh, so now he's your client, not your employee? Wasn't he working for you, trying to spook Paige Vallis?"

"This interview is over," Robelon said. "And Alex, don't ever try to sandbag me again, okay? You want me to answer questions, there's a proper way to do that. I didn't see Webster on Wednesday and if he had anything to do with you and some kind of chase, I can promise you I don't have the first clue about it."

Mercer's pager went off and he reached into his pocket to shut it down. The loud beeps seemed to signal the meeting's end.

Peter Robelon was holding the door open for us. It was probably the wrong time to ask another question but I gave it a shot.

"Do you know where Andrew Tripping is?"

He looked down at his right foot as he pawed at the carpeting. "You guys don't get it, do you? I represent him, Alex, remember?"

"No, no, no. I'm not going to do an end run. I mean, can we get to the courtroom in a couple of weeks and put this whole thing to bed?" I asked.

Peter seemed surprised by my offer, debating whether to talk with me. "There's a—there's a meeting this morning. Andrew and the child welfare agency lawyers—they're getting him together with his son. It's all supervised. Planned for today so he wouldn't miss another school day. Don't worry, Dulles won't be alone with him. Give me a call later on."

The elevator doors opened and the three of us got on.

"What do you think?" Mike asked. He lighted the cigar as we hit the sidewalk.

Mercer retrieved the number on his pager as I answered. "That we can't trust him. He's the target in an investigation pending with my office, remember that? I just don't think you can believe what he says. Who's the beep from?"

"Unfamiliar number. I'll call it now," Mercer said.

"You sure that was Robelon behind the wheel on Wednesday?"

I rolled my eyes at Mike. "Please don't start second-guessing me. If you two don't believe in me, who will? I had a pretty good look at the guy and yes, it was Peter Robelon."

"This is Mercer Wallace. Did you call me?" He was leaning against Mike's car and talking into his cell phone. He stood straight and gave us a thumbs-up. "Sure, I've got time to help you, Mrs. Gatts. No, no, I don't blame you for not wanting to talk to that homicide detective. Yeah, I can. Sure."

"What kind of stroke job is he getting now from that tub of lard?" Mike asked.

"The numbers joint on One Hundred and Eighteenth and Pleasant? You stay put in your house. I'm on it."

"What's she got?"

"Bessemer's back," Wallace said, pounding his fist on the hood of the car. "C'mon, unlock your batmobile and run me over to One Hundred and Eighteenth. Kevin Bessemer just showed up, high as a kite and looking to score. Drugs and the daily number. Sooner or later they all come back round."

"You, blondie. Backseat. Buckle up and keep your yap shut. Maybe Kevin'll tell you who the real money-bags is behind the whole operation. Find who paid to hire Helena Lisi for Tiffany."

Mike reached under his seat and lifted the red bubble dome to the dashboard. He tested the whelper to make sure it was working and wheeled out of his parking space, headed back to the northbound FDR Drive.

Mercer was on the phone, calling the precinct to talk to the squad lieutenant. "Get your men over to Limpy's place. Kevin Bessemer, the snitch who—"

The lieutenant didn't need a scorecard. He knew the players. Especially the one who'd taken himself out of the lineup.

"Don't you want to grab him yourselves?" I asked.

"And take the chance we knew where he was and let him get away again?" Mike said. "They'll hold him there for us and then we'll get to eyeball him."

Mercer dialed again. "Limpy? Wallace here. That scumbag you got hanging out? Yeah, that's the one. The cavalry's coming. No, no, not to worry. They're not there to break your balls—they just want Bessemer. Don't let him outta your sight, okay?"

"Why'd you give him a heads-up?"

"Good guy, Alex. He's worked with us for a long time. Runs a pretty clean operation. Does numbers on the side. Just didn't want him to panic when the men in blue burst in. Limpy's bigger than I am, so Bessemer won't be going anywhere."

"How's he going to hold down an out-of-control junkie, high on crack? He limps, no?" I asked.

"Not his leg," Mike said. "Limp dick. That's how he got his name. Ex-wife gave it to him and it stuck."

We were almost there when Mercer's cell rang.

"Be there in two minutes," Mercer said. He repeated the rest of the conversation to us. "Bessemer's acting like a wild man. Limpy has him pinned in a chair in the basement with the cops at the top of the stairs."

We pulled up to the building that housed the newsstand that was the front for the illegal numbers business. Mike and Mercer got out and went inside. I stepped onto the curb and explained to the two uniformed cops posted beside the open door that I was just waiting for the detectives to bring the prisoner out.

I could hear Kevin Bessemer screaming at the top of his lungs. There was a sound like furniture crashing around the room, and Wallace's deep voice telling him, "Stop kicking, man. Stop breaking up the place. Calm down."

They were on the staircase now and the scuffling noises continued, getting closer. Bessemer was kicking the walls and cursing.

One of the cops felt it necessary to apologize to me for the perp's foul language. "That's the crack talking, ma'am. Sorry you have to hear it."

Mike backed out of the store before the two detectives holding the cuffed prisoner. "You're the Kentucky Fried Chicken man, no? Two breasts and some wings—to go. Right out the fire escape with Tiffany. You ought to watch the Food Network more often, Kev," Mike said, faking a punch in his direction. "*Bam!* Take it down a notch, Kev."

Mercer came out behind the prisoner. "Let's get

him over to Met to sleep off his high. Psycho him before we think about going to court."

Metropolitan Hospital was only a five-minute
drive. The psych ward there had seen far worse than
Kevin Bessemer.

"So, Kev, tell the nice lady who your lawyer is.
Your real lawyer."

"I got the best money can buy," Bessemer
screamed, twisting against his captors and kicking at
the car tires on the RMP. "I got Clarence Friggin'
Darrow. I got Johnnie Friggin' Cochran. I got
Clarence Friggin' Thomas working for me. They
gonna 'peal my case up to the Supreme Court."

One of the cops grabbed the crown of his head and
pushed it down, trying to get Bessemer off the street
and into the patrol car as a small crowd began to
gather.

"What about Tiffany?" Mike asked. "Tell me who
to talk to so Tiffany isn't left out there to swing in the
breeze."

"Fuck Tiffany," Bessemer shouted, lying back on
the rear seat of the car and hurling his feet against the
door as the cop tried to close it. "Tell that Spike Logan I'm coming back for a piece of what *he* got."

37

"I'll catch up with you two later in the day. Let me go on down to the hospital and sit by his bedside. Maybe when Bessemer sobers up, he'll be willing to talk to me," Mercer said.

I got into the passenger seat and while Mike drove downtown toward my office, I tried to page the child welfare lawyers—Irizzary and Taggart—to learn what had happened at the meeting with Andrew and Dulles Tripping.

The phone was ringing as I walked in. It was Peter Robelon. "You've got news?" I asked him.

He was still angry about this morning. "Can we strike a deal? I act like a gent and you keep your goons away from me when you want to talk."

"Depends on whatever deals you've worked out with Jack Kliger."

Robelon was silent. It was obvious he had thought I didn't know that he was the target of an investigation in our office. "That's below the belt."

"So is everything that's happened to this poor kid for his entire life. Don't use Dulles as a pawn, Peter.

Why are you fighting to keep Andrew Tripping out of jail?"

Why hadn't I played hardball earlier in the day? He seemed to be loosening up.

"Look, Alex, the boy's meeting with Andrew didn't go as well as expected. Mr. Irizzary told me Dulles was—well—was kind of freaked out by his father."

"And that surprises you? Your client's a very weird guy. So what's next?"

Robelon was squirming. "The lawyers are considering another possibility."

"Giving the Hoyts temporary custody?"

"Yeah. They're taking him over to the Chelsea Piers where Hoyt's docked. Play some ball, shoot some hoops, let him go out on the river for the weekend."

"Don't you think that's good for Dulles?"

He was silent again.

"Put aside your personal feelings for Graham Hoyt," I said. "Do you think he and his wife are sincere about wanting to adopt the boy?"

"Actually, I do. Hoyt's a pretentious bastard, but he adores Jenna, and she's devastated about being childless. She'd be a great mother, and they both have a lot to give to Dulles—between Jenna's warmth and Graham's, well, material blessings."

"Look, Andrew's your client, so I'm not asking you to say anything about him. But he's the last guy I'd want to see playing Mr. Mom."

"Doesn't mean he killed anyone, Alex. Doesn't even mean he raped anyone."

"We're just going around in circles. Thanks for letting me know the conversation is over," I said, ready to end it.

"That's only part of the reason I called."

"What's the rest?"

"Any chance I could meet with you alone, just to talk over some ideas I had about Paige Vallis's murder? Just the two of us—no cops?"

Not a prayer. "We're alone right now, Peter. Why don't you tell me what's on your mind?"

"I'd prefer not to do it on the phone."

"That's all I have time for at the moment."

He didn't pause for very long. "Andrew has a theory."

"I was almost ready to go along with you," I said. "His theories don't really interest me all that much, Peter."

"Hear me out, Alex. The reason Paige Vallis left her apartment and went downstairs the night she was killed? It's about you."

I sat up and started writing notes as he spoke. "That's ridiculous, Peter. If you're trying to make me feel worse about her death than I already do, then just keep on talking full-speed ahead."

"It's true. We're sure of it."

"'We' being you and that terribly unhinged psycho you represent?"

"Listen for a minute. Andrew thinks he can prove that the reason Paige went downstairs from her apartment last Friday night was to mail a letter to you, to send something she needed you to know, to have."

I was sweeping aside documents and law journals

and case reports that had stacked up on my desk while I was out of town. Laura had sorted the mail from the past two days but I had buried it under the papers I had carried in this morning, so I looked for return addresses or unmarked envelopes that might possibly be from Paige Vallis.

"Like what?" I was making more of a mess, agitated by Peter's suggestion.

"I'm not sure, Alex. But Andrew—well, when I see you—"

"I'll call you back later. Let me look around." There was also three days of mail at home that I had not even touched, other than to pay some of the bills.

Mike had followed me in. "What'd that loser want?"

"To see me alone. Without you—or my goons, as he so politely implied. He says Tripping thinks Paige Vallis ran into her killer on her way from sending some midnight missive to me. Does that make sense to you?"

"That I'm a goon?" Mike was lifting papers and shuffling through things on my desktop. "Nah."

"I mean the letter to me."

"Like a suicide note? Like she sent you an apology for causing you such a hard time at the trial and then choked herself to death in her hallway? I don't think so."

"I don't either. Wouldn't she have called to tell me what she wanted to say, or if she was frightened, left me a message that she was mailing me something?"

"He's a whackjob, the Tripping guy. A complete paranoid. Next thing Robelon's going to tell you is that she sent you a letter recanting her allegations, saying she made up the whole story about the rape. That's what he and Tripping want you to believe. That and the fact that the mailman lost the letter."

"You're probably right."

"Sure I am. This way, you don't just dismiss the indictment against him in a couple of weeks, you get to exonerate him completely, with Vallis permanently out of the way."

I looked up at Mike. "Good thinking."

"Yeah, that one goes in the dead-letter department. What's next?"

"I thought we'd take a ride over to Chelsea Piers. Try to catch up with the happy campers before the child welfare agency lawyers cut out. See what went wrong at this morning's meeting between Dulles and his dad, and what the thinking is about the Hoyts as prospective parents," I said, and filled him in on what Robelon had told me.

"Nice day for an outing. Saturday afternoon on the river. Sure you didn't have enough water this week?"

"The sun's out now, it's a crisp fall day. I'll spring for hot dogs. If we get lucky, Hoyt's chef'll cook you a meal."

It was a little after one o'clock when we left the office and drove across Canal Street to get to the West Side Highway. "Don't ever tell my mother I took you to the Chelsea Piers. You know her and her superstitions. All bad things come in threes," Mike said.

"So what were the first two?"

"That's where the *Titanic* was supposed to dock on

its maiden voyage, before that ice cube got in its way. And the *Lusitania*? She sailed from Chelsea on her regular run to London when the U-boat got her."

"You look at the place now and it's hard to believe it was the world's premier passenger ship terminal once." We drove north to Twenty-third Street, crossing onto the Hudson River Boulevard and parking in one of the large lots.

The Chelsea Piers, opened in 1910 to house the Atlantic's luxury liners, were a stunning urban design complex by the same firm that built Grand Central Terminal. The elegant row of gray buildings, edged with pink granite facades, took the place of a mess of crumbling, old waterfront structures of the nineteenth century.

In both world wars, the piers became the embarkation point for soldiers heading off to battle. By the 1960s, when air travel had made most ocean crossings obsolete, the decaying buildings were converted to cargo facilities. And when that part of the business relocated to the ports of New Jersey a decade later, the once-grand piers were demoted to use as warehouses, car pounds, and sanitation-truck repair stations.

By 1995, after a few years' work based on a proposal by three smart developers, the four surviving Chelsea Piers—numbered 59 through 62—were transformed through a $100 million project into a spectacular center for public recreation right on Manhattan's waterfront. Golf driving ranges, batting cages, roller rinks, bowling, an equestrian center, and a marina that could handle yachts like Graham Hoyt's were only some of the amusements available on the Piers.

"What's your guess?"

"Let's start at the boat. At least the crew is bound to be there, someone who should know where Hoyt and the kid are," I said.

We took the promenade south of what they called the golf club and walked along yachts in the marina, looking for the *Pirate*. There was a warm breeze coming off the water, and although it seemed a bit choppy, it was deep blue and clean. A maze of small boats crisscrossed the river, and the commuter ferries worked the waves in both directions.

Graham Hoyt saw us before we spotted him. He was behind us, coming from one of the other parking lots. "You have any jurisdiction on the high seas, Detective?"

"Aye, aye, Cap—what do you need?"

"Left here twenty minutes ago to take Ms. Taggart back to her car and answer some questions for her. Could have sworn I had ninety-eight feet of a fine-looking boat sitting right at the end of that dock," he said, pointing. "Grand larceny, I think."

The small tender, the *Rebecca*, was tied up, but the slip for the larger vessel was empty.

"Are you serious?" I asked.

"Either that or my crew has mutinied, Alex. Maybe I worked them too hard on the way down from the islands."

He was laughing, so it was clear that no one had made off with the boat.

"Where's the boy, Mr. Hoyt?" Mike asked.

"Jenna took him over to one of those buildings in the sports complex. Todd, our first mate, was going to hit some balls with him, just play and hang out. Let him be a kid for a change. Guess the captain decided to go for a ride in the meantime. Want to go have a look for Dulles and my wife?"

"Sure."

We retraced our steps at Mike's suggestion. "The batting cages are in the field house, up between the first two piers. Eighty thousand square feet of pure heaven for a kid. This was a good idea of yours. They've got hoops there as well as baseball and gymnastics equipment. You ever been here before?"

Hoyt shook his head. "Only the marina."

Mike was leading the tour. "That's the building where they film all the TV shows, you know, like—"

"*Graham!*"

A woman was screaming Hoyt's name at the top of her lungs. The first two times we each heard it and looked around, unable to find her among the hordes of adolescents who had taken over the Piers' activity centers on the busy weekend.

"Jenna—what is it?"

I turned and saw a diminutive woman running toward Hoyt. She was dressed in a T-shirt, cotton slacks, and sneakers. Her face was contorted into an expression suggesting she was in pain, and she was weeping as she came at us.

"What's the matter?" he said, grabbing both arms and trying to calm her down. "Is it Dulles? Where is he?"

She caught her breath and tried to speak. "He's okay. But it was frightening, it was terribly frightening."

The more she tried to talk, the harder she cried.

"Tell me what it is," Hoyt said, sternly now, enunciating each word between clenched teeth, ordering her to explain whatever had happened.

"Mrs. Hoyt," I said, trying a softer approach by putting my arm around her shoulder and taking her hand in mine. "Please tell—"

She ignored me and talked to her husband. "It was Andrew. That meeting he had with Dulles this morning, before Nancy Taggart brought him here? Andrew was angry that it broke up so abruptly."

She stopped again to take some deep breaths.

"Damn it," said Graham. "He just can't let go of the boy."

"Andrew actually followed them here. That Taggart woman must be an idiot," Mrs. Hoyt said, her tears replaced by anger. "She led him right to us."

"Did Andrew do anything? Did he go anywhere near Dulles?"

"No, not that close. But—"

"Where the hell were you? What was going on? Where's Dulles?"

"I was sitting in the stands on the side, watching him play. I didn't even see Andrew." She was beginning to whine now, seeing that Graham was getting frantic over something that she had not been able to control. "Next thing I know Dulles looks up and just freaks out. He saw his father standing twenty feet away, just staring at him, holding on to the wire cage."

Hoyt was looking all around now. "Where are they?"

"It's okay, Graham. Todd scooped Dulles up and started running. Right to the boat. I—I couldn't keep up. I decided to try to block Andrew, to get in his way so he wouldn't be able to catch them."

She pointed down at her torn slacks. She must have fallen and scraped her knee. There was still fresh blood. Hoyt didn't seem interested in her bruise.

"Todd and the boy?"

"I saw them get on the *Pirate*. I saw the captain pull out into the river."

"Which way?"

"North."

"You sure?"

She was pointing now, and the magnificent steel bones of the George Washington Bridge stood in the distant background as if they were painted against the sky.

Mike and I were more worried about the fact that Andrew Tripping had begun to stalk his own child.

He spoke before I did. "Tripping? Did you see which way Tripping went?"

"We got entangled in each other. That's how I fell. He got up and started running—"

"After Dulles?" Graham asked.

"No, no. The other way. He ran toward a black car that was parked near the taxi drop-off area," Jenna said. "Over that way."

"You see him get in?" Mike asked.

"Yeah."

"Driver's side?"

"No, no. Someone was already waiting there, in the car. Another man."

Mike and Graham Hoyt were speaking at the same time, with different concerns.

"That son of a bitch was coming after Dulles, to take him away from us. To kidnap him. Had a car waiting and everything," Hoyt said, turning away from his wife.

Mike wanted to know what the man in the car looked like.

"He was a white guy. Short hair, thin face."

"Lionel Webster."

"Who's got a gun, Mike," I reminded him.

"She's yours," he said, telling Jenna Hoyt to stay with me till he got back or got word to us later.

Mike jogged in the direction of the parking garage, talking into his cell phone as he did.

Graham Hoyt took off the other way, toward his sleek-looking speedboat, the *Pirate*'s tender tied up at the end of the dock. Jenna followed behind him, favoring her bruised leg. I ran after them, overtaking her quickly and trailing behind her husband.

Halfway down the pier, Jenna let out a groan. I looked back and saw her doubled over, kneading a cramp out of her calf. She waved us on.

Graham Hoyt took care of the slipknot and tossed the rope onto the clean white rear seat of the boat, bounding in after it. "We're going for the boy," he called out to his wife.

He held out his hand and I jumped on as he juiced the motor and headed upriver.

38

The bow of the Whaler crashed against the waves, and the second speed bump threw me down onto the seat. Graham Hoyt was holding the wheel, driving the powerful craft hard, running it between and around the river traffic. Spray from the cold river was splashing over the sides, carried by the wind, soaking my hair and face.

Hoyt looked back at me. "Stay down, okay?"

I nodded that I would.

With his left hand he picked up a walkie-talkie device, trying to raise his captain on it.

Seconds later came the reply that he could be heard.

"We're in the tender, trying to catch up to you. Is Dulles okay?"

The machine crackled as the answer was transmitted. I could hear the captain say that the boy was "just fine."

Hoyt asked how far ahead they were, and I thought I heard the words "Spuyten Duyvil," which was just a few miles north. He replaced the device on the dashboard and turned to me with a smile, slowing the speed a bit. My stomach had been churning as the boat slammed against the water over and over. Now I was able to let go of my firm grip on the edge of the seat.

"He's good, Alex," Hoyt said, flashing me a grin. I could barely hear him over the sound of the engine.

I called out from the back of the boat, "You're both really determined to get him through all this. That's clear."

He was relaxed now. "I only hope Jenna can put up with Andrew's nonsense until we get a judge to formalize the arrangement. I've raised a lot of money for children's organizations around the world, Alex. It's Jenna's passion, and we've been pleased to do it. All those orphans in Bosnia and Afghanistan and East Africa. What the hell else is there but kids, in the end? I've thrown a lot of my money into making kids' lives better."

Somebody had just been talking to me about a corporate lawyer who donated money to children's charities. The wind whipped my hair into my eyes and mouth, and I tried to recall the conversation. I remembered, too, there was a scam involved.

We had passed the Seventy-ninth Street boat basin and were parallel with the West Side Highway. I took my cell phone from my pocket and called Mercer Wallace to see whether he had any word from Mike.

"Hey, where are you?"

"With Graham Hoyt, trying to catch up to the big boat to find Dulles. Halfway between Hoboken and Harlem, on the water. You heard anything from—"

"I'm telling you right this minute, Alexandra, lower yourself into the drink if you have to, but get yourself back to shore this very minute."

"What's wrong?"

Hoyt must have heard the change in my voice and looked around at me. I smiled at him and shrugged my shoulders. "Just checking with my deputy to make sure nothing serious came up while I was on the Vineyard. She's home with her kids."

"Is anyone else with you?" Mercer asked.

"No."

"You close to any place he can dock or pull in?"

"Not far."

Hoyt kept checking back on me.

"Is it Mike? Did he get Andrew Tripping?"

"I haven't heard a thing from Mike. I got another glitch."

"Like what?"

"Just you come home."

"You've got to tell me so I know what I'm dealing with here," I said, hoping the concern in my whispered words hadn't been carried to Hoyt by the wind.

"After I left Kevin Bessemer at the hospital, I stopped by to see Tiffany's mother. Thank her for calling in the tip."

"Yeah."

"Remember Tiffany told us she took something from Queenie's apartment, after she got there and found the old girl was dead?"

"A photograph. She took a photograph of Queenie with her son."

"That's who all of us believed was in the picture,

when Tiffany said it was a young boy, right? We just assumed it was Fabian because it came out of Queenie's apartment."

"It's not Fabian?"

"Mrs. Gatts had the picture at her place, 'cause she took her daughter's purse home with her the day Tiffany was arrested. It was a ten-year-old boy in the picture, all right, but it wasn't McQueen Ransome's son and it wasn't taken forty years ago."

"What?"

Hoyt had slowed the boat even further, and I continued to fake my lack of concern.

I needed to listen to Mercer and not panic. I needed to let him tell me what he knew.

"The kid in the photograph is Dulles Tripping—it's a Polaroid and he signed his name right on the back, thanking McQueen Ransome for something, maybe something she gave him."

"Um, hmm, I understand," I said, beginning to see the light.

"And it's dated. It was taken on the afternoon Queenie died, just hours before Kevin and Tiffany got there and claimed she was already dead."

"I see," I said, still pretending to be talking to Sarah Brenner. "I'll take care of that next week."

"You'll take care of it right now, Alex. Whoever the agency had let Dulles go off with that afternoon, whoever he was allowed to visit with, might be the person who killed McQueen Ransome. Now maybe it's not Graham Hoyt, but until I can get an answer to that from the child welfare agency, I don't want you alone with him for another nanosecond."

"It's okay, Sarah. We're just a couple of minutes away from the yacht. I'm counting on a delicious lunch from Mr. Hoyt's chef." I wanted Mercer to know there was a crew on board the boat with Dulles, so I wouldn't be alone for long.

"Call me when you get there, right?"

Hoyt had picked up the walkie-talkie again and was speaking to someone on the *Pirate*.

"Would you do me one more favor?" I said to Mercer. I had shifted my body now so that I was holding the phone to my left ear, my back to Hoyt, with the magnificent skyline of Manhattan receding before me.

"Shoot."

"Call Christine Kiernan, will you? She triangulated a phone number for a new case last week. Tell her it's urgent. Ask her to do a trap-and-trace on my line immediately. She's got all the forms and the contacts at TARU. She can do it in minutes. Keep an eye on me till we get back. Track my coordinates, please?"

"Stay on with me, Alex. Just stay on the line."

Hoyt shut off his receiver and hung it in its cradle. He jerked the steering wheel as hard as he could and pushed ahead on the throttle, turning the boat completely around, a full one-eighty, heading back to the mouth of the great river. I fell down against the seat and the small phone flipped out of my hand onto the wet floor, sliding across out of reach to the other side of the tender.

Find me, I prayed silently to Mercer. Find me before I'm sleeping with the fishes.

39

I hugged the leather seat cushion and tried to balance myself against it on my way to grab the cell phone. Hoyt had let go of the wheel for a few seconds. Steadier than I as the boat crossed its own wake, he stepped ahead, leaned over, and picked it up before I could get to it.

"Is there some change in—?" I tried to ask without broadcasting my alarm.

"We're going back to the Chelsea Piers. Just stay where you are. I'm going to bounce us around a bit." He was looking angry now, under way at excessive speed and rolling me across the stern of the sturdy Whaler.

He pressed a button on the phone and held it to his ear with one hand. He must have hit redial. If he heard Mercer's voice and not Sarah's, he'd know I'd been lying.

Mercer probably answered immediately, since we had been disconnected abruptly.

Hoyt turned to me and sneered, throwing the

phone into the water and laughing as he spoke into the breeze, "Sorry, wrong number."

There were craft of all shapes and sizes zigzagging across the Hudson on this fall afternoon. I wasn't able to stand up without falling at the speed we were going, no one could hear me over the noise of the various engines if I were to call out for help across the water, and the only option left—waving my arms in the air—would look like a friendly greeting to most boaters out on a sunny afternoon.

"Don't even think about it, Alex. Just sit nice and still."

I was anything but still, tossing around on the seat cushion as Hoyt purposely steered the boat back and forth, almost hot-rodding it on the chop to keep me off-balance.

"Over here," he said, snarling at me. He pointed to a spot directly next to his feet.

I didn't move. Hoyt spun the wheel sharply to the left, hard enough to knock me across the length of the rear seat and send me crashing onto the floor.

"Damn it. I said I want you over here."

I crouched and started moving in his direction, looking everywhere for some kind of tool that I could use to defend myself.

We were below Forty-second Street now—I could track the West Side Highway ramp descending and the roadway curving—but Hoyt gave no sign of slowing down as we came into striking distance of Chelsea Piers.

"We're going to let the boy be for a while, Alex. You and I have things to talk about."

There wasn't going to be time for a long conversation before we passed the southern tip of Manhattan heading into Upper New York Bay and the ocean that stretched out forever beyond the Verrazano Bridge. The Atlantic was a massive graveyard that I didn't want to visit today.

"Your captain will be back—"

"I know, I know. And your buddies will be looking for you all the way from Chelsea to the Dover cliffs. But I just told my crew that the damn engine in this boat is acting up again. And my unreliable steering column—I meant to have it repaired in Nantucket. It would be a terrible thing if I lost control and it crashed up on the rocks," he said, pausing to glance down at me. "With one of us still aboard."

There had to be a knife or bottle opener or sharp-edged object in some compartment or other. Everything seemed to be stowed tightly in place, and I saw nothing loose that I could grasp for protection.

Hoyt went on. "I just told the captain that you insisted on seeing the Statue of Liberty up close. So this excursion will be, after all, your very own idea, Alex. That's the way he'll tell it."

I was sitting in a puddle now, and when Hoyt dipped the boat on its side to throw me off-guard from time to time, I shivered from my thighs to my shoulders as the cold water saturated my clothing.

With one hand, he unlatched a drawer beneath the windshield and reached in, removing a short length of rope and dangling it in front of my face.

Paige Vallis. What had Squeeks told me about her

cause of death? She'd been strangled by some kind of ligature. Probably a thin rope.

Hoyt let go of the wheel for a few seconds while he made a sailor's knot, deftly, as if he'd done it hundreds of times before. Maybe even in the laundry room of Vallis's apartment building. Again he let it swing before my eyes.

"What was it that changed your mood, Alex? What did the detective tell you that seemed to frighten you so terribly?"

"Nothing scared me. I—uh, I was just worried about Mike. He was talking to me about Mike Chapman. Nobody's heard from him since he ran off after Andrew Tripping. Mercer's concerned, too."

Hoyt grabbed a handful of my hair in his left hand and smashed my head backward against the edge of the cockpit door.

"Lying never helps, Alex. You're smart enough to know that. I heard you say the name Fabian. Now why in the world would you be talking about him right now?"

I didn't answer. I had found the man who was the missing link between the two murders—McQueen Ransome and Paige Vallis.

"Something the friendly detective said shocked you. Why don't you slip this rope over your ankles while you think about telling me what it was exactly?"

He lowered the noose and I fumbled at putting my feet through the opening. Though I was a very strong swimmer, I couldn't do anything if I went into the water with a restraint around my legs.

"I thought about putting it over your neck instead, but then if one of us survives this little accident—and surely one of us will—I wouldn't want to have to explain those burn marks that would have been on your throat." Hoyt pulled up on the end of the rope and it tightened over the cuff of my pants, jerking me closer to him and lashing my head against the boat's floor.

My hands were free, and I thought about striking at his knees to bring him down with me. But the cord on my legs limited my mobility, and although he was shorter than I, he seemed to be strong—and determined.

"So you were saying to Mr. Wallace—something about a photograph and a boy—possibly Fabian Ransome?"

I couldn't speak. I didn't know what kind of answer Hoyt was looking for.

"Now's the time to talk," he said, lifting his leg to deliver a swift kick to my side. "Heard you're never at a loss for words in the courtroom."

I looked up at him, everything coming into focus. "So you're the one paying for Tiffany Gatts's lawyers. You're the one she's afraid will have her killed if she talks."

He was weaving between a ferry and some smaller boats, maneuvering through heavier traffic as we got down to Battery Park City and its busy marina, nearing the southern tip of Manhattan.

I could see the majestic statue of Lady Liberty straight ahead of us, green copper skin glinting in the sunlight, her torch raised high as she appeared to be striding forward. She loomed over the harbor, welcoming the tired, poor, and huddled masses, her "mild eyes," as Lazarus described them, blind to my dilemma.

I thought of the image of Liberty on the face of the Double Eagle. Was I going to die because of a useless twenty-dollar piece of gold?

Hoyt was clear of some of the traffic and ready to talk again.

"All this for what?" I asked. "You and Peter Robelon are both chasing after the same thing, aren't you?"

"Don't spend too much of your time thinking, Alex. You should be admiring the view."

"I can figure out Tiffany's role in this. Tiffany and Kevin Bessemer. Who's Spike Logan working for? Which of you sent that bastard after me?"

"Watch how you speak of the dead."

I looked up at Hoyt.

"The sea is a treacherous place, Alex. I told Spike I'd pick him up in the tender, from Stonewall Beach, the morning after the storm. He seemed to have lost his footing on the swim platform when he tried to get on board. I went to save him with the grappling hook, but—well, I missed the mark."

That must have been just shortly before I saw Hoyt on the *Pirate* yesterday, gassing up in Menemsha. "You killed him because he didn't bring back what you sent him for?" I was rolling the words slowly off my tongue, trying to understand what had been going on around me. "You killed him because his mission was to get from me whatever it is you think I have?"

"Paige set you up, Alex. Right before she died. I know you've got it."

I could see the seven points in Liberty's diadem, one for each of the world's seas and continents. "That's not true, Graham. She didn't send me anything. She—"

He kicked my side again with the bottom of his shoe. "It's ugly when you dissemble. Think about it. Paige didn't want to die, Alex. She really didn't. She pleaded with me, on her knees, on the cold cement of the basement floor. I gave her one chance, and she told me she sent it to you. Help me, Alex," Hoyt said, patting me on top of my head. "Help yourself."

"What is *it*, Graham?" I pleaded. "How the hell can I tell you when I don't know what you're looking for?"

We were almost in front of Bedloe's Island now, circling the star-shaped foundation of Fort Wood, on which the great lady stood. I could see the broken shackles at Liberty's feet, and envied her escape from tyranny, when all that held me was a length of rope.

I tried again. "The coin. Is it the Double Eagle you're looking for?"

"Not anymore, Alex."

I put my head in my hands and tried to shake the image that had appeared. I was thinking of the photograph of Queenie and the Tripping boy, taken just before her death. "You took Dulles with you when you killed McQueen Ransome? That's how you—"

Liberty was behind us now, and Hoyt was going full throttle into Upper New York Bay, with Staten Island straight ahead. If he veered left, under the Verrazano to the ocean, I would be running out of shore-line as fast as I was running out of ideas.

"Don't be stupid, Alex. You know how I feel about kids. He just came in for a bit of a tease, to warm the old lady up, remind her of her lost little boy. See if she'd part with her precious gold treasure, which was worthless to her anyway. That's what she'd promised me, as long as I'd bring the kid by every now and then to visit her. Pay some of her expenses. Find her a nicer place to live. Dulles performed like an angel. Then I sent him out to the car, and—"

"And Queenie changed her mind, didn't she?"

"Tough old bird. She struck a hard bargain, then tried to welsh on it. She knew something was up."

"So Kevin and Tiffany were just the fall guys. You sent them to break in later on, and if caught, they'd take the weight for what you had stolen—or who you had killed."

"Every plan needs a backup, Alex. I never intended to hurt Queenie. Why should I? She was playing into my hands. I made a big contribution to the Schomburg just to mount a permanent exhibit of her pho-tographs."

Contributions to child refugee organizations, con-tributions to inner-city art museums. Hoyt was the desperate lawyer Justin Feldman had been telling me about as we talked on the plane on the way to the Vineyard. The guy so far in over his head that he was now killing people to support his lifestyle, to make the one big score that would save his own neck.

"So you have the Double Eagle," I said, "and the only thing you need is some way to make it legiti-

mate, some way to make it worth seven or eight million dollars."

"Go to the head of the class."

"And you think that I have that? You're wrong,
Graham. Paige never gave me—"

I was twisting, trying to roll onto my knees so I
could wrestle with Hoyt for the steering wheel and
turn the boat back toward the city.

Of course Paige had given me something, I realized, as I fell sideways and cracked my head against
the handle of a fishing rod stowed under the gunwale
of the boat. She never *mailed* me anything—didn't
send it to me that last night of her life—which is what
both Hoyt and Robelon were assuming. But she'd
brought something to my office earlier that same day,
something that was sitting in a drawer of my file cabinet. Maybe that concealed whatever it was that this
man would kill to obtain.

I struggled back to my knees, trying to loosen the
rope on my feet while Hoyt steered the boat. "I have
an idea, Graham. Tell me what it is you're looking for
and maybe I can figure out where it might be."

Hoyt looked down at me and laughed. A second
later, he swerved the wheel to the right, turning and
turning as furiously as he could, sending me lurching
backward again.

"Why don't you start, Alex? Paige obviously gave
you something—that's where you ended your last
thought, midsentence. Hurry up, Alex. Tell me what
she gave me. We're almost there."

I picked my head up, relieved to see that the turn
had taken us away from the direction of the Ver-

THE KILLS

razano. Instead of going to the ocean, he had steered to the right, to the body of water that separated Staten Island from New Jersey.

There was land on both sides of us rather than endless fathoms of water, and I was unrealistically euphoric at that thought. Then I made the mistake of asking where he was taking me.

"The Kills, Alex. Don't you know your geography? We're going to the Kills."

40

What a fitting place to meet a violent end. The Kills. Much smarter of Hoyt than heading out to the Atlantic, which had been my greatest fear. He probably figured that Mercer Wallace would have marshaled every coast guard boat and NYPD harbor launch in that direction. So vast and far too obvious. I had to give Hoyt credit for his quick thinking.

The green sign posted at the entrance to the waterway said KILL VAN KULL. I knew there once were "kills" all over Lower Manhattan, a vestige from the Dutch colonization that meant "channels" or "creeks." This one was obviously a viaduct to the shipyards along the Jersey shore, so busy with traffic that no one would give special notice to an innocuous little Whaler weaving among the mix of commercial and sport vessels.

"Why don't you anchor somewhere?" I asked, my voice trembling. "I can call my office and someone can search for whatever it is you want."

"You're not going back, Alex. You know that. And I'm not looking for a plea bargain here. It's very simple. You tell me what I need to know, or you don't.

And if you don't, more people will have to die, don't you think?"

He was talking about Mercer and Mike. Hoyt had to kill me, whether I told him what he wanted or not. I knew too much about what he had done. He could still hope the others hadn't figured everything out.

But if he wasn't just going to dump me in the water, on the open seas, he must be figuring to torture me before he finished me off. That's why he chose this route.

There was a small bridge ahead and a sign that said SHOOTER'S ISLAND. Hoyt opened the deep compartment on the dashboard in front of him, the one from which he had pulled the rope. He lifted something out, a metal tool that looked heavy as he hoisted it and let it fall with a loud clang on the countertop. I guessed it was a wrench.

"So what's your plan?" I asked, sitting back on my heels, my arms bracing me against the side of the boat behind me.

"To find out where you've got it, Alex. A simple piece of paper. That's all I want. Then no one has to get hurt. No one else, I mean."

So Graham Hoyt and Peter Robelon both thought Paige Vallis had the means to legitimize the little gold coin that they both coveted. A legal form, signed by the secretary of the treasury more than half a century ago, that would monetize the Double Eagle. One sheet of paper, smuggled out of Egypt by Paige's father, perhaps, after King Farouk was deposed. The document that together with Queenie's coin would make their possessor a multimillionaire.

Why couldn't there have been two Eagles validated

for the great Farouk? An identically matched pair, one of them undiscovered until now? No one had ever been sure of the exact count of the handful of coins smuggled out of the Mint, then or now.

"I meant your plan for me," I said.

Graham Hoyt had studied the lives of the great collectors, the greedy Farouk among them. There were newspaper accounts at the time of the king's lover, the exotic dancer from Harlem. He had schoolmates like Tripping and Robelon, who also knew the legends and the myths of the accumulated treasures. They'd all heard the story of the tutor who didn't want gold or jewels, but who busied himself with Farouk's documents. Then, too, Hoyt must have followed the great auction, the amazing story of a twenty-dollar piece of gold that fetched millions because of the paper that made it legal.

He was slowing the speed as we neared Shooter's Island. There was no sign of any human life ahead. No people around, no one to call out to. It looked like a wildlife preserve.

"Terrible place for an accident," he said, steering with his left hand and picking up the wrench in his right.

"The cops won't buy it. You told your captain I wanted to see the Statue of Liberty, not some goddamn bird sanctuary." I was fidgeting wildly now, trying in vain to make him worry about people doubting why we were here. I glanced at the desolate scrap of land, nestled off the northern coast of Staten Island, New Jersey's border in the distance, and nothing but the Kills behind me.

"Funny thing about that. My captain will probably remember—once I remind him—that when you were on board yesterday I mentioned this little island to you. How curious you were about its spectacular hey-day a century ago, when Teddy Roosevelt came here to launch the *Meteor III*—Kaiser Wilhelm's racing yacht. You asked to see it and I obliged."

"So now you have a problem with the steering, you crash-land on the shore, and I go overboard, which accounts for the terrible crack in my head," I said, pointing at the wrench. "An accidental drowning."

"Save a friend, Alex. Just tell me what Paige gave you, one last time?"

He was maneuvering the boat into place, looking around behind him to make sure that no one was any-where near us on the wide side of the Kill, far from landfall in Jersey. On my right, the only living things were egrets and herons, surrounded by tall stands of salt-marsh cordgrass.

Hoyt was making his last reconnoiter before, I assured myself, he got ready to use the wrench to tor-ment me into some kind of cooperation.

With my left arm balanced on the side rail, I pulled on the plastic line of the fishing rod that I had found when I cracked my head against it, stowed in its place along the length of the boat. I yanked it until I could grasp the cold metal hook in my right hand. Sitting back on my haunches, I lunged at Hoyt's left hand, ripping the skin with the long, sharp claw of the silver hook.

He screamed, and the wrench dropped to the floor as he reflexively grabbed at his bloody left hand with his right. I stabbed again, catching on a bone in his right wrist this time, doubling him over and bringing him to his knees as he shrieked in pain. A cacophony of birds began mocking him from the island, screeching in reply to his ungodly sounds.

I reached behind me and pulled my feet out of the noose he had made. I looked up and there was blood everywhere. Hoyt had buried his face in his hands and was trying to bite out the hook that was embedded in his wrist.

I didn't know how to stop the boat, which was moving slowly past the tip of Shooter's Island, headed south into the next kill that separated Staten Island from New Jersey. I crawled across the floor and picked up the wrench, striking Hoyt on the back of the head. He collapsed onto the floor and continued to writhe and moan.

Once on my feet, I checked our distance from the small island preserve, which was blessedly close. I sat on the side of the boat, swung both legs over, and, careful to avoid the engine, kicked away and threw myself into the water. I swam the ten feet to shore, startling all the wildlife, and pulled myself up onto land to catch my breath.

I looked back and the boat was still moving, farther away, with no sign of Hoyt at the wheel.

As fast as I could travel in my bare feet, I ran in the opposite direction from which we had come. The brush and rocks were rough on my soles as I tried to pick my way through the undergrowth. Bird droppings were everywhere, and my feathered companions squawked and flew off as I invaded their habitat.

Gulls circled overhead in protest, and I plugged along as best I could, until I finally caught sight of a tanker coming toward the entrance to Arthur Kill.

My frenetic gesticulations did nothing to stop the larger vessels that passed through the channel, but someone must have radioed to the authorities the sight of a human trespasser on Shooter's Island. Fifteen minutes later, an NYPD harbor launch was steaming at me, and I waded out into the chilly water to greet it.

41

I only had to say my name and the cops on harbor patrol knew what to do with me. Mercer had called headquarters when Hoyt cut off my cell phone, which started a search of the waterfront. Then he'd spoken with the *Pirate*'s captain, who mentioned the Statue of Liberty as a possible destination. Mercer and Mike had met up at the East Thirty-fourth Street heliport and been choppered to Liberty Island to set up a command post there.

When we docked at the small pier on the southwest side of the statue, Mercer was waiting for me. He lifted me down from the rear of the boat, embraced me, and held me close against him. I couldn't control my shivering as I rested my head against his chest.

"Let's get her inside," he said, passing through a group of other cops and security agents who wanted to be helpful. "You," he said, pointing at a National Parks Service officer, "get into the gift shop and—"

"It's closed for the day, sir."

"Get in it. Bring me a sweatshirt and anything

else that's dry and clean. I don't care if you have to break in."

One of the cops had covered me with his own windbreaker. It hardly mattered. Cold, wet, and numb were feelings I was getting accustomed to this week.

We walked into the entrance of Fort Wood, the War of 1812 garrison that formed the statue's base, and Mercer guided me to an office door down a long corridor.

"What happened?" Mike asked, hanging up the phone and flashing me one of his priceless grins. "Hairdresser couldn't take you today? Look like that, it's no wonder you can't hold on to a man."

There were six other cops in the room, working phones and computers, now calling off the search and alerting the patrol boats that I was safe.

"Tried my best to hook a guy just half an hour ago," I said, knowing that if I didn't keep up the banter, I was likely to dissolve into tears. "Did he get away, too?"

"Glad to see you haven't lost your sense of humor entirely, blondie. Nope. Mr. Hoyt is in an ambulance on his way to the hospital. Mild concussion and a couple of holes in his hands. The Port Authority cops picked him up on the Jersey side."

"C'mon next door," Mercer said. "There's an empty office."

"Figures," Mike said. "Coop's the only little girl I ever knew who preferred Captain Hook to Tinker-Bell."

The parks service guard returned with a large fleece shirt, a huge logo of Liberty's torch on the front. I went inside first and changed into the dry top before opening the door for Mercer and Mike. They wanted to know what had gone on this afternoon with Graham Hoyt and how I had handled it. I gave them a clinical version. The prospect of what could have happened on the river was overwhelming.

"You've got to call security at Hogan Place," I said. "The DA's squad has a skeleton crew on Saturday. Get some of the guys to go down to my office. The key to the file cabinet is in Laura's desk. Tell them to examine the Yankees jacket that's behind the Tripping file in the first cabinet, second drawer—check the pockets or, more likely, cut the seams open and look inside the lining."

"Why?"

"Because I'll bet that's where Paige Vallis hid the piece of paper that her father had been holding on to for fifty years, thinking it might someday be his passport to a fortune, if he could ever match it up with the gold coin it would legitimize. The paper Victor Vallis took from King Farouk's palace."

Mercer got on the phone while I settled in and warmed up.

"But you'd told Graham Hoyt about the kid's baseball jacket, hadn't you? I remember you telling him that you were going to give it back to Dulles. Why didn't he figure it out?"

I shook my head. "No, I told him the kid left the jacket at the hospital. It was logical for him to think it was vouchered there that same day as police property, as something that came out of the crime scene, maybe had the kid's blood on it. I never mentioned that it was Paige who took it home from Bellevue with her and held on to it for all those months."

"And Paige put the document in your hands because she knew that her life might be in danger."

"Probably so."

Mercer flipped his phone closed. "They're on their way down to your office. They'll call me back as soon as they've checked the jacket."

Another ranger knocked on the door and came in with a tray of hot coffee and sandwiches left over in the cafeteria at the end of the tourist day.

Mike stood behind me, massaging my shoulders and neck, trying to calm me while we talked. "You got this all figured out? You sitting in that rowboat with Hoyt and all of a sudden get one of those 'Holy shit!' moments?"

"I think I've got a good idea of what was going on, don't you?"

"I guess it all got into high gear in the summer of 2002. Sotheby's holds the auction of the only valid Double Eagle known to exist and sells it for seven million dollars."

"And that," I said, "probably revived old rumors that had swirled around expatriate types after World War Two about the most famous coin in history. The myth of a second Double Eagle. The possibility that Farouk's delegation had gotten two of the fabled birds out of the U.S. at the same time."

"You mean, that had been gossiped about in 1944?" Mercer asked.

"The feds can tell us that. It was such a great embarrassment to the government that a group of the gold pieces had survived the presidential order to have them destroyed, no one could put an exact count on how many there actually were."

"So who was aware of the second Double Eagle?" he asked again.

Mike answered him. "Graham Hoyt must have known. He made a practice of examining the lives of the world's greatest collectors, so he certainly knew all about Farouk."

"I got another piece of the puzzle today. It was Spike Logan who came to my house on the Vineyard. He was working for Hoyt."

Mike let go of my neck and came around to sit in front of me, waiting while I inhaled some of the coffee. "What?"

"Figure it out. Hoyt gave money to the Schomburg. You think it was an accident that Spike Logan was interviewing Queenie Ransome? Graham Hoyt knew exactly who she was, from his interest in Farouk. He hires Logan to get inside, to gain the poor old dame's trust. He hires Logan mainly to learn whether that precious piece of gold was actually one of the things she spirited out of the palace."

"Will Logan talk to us, you think?" Mike asked.

I looked over at Mercer. "Call Chip Streeter. When Logan showed up empty-handed after ransacking my house during the hurricane, Hoyt realized he already knew too much. Tell Streeter to expect what's left of Logan to wash up on South Beach, near Stonewall, any day now."

"You think Hoyt sent Logan to spook you during the storm?"

"Worse than that. It was Hoyt who set me up all week, telling me how bad the hurricane was going to be, why I needed to get to the house. You see," I said, "I think he really believes I knew what Paige gave me. He thinks she confided in me—since she had been so candid in telling me about accidentally killing the man in her father's house. Hoyt's sure I had this priceless piece of paper from the Treasury Department, and that once Paige was dead, I would have kept it with me for safekeeping, even if I wasn't entirely sure what it was."

"He sent Logan to the house to get the document, and get rid of you," Mercer said.

"So then there's Hoyt's competition," I said.

Mike was gnawing on one of the sandwiches. "That would be Peter Robelon. He knew about the coin because his father was top dog in the British Secret Service, attached to Farouk's group when the king was living in exile. Lionel Webster—the guy who pretended to be Harry Strait—he's a mercenary who was hired by Robelon."

"So you had two professional teams working against poor, whacky Andrew Tripping, who knew the whole story from his own Agency experience but just couldn't put together a plan that worked," Mercer said. "You think his effort to meet and date Paige Vallis was a setup?"

"From the get-go. Same with Lionel's 'Harry Strait' character." I was certain that was no chance meeting.

"And Paige?" Mike asked. "You think she knew the whole story?"

"I can't imagine she did. I'll give you some more

homework, guys. You remember the burglar who died in the struggle, the one she confronted when she got home after her father's funeral?"

"Yeah."

"Get phone records and bank records and anything else that left a paper trail. Bet you almost anything that guy was hired by Graham Hoyt. Smart enough to pick an Arab to do the dirty work. That way, if the plan failed, it would look like the break-in was related to the consulting job on terrorism that Mr. Vallis was involved in when he died."

"You think he went in to steal the document that made the Double Eagle a legal coin?"

"Yes, I do."

"Then you also think . . ." Mike was mulling my theory over as he chewed.

"I'll bet that Paige found the paper on the burglar's body—maybe they even fought over it when she interrupted him."

"She realized what it was?"

"I'm not sure that she knew its value or meaning, but she was smart enough to figure out it was so important that someone might kill for it. Who knows, maybe her father had explained its significance, figuring the stolen coin that it referred to would eventually surface somewhere in the world. And that he—and then Paige—was the only person who held the key to turning twenty dollars' worth of gold into seven or eight million."

"Assuming we find the document in Dulles's jacket, why do you think Paige gave it to you, Alex?" Mercer asked.

I shrugged. "I don't think she had anyone else in her life she could trust at that point. The evening before she testified, she got a phone call from Harry Strait. So the morning she came to my office, she was scared enough to tell me something about him. But she didn't give me the baseball jacket then."

"Wasn't Strait in the courtroom, too?"

"Yeah. She gets on the stand and not only is she facing Andrew Tripping, who was way too interested in her father and his career for it to be coincidental, and there's Strait again."

"That ratchets up her fear factor," Mike said.

"So then we went back to my office, and before she left, she made her decision to pull out the Yankees jacket from her bag and give it to me."

"But didn't even give you a hint that she's hidden something in it."

"She was frightened, Mike, but I don't think most people cope with the fact that their lives might actually be in imminent peril. She had been flirting with this particular danger for months."

"Besides," Mercer added, "she was never too direct with Alex unless she was pressed to be. She let everything come out piece by piece, when she was ready to tell it. Right up to the minute she testified."

"Step one was giving me the jacket for safekeeping. Getting it out of her possession and into the hands of the law. Step two would be swearing that she no longer had it to anyone who tried to get it from her over the weekend."

"Not too successfully, obviously," Mike said.

"You know, when Hoyt lured her out of her

apartment by telling her she could see Dulles, and then waylaid her in the laundry room," I thought aloud, "I'll bet she pleaded for her life by telling him she had given me—sent me is what he thought—the paper."

"Once she admitted that," Mike went on, "she was as good as dead. He didn't need her anymore."

"I think she figured if someone hassled her over the weekend, she had a chance to unload the whole story to me on Monday. She just didn't know how very dangerous Hoyt was."

Mercer's phone rang and he took the call. It was a short conversation but it confirmed what we had already guessed. Paige Vallis had sewn the mistakenly issued 1944 document that made the second Double Eagle legitimate legal tender into the lining of the pocket of Dulles Tripping's favorite Yankees jacket.

"That Polaroid photo of Queenie and Dulles that Mrs. Gatts gave me today, Alex," Mercer asked. "Did Hoyt talk about that?"

I smiled at him. "Me and my big mouth. Hoyt overheard me talking to you about Fabian and the picture. That's what almost bought me a piece of muddy real estate at the bottom of the Kills."

Mike hadn't heard Mercer's news yet.

"Get somebody good to sit down with Dulles, as soon as possible. I think whenever Hoyt had a visitation period with him, they were keeping a little secret between themselves. Hoyt was taking the boy to visit McQueen Ransome."

"But why?"

"She was a sucker for kids. We know that from the neighborhood. Here comes Hoyt, pretending to be a great admirer of her career, full of stories he knew about Farouk, ready to dignify her glory days by funding an exhibit at the Schomburg. And he brings along a fair-haired boy—the exact age of her son when he died—with a sad story to go with the kid. Who does Queenie have to leave her few belongings to? Why not this deserving child, who had no mother?"

"Something misfired, though."

"Yeah, I think Queenie was every bit as smart as Graham Hoyt, and even tougher. I don't think she liked the smell of his offer. She probably realized that what he wanted from her had more value than he was telling her."

I could barely hear Mike when he spoke. "So he killed the old lady."

"And was ready to let Kevin Bessemer take the weight. After all, who's going to believe a convicted felon—and a crackhead to boot—that Queenie was already dead when he got there?"

"He even controlled all the legal proceedings, all the players."

"That's it."

"Why does anybody with his kind of dough need another seven million?" Mercer asked.

"Because he really didn't have the money you think he did," I said.

"The art collection, the yacht, the country house—"

"Graham Hoyt had been stealing from his law firm for years. He has an addiction every bit as pathological as Bessemer's addiction to cocaine. He needed to own, to possess, to collect, like all the men he idolized. It was a sickness with him."

"None of it fit on a lawyer's salary. You said that when he first showed up in the case."

"He's been stealing money from his law partners for years, claiming he was writing checks to his favorite charities and getting the firm to reimburse him. Only, those checks went right into his own pocket, right into the gas for his yacht and the art on his walls."

"So get the Double Eagle, get the sheet of paper that makes it legal, and with one auction, he'd make a seven-million-dollar score that would get him out of hock and keep him afloat for a lot longer. Phony little prick."

"Think about what else he was telling me. Hoyt was really anxious for Tripping to take the guilty plea. That way, Andrew would be in jail and out of the chase for the golden bird."

Mercer also remembered what I was talking about. "It was Hoyt who stopped by your office late one evening and made a point of telling you that Robelon was dirty, that Robelon was a target of an investigation in the DA's office?"

"True, he delighted in diverting me by painting a tinge of guilt on each of the other players. And I fell for it."

"We all fell for it," Mike said.

Another knock on the door and the ranger came

in. "We're losing the daylight, Mr. Wallace. You've gotta get that helicopter out before the sun sets. We aren't equipped for flying after dark."

Mike got to his feet. "What do you say, Coop? We got our own wings right outside. Take you anywhere you want to go."

I leaned my head back and tried to clear my mind of its deadly whirling images of the past week. Dark shadows in the hurricane, Hoyt's sneer as he reached for the wrench in the cockpit of his boat, the sailor's knot that was probably looped around Paige Vallis's neck.

"Fly you to the moon?"

I ignored Mike's chatter. "Where's the boy? What's going to happen to Dulles?"

Mercer took me by the hand and helped me up. "Ms. Taggart and the folks at child welfare have been looking into that for weeks. They never much cared for Hoyt or his wife. Seems Mrs. Hoyt was always too worried about Tripping's involvement and probably afraid of her husband, too."

"I can't bear to think of what becomes of the child in all this."

"Could be good news. Tripping's second wife— the one who left him because he beat her? She always had a good relationship with Dulles. She's married now, living in Connecticut with her husband and two kids. Says if Andrew is ready to do the right thing and let go for good, she'd be willing to adopt Dulles."

Mike wouldn't stop. "See, there's nobody to worry about anymore except you. Forget these sandwiches.

They're already stale. We'll pack a picnic basket and fly—um, can we make it to Paris in this buggy? Anybody know?"

"The coin, Mercer, is anybody looking for the coin?" I asked. "Hoyt must have taken it from the apartment the day he killed Queenie."

Mercer hooked his elbow in mine, as we walked out of the building toward the blue-and-white helicopter with the NYPD logos on it. "Teams have blocked off Hoyt's apartment, his office, and the yacht till they can get warrants for all that and his bank vaults. We'll find it."

Mike took my other arm and guided me down the path as the pilot started the engine and the rotors began to spin. "It's going to be a perfect night. The moon is waxing to full; we can set this baby down in the middle of Times Square and dance till dawn."

Mercer made a signal of some kind over my head, probably telling Mike to cut it out.

"It's okay," I said. Mike Chapman knew me every bit as well as I knew myself. I didn't want to go home just yet. I didn't want to spend the night alone.

I ducked under the blades and climbed up on the pontoons, into the seat behind the pilot. I had been in a similar chopper scores of times, riding with the DA's office photographer to take aerial photos of crime scenes. Someone would return tomorrow to do that over the river and bay, down to the Kills.

After Mike and Mercer got in, the pilot lifted the helicopter in the air, hovering behind the great green lady. He swooped down and to his left, circling from behind her enormous arm holding the torch aloft, past her strong face, illumined at dusk by the lights in her crown.

"Lady Liberty, Coop. She watched over you today. Quite a beauty."

My head rested against the window and I stared back at her, saluting her silently in gratitude.

"Personally," Mike went on, "the Liberty on the gold piece is a bit sexier, in my book. This one's got her hair all tied up neat in a bun. The one on the Double Eagle? Hers is all loose and wild, kinda like yours looks right now."

The sun was setting behind us, west of the Hudson, and straight ahead the elegant Manhattan skyline was showing off its stunning array of lights.

We were over the river, then above the Chelsea Piers, passing close to the Empire State Building and the Art Deco spire of the Chrysler Building, coming in for an easy landing along the East River, in sight of the old deadhouse at the tip of Roosevelt Island.

A phalanx of detectives was waiting at the heliport to brainstorm with Mike and Mercer, and to hear my story of the day's events.

"The commissioner wants to see Ms. Cooper before he goes home tonight," one of them told Chapman as he brushed them out of the way.

"Give me an hour. I gotta buy her a new pair of shoes. Then we'll have her down to headquarters." He spotted a friend in the crowd. "Joey—get us uptown fast as you can, lights and sirens. The broad needs a bath bad. She got too close to Jersey today—smells like Secaucus."

We were at my front door fifteen minutes later. I unlocked it and the three of us went inside. "Clean yourself up, blondie. Go heavy on the perfume."

"Do I really have to go to headquarters tonight? I'm drained," I said, opening the bedroom door and pausing there while Mike and Mercer headed for the ice cubes and the bar glasses respectively.

"You bet your sweet ass you do. The commish had all of Manhattan South scouring the town for you—air, sea, scuba—every hand on deck. And after you're done thanking him, you've got the two of us to deal with."

I called back out to Mike, "What do you mean by that?"

Mercer answered. "It's payday. We're going to keep you out all night. Dancing, wining and dining, hanging out with your friends."

"And when we deliver you back here at daybreak, you'll be so exhausted you won't be able to give me any orders for at least a month. You'll sleep like a baby," Mike said.

"I'm not sure I can keep up with—"

"Unless you'd rather we go on ahead and you just take your shower, pull the covers up over your head, and stay here feeling sorry for yourself. Sulking, pouting—your usual MO."

"Give me half an hour," I said. "Don't leave without me."

I went into my bedroom and stripped off the sweatshirt and damp pants. The message light was flashing on the answering machine, and I could see there were seven calls. I pressed the erase button and held it down until every one of them was deleted. Whoever had been looking for me today could try again tomorrow.

Acknowledgments

The rare and magnificent object that captured my imagination—"such stuff," the Bard once said, "as dreams are made on"—first came to my attention in an article in *The New York Times*. Other helpful sources included William Stadiem's *Too Rich—The High Life and Tragic Death of King Farouk;* the Sotheby's/Stack's catalog of the July 30, 2002, auction of the 1933 Double Eagle; John Rousmaniere's history of the New York Yacht Club; and Seitz and Miller's *The Other Islands of New York City.*

I am grateful to Susanne Kirk and all my friends at Scribner and Pocket Books who have made my transition from the prosecutor's office to my writing room such a delightful step.

Esther Newberg is the best friend any writer could hope to have.

My friends and family give me more joy than I can express. And although Justin Feldman is only a cameo in the world of Alexandra Cooper, he is everything to me.

ABOUT THE AUTHOR

LINDA FAIRSTEIN, America's foremost expert on crimes of sexual assault and domestic violence, led the Sex Crimes Unit of the District Attorney's Office in Manhattan for twenty-five years. A Fellow of the American College of Trial Lawyers, she is a graduate of Vassar College and the University of Virginia School of Law. Her first novel, *Final Jeopardy*, introduced the critically acclaimed character of Alexandra Cooper and was made into an ABC Movie of the Week starring Dana Delaney. Her celebrated series has gone on to include the international bestseller *Likely to Die* and the *New York Times* bestsellers *Cold Hit*, *The Deadhouse* (chosen as a "Best Book of 2001" by both *The Washington Post* and the *Los Angeles Times*), *The Bone Vault*, and *The Kills*. Her nonfiction book, *Sexual Violence*, was a *New York Times* notable book in 1994. She lives with her husband in Manhattan and on Martha's Vineyard.

Visit her website at www.lindafairstein.com.

POCKET STAR BOOKS
PROUDLY PRESENTS

THE BONE VAULT

LINDA FAIRSTEIN

Now available in paperback
from Pocket Star Books

Please turn the page for a preview of
The Bone Vault. . . .

1

I spent a long afternoon at the morgue. I had left my desk at the Manhattan District Attorney's Office shortly after lunch to review autopsy results on a new case with the deputy chief medical examiner. A nineteen-year-old, dressed in an outfit she had bought just hours earlier, was killed outside a social club as she waited on a street corner for her friends.

Now I walked a quiet corridor, again surrounded by death. I did not want to be here. I paused at the entrance of an ancient tomb, its painted limestone facade concealing the false doorway to an underground burial chamber. The faded reliefs that decorated its walls showed offerings of food and drink that would nourish the spirit of the dead. I didn't harbor any hope that the young woman whose body I had seen today would ever be in need of the kind of good meal displayed before me.

I made my way past a granite lion and nodded at the uniformed guard, who slouched on a folding chair beside the elegantly carved beast, once the protector of a royal grave. Both were sleeping soundly. The outstretched arms of the neighboring alabaster monkeys held empty vessels that had no doubt been receptacles of the body parts of some mummified dignitary of the Old Kingdom.

Voices echoing from behind me suggested that I was not to be the last arrival at this evening's festive dinner. I quickened my pace and swept by cases filled with goddesses' stone heads, perched on shelves holding jeweled sandals and golden collars that had been buried with them for centuries. A sharp left turn brought me face-to-face with the enormous black sarcophagus of a thirtieth-dynasty Egyptian queen, held open by two iron posts, so that passersby could see the image of her soul portrayed on the inside of the upper lid. The dark, heavy casket with a faint outline of the slender body it once housed chilled me, despite the unseasonal warmth of the late-spring night.

Then I turned the last corner, where the darkness of the funereal rooms gave way to the glorious open space that housed the Temple of Dendur. The northernmost end of the Metropolitan Museum of Art was a sloping, glass-paned wall soaring above the sandstone monuments, opening the vista into Central Park. It was almost nine o'clock, and the streetlamps beyond the windows lightened the night sky, giving definition to the leafy green trees bordering the great institution.

I stood at the edge of the moat that surrounded the two raised buildings in this stunning wing, searching the crowd for my friends. Waiters in sleek black suits zigzagged back and forth among the guests, stopping to dispense smoked salmon on black bread and caviar blinis. They were trailed by others who carried silver trays filled with glasses of white wine, champagne, and sparkling water, dodging the elbows and arms of the assembled museum members and supporters.

Nina Baum saw me before I spotted her. "You came just late enough to miss most of the speeches. Smart move."

She signaled to one of the servers, and handed me a flute of champagne. "Hungry?"

I shook my head.

"The morgue?"

"Not a very pleasant afternoon."

"Was she—?"

"I'll tell you about it later. Chapman thought he had a lead on a case he's been handling that's reached a dead end, so I wanted to get a clear understanding about the pattern of injuries and how they'd been inflicted. That way, if he picked up a suspect and I got a chance to question the guy tonight, I'd be ready for him. Turned out to be a bad tip, so there's no interrogation, no arrest. It's on the back burner for a while."

Nina looped her arm through mine and started to walk me toward the steps. "Why didn't you bring Mike with you?"

"I tried. Once I told him it was black tie he sent me home to shower and change. No penguin suit for him, not even to see you. He'll catch you later in the week."

Mike Chapman was a homicide detective. Best one on the job, in my view. Nina Baum was my closest friend, and had been for exactly half my life. We were eighteen when we met, assigned to be roommates at

Wellesley College when we arrived freshman year. She was married now, living in California with her husband and young son. She had met Mike many times during the decade that he and I had worked together on cases, and she looked forward to spending time with him whenever she was in town.

"First we'll find Jake." She led me up the steps, past the lone palm tree that stood on the platform below the great temple. "Then I'll introduce you to my boss and all the museum heavyweights."

"How's Jake behaving? You still have a job after tonight or is he hounding everybody here, looking for scoops?"

"Let's say we've raised a lot of eyebrows around town. I keep telling people that I've only borrowed him for the evening, but when you read tomorrow's gossip columns, you might begin to wonder. You must have a lot of friends here, 'cause they can't figure out why I'm hanging on to him and why you're nowhere to be seen."

"'Who is that auburn-haired beauty who whisked in from the coast and stole NBC correspondent Jake Tyler right out from under the long arm of the law? Prosecutor Alexandra Cooper has a warrant out for her arrest. And also for the return of the terrifically sexy—and backless—navy blue sequined dress that this interloper slipped out of Alexandra's closet when she wasn't looking.' That's what I'm likely to see in the tabs?"

"I figured you loaned me the guy for the evening, how sore could you be about the sexy, backless gown?"

Nina had arrived in New York a day earlier. She was a partner in a major L.A. law firm, where she had developed an expertise in packaging large entertainment projects for screen and television movies. Tonight's event was staged to announce a historic occasion for the two great New York institutions. The Metropolitan Museum of Art and the American Museum of Natural History, with some help from Hollywood, would hold the first cooperative exhibition in their histories.

The controversial mix of scholarship and show business had had a difficult birth, struggling to overcome resistance from trustees and curators, administrators and city officials. But blockbuster shows like the Met's "Treasures of Tutankhamen" and the Costume Institute's collection of Jacqueline Kennedy's White House clothing filled the museum coffers and argued for the drama of a spectacular twenty-first-century display of the two museums' collective greatest hits.

Nina's California client, UniQuest Productions, had successfully bid on all the media marketing rights to the new project. "A Modern Bestiary," as the show had been titled, would feature all the fantastic animals of the world, as represented in both collections, from hieroglyphs, tapestries, and paintings to mounted specimens and stuffed mammals. There would be dazzling, high-tech creations and virtual dioramas, IMAX time trips through the ages to examine artists and artifacts in their natural habitats, and commercial tie-ins for souvenir sales in museum shops and on the Web. There would be Rembrandt refrigerator magnets, triceratops lapel pins, plastic human-genome Slinkys to bounce down staircases across America, and snowglobes with endangered species of the Amazon being doused by acid rain.

Nina steered me toward a short, dark-haired man with too much facial hair and a collarless tux shirt. "Quentin Vallejo, I'd like you to meet Alexandra Cooper. She's—"

"I know, I know. The best friend." Quentin did the up-and-down thing. My five-ten frame towered over him, so his eyes just focused at the level of my breasts and worked their way south to my knees before lifting back up to meet my glance. "The sex crimes prosecutor. Nina talked about you for the entire flight yesterday. That's an interesting job you've got. We ought to have a chat some time, just the two of us. Like to hear more about what you do."

Quentin turned to exchange his empty wineglass for a full one, and I gave him a nod as I walked away. Nina blew him a kiss and followed after me.

"That's the guy who's running this show?"

"Worked with Spielberg for twelve years. He's absolutely ingenious at designing interactive materials and futuristic movie images. Makes inanimate objects look like flesh and blood. He sees things in ways that nobody else does."

"That much was obvious to me." I stood on tiptoes, looking over heads and shoulders for any sign of Jake. "Did the big guns at the Met and Natural History ever meet Quentin before today?"

"You think we wouldn't have a done deal if they had?"

"Have you lost your mind? This museum was founded by old men. Very rich, very white, very Presbyterian. Natural History was pretty much the same. The good old boys may be dead and buried, but this place isn't exactly run by the most diverse crowd in town."

"Somebody on the project did his homework. Our advance group managed all the hands-on work to get this event up and running. Probably the preppiest-looking film team I've ever seen west of the Mississippi. Hired a white-shoe law firm here to handle the contract work. Saved the outing of Quentin for tonight's gala, the big announcement."

"How'd that go?"

"Listen to the buzz. The trustees, the press, the upper crust—whoever these people are, they seemed thrilled about the news." Nina steered me to the small recess at the center of the taller building, the gateway to the Temple of Dendur. She was looking for a quieter place to tell me about the presentation that I had missed.

"Do you know Pierre Thibodaux?" She pointed to the podium, where a tall, dark-haired man was being led away from the small group of museum officials. He motioned back to his colleagues with a raised finger and stepped into the adjacent corridor.

"Only by reputation. New guy in town." Thibodaux had replaced Philippe de Montebello as director of the Met less than two years ago.

"He's taken all the meetings with our advance crew himself. This show is his baby. Brilliant, mercurial, handsome. You've got to meet him—"

"Ladies, you can't be leaning against the building, y'all hear me?" a security guard said.

We walked out of the narrow opening and searched for another quiet nook.

"Let's get out of this wing so we can have a normal conversation. There are as many living, breathing jackals in here tonight as there are limestone ones standing sentry over all the Egyptian galleries. I somehow think poor Augustus didn't foresee, when he built these monuments, that they would become the most prized cocktail space in Manhattan."

I could tell that Nina was annoyed with me, as she tried to follow me back down the steps.

"Who's Augustus? What the hell are you talking about? The temple is Egyptian, right?"

I had been coming to the Met since my earliest childhood, and knew most of the permanent exhibits pretty well. "Half right. It was built near Aswan, but by a Roman emperor who ruled that region at the time. Augustus had it erected in honor of two young sons of a Nubian chieftain who drowned in the Nile. I hate to dampen your enthusiasm, Nina. I've just been around too much death today not to wonder why we find it appropriate to organize our festivities in and around the tombs of all these ancient cultures. Wouldn't people find it offensive to have the next cocktail party at Arlington Cemetery?"

"Sorry they're not serving scotch tonight, Alex. Take it easy, will you? We can leave any time you'd like. Who's the old dame hanging on to Jake?"

He had spotted the two of us and was making his way to the foot of the platform on which we stood. A silver-haired woman with lots of dangling sap-phires—earlobes, wrists, fingers—had grasped Jake by the arm and was bending his ear about something. I stopped on the bottom step and fished in my purse for some coins to toss in the moat.

"Look out for that crocodile, darling. The most dangerous creature in Egypt, the embodiment of the essence of evil." Jake held out his hand to lower me down as I tossed a few quarters in the water, for good luck. The ebony croc mocked the gesture, his gaping mouth poised for eternity, seeking something meatier than the quiche that was being circulated around the room.

I kissed Jake's cheek, which was already covered with the shapes of pursed lips in a variety of colors. "I don't mind that you're *in loco husband* for Nina, but who's the rest of my competition?"

"That last woman? Just one of the trustees. Didn't catch her name. Gushing about how exciting the joint show is going to be and asking whether the networks are covering the fireworks tonight."

"Fireworks?"

"There's supposed to be a preview, a five-minute sound-and-light show to kick off the news about the bestiary exhibition. Here comes Thibodaux. He'll do the honors."

Instead, the director walked straight toward us, smoothing his jacket with one hand and his hair with the other. "Nina, may I have a word with you? Do you know where Quentin is?"

"I'll find him for you. Pierre, I'd like you to meet my—"

"Enchante." He greeted us tersely but his eyes searched the room over my shoulder. He and Nina broke away, retracing their steps to look for the producer.

I glanced at my watch. "Soon as we tear her loose, think you'd treat your two dates to burgers at '21'?"

"My chariot awaits you, madam."

Nina, Quentin, and Pierre had their heads together at the top of the stairs. The director did a double take over his shoulder as Quentin pointed down at me. Nina was shaking her head in the negative and trying to block me from Quentin's line of sight. You're right, pal. Whatever it is, keep me out of it.

Pierre Thibodaux didn't wait for the others to descend the two tiers of steps.

"Miss Cooper? Mr. Vallejo just told me that you're a prosecutor. May I have a moment with you, alone, for some advice? Do you mind, Mr. Tyler?" This time, no guard admonished us as Thibodaux led me back up to the platform, removed the rope between the two pillars at the entrance of the Temple of Dendur, and stepped into the quiet archway.

"You're a bureau chief in the Manhattan District Attorney's Office. I need your help in dealing with the police tonight."

"Here, at the museum?"

"No, actually, in a freight yard. I'm going to make a few remarks to close the evening and send all these people on their way. We'll forego the drama of the UniQuest Productions pyrotechnics. The last thing we need tomorrow is any bad publicity linked to our splendid new show."

"Perhaps I can make a call to the proper—"

"There's a shipment of exhibits going abroad, stored in containers for transit. It's a very routine occurrence for us. Crates go in and out of the country all the time. Exchanges with other museums, items we've de-accessioned or loaned to foreign institutions. Happens regularly."

"I doubt there's anything that I can help you with. If you've got a problem with Customs—" I said, as Thibodaux continued to speak over my objection.

"What doesn't usually happen is that one of the ancient sarcophagi was opened for inspection a few hours ago. There was supposed to be a mummified princess in the coffin, Miss Cooper. Twelfth dynasty, Middle Kingdom. A couple of thousand years old and quite valuable. Instead, there's a corpse inside. Someone has substituted a body, I'm afraid. A few centuries younger than my princess, no doubt, but just as dead."